Praise for *Claiming Her Legacy* by Linda Goodnight

"Step into adventure in Goodnight's new book *Claiming Her Legacy* and you'll fall in love with the characters."
　—Jodi Thomas, *New York Times* and *USA TODAY* bestselling author

"At the center of *Claiming Her Legacy*—a novel that is both sweet and adventurous—is a tender story about the kind of love that can heal deep wounds. I lost my heart to Willa and Gideon and thoroughly enjoyed the twists and turns that led them to a much-desired happily-ever-after."
　　　　　—Robin Lee Hatcher, Christy Award–winning author
　　　　　of *Make You Feel My Love* and the Legacy of Faith series

"Willa Malone must hunt down her father's killer. Justice demands it and the reward money would save the farm for her and her sisters. Gideon Hartley would be the perfect guide for Willa if he weren't a drunk. Realizing that Willa's life is in jeopardy without his protection, Gideon must deal with his addiction as well as the pain he is trying to mask. Written in the tradition of a classic western with a flawed hero, a stubborn heroine and a perilous quest, Linda Goodnight takes readers on a thrilling ride they'll never forget."
　　　　　—Regina Jennings, author of *Courting Misfortune*

"I loved everything about *Claiming Her Legacy*. Willa, the heroine who has the weight of the world on her shoulder. Gideon, the hero that comes through after a bad beginning. Linda Goodnight sharing her talent with us is a blessing."
　　　　　—Mary Connealy, bestselling author of *Braced for Love*
　　　　　(Brothers in Arms series, book 1)

D0059079

CLAIMING

Her

LEGACY

LINDA GOODNIGHT

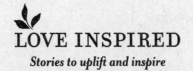

LOVE INSPIRED

Stories to uplift and inspire

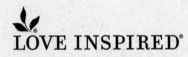

LOVE INSPIRED®

Stories to uplift and inspire

Recycling programs
for this product may
not exist in your area.

ISBN-13: 978-1-335-41876-0

Claiming Her Legacy

This edition published by arrangement with Harlequin Books S.A.

For questions and comments about the quality of this book, please contact us at CustomerService@Harlequin.com.

Love Inspired
22 Adelaide St. West, 41st Floor
Toronto, Ontario M5H 4E3, Canada
www.LoveInspired.com

Printed in U.S.A.

To Jesus be all glory, always.
I am eternally grateful that, like Gideon in the book,
You took me out of my darkness and into Your marvelous light.

But God commendeth his love toward us, in that,
while we were yet sinners, Christ died for us.
—*Romans 5:8*

CLAIMING
Her
LEGACY

Chapter One

Oklahoma Territory, 1890

Papa was dead.

Murdered.

Even with a month passed and green grass already sprouted atop Finn Malone's lonely mound of red dirt, Willa Malone and her two sisters could scarce take in the desolate truth.

"He was a good papa." With tears glistening in eyes as blue as cornflowers, Savannah, a blond vision in a yellow cotton dress, placed a bouquet of wildflowers next to the simple wooden cross.

At twenty, Savannah was the baby of the family, protected, coddled and educated in the east because of her delicate health. How would a fragile butterfly like Savannah survive for long in a place as wild and lawless as Oklahoma Territory?

"He loved us," Savannah declared as if trying to make herself believe it.

Willa had her own opinion about Papa's devotion. If their

father had loved them enough, he'd have made provisions for them. If he'd loved them enough, he wouldn't have gallivanted off to search for gold, leaving three young women to farm a fledgling homestead alone on the Oklahoma prairie.

And he wouldn't have left them owing a loan they couldn't repay.

Willa was the oldest. Caring for the family rested on her shoulders. It always had.

At the moment, she didn't know how to move forward. And there was no going back.

A crow flapped to the bare earth nearby and pecked, his iridescent blackness gleaming in the bright spring sunshine. The air smelled fresh and clear, of yesterday's rain and windswept prairie grasses. Thick droplets of dew glistened on the meadow surrounding Papa's grave. Above, in the blackjack tree, a twitter of songbirds serenaded the Irishman who'd loved music.

Swallowing a lump of grief thick enough to choke a horse, Willa turned abruptly and bumped into Mercy, the middle sister with the gift of healing who did not know how to heal herself.

Anger stirred in Willa. At Papa for leaving and dying. At the man who'd taken his life for a pack mule and a pocketful of gold dust. At whatever had broken Mercy's spirit. Most of all, she was angry with herself for being helpless to change any of it.

"We have work to do," she said in her no-nonsense voice. "Best get on with it."

With a yank at her heavy brown riding skirt, Willa marched down the incline and away from the ragged rows of wooden crosses denoting the dead of Sweet Clover. In the little more than a year since the settlement had sprung up along this branch of the Cimarron River, death had forged its mark on the settlers and the quiet hillside.

Silent now, the sisters walked as one toward the little farm on the edge of town—a town that had yet to produce much of anything except a handful of hopeful businesses and a weekly mail delivery.

Their farm had produced even less.

A dozen scrawny chickens pecked the ground behind their one-room cabin. The Guernsey cow, udder full and dangling, stood beneath a shade tree and mooed hopefully at their approach.

Here at least was something to be thankful for. Chickens and a cow bartered from a man returning to his native Virginia after his wife died of childbirth last winter put food on the table. The woman's grave and that of her child, like Papa's, testified to the harshness of this new territory.

"I'll gather the eggs and make custard," Savannah said with forced enthusiasm. "Won't that make a grand breakfast?"

What she wasn't saying was that they had little else to eat but eggs and milk until the early garden began to produce, and no money remained for provisions to tide them over until that happened.

Willa was loath to ask the mercantile owners for more credit. Hank Fleming knew as well as she that the Malone sisters had little in the way of repayment.

In an effort to encourage her sunny sister, though discouragement rode her own shoulders, Willa nodded, her tone kind, if solemn. "You make good custard, Savannah. I'll get Brownie milked."

Worrying was not Savannah's job.

"Would you rather have biscuits and eggs? Or pancakes topped with Brownie's butter and a whip of fresh cream?"

Mercy shook her head, her smile tender. "Our Michelangelo at the stove."

"Oh, not me," Savannah said with all modesty. "Aunt Francis. She was a true artist in the kitchen."

More than once, Willa wished her youngest sister had stayed in St. Louis. Though aging and not in the best of health themselves, the godly aunt and uncle had welcomed Savannah while she'd attended Miss Pennington's School for Young Ladies. Theirs was a much better situation than rugged, dangerous Oklahoma Territory for a delicate young woman.

Savannah's crippled leg and frail disposition were a constant concern to her sisters.

"You should go back to St. Louis. Your aunt Francis would welcome your company."

Francis had been especially fond of Savannah's mother, Papa's third wife, and had delighted in sharing her home with her adored niece's child. Even now, Francis wrote frequent letters urging Savannah to "come home."

Willa wished she would.

Savannah, lagging behind from the brisk walk, waved away the comment.

"No, Willa, I do not wish to return to St. Louis. I am perfectly content here with my dear sisters."

Willa slowed her steps to allow the now limping Savannah to catch up. Suddenly, she heard the pound of feet on packed earth.

"Miss Mercy!"

All three women whirled at the shout. Aiden O'Shea, the towheaded son of the livery owner, raced across the bare front yard and huffed to a stop three feet away.

Panting, hands to his threadbare knees, the spritely child motioned behind him toward the clapboard town. "Miss Mercy, come quick. Some feller's been shot."

Green eyes intense, Mercy's hand went to her heart. "Shot? Where? Let me retrieve my bag."

Willa touched her sister's shoulder. "Go with Aiden. I'll fetch your gear."

"In the cupboard. Bring my gunshot kit, as well." Mercy whipped toward the boy. "Where have they taken him?"

"The saloon. Pa said to hurry." Aiden's eyes were wide and worried. He glanced toward town and then back to Mercy. "The fella's bleeding bad. I saw him come ridin' in. He fell off his horse right smack in the middle of the street."

"No time to waste then." With a jerk of her chin toward the buildings in the near distance, Mercy hiked her skirts to the tops of her boots.

Message delivered, the young lad spun on his heels and ran, bare feet eating up the dirt path.

"Take Jasper," Willa said. The draft horse was docile enough to ride bareback and easy to catch.

In an answering swirl of brown calico and relentless dust unsettled by last night's rain, Mercy raced toward the horse, pastured in the grass behind the cabin. In the rush, her bonnet slipped from her head. A pile of glorious cinnamon-colored hair gleamed beneath the bright sunshine.

Both of Willa's sisters were beautiful women. She, on the other hand, was practical and hardworking. Fine attributes, her two stepmothers had promised, though the terms had seemed lacking to a young girl hungry for approval.

Willa hurried inside the cabin for the bag containing Mercy's medicinal herbs, bandages and sewing tools. With the nearest doctor more than twenty-five miles away, folks in Sweet Clover called on Mercy Malone's natural gift of healing in times of sickness or injury.

Mercy, a far better Christian than Willa could ever be, never asked who was sick or wounded or how far she might have to travel. She simply went. Though at times the personal cost was great, God had given her a gift and Mercy would not let Him down.

Willa often wished she shared her sisters' steadfast faith. Not that she didn't believe in the mighty power of God. She did.

She also believed God helped those who helped themselves, even if Savannah insisted no such Scripture existed. Willa wouldn't know about that, never having read a single word of the Holy Bible.

By the time Willa and Savannah arrived in town—a double row of upstart buildings along a wide dirt lane—the injured man had been laid out on the gambling table inside the saloon.

As much as any civil woman disliked entering the confines of such an establishment, both the space and the whiskey proved useful in times such as this. Thankfully, business was slow this morning and, other than those who'd carried in the wounded man, only the barkeep and owner were inside, clearing away last night's mess.

Willa sucked in an inadvertent hiss at the stench of stale liquor, unwashed bodies and, most troubling of all, the overpowering scent of perfume, a testament to the unholy truth that more than liquor was sold inside these walls.

Savannah held a handkerchief to her nose and moved toward a straight-backed chair. Willa winced to watch her, the limp more pronounced after the unrelenting rush to the saloon.

Bent over the silent bleeding man, Mercy was already at work, her face a study in concentration. Her long gentle fingers moved at breakneck speed.

Two men stood on the opposite side of the table. Willa recognized Jim Woolsey, a goosenecked cowboy with a knack for rope-making, but the other man was a stranger.

"Your bag." Willa scraped another chair closer to her sister's side. "I'll set it here. Tell me what to do."

Mercy's nod was short and without eye contact. Her focus

remained on the injured party. From her sister's expression and the man's limp stillness, Willa reckoned the situation was grave.

"Help me remove the shirt," Mercy said. "I can't find the exit wound. If there isn't one…"

No exit wound meant trouble. Willa knew that much about doctoring from the times she'd tried to assist Mercy. Gunshot wounds were as much a fact of life here in lawless Oklahoma Territory as dust and wind. Most recovered. Some didn't.

Her jaw went tight. Men. They fought over everything, and expected women to clean up their messes.

Though she'd rather be horsewhipped than deal with bleeding bodies, Willa moved into place to do her sister's bidding.

Her empty stomach protested. Sweat broke out on her upper lip. Mercy, accustomed to the smell and sight of blood, didn't notice that her oldest sister was about to humiliate the Malone name.

Willa clenched her teeth and swallowed hard. She could do this. Didn't she wish someone had been there to care for Papa when he'd been shot?

Instead, he'd died in the dirt beside his campfire, alone.

She gulped again, fighting nausea and grief in equal amounts. Careful to breathe through her mouth, she reached for the patient's shirt buttons. Her outstretched fingers trembled. She clenched her fist, fighting for control.

Someone's strong presence eased into place beside her. A masculine hand pushed hers aside. "I'll do this. You ladies shouldn't even be in here."

Willa wanted to laugh. Did he know how many times she'd "assisted" her singing Papa home from saloons? She turned her head to tell him so, but the words died on her lips.

The sick stomach fluttered with some new symptom that was not altogether unpleasant. Eyes as blue as Savannah's, though rimmed in red and full of secrets, gazed at her from a very handsome face. There was something else in that face, too, something that stirred the woman in Willa.

She, an old maid of thirty and a tomboy to boot, considered herself long past experiencing vapors when in the presence of a handsome man.

Perhaps she'd considered wrong.

So shocked was she at the untoward reaction, she forgot to be stubborn and, instead, stepped back.

"Thank you." With another gulp, this one having nothing to do with the smell of a stranger's blood and everything to do with the strange buzzing in her own, she muttered, "Mercy, I'm here if needed."

As she moved away from the sick bed, the handsome man in a black vest and trousers took her place and began the swift job of removing the wounded man's shirt. Willa caught the faintest whiff of some woodsy citrus scent with the underpinnings of whiskey. Or was that the saloon itself? It was hard to tell. Nonetheless, she was grateful to the stranger. Grateful and disturbed.

The bartender leaned on his broom to watch, but when the procedure took more than a few minutes, he moved on in his white apron, sweeping up last night's debacle.

Why would a man spend hours of time and all his money in such a place?

She wondered, too, at the attractive man quietly assisting Mercy.

Sun wrinkles spoked around his eyes. His skin was tanned and his longish black hair neatly combed. Although his linen was pristine white, the shirt looked rumpled as though slept in and his boots could use a good shine. Not overly tall or overly broad, he, nonetheless, had a presence. A very manly presence.

Goodness! What was wrong with her?

She pressed both palms to her burning cheeks. Who was he, anyway?

As if he'd assisted in repairing broken bodies before, the disturbing fellow followed Mercy's orders precisely and quickly. At one point, he signaled to the barkeep to bring a bottle of whiskey and a glass. The gunshot victim had not regained consciousness and thus was in no need of pain relief, but Willa reckoned the whiskey was to cleanse the wound.

The stranger poured a shot and tossed the amber liquor down his throat, shuddering once before resuming his role as Mercy's assistant.

If Mercy noticed, she didn't react. Willa frowned, shocked and disapproving. So, she *had* smelled whiskey on him.

At nine in the morning?

"He's lost too much blood," Mercy said at last. "I don't think…"

She bent to her patient's chest and listened. She pressed bloody fingertips to his neck and then to his wrist. Finally, she stepped back with a shake of her head. Her sigh of surrender pierced the silent company with finality.

"Is he dead?" the barkeep asked.

Dead. Such a harsh word. And all too common on the frontier.

"Yes." Mercy leaned the back of a bloody wrist against her forehead for one long silent, aching moment, eyes closed. Today, she'd battled the grim reaper and lost. She'd take the death hard. She always did.

Savannah made a small noise of distress and turned away from the bloody sight. Willa, too, glanced to one side and fought off a rising sickness.

The heavy, acrid scent of death, violent and needless, rose in the somber silence of mortals facing mortality. Perhaps they pondered their own deaths, for it was mankind's lot in the end. An appointment with death, though none of them knew the day nor the hour.

With a heavyhearted exhale, Mercy spoke to the two men hovering near the gaming table. "Gentlemen, I'd be grateful if one of you would inform Mr. Whitaker. Perhaps he can find time from his barbering duties to prepare a coffin. Ask if he'll take the man's horse in exchange for his usual fees."

"The big gray outside is a fine animal, Miss Mercy. Whitaker will take her, all right." Boots shuffled as cowboy Jim donned his hat. With a respectful nod to the ladies, he turned to leave.

The disturbing stranger said nothing, though he accompanied Jim out the door. In spite of her better judgment, Willa followed him with her gaze. He was hatless, and his hair, black as a raven's wing, gleamed in the morning sun.

There was something unsettling about the man, something more than the shot of whiskey at nine in the morning and the ridiculous feminine flutter he'd caused beneath her breastbone.

In his well-made vest and black trousers, he was neither cowboy nor farmer.

A mystery. That's what he was, though why she should think of him at all was the greater mystery still.

A passel of town folk who had gathered outside the saloon closed in around the cowboy and the mystery man. Through the window glass she heard voices rise and fall in question.

An unexplained death stirred fear in the hearts of peaceful settlers.

Behind the bar, glasses clinked as they were washed and shelved for the day ahead. Feet shuffled. Conversation returned.

Strange how a man could die before their very eyes and after a moment's curiosity, people returned to business as if nothing had occurred.

A man's life is like grass that withers quickly and is soon forgotten. Didn't the Good Book say that somewhere?

"He's with God now," Savannah said quietly, her hands folded as if she'd been in prayer. Likely she had been, and the fact that Willa had not even thought of praying shamed her a little.

Still, any man who'd been shot in the back had probably done something to deserve it.

"Is there any identification on him? If he has family…"

Weeks had passed before they'd heard about their father's death. Families deserved to know what had happened to their loved one before a wagon rumbled up to their door with a wooden coffin in the back.

She reached for the deceased's bloody, battered leather vest lying on a nearby chair.

"He looks familiar." Savannah rose to peer intently at the dead man. "Mercy, look at his face. I think we know him from somewhere."

"I was so busy seeing to his wound…" Mercy said.

The ashen face, peaceful now in death, *did* look familiar but Willa couldn't place him.

"Maybe something in here will identify him."

Inside the vest pocket, Willa found a few coins, a letter from someone in Illinois and a tarnished pocket watch.

She handed the letter to Savannah. "Read this. Look for a name or a place of residence."

Savannah took the letter without comment. Willa's sisters knew her secret shame. They could read. She couldn't.

The failing didn't have a thing to do with lack of teaching. Savannah's mother, their father's third and final wife, had tried for two years, but Willa had been too stupid to learn.

As a child she'd wondered if her ignorance had driven her last stepmother to run away. That, and trying to deal with a sick and crippled baby in a harsh land so different from her genteel Georgia upbringing.

"What else is in there?" Mercy gently covered the dead man's face with a towel provided by the barkeep.

"A wad of papers." Willa unfolded the printed sheets. "Well, look at this." Even a dunce who couldn't read recognized the documents. "Wanted posters."

"I remember him now," Mercy said. "He's the bounty hunter, Mr. Smith."

Though Willa doubted the lawman's real name was Smith, she, too, recognized him as the bounty hunter who'd come through Sweet Clover a few weeks ago with a promise of bringing Finn Malone's murderer to justice.

Now even that small hope of retribution was gone, bled to death in the Red Diamond Saloon in Oklahoma Territory. Papa's death would go unpunished.

Mercy rifled through the posters until she found the face she sought. "Here he is. The scoundrel who murdered Papa."

All three sisters stared down at the drawing of the outlaw.

Charlie Bangs, the cowardly snake who'd murdered her father. Cold beady eyes, dark unkempt hair and a droopy handlebar mustache.

Hatred curled in the pit of Willa's stomach. She'd never forget that face as long as she lived. Charlie Bangs deserved to die.

According to the prospector who'd brought him home, Papa had befriended the man who'd taken his life. He had even shared his camp and grub. Unlike his cynical daughter, Finn Malone believed the best of people.

His friendly nature had gotten him killed.

Oblivious to the dried blood staining her fingers, Mercy smoothed the poster flat. "Would you look at this? A thousand-dollar reward. No wonder men take to the bounty trails."

"Papa's life was worth more than that!" Savannah exclaimed hotly.

"Indeed," Mercy said, "but a thousand dollars is still a great deal of money, Savannah. Enough to pay off Papa's bank loan with plenty left over to order that sewing machine you've been mooning over in the mail order catalog."

"I wasn't mooning. The machine is a thing of great use. I could sew for the ladies of the community as well as for us."

Willa didn't think many in their fledgling settlement had an extra penny to spend on tailored yard goods, but Savannah needed her dreams. She was a good hand with a needle and took in mending here and there. The pay wasn't much. Certainly not enough to repay the bank loan.

Finn Malone in his great rush toward the gold fields had borrowed against their land claim for a grubstake. Now that he was gone and the dab of gold with him, she and her sisters must either repay the loan or find themselves on the streets.

A step on the stairs drew her attention to a bleary-eyed woman with the dregs of last night's rouge smearing her cheeks. At Willa's glance, the saloon girl quickly receded into the dark confines of the stairwell.

With a shudder, Willa said, "Bounty hunting beats working upstairs for Madam Frenchy."

"Willa Malone!" Mercy's eyes widened. "We could never do such a thing."

"Maybe that's what the girls upstairs thought, too, at one time. We need money, and there's hardly any way for a woman to survive out here unless she has a man to support her."

The admission galled her.

"I could marry Mr. Baggley," Savannah said, but the dread in her eyes cut Willa to the bone.

"Don't be ridiculous. You're not marrying that old goat to

put food on the table." Homer was sixty if he was a day and only washed once a year if the creek was high and warm.

Worse still, he had the manners of a billy goat, blatantly making his attentions clear one afternoon in the mercantile for the whole town to hear. As long as Savannah could cook and *bear him a passel of young 'uns*, as he put it, he didn't care one whit if she was *gimpy*.

"He is rather repulsive," Savannah admitted. "But I'll marry him if I must."

Willa's jaw hardened. "You won't."

Doubt gnawed around the edges of her mind. What if they had no choice? What if her baby sister was forced to marry a rich old man who had only one thing on his mind?

Marriages of convenience were not that unusual for women alone, but how different were they from Madam Frenchy's girls?

Willa shuddered, fingering the wanted poster. She'd do about anything to keep her sister from being sold off like a brood mare. Savannah was a beautiful educated Christian woman. Any man worth marrying would love her for those wonderful qualities and ignore her damaged leg.

But no such man was pounding on the door.

Mercy, too, was beautiful and smart. Willa's thoughts skittered to a halt. Something untoward had happened to Mercy, something that had changed her view of marriage and family.

They were three women in a territory brimming with males and not a one of them could attract a suitable husband.

Unlike other ladies, the Malone sisters could not depend upon a man for help. Their future would be up to them and the Good Lord.

A tomboy out of necessity, Willa had never had a beau and never expected to at this great age, though she'd once cherished such romantic hopes.

The thought of the handsome stranger circled around in her head like a pleasant dream. Pleasant, yes, but too much trouble. Whiskey at nine in the morning?

Then there was Papa, always looking for the pot of gold at the end of the rainbow and full of wanderlust without a bit of sense for money. The fact that he'd come west for the '89 Land Run and then promptly headed for the rumored gold discovery was proof of that.

Men, in general, did not impress.

The Malone sisters were on their own.

Mercy's doctoring was usually repaid with jars of jam or a slab of meat. Rarely a coin crossed her palm. Savannah had her mending.

Willa, as usual, felt useless. She'd tried hiring out to farmers. She could plow and plant and work cattle as well as any man, but her offers were refused. After all, she was naught but a woman.

She took heart that in a few years' time the homestead would supply their needs.

But they didn't have a few years. The bank loan hung over their heads like a noose.

Her gaze fell to the wanted poster.

Suddenly, a new resolve came over Willa. A chance to finally and forever have a home of her own that no one could take away. A chance to avenge her father's death.

"I'm going after him."

"What? Who?" Two furrows appeared between Mercy's sleek ginger eyebrows. "Whatever are you talking about, Willa?"

"Him. Charlie Bangs." She stabbed a finger against the outlaw's handlebar mustache. "I'm going after Papa's murderer."

Chapter Two

The three sisters still argued come bedtime.

Willa divested herself of dusty boots and set them by the cabin door with a resolute *thunk*. "I'm going to hunt him down and collect that bounty and neither of you will convince me otherwise."

"This is crazy talk." Mercy, already in a long nightdress, loosened her hair and let it fall over one shoulder. "A woman can't go bounty hunting."

"Why not? I can ride and shoot better than most men."

"It is simply not done. Women don't ride off alone after outlaws. Lawmen do."

"I staked this claim alone, didn't I?"

Mercy had stayed behind at the rail depot with Savannah, who could no more run for land than she could leap over the moon. Papa had run with Willa, hoping for a double portion, but he'd come up short. Willa hadn't.

"There were plenty who tried to take it away because I was a woman."

She'd faced the claim-jumpers with a loaded rifle in hand, dead set on keeping what she'd staked until Papa and the sisters arrived to set up camp.

"Yes, and now we have to find a way to keep it." Worry weighed Mercy's soft words. "But bounty hunting is not the way, Willa. Riding after an outlaw alone, a known killer, is too dangerous. Even for a man."

Mercy reached for a brush, and with more than the usual vigor, began the first of one hundred strokes of her glorious hair.

Willa had given up such feminine niceties long ago. A braid down the back was sufficient. Practical.

No one would notice if she primped anyway.

Willa's chin jutted. "I'll hire someone to go along. A tracker."

Mercy's brush paused. "Who?"

Willa's heart rattled at the truth in Mercy's statement, though she didn't dare let either sister see her concern.

Finding a knowledgeable guide with the grit for bounty hunting would be difficult enough. Finding one who'd agree to a share of the bounty in return for his services might be next to impossible. And riding the trail with a woman? Even she saw the futility in that.

Yet, what other choices did she have?

"I'll find one," she said with false bravado. "With the many settlers coming and going in this territory, someone will know a guide."

"Even if you find one, how will you know where to go?" Mercy resumed her brush strokes, the red hair gleaming in the lamplight. "This is a big country. A man on the run can hide many places."

Willa shivered, her heart jittery in her chest as she slipped into her nightgown and turned back the quilt Mercy's mother had pieced from scraps.

She didn't remember her own mother but she fondly recalled Papa's second wife, Maeve, a gentle soul who'd nurtured a needy, motherless six-year-old. Maeve, as Irish as Papa, had been the balm that soothed Papa's wanderlust for a while. Those were the good days when Papa had worked the railroad and Maeve had turned a sod house into a loving home.

Emotion knotted in Willa's chest. At times like this, when life was hard and decisions were harder, she missed having a mother to lean on. She missed Maeve.

She recalled Papa playing his fiddle by the firelight as Maeve's work-roughened hands put together the tiniest pieces of scrap cloth until a pattern emerged, amazing Willa.

She also remembered Maeve's swollen belly and the promise of a brother or sister. She'd gotten Mercy and lost Maeve in the same pain-filled day.

Months later, while Papa awaited wife number three, a mail-order bride from Georgia, he had given the quilt to Willa.

Now, with the enormity of what she planned tight in her chest, she pulled the precious cover closer, imagining the comfort of Maeve's biscuit-and-rosewater scent.

"The bounty hunter had a good notion Papa's killer was headed to Indian Territory to hide out for a spell," she murmured. "I'll start there."

"Willa, stop! Put this out of your mind." By the light of a coal oil lamp, Savannah's slender fingers jabbed a needle in and out of a ripped chemise. "A woman traveling out there, even with a man's protection, would be in terrible danger."

The Territories, both Oklahoma and Indian, had become strongholds for every kind of criminal. She'd heard the stories. Desperados roamed these parts as if they owned them, taking what they wanted and killing to get it.

Men like Charlie Bangs.

"She's right, sister. Even though the Indians are mostly peaceful, the Territory is a dangerous, lawless place. Men of all ilk, men who'll do *anything.*"

The prospect of such men silenced the conversation.

A pulse beat thrummed in Willa's neck. Fear of going. Fear of staying. Fear of losing everything.

Willa rolled onto her side, considering all that had happened today. Considering her options. Which were few.

Mercy parted her lustrous cinnamon-colored hair into three strands and began the task of braiding. Her nimble fingers made quick work of the process.

"Let's go to bed," she said. "Forget this crazy notion and pray the Lord shows us a better way to pay off Papa's loan."

Her sisters' protests only strengthened Willa's resolve.

In his string of crimes, Charlie Bangs had killed more than one man. He deserved to hang. And the Malone sisters needed that money.

"There is no other way. If there was, I'd do it. We've been praying for weeks. Today, the bounty hunter arrived and we found the wanted poster. This *is* the Lord's answer."

The room fell silent.

Savannah finished her mending, bit off the thread and jabbed the needle into a pincushion. Mercy tied a strip of rag around the end of the thick glossy braid.

Willa lay beneath the comforting quilt, silent, too, watching her sisters, hoping she wouldn't lose her nerve.

She was the strong one, the head of the family.

The world had wounded her sisters. Willa couldn't let them lose anything else. They needed this home as much as she did.

Without it, where would they go? How would they live?

"Please understand," she whispered as much to herself as to them. "I have to do this. I *must*. For all of us. And for Papa."

Savannah hung the mended chemise on a nail pounded into the wall and turned to stare at Willa. The lamplight cast strange lights from her pale blue eyes. *Fairy eyes*, Papa had called them. Eyes that glowed in the dark.

"Aren't you afraid?" Savannah whispered.

Willa didn't want to consider that what had happened to Mr. Smith could happen to her. Or worse. "I'm afraid of losing our home. I'm afraid of that more than anything."

"Oh, Willa." Mercy's hands twisted together in her lap. "What if…"

"I'm scared," Savannah said.

Fear couldn't enter into the decision, though Willa's insides rattled and the dangers pushed into her mind, real and terrifying.

"'For God hath not given us the spirit of fear,'" she quoted, more to brace herself than because she believed it. "I'm going after Charlie Bangs, and no one is going to stop me."

An eye for an eye. A tooth for a tooth.

As long as she remained angry and determined, she wouldn't back down.

The quiet descended again, but the air was thick with thoughts so strong Willa could almost hear them.

"Will you talk to the bank? Ask for more time." Savannah's tremulous voice caused an ache in Willa's chest.

Her mouth twisted bitterly. She'd found little sympathy in Theodore Pierce. "I already have. We have until October."

At last, Mercy whispered, "When will you leave?"

"As soon as I can find a guide and gather provisions. A few weeks, a month."

Savannah limped across the plank floor to where Willa lay. Without the stuffing in her shoe, one leg was at least an inch shorter than the other. She never complained, but Willa had watched her rub the twisted, shrunken limb and knew she suffered.

"We'll go with you. Three bounty-hunting sisters."

"No!" Willa sat up in the bed, covers grasped tight against her chin.

Putting her sisters in jeopardy was the last thing she wanted.

"You're needed here to keep the farm going. There are crops to plant and animals to care for."

"It's because I'm lame." Savannah sank to the edge of the bed, her voice small. "You won't let me go because I'll slow you down."

Aching for her beautiful sister, Willa stroked Savannah's slender arm. "No, dear one. I need you here. Truly."

"She's right, Savannah. We have to stay and protect what's ours."

Willa cast Mercy a grateful look. "Get to bed. It's been a long day."

Savannah rose and limped to the nightgown hanging on a peg. Despite Willa's claim to the contrary, she could tell Savannah still believed her disability was the reason for Willa's rejection.

Her assumption was, of course, correct.

Willa lay back again, quilt at her chin, and stared up at the rough-hewn ceiling. A shiver of sorrow wracked her body. She and Papa had built this room.

With such high hopes and good humor, the sisters had worked alongside them, chinking the holes and spaces between the logs with the abundant red clay. They were certain that, finally, they had a permanent home, a farm that would provide all their needs.

A fine home it was compared to soddies and dugouts peppering land claims outside the fledgling town. In addition to the iron bedstead, the Malone cabin boasted a fireplace and a table. Maeve's cookstove, hauled all the way from Kansas, crowded one corner with a shelf above and a cupboard along one wall. The trunk holding all their possessions doubled as seating.

The one-room cabin was the nicest home Willa had ever known. A home worth fighting for.

Mercy's hairbrush clattered against the washstand.

The outer edge of the straw-ticked mattress dipped as she slid into bed next to Willa and settled. She said nothing but Willa could hear the whispered prayers. Prayers for direction. Prayers for a miracle.

Willa added her own silent pleas, but in her experience, the Lord helped those who helped themselves.

The shadow of Savannah's slender hand appeared on the ceiling just before the light flickered and died in the lantern. The smoky smell of extinguished coal oil drifted to her nostrils.

Darkness collapsed around the silent sisters, absolute, as Savannah crawled into bed on the opposite side of Willa.

Worry pulsated, a loud voice in the silence, though the three didn't speak again of what was to come. There was no need. The sisters knew Willa. They knew she'd do what she believed was right.

She would go after Charlie Bangs, she'd avenge their father and she'd return with that bounty.

Somehow.

Gideon Hartley awakened facedown across the bed, fully dressed, with a splitting headache and the voice of some harridan demanding he get up. He pulled the pillow over his head.

Stout hands jerked it away.

"Mr. Hartley, wake up."

"Go 'way," he managed, though his tongue was thick and the words slurred.

A three-second pause ensued, giving Gideon hope that the woman, whoever she might be, had given up the quest to awaken him from a much-needed day of recuperation.

Just as at the gaming tables last night, his luck did not hold.

"You're drunk." Disgust dripped from the harridan's voice.

Gideon sighed into the foul-smelling sheets. The nightmare was disgusted? So was he. Anytime he became the least bit sober, he was completely disgusted with himself.

"Mr. Hartley, did you hear me? Please. Wake up."

Persistent female. Like a buffalo gnat.

He was wearying quickly of the woman's voice, though it was, all in all, a pleasant one, but not one accustomed, apparently, to being denied.

Her footsteps moved away, a soft thud on the heart-pine floor of his hotel room. The sound jarred his aching head. Wood scraped against wood, and suddenly fresh air rushed into the room. She'd opened a window.

Thunderation! Had she no mercy?

"Please, sir, I must speak with you. It's quite urgent."

With a groan, he rolled onto his back and squinted up with one eye. Like a vicious sledgehammer to the skull, the back of his head protested against the movement. His stomach rolled.

Oh, to return to his dreamless slumber, where nothing encroached, no memories, no demands, no noisy females. He let his eyelid flutter closed.

"'Come Sleep! O Sleep, the certain knot of peace,'" he muttered, for truly Sir Philip knew of what he wrote.

"I beg your pardon?"

Both his eyes flew open again like creaky shutters too long disused.

She was still there, the harridan, staring down at him as if he were the bottom of a horse's hoof. He stared back through slits that once had been eyes. He'd seen her somewhere, though where and when he didn't remember.

She wasn't the typical female, nor was she particularly beautiful, but she enthralled him just the same.

He glared at the woman. Both of her.

She was too intriguing to shoot even if he could decide which one of her to aim at.

Above a buckskin skirt and a white shirtwaist that nipped a narrow waist, eyes the color of good whiskey glowed with a fearsome determination. A glossy teak-brown braid fell across one shoulder. Bits of stray hair caught the light from the window behind her and radiated like Medusa snakes from the sides of her high-held head.

Her chin jutted perhaps a bit too much and her mouth was overlarge. His shuttered gaze focused on that mouth for a tad too long. The bottom lip protruded in a permanent pout.

A bizarre, unwelcome stir of attraction shifted through the haze of alcohol.

With a defiant hand perched on one hip and a rifle fisted in the other, she was not a temptress. No, not that at all. She was an avenging angel come to claim him.

"'Stern Daughter of the Voice of God,'" he murmured.

"What?" The woman blinked, baffled, so it seemed, by his predilection for poetic outbursts.

Gideon tried to wave away the line from Wordsworth but the motion shot more pain through his head. His hand fell to the coverlet with a jarring flop.

"What do you want?" His voice sounded like a rusty meat grinder.

"I need your help."

The pounding in Gideon's brain grew louder. He blinked,

and his eyelids slashed against memories sharp as a barber's blade.

Help, Gideon. Help me!

To silence the long-dead voice, Gideon jerked from the bed, a regrettable action because he staggered against the woman. She thrust out a hand to steady him. A strong, calloused female hand with more strength than he had, at the moment, in one finger.

Shame coursed through the fog of last night's libations.

Mustering a dignity too frequently abandoned, he pulled away and stalked to the washstand, weaving only slightly, though his hand shook as he reached for the decanter to pour himself a drink.

Four slender female fingers clapped over the opening on the tin cup.

Gideon spoke through clenched teeth, "Kindly remove your hand."

"Kindly put away the liquor."

He snarled, "Move. Your. Hand."

"Put. Away. The liquor."

"You're trying my patience."

A gun cocked. "No liquor until we talk."

With studied control, Gideon capped the decanter.

Shooting him would do the world a favor, but as much as he'd contemplated death, his distant respect for the Almighty and the promise of judgment day served as deterrents.

"Put the gun away, madam. There is no need for weaponry."

He turned to face her, hands slightly aloft as he weighed the option of wrestling the rifle away or mustering up the dregs of his charm.

She didn't seem the type to succumb to charm, and while

wrestling with this enchanting warrior held a certain appeal, Gideon opted for civil discourse.

A man with a violent hangover was in a position neither to charm nor to wrestle. "I am at your disposal."

She lowered the Winchester in a shockingly feminine movement that belied her tough expression and her choice of weapon. "Where shall we talk?"

He made a grand sweeping gesture toward the only chair in the room, a straight-backed cane bottom he'd never used for anything other than a hanger for his clothes—when he was sober enough to undress.

She shook her head. "I'd prefer we speak somewhere other than your hotel room."

Gideon arched an eyebrow. Even his hair hurt. "Why?"

"It wouldn't be proper for an unmarried lady to have a conversation in a gentleman's room."

He laughed. And instantly regretted the action. The throb in his head deepened. "Proper, madam?"

"Stop calling me madam," she snapped. "I don't run a bordello. I'm Willa Malone, plain and simple."

His laugh barked again, and the pain that shot between his eyeballs was enough to bring an ox to his knees.

Willa Malone was neither plain nor simple. She was, however, trying his patience and causing him considerable pain.

The woman had stormed into his room, awakened him from a deep, if inebriated, slumber, pulled a gun on him and now she was worried about proprieties.

She was the most confounded female he'd met in a long time.

Which intrigued him even more.

How curious.

"Need I remind you, Miss Malone—" he shot her what he

hoped was a devilish grin "—we are already having a conversation in my hotel room."

She ignored the pure logic. That beguiling chin tipped upward. "We can speak in private in the hotel's parlor downstairs. I took the liberty of securing Miss Hattie's approval in advance."

If Miss Hattie was on this harridan's side, he didn't stand a chance. A man with a raging hangover knew when to cut his losses.

He tilted his head in resigned acquiescence. "As you wish, madam—Miss Malone."

With a quick nod and a flicker of relief, his tormentor strode with purpose to the door, turned the knob and stepped into the hall.

Gideon dove for the whiskey, knocked back a shot faster than he'd have believed possible and prepared to gloat in triumph.

No one, certainly not a small brown sparrow of a woman, steered his ship.

The fiery liquid shuddered through him at the exact moment Willa turned back toward him. Her mouth opened. Her shoulders slumped. Disappointment darkened her eyes.

Even as the whiskey did its work, bolstered him, settled his stomach and his shaking hands, Gideon's moment of triumph withered into shame.

He was sorry she hadn't shot him.

Chapter Three

The man was a drunk.

In shocked dismay and with hope dwindling, Willa twisted her hands in her lap beneath the round parlor table. The guide and tracker she wanted to hire sat across from her, nursing a cup of coffee and a hangover.

Now she understood the sly warnings she'd received about Gideon Hartley.

Having taken only the time for that one drink of whiskey before stumbling down the stairs behind her, his longish black hair was mussed and his clothes badly rumpled. He had, however, tucked in his shirt, though Willa feared the courtesy had only added to his roguish appearance.

Her heart had ricocheted like a bullet on a boulder when she'd tromped into the hotel room and recognized Hartley as the man from the saloon. He was, she feared, every bit as handsome as she remembered.

A handsome rogue who drank too much.

While she fidgeted, afraid he'd refuse her request and even

more afraid he wouldn't, he took his slow, sweet time doctoring his coffee. First, a spoon of sugar, followed by a taste and a grimace. Then a dollop of cream followed by yet another sip.

Tapping her foot in impatience, Willa glanced around at the lovely rose-papered parlor furnished with a settee and a small table to accommodate the hotel's guests. A man and woman occupied the settee, thankfully far enough away not to overhear her conversation with Gideon Hartley. If she ever got to have one.

He reached for more sugar.

"Mr. Hartley, while I appreciate the flavor of well-prepared coffee as much as anyone, I have an important matter to discuss with you."

The spoon clinked against the saucer, leaving a dot of brown liquid on the white china.

"All right, then," he said with a heavy sigh. "To what do I owe this disgustingly early morning visit?"

"It's afternoon."

He flinched and turned slowly to squint out the broad window. Afternoon shadows pointed toward the east.

"So it is." His dark eyebrows drew together in a frown. "You seem familiar. Have we met?"

"You helped my sister a few days ago."

"That doesn't sound like me."

With studied nonchalance, he poured more cream into his coffee. And stirred. Again.

Willa found his self-deprecation less than amusing.

"You weren't drunk at the time," she snapped. "Perhaps that's why you don't remember."

He arched an eyebrow. "Such a viperous tongue from such an enchanting source."

Willa struggled not to roll her eyes. The man was not only half-drunk, he was a slick liar. She knew her shortcomings as well as her strengths. Savannah was enchanting. Willa was merely determined.

"The man my sister tried to save was a bounty hunter. He was tracking the murderer who killed my father."

"Ah. Now, I remember. The ladies in the saloon. One fighting with death while the other fought not to lose her breakfast."

She'd had no breakfast to lose. "How chivalrous of you to mention it."

He showed his teeth. "How else may I be of assistance?"

Though his tone indicated less than cooperation, Willa leaned forward, determined to forge on. He was her only hope.

"I'm told you're a tracker and a guide. I want you to help me find my father's murderer."

The coffee cup stilled halfway to his mouth. Fragrant steam circled a lip in need of a razor.

"I don't do that anymore."

"Why not? I'll pay you part of the bounty."

His gaze slid to the fireplace at the end of the room. He set the cup carefully onto the saucer and avoided eye contact. "I have my reasons."

"People say you're the best."

Not that she'd had many choices, but his name had surfaced three times in her search. They'd also said he wouldn't do it.

But Gideon Hartley had been the only guide around other than Rupert Johnson. At eighty and mostly blind, Rupert was out of the question.

"I'm told you scouted for the army, that you can track anyone into any place."

"But now you have your doubts." He saluted her with the cup. "Quite wise of you."

His insolence annoyed her. "Do you drink on the job?"

"I have no job." He shoved back from the table with a great

scraping of wood against wood. "Would you care for coffee, Miss Malone?"

"Willa," she demanded again. "Plain and simple Willa."

A small smile tilted the corners of his lips. "So you said."

She amused him? Did he think this was some kind of foolish game concocted by a weak-minded female with nothing better to do?

The burr in her saddle dug deeper.

"I am completely serious, Mr. Hartley. I need your help, and I'm willing to pay you." Hoping to sweeten the deal, she gulped and declared, "Half the reward."

"It's Gideon. Plain and simple." He took the coffeepot from the sideboard along one wall and carried it back to the table.

Hefting the pot, along with one wicked-looking black eyebrow, he asked, "Coffee, plain and simple Willa?"

Willa clenched her teeth. If she let him rile her, she might do something foolish. Like shoot him.

"Coffee would be lovely, thank you."

He poured her a cup and set the pot aside. His hand shook.

As if ashamed—as he should be—he balled his hands into fists.

A niggle of sympathy tried to push in, but Willa squelched it. If his hands shook, he had no one to blame but himself. No one forced liquor down his throat.

She added thick cream to her cup and stirred, more for something to do than for the want of coffee. The fact that he was studying her over his own cup made her nervous.

Outside the hotel, a buckboard rumbled past loaded with sacks of grain while a barefoot boy chased another boy across the dirt street. A woman toting a basket toward the mercantile stopped to speak to a man tying his horse to the rail.

Willa was sharply aware of these things, all the while praying for the Lord's guidance. Gideon Hartley was not what she'd expected. Even if he had been, he didn't seem interested in her offer.

At long last, he clinked the coffee mug onto the saucer and said, "I suggest, plain and simple Willa, that you abandon your quest for revenge."

Her heart fell. "I can't."

"And I cannot guide you." He started to rise.

Tired of the cat and mouse game he'd been playing since they'd entered the parlor, Willa grabbed his forearm. The man might be given to drink but his arm was as strong and hard as a tree trunk.

"Hear me out."

He gazed down at her hand with a pointed look and an elevated eyebrow, black as midnight. Willa stubbornly held her grip.

"Please. Gideon." The name felt strangely sweet on her tongue. "At least let me explain."

Bloodshot eyes held hers for a long uncertain moment before he sank back into the chair.

He crossed his arms over a surprisingly impressive chest. "I'm listening."

She released a held breath and quickly told him the story of her father's death and of the bank loan hanging over her head like a noose.

"So you see, finding Charlie Bangs is not about revenge." At least not completely. "My sisters and I need that bounty money in order to keep our homestead."

Filled with renewed hope, Willa awaited his answer. Surely, now that he knew the reasons, he wouldn't refuse her.

He did. "The answer is still no."

"Why?"

"I am no longer for hire."

Willa could see that he meant every word, and she wondered if perhaps his refusal was for the best. Surely, she could find another more sober, more agreeable guide. Somewhere.

But she knew better. She'd tried. And failed.

She rested her gaze on him, a handsome rogue, a debauched and troubled stranger. Though he was as darkly beautiful as Lucifer before the fall, Gideon's puffy eyes and shaky hands served as fair warning.

A man with a drinking problem could be more trouble than he was worth. He could get her killed.

She could do that all by herself.

"Thank you for your time, Mr. Hartley, and for the coffee." Willa rose from the table and took up her rifle, disappointed but undaunted. "If you won't guide me, I shall do what I intended in the first place."

Stomach trembling, she drew to her full unimpressive height, head high, voice strong.

"I shall go alone."

Gideon left the hotel, intending to head straight for the saloon. He contemplated a meal first but, considering the foul mood he was in, opted instead to drink his dinner.

Self-loathing rose in his chest, the taste of sour whiskey and coffee ripe on his tongue.

There had been a time he would have leaped at the opportunity to guide anyone anywhere for any reason. He was good at it, and he loved the open skies, the wide prairies, the rocky hills and muddy rivers, the chance encounters along the trail.

The West remained wild and beautiful. And free. A freedom Gideon craved but could no longer embrace.

Even if he wanted to help the fearless lady with her quest, he couldn't.

"'This mighty empire hath but feet of clay,'" he muttered. "Feet of clay."

The memory of Willa Malone's disappointed face followed him as he crossed the street. Her quest was noble and self-sacrificing, qualities he admired, though a warrior woman like her was bound for revenge whether she admitted it or not.

Plain and simple Willa and her sisters were in a bad spot. A thousand dollars was a fortune for most.

"Gideon. Oh, Gideon, hold up." To his great relief, the feminine voice was not the warrior woman's.

He stopped at the railing in front of the bank. Though his head pounded and he longed for a drink, Gideon smiled at the woman in a faded calico dress and bonnet.

"Hello, Mary," he said kindly. "How's Isaiah?"

Lines of perpetual worry deepened in the woman's face.

Mary Baker couldn't be much older than Gideon, but the harsh prairie conditions and pioneer life had aged her mercilessly.

"Progress is slow and Isaiah is impatient. But he wants you to know how obliged we are for all you've done." She put her weathered hand on his arm. "We are deeply grateful."

Gideon shifted under her admiring gaze. He was nobody's hero. Men like Isaiah Baker were the heroes, struggling to establish a homestead and to provide for his family after a wagon accident had mangled his leg and set up an infection that had threatened his life.

"No need for gratitude, ma'am. Isaiah's a good man."

"This accident has brought him lower than I've ever seen, but we got faith, Gideon. We'll get through. God always provides."

"Yes, ma'am." Gideon didn't feel all that comfortable with the Lord Almighty anymore. Likely, the Almighty wasn't too comfortable with him, either.

"Isaiah coulda laid out there in the woods 'til the wolves got him or 'til he bled to death, except for you. You saved his life."

"Happenstance, Mary."

"No, sir." She shook her head hard enough to wiggle the ribbons on her faded sunbonnet. "You came ridin' along in the nick of time. That was God right there. God and Gideon."

Gideon considered himself the fortunate one, to have ridden upon the settler that fateful day. If that was God's doing, he was grateful. The budding friendship brought him a strange kind of peace. He didn't understand or question it, lest it disappear.

Mary put a hand over her heart. "We Bakers owe you. We don't never forget something like this. Someday we'll repay your kindness."

"You don't owe me anything," he said gently, understanding pioneer pride. "But I wouldn't turn down a slice of your pie."

Beneath the tired bonnet, her weathered countenance brightened. "What's your favorite?"

He searched his aching brain for the ingredients she'd most likely have on hand. Trying to think with a hangover didn't make thinking easy.

"I'm partial to buttermilk."

"Buttermilk it shall be." She squeezed his arm and smiled up at him. "Ride out soon. I can whup up a pie in a jiffy while you and Isaiah jaw."

The change in her, with only a smile, was stunning. Beneath the weariness, Mary Baker was a comely woman.

"Give my best to Isaiah. Tell him I'm coming out real soon to eat up all his pie." While he was there, Gideon would see to the woodpile and whatever else needed a man's hand.

Men like Isaiah would build this new land if given the chance. Gideon aimed to see he got it.

"He'll be mighty pleased to see you again."

With a bounce in her step, Mary moved on down the boardwalk to enter the mercantile. In a way, she reminded him of Willa Malone, battered by this hard prairie life but determined to survive. A small warrior fighting for life and livelihood.

Women. They were the strong ones.

Sweat beaded on Gideon's face, a mix of sun and the gnawing in his gut for a drink, the need to drown his thoughts.

He stepped up on the boardwalk, touched the brim of his hat toward a passing lady and headed for his original destination.

He didn't want to think about the past or even the present. He sure didn't want to think about plain and simple Willa. He couldn't help her even if he'd wanted to. And he didn't want to. The risk was too great.

He shoved open the double doors leading into the saloon. They shut behind him with an echoing flap.

Nothing much stirred in the Red Diamond this time of day. Activity came later toward sundown, along with the music and the card games.

A couple of cowboys at the bar nodded in his direction.

Gideon wasn't in the mood for conversation. Willa had worn him out on that account.

Willa. Pretty name for such a fierce woman. Strong but flexible, able to bend with the storms of life. He wondered if the storms would eventually break her in half as they did so many. As they had him.

Salty, the barkeep, caught his eye and thumped a bottle and glass onto the bar. Gideon's parched mouth watered.

Belly to the bar, he took up the glass and was silently shamed when his hand trembled. The shaking was a recent development.

He'd never intended for whiskey to take such a hold. He simply sought peace and dreamless sleep, and he had found them at the bottom of a glass. He'd never expected the price to be so high.

The first drink would ease the shakes. The second stilled the gnawing. The third quieted the noises in his head.

He stared in loathing and longing as the second glass was poured. Then he tossed it back and hissed between his teeth, welcoming the burn as a much deserved punishment.

On this particular afternoon, following more drinks than he cared to count, he could still envision Willa's stubborn thrust of chin, that fetchingly pouty lip and the way she'd straightened her small shoulders, determined to take on the whole territory to care for her sisters and save their home.

Had he ever been that brave, that resolute, that impassioned?

He shook his head, knowing full well he had. Once, someone had mattered more than whiskey and himself.

Didn't Willa understand what he'd learned the hard way? Her heart would be wounded even more than it already was. She could not succeed. A woman tracking an outlaw into Indian Territory—Gideon shook his head again and washed down the preposterous thought.

"Hartley." A cowboy clapped him on the shoulder. "Join me for poker?"

Glad for the distraction, Gideon swiveled from the bar, bringing the bottle with him. "Have money to lose, do you, Pete?"

"Planning to win back what's mine." The amiable cowboy tossed his hat on a chair and slid his long legs beneath the table.

"I'm not that drunk."

Pete laughed, and the game commenced with each of them taking a hand. For a while, Gideon forgot about the earnest woman who'd roused him from his sleep and reminded him of who he'd once been.

Then, halfway through the third hand, Pete said, "A woman was asking around for a man to guide her into Indian Territory. One of the Malone sisters."

"I don't do that anymore." He discarded a three.

With a start, Gideon realized this had become his living. His life. Skinning friendly cowboys of their paychecks.

"Just thought I'd mention it. Hear you used to be real good."

Used to be.

Gideon pretended to study his cards, but his mind had returned to Willa. In one conversation, she'd made him look at himself through her eyes.

He didn't much like what he saw.

"Your turn, Hartley. You gonna play or fold?"

"Fold." Gideon tossed three aces upside down on the table.

With a cry of victory, Pete raked in his money. "Play again?"

"Not now, Pete." Gideon rubbed his bottom lip in thought.

He couldn't do what Willa asked, and regardless of her persistent bravado, he was fairly certain she wouldn't attempt the journey alone.

Would she?

Tired of his own troubled thoughts, he lifted his empty glass and motioned to Salty at the bar.

Chapter Four

Rupert Johnson might be blind, but his mind remained as sharp as a well-honed knife. It was this sharpness Willa depended upon the afternoon she'd come calling.

The old trail guide sat in the bright spring sunshine outside his daughter's pretty two-story home at the north edge of Sweet Clover, his straight-backed chair turned toward the town and the people on the nearby road coming and going like red ants after a corn muffin.

Willa supposed the blind man, accustomed to moving freely around the countryside, occupied his days listening to others do what he no longer could.

"Papa, you have a caller." The old man's daughter, Sadie Faragate, placed an affectionate hand on her father's shoulder. "Willa Malone is here to see you."

"Malone. Malone." Rupert frowned as his sightless eyes turned toward his daughter's voice. "Wasn't there a feller named Malone got hisself killed by claim-jumpers a while back?"

"Yes, sir." The familiar hand of grief clutched Willa's throat. She swallowed, though the action didn't assuage the sorrow. "That was my father. He's the reason I wanted to talk to you."

Rupert rotated back to Willa. "That a fact?"

"Yes, sir." She gripped the arms of the offered wooden chair and lowered herself to a rest. "I understand you used to be the best guide and tracker in this part of the country."

He stared into the distance with a kind of sad nostalgia. "That was the rumor. One of the best, anyway."

"He was, indeed," Sadie said proudly. "Willa, would you care for tea?"

The elegantly offered refreshment was not unexpected. Sadie Faragate, along with Agnes Pierce, the banker's wife, held sway over Sweet Clover society and strove to create a genteel community.

Sadie and her husband, George, who owned the sawmill, were among the founders and builders, the handful of people in Sweet Clover with more than two nickels to rub together. They'd come here, according to common knowledge, eager to make their mark in this new land and to fill their already well-lined pockets by bringing sorely needed building materials to the community.

Papa had bought lumber from Faragate Mill for their cabin. The memory pinched a bruise on Willa's heart.

"Kind of you to offer, Mrs. Faragate. Thank you."

Maeve, the stepmother Willa still mourned, would be pleased to know the ragtag tomboy with the grubby hands and dirty face hadn't forgotten every social convention. Though, for the most part, Willa found no value in fancy manners.

Sadie's day dress of rust-colored taffeta rustled as she paused to add, "Mr. Faragate and I are hosting a community barn dance a week from Saturday. I do hope you and your sisters will attend."

Savannah had twittered on about little else since the event was announced at church. Accustomed to a more refined environment, she missed the social activities found in the city. If only she missed them enough to return to the safety of St. Louis.

"My sister is looking forward to it, Mrs. Faragate."

"Oh? What about you, Willa?" With a sparkle in her eyes, Sadie gave Willa a meaningful look. "There will be plenty of eligible men."

Fighting back a sigh, Willa hung on to her smile. Sadie meant well. They all meant well. They just didn't understand what she knew.

"It's nice of you to throw a social for the town. We'll be there."

Sadie pressed her hands together in a happy silent clap. "Wonderful. Now, to that tea."

When Sadie had traversed the wide wooden porch, entering the house through a door that sported real glass on either side, Willa turned her attention to the reason she'd come.

"Mr. Johnson, we were discussing your time as a trail guide."

"Why would a young lady such as yourself be asking about an old man like me?" He leaned forward in his chair, hands clasped between his knees. "You looking to do some tracking?"

"I am."

"I see, I see. Uh-huh." Rupert scratched an itch below his chin. "Going after your pa's killer? Is that it?"

He was, indeed, sharp of mind.

"I've come to ask your advice to that end. What supplies I need to take, how to track a man and learn his whereabouts."

The old guide stroked a hand over his thick salt-and-pepper

beard. Once. Twice. "Dangerous game. You taking a deputy with you?"

"No, sir."

He spit, barely missing Willa's boots. "No job for a woman."

She'd expected his response. In her daily search, she'd heard the phrase many times. She had also learned some basic facts about the man she hunted, which she deemed worth listening to the naysayers.

One thing she'd learned in life—if you wanted something done, do it yourself. The Lord would be with you if you asked, but He expected you to pack the mule and put in the sweat.

She'd become proficient at packing and sweating.

"A woman without a man has few choices, Mr. Johnson. I tried to hire a tracker. He refused."

"Who?" The old man's face grew intense. "Hartley?"

"You know him?"

"We've crossed paths."

She couldn't tell if this was a good or bad thing.

A vision of the handsome, debauched trail guide flashed in Willa's mind.

Gideon Hartley was not available.

"He says he doesn't track anymore."

Mr. Johnson leaned back, sighed, nodded. "Understandable."

"Why is that?"

The pale sightless eyes turned on her. "Has his reasons, I reckon. You're better off without him."

Willa waited for more, but whatever Rupert knew, or thought he knew, about the mysterious Gideon Hartley, he chose to keep to himself.

"I have no choice but to find Charlie Bangs myself. Will you teach me what I need to know?"

A long pause ensued. Willa sucked in a lungful of air,

scented by the wild roses growing along the three-sided porch, and held her breath. Waiting. Hoping.

The old tracker pondered, mulled, twisted his mouth from one side to the other before finally ruining her day.

"And carry your life on my conscience? No, ma'am. I will not."

Three days, dozens of poker hands and too many glasses of whiskey to remember—if he remembered anything at all—passed. And yet Gideon was as haunted by Willa Malone's disappointed brown eyes as he'd been the day she'd harangued him in his hotel room.

The woman was a pest, a mosquito buzzing in his head. A reminder of the life he'd loved but couldn't return to.

Everywhere he went in Sweet Clover, someone mentioned her name or shared the gossip that some fool woman wanted to take up bounty hunting. The guffaws that followed these statements irritated him, though he couldn't say why. The gossipers were correct. Any female who'd consider such a thing was foolish.

Or desperate.

He understood desperation.

"Plain and simple Willa," he murmured with a huff of aggravated laughter.

Trying to drown the pesky woman with liquor clearly had no effect.

Even now, when he was sober as a preacher and standing in a stall at O'Shea's Livery Stable, Willa Malone nagged him. She would not go away.

Sucking in a breath of warm horseflesh and fresh hay, Gideon stroked a hand over his steadfast bay.

On Traveler's strong back, Gideon had scouted for the army, guided settlers, and led posses and detectives across the West in search of horse thieves, murderers and robbers. Where others balked at guiding through the wild, wooly territories, he'd leaped at the opportunity to see new country, to outrun his past.

Trouble was, the past moved faster than he did. It was always there, waiting, when he arrived.

Moving on from Sweet Clover to some other outpost would make no difference. He might ride far enough to forget Willa Malone and her bravado, but he'd never leave behind the rage, the guilt, the yawning black hole inside his soul.

"Eager for a run, old man?" he murmured to the horse.

Traveler thrust his head upward, ears pricked.

"He's a fine one, Mr. Hartley," said Liam O'Shea. The livery owner's Irish lilt sent Gideon's thoughts tumbling right back to Willa Malone. Malone, a name as Irish as a shamrock. "Would you be wanting me to bring your saddle?"

"I'd be obliged."

The wiry Irishman with the quick smile nodded once and disappeared around the corner. Gideon heard him talking, likely to his young son, who groomed the horses and ran errands around town.

Gideon inspected the bay, running his hands down each leg, lifting feet. Traveler was in good condition from O'Shea's caring hand. Even the horse's hooves were trimmed and clean.

The Irishman returned, toting Gideon's saddle. The young boy, Aiden, came behind, tack in hand, the long reins and bridle lofted high to keep them off the ground.

In no time, he'd saddled the animal and was ready to ride.

"He's in fine shape, O'Shea." Gideon looped the reins over the saddle horn and prepared to mount. "You've a way with horseflesh."

"Me da was a stable lad back in the old country." At Liam's voice, Traveler turned soft eyes in his direction and whickered in quiet recognition. The liveryman reached for the horse's ears. The animal dipped his head lower to receive the scratch.

"You've earned his trust." The horse's behavior told Gideon a lot about the Irishman. Animals sensed a man's character faster than another man would.

Liam's ready smile flashed. "I could say the same for him. Horses, I'm thinking, are more reliable and honest than most men. Treat 'em kind, and they won't be turning against you."

Gideon settled a thoughtful gaze on his companion. A story lurked behind such a statement.

Liam O'Shea, he'd wager, carried a secret or two, though no one would notice unless they looked closely. Successful gamblers learned to look closely. A man's secrets were his weakness.

But this wasn't a poker game. Nor was O'Shea's life any of Gideon's business.

Plenty of men—and women—came west, especially to the territories, to escape one thing or the other. Hadn't he?

The less a man pried into the past of another, the longer he kept breathing.

He stuck a booted foot in the stirrup and swung into the saddle, light and easy.

With a tug of his hat, he said, "A good day to you, O'Shea."

"And to you, sir."

Sir. The term never sat well with Gideon.

Visions of his father's sunbaked cotton fields flared, scorching him. Visions of freed slaves, now poor sharecroppers, struggling to make a living in the Texas heat while Thomas Hartley grew richer and meaner.

Hatred stirred in Gideon's belly, stronger than boiling lye, eating him inside out.

The urge for a drink pressed in. He bit down on the inside of his cheek, a distraction that did little to quell the hunger and nothing to quell the hate.

He tapped his heels to Traveler's sides, urging the responsive steed to a run. Let the prairie wind blow away the ugly thoughts today. Ignore the liquor. Prove he still could.

Though he didn't know why resisting mattered anymore.

Maybe it was the sorrowful look in Willa's eyes the day he'd tossed back the drink to spite her.

For one stunning moment, he'd wanted to be a better man.

In the next, he'd wondered why God allowed him to keep breathing.

With a thousand pounds of powerful horseflesh beneath him, the rolling landscape flew past, clumps of cottonwood and hickory, scrub brush and cedar. The air was rich with fragrant blooms of spring and the lush green scent of prairie grass whispering against Traveler's strong legs.

These sights and smells and sounds had once fulfilled him. Once, the tracking had given him purpose and made him feel worthwhile.

What was his purpose now?

Teeth tight, stomach burning, he bent low over the saddle. As man and horse thundered past, quail flushed and whirred upward from the tall grass. Rabbits scattered and crows scolded, insulted by the interruption.

Here and there, a homestead sprouted from the landscape. Sprigs of a summer crop peeped above the fertile ground. These were the early arrivals who knew the importance of getting shelter erected that first year. Newer settlers lived in tents, covered wagons or dugouts—living like prairie dogs until they could do better.

He'd never considered settling down in one spot. If he wanted a house, he had one. Not that he'd ever see it again. Didn't want to.

If he ever settled, it wouldn't be in Texas.

Gideon smelled the river before he saw it, the heavy scent of salt and mud.

By the time he reached the wide Cimarron, Traveler's bloodred coat gleamed dark with sweat. Sweat beaded on Gideon, too, though not from exercise. His insides gnawed like rats at a paper house, craving liquor and shredding his resistance little by little.

As he slowed his mount to a walk, he heaved a disgusted sigh of surrender, fumbled in his saddlebag for the whiskey flask and shivered down two long pulls. The devil in a bottle, he'd heard it called, and knew this to be true.

He just didn't know what to do about it.

His mother had taught him that a strong faith in God could conquer any difficulty. Which proved how far away from his mother's faith he'd fallen.

He often thought about the Almighty, wondering if there was still a chance for a man filled with nothing but hate and self-disgust.

Did the Lord ever think about him?

Nearing the river's edge, Gideon dismounted and led the horse to the red water. The bank stank of mud and dead fish, but Traveler drank deeply.

While the horse refreshed himself, Gideon walked along the bank, breathing in the sights and smells. A river teemed with life. Deer, raccoon and turkey tracks littered the wet sand.

Horse tracks, too.

He squatted, studied them. Three riders heading west less than an hour ago. Traveling fast.

A noise pierced the landscape, echoing through the many canyons carved by this wayward leg of the Cimarron.

Gideon turned his head toward the sound.

An animal's cry? An outlaw's signal?

Tension gathered the hairs at the base of his neck.

Was he being watched?

A man never knew who or what he might encounter here in the territories. Horsethief Canyon lay a few miles west, a sanctuary for men following the Owl Hoot Trail. A likely source of these tracks.

Was one of those riders Charlie Bangs?

He'd encountered plenty like Bangs in his scouting days, desperate men who wore their six guns for all to see and caused trouble in peace-loving settlements like Sweet Clover.

Staying low, treading light but quick, Gideon slid his Winchester from the saddle holster. He cast a wary eye into the thick mat of scrub trees growing on both sides of the river. Knee-high grass waved in the breeze. Overhead a red-tailed hawk circled, round and round, on the hunt.

Traveler slept, head low, one back foot raised, unperturbed.

Gideon moved around the horse, rifle ready, scanning in a slow circle, before letting himself relax.

The sound came again. Closer. This time he recognized it.

He aimed his rifle, ready when a fat tom turkey strutted into sight. Gideon's hand trembled the slightest bit, but he managed to steady the gunstock against his shoulder.

In minutes, he'd downed the fowl, strung it onto his saddle, taken a drink—only a small sip to prove his control—and remounted, his destination now determined.

He had no need of wild game, but he knew who did.

He would also welcome another visit with Isaiah Baker. The man's wisdom and steadfast faith in God even in the face of hardships spoke to something deep in Gideon. Something he'd long ago abandoned. Something that drew him.

Nearing the Baker farm, Gideon gazed over the property, one hundred and sixty acres of prime farming land, flat and fertile. Last fall, Isaiah had cleared and plowed ten acres, but now the fields lay fallow, waiting for the farmer's leg to heal.

Isaiah had begun building a second room onto the one-room cabin, this one with an attached lean-to for the animals. Like the fields, the much-needed addition waited.

The woodpile next to the house was abandoned, too, the ax handle poking up from a tree stump. Mary tried, but she couldn't manage a farm with five children and an injured husband.

The garden in back, at least, showed signs of progress. Mary and the children, he supposed. Green plants sprouted from the dry soil, hopeful of enough rain to produce a crop.

Gideon took a final swig from the liquor flask before sliding it into his saddlebags and fumbling in his vest for a peppermint candy.

He'd seen the admiration in Mary's eyes, felt the warmth of Isaiah's handshake. For once, Gideon didn't want to be drunk.

At his approach to the house, the chickens scattered, squawking in protest. A passel of children came running from all directions, insulting the chickens even more. One child ran from the garden, some from inside the cabin and one from the creek flowing through the woods along the back of the property.

Five blond stairsteps, all barefoot, the youngest was a shirtless toddler in a baggy diaper, the eldest no more than nine years old, if he was that.

It was this oldest lad, Matthew, who toted two buckets from the creek, his load weighing him down so that the wooden pails kissed the grass.

"Mama, Mama, somebody's here!" This robust yell erupted from a tiny girl with pale braids and a pug nose, her face as dirty as the ground. Hannah, if he remembered correctly.

The eldest boy set his buckets down and strode near, taking Traveler's reins as Gideon dismounted.

"Howdy, Mister Hartley." The lad stuck out a hand. The

marks of the bucket handle scored his small palm. "Mighty glad to see you again."

Gideon hid a grin as he shook the boy's damp, bony fingers. Nine years old and the man of the house. Strong, country stock, like his father. In Gideon's previous visit to the farm, Matthew had latched on to him like a wood tick on a hound. Followed him around, peppered him with questions.

The boy's admiration was downright discomfiting.

"Good to see you, too, Matthew."

"Mama said she saw you in town. Said you'd be out soon 'cause you was a man of your word." Matthew whirled toward the other children, who'd gathered in a bunch around him. "Tell Mama. It's Mr. Hartley, the saving man."

The saving man. Gideon's chest pinched at the sweet, inappropriate words.

He couldn't save anyone. Life had taught him that. Even now, he could envision the dead faces as clearly as if they hadn't been buried for fourteen years.

Mary Baker flew out the cabin door, her apron strings sailing behind her. "Gideon, you're here. Oh, this is a right treat. Children, wash those nasty faces. Hannah, see to Biddy's diaper."

The chattering children latched onto his hands and arms, clinging like baby possums as they ushered him through the narrow doorway.

"Isaiah, dear, Gideon's come to see you."

The tender love in Mary's voice touched a chord in Gideon. What would it be like to have a love this strong and faithful? And why, suddenly, were such questions tormenting him? He deserved nothing of the sort.

Not a man who dared contemplate such improbabilities, Gideon blinked his eyes against the image and the cabin's dim confines.

The interior was divided by curtains for the sake of privacy, though they were open this time of day as was the door and single window. Although crowded with bits of rugged furniture and the children, the cabin was clean and as tidy as possible, the air redolent of food on the fire.

There was love here, love and family. A man felt it the minute he stepped through the doorway.

Hat in his hands, Gideon crossed the rough puncheon floor, the sound of his boots as hollow as his soul, to where Isaiah rested on the iron bedstead, one leg propped on a folded, faded quilt.

As long and angular as Mr. Lincoln, Isaiah Baker sported a reddish-blond beard and wore his pale hair slicked back from his face, his hazel eyes warm and direct.

His was a good face. An honest face. A man could trust Isaiah Baker.

"Let me get up." Isaiah's smile greeted him. "Hand me that stick, will you, Gideon?"

Gideon motioned him to stay where he was. "Not on my account. Keep that leg up."

"You listen to Gideon, Isaiah," Mary said, her faded blue eyes worried. "We can't have you busting that sore open again. You know what Mercy said. You stay put."

Isaiah gave his wife an affectionate glance. "Feisty, isn't she? The best there is." He winked, his countenance merry. "Get a woman like this one and your life's a feathered road."

Blushing a little, Mary flapped a hand toward her husband.

Again, the love between the couple swarmed Gideon. He, who was immune to such emotion, recognized it when he saw it.

His mother had loved his father like this.

At Mary's bidding, Sam, a five-year-old silent grinner,

dragged a cane-bottom chair to Gideon. Gideon sat, gripping his hat, anxious lest his hands tremble and Isaiah notice.

There were some secrets a man needed to keep in his pocket.

"Sure is good to see you, Gideon," Isaiah said. "The Lord always knows what we need before we even ask Him." Expression gentle, his teeth barely showed in the crop of whiskers. "We did ask, though. Prayed He'd pour you out a blessing you couldn't contain."

Gideon shifted uncomfortably under talk of the Almighty. He recognized the Scriptures that flowed out of Isaiah like water from a spring. He'd once believed as strongly as his mother had. But that was before.

Deftly switching topics, he said, "How are you, Isaiah? The leg healing?"

"Well enough. In a few days, I'll be in the fields again. Time's wasting to get that crop in or pay the price this winter."

In the weeks since the accident, the farmer had improved, thanks to his wife's tender care, but he was nowhere near ready to walk behind a plow.

Mary cast a worried glance at her husband. "The Lord will provide, Isaiah. We cain't afford for you to take a setback. Matthew and me can plow."

The other man frowned but didn't argue. He knew he was in a fix. A family to feed and a busted leg didn't go together very well on the prairie.

Something in Gideon that he barely recognized rose up, pecking away at the conscience he tried to keep well seared. "I could plow a few acres while I'm here."

Isaiah shook his head. His beard whispered over his muslin shirtfront. "We couldn't ask you to do such a thing."

"You didn't. I offered." A few hours in the hot sun might

take his mind off the bottle in his saddlebags. He sorely wanted a drink.

Gideon saw the struggle on Isaiah's face. Pride and independence warred with need and practicality. Need won out. "I'll repay you when I can."

"I'll hold you to it," Gideon said to settle the matter, though he had no intention of collecting the debt.

"All right, then. Obliged."

As if she'd been holding her breath, Mary let out a relieved sigh and went briskly about the business of a farm wife, work he'd seen his mother do a thousand times, though she'd had paid help and Mary did not.

What he'd give for one more day with the gentle woman who'd bore him and his siblings and raised them right. The truth of that dug into his conscience and increased his desire for a glass of whiskey. Just one. Only one.

"I've got rabbit stew in the pot." Mary broke into his thoughts as she aimed a proud look at her son. "Matthew set some rabbit traps, and the Lord did the rest."

Matthew puffed out his small chest. "Got two fat ones yesterday. None today, but Ma says we had plenty of leftovers."

Gideon doubted the plenty part.

"Sounds delicious."

"Mary's biscuits will make your mouth water."

He hadn't come to eat their meager rations and add to their troubles. Truth was he hadn't intended to come here today, but he'd felt compelled, as if their wholesome goodness could rub off on him and change who he'd become. The turkey had simply given him an excuse.

"We got fresh butter, too," Mary was saying. "Mercy brought it when she come to check on Isaiah's injury. Willa sent it. Claimed they had plenty of milk to spare." Mary chuckled, shaking her head. "That's a stretch of the truth if ever I heard it, but I figure the Lord will forgive her."

Gideon crushed the brim of his hat. He sat up straighter. "Willa Malone?"

There she was again, his nemesis, right back in his head, golden brown eyes blazing with a passion that would likely get her killed, or at the least leave her bitter and disappointed.

Of all the names for Mary to say, this was the one he least wanted to hear.

Mary dipped her hands in a washbasin and dried them on a rough flour sack. "Do you know her? She and her sisters have a cabin about a mile through the woods. Closer into Sweet Clover. They been a real blessing to us."

He cleared his throat. "We've met."

Mary dumped flour into a clean blue-speckled dishpan. "Terrible how some feller killed their pa, but those girls are made of strong stuff. Stubborn like the rest of us, I guess. Made up their minds to stay in Sweet Clover and make the best of it."

"Sure glad they did." Isaiah motioned to the leg sticking up from the pile of blankets, the toes bare and puffy from swelling. "With no doctor around, Mercy is a godsend. She's got a gift. A healing touch. I coulda lost this leg without her."

"We couldn't afford no doctor, anyway," Mary said. "Mercy takes whatever we can pay. Usually nothing."

"I'll pay her better once I'm on my pegs again. Told her I'd work her land in trade."

"I know you will, dear," Mary said, soothing wounded pride. "Mercy knows, too."

"She mentioned some notion about Willa going after her pa's killer," Isaiah said. "Mary dispossessed her of such foolishness right quick."

Gideon doubted that very much. Willa seemed set on getting herself killed.

Not his problem.

He wished she'd leave him alone.

Mary turned from her biscuit dough to poke a stick into the fireplace, stirring the flame beneath the stewpot. "Willa is strong, but that's downright dangerous. What good is bounty money if you're dead?"

He sighed, annoyed and troubled that Willa had followed him here.

Worse than a dog on a steak bone, plain and simple Willa had not given up her quest.

"Now, Miss Willa, you know I hate to turn you down, you ladies being alone and all, but I can't give you any more credit until you pay what you owe."

Hank Fleming, owner of Fleming's Mercantile and General Store, spread his thick, fleshy hands in helplessness.

"I'm sorry. Truly sorry. Your daddy, God rest his soul, ran up quite a bill before he left, and I have a family to feed."

Willa struggled against defeat.

"I'll repay you for everything, including Papa's bill, as soon as I return with the money. You have my word."

Ruby Fleming, her brown bun nestled high on her head like a bird's nest, popped out from behind the yard goods. "Where are you going, Willa? Visiting wealthy relatives?"

The fact that Mrs. Fleming had not already heard about Willa's quest was a surprise.

Willa searched for an evasive answer that wouldn't be a flat-out lie. She was reluctant to tell another soul of her bounty-hunting plans. All she'd heard so far was laughter, disbelief or dire warnings of her certain demise.

Finally, she huffed out the only kind of answer she knew how to give. An honest one. "To collect the bounty on my papa's killer."

"Land O' Goshen!" Mrs. Fleming's fleshy jowls wobbled. She gripped the bib of her white apron as if to hold in the shock. "George Radcliff was in here yesterday, telling that, but I thought he was in the sauce again." She leaned in as if to share a confidence. "He nips the bottle, you see, though he hides it from his wife. You can smell him, though. He's not fooling a soul."

Like Gideon Hartley. A man couldn't long hide his penchant for strong drink.

Willa's fingers clenched on the folds of her skirt.

Thinking about Hartley made her mad enough to spit. There was a man who could guide her, who knew the territory like the back of his hand, and he'd rather sit in a saloon and drink and gamble than earn an honest living.

He could full well drink himself senseless. She didn't need him or anyone else.

Her mind was made up. She'd prayed, figured, wheedled dabs of information out of Rupert Johnson and, guide or no guide, she would not be deterred.

Though her whole body quaked if she let herself think too hard on the issue, she saw no other choice.

Mr. Fleming's perpetual frown deepened. "Your pa would be beside himself."

More likely Papa would saddle up and go with her. To Finn Malone, adventure was worth the risk.

Look what that got him, a little voice whispered in her ear. *Look what it got all of you.*

Willa shushed the voice.

"I appreciate your concern, Mrs. Fleming. Now, about those supplies." From her skirt pocket, she extracted a list written in Mercy's flowing hand and placed it on the counter along with a pound of butter.

With an increase in Brownie's milk output, Willa had extra

butter to barter. Savannah claimed the Lord had seen their need and provided in the most practical way.

She hoped the Good Lord would also see her need for these supplies. She couldn't very well ride into Indian Territory, wherever it was, without food and ammo.

"Willa, child," Mrs. Fleming said, owl-eyed behind her spectacles, as her husband studied the list, "if something un-toward should happen to you, your poor sisters…"

The woman let the words trail away but Willa got the mes-sage. Her sisters had lost both mother and father. Losing their eldest sister, the strongest of the lot, was unthinkable.

Hadn't she fretted about this? Prayed about it? Pleaded with God to show her another way to earn that money?

"Mercy and Savannah are resilient. They'll be fine."

Ruby sniffed, the line of her mouth tightening. "What about your pa's bill? If you get killed, who will pay?"

Ruby Fleming didn't care one whit about her sisters or if Willa ended up dead as long as she got her money.

All Willa had of value was her land and the cabin—which were already in jeopardy—Maeve's stove, a cow, a horse and some chickens.

"Would you consider a promissory note?" she asked. "If I don't have your money by autumn, you can take my dozen chickens."

The idea heartened her. Chickens could be replenished. She could set a hen and start another flock right away.

"Well." Hank stroked his short salt-and-pepper beard again, considering the note in his hand. "This is a mighty long list you got."

Mrs. Fleming's ample form leaned over the counter, sharp eyes sparking. "What about your cow?"

Willa blinked, taken aback. "She's worth more than a few groceries and a box of rifle shells."

"Tell you what." Hank tapped the list. "Sign a note for your cow, and I'll fill your order and allow your sisters to make necessary purchases while you're off on this wild goose chase."

Brownie. The dependable Guernsey.

Without the cow, they'd have no milk, no butter, no baby calf to sell each year. Brownie was a big part of their future plans.

Willa weighed the options and didn't like what she saw. If she signed a promissory note and didn't find Charlie Bangs, she'd lose the cow and be worse off than she was now. If something terrible happened and she didn't return at all, her sisters would not only lose her, they'd lose a good portion of their livelihood when Mr. Fleming took Brownie to pay the bill.

On the other hand, if she didn't barter the cow, she'd have no chance at all of repaying Papa's loan.

She simply had to find Charlie Bangs and collect that reward.

With a shaky gust of resignation, she agreed.

"All right. My cow. In exchange for supplies for me and for my sisters until I return."

"Only until October." Mrs. Fleming offered a narrow smile. "In case you don't return at all."

Willa shuddered at the cold, but too true, prospect.

Faster than Willa could rethink the impetuous decision, the other woman whipped out a pencil and paper. Mrs. Fleming scribbled something, then turned the note to Willa and tapped the pencil end. "Sign right here."

Willa's heart clattered. She stared at the squiggles on the page. They swam and moved before her eyes.

She had no idea what the proprietress had written.

Humiliation burned her face. With a shaky hand, she scribbled the only words she knew, *Willa Malone*.

She returned the stubby pencil, her hands suddenly clammy. What had she done? Would she lose her home *and* the cow?

Mr. Fleming studied her list again. "Don't have everything on here. It'll take me two weeks, maybe more, to get all these things ordered in."

Another few weeks of waiting and worrying that Charlie Bangs was too far away to catch. Or that he was dead and someone else would collect the bounty on his sorry head.

Another choiceless decision.

Mrs. Fleming pushed her spectacles up on her nose and placed a spool of thread on the counter, her mood cheerful now that she thought she would inherit a fine milk cow.

"Tell Savannah, if this isn't the right color, she can come in and trade."

"Thank you, Mrs. Fleming. I'm sure this will be fine."

Willa was only serviceable with a needle and thread. Another of her womanly failings. Even her weekly visit with Belle Holbrook and the quilt they were making hadn't improved her stitches.

All the more reason to prove she could do anything a man could do. Which included bringing in Charlie Bangs.

Gathering her merchandise, Willa turned to leave as the bell over the door tinkled and Theodore Pierce stepped inside.

Her belly dropped to her dusty boot tops.

Sweet Clover's only banker. An arrogant, handsy sort who made her uncomfortable. The man who held the lien on her home was no one's friend but his own. She'd learned that the hard way when, to satisfy her sisters, she'd pleaded one last time for an extension on Papa's loan.

Mr. Pierce had smirked at her. Smirked and uttered discomfiting innuendos about her sisters.

She'd been tempted to shoot him.

Theodore Pierce also ran the land office and bought up

widows' claims for a few dollars, squeezed out struggling farmers for a few more and was ever eager to loan money against a land claim. A loan he knew a settler likely couldn't repay and that would, eventually, profit him greatly.

Theodore Pierce was a well-dressed thief, that's what he was.

Still fretting over the corner she'd backed herself into with the Flemings, and hoping to sidestep the banker, Willa dipped her chin low, hiding her face beneath her wide-brimmed hat, and hastened toward the exit.

As she reached for the door and escape, Pierce's imperious voice froze her in place.

"Miss Willa Malone. Is that you, my dear?"

Theodore's syrupy endearment made her stomach churn worse than it did at the smell of blood.

With reluctance, she turned to face the man who held her future, quite literally, in the palm of his greedy hand.

Always dapper in a dark suit, string tie and vest, the banker tipped his bowler hat and bowed.

He should have been a handsome man. Yet, his condescending manner and razor-sharp stare made her skin crawl. Perhaps she disliked him so much because of the awful awareness of his power over her and her sisters.

Power to take everything. Power to leave them destitute.

Why, oh, why, had Papa mortgaged their land claim to this opportunist?

Because Papa was a trusting soul.

Rich men put their britches on just like us poor ones, me lass, her father's voice echoed in her head. *There's no need to fear.*

Willa's chin shot up.

Refusing to let the banker see her anxiety, she offered a curt nod. "Good day, Mr. Pierce."

She reached for the door, but the banker blocked her way.

"Now, Willa dear, you aren't trying to avoid me, are you?" His smile was feral. "Something's come up. We need to talk."

"I'll try to stop by the bank later." She made another effort to go around him.

He blocked her way. "We'll talk now."

Bidding farewell to Margaret Muller, a pleasant lady who'd just enlisted his aid and pocketbook in hopes of hiring a schoolmaster, Gideon headed down the mercantile stairs. He'd somehow promised to talk to friends, especially the wealthy Belle Holbrook, about donations, though how the affable Mrs. Muller had roped him into such a thing baffled his brain.

However, the prospect of a tamer town with a school would have pleased his mother.

He rubbed the sore spot in the middle of his chest that always ached when he thought of her. Susannah Hartley treasured education, had seen he'd had plenty, though he'd used it poorly.

Another failure on his part.

At the bottom of the steps, he cast a glance at the clear glass jars of lemon drops and peppermints next to the cash register, planning to buy a few. Peppermint freshened the breath and hid the whiskey.

At the counter, a sunburned man in red suspenders spoke to Ruby Fleming, hat twisting and twisting in his beefy hands as he inquired of a letter from home.

When none was found, the farmer left, dejected.

A frisson of pity slid through Gideon, unexpected and unwanted. A letter from home. Something he'd never had. Never would have.

His gaze followed the man's departure, but his attention caught and held on the duo near the exit.

The banker, Theodore Pierce, allowed the farmer to pass,

but barred the way of one small woman in a wren-brown dress and men's heavy worn boots.

Willa Malone.

Stroking his bottom lip, eyebrows tugged inward, Gideon observed momentarily. The banker with plain and simple Willa?

The stiffness of Willa's shoulders told him this was not a friendly conversation.

He knew Theodore Pierce. Knew he preyed on struggling settlers to line his already fat pockets and grow his banking business. Half the town owed him money.

Gideon had also heard the disturbing rumor that the pompous banker had roughed up a girl or two at the Red Diamond Saloon. He didn't know if it was true. Yet.

His fists clenched and unclenched.

He eased closer, careful to remain out of sight. He pretended to browse the shelves of toiletries, though his eyes and ears drifted to the conversation that was none of his business.

Theodore considered himself a ladies' man, irresistible to women.

Gideon's gaze stumbled over Willa. She was definitely a woman.

With a narrow smile that could only be termed malicious, the banker was saying, "As you know, Willa, I am deeply concerned about you and your lovely sisters. Alone since the unfortunate death of your father. Sad, very sad."

Gideon's lip curled. Pierce wasn't sad at all. He was a vulture circling the wounded.

"Thank you. Now, if you'll excuse me." Willa made a reach for the door.

Pierce covered the door handle. Willa snatched her hand away and clenched the little fist at her side.

Gideon read the tension in her slender form and pitied her.

He pressed the spot on his breastbone again.

"Though I am reluctant to bring up the topic during your time of grief, we have financial matters to discuss." Pierce smacked his lips in irritating *tsking* noises that set Gideon's teeth on edge.

Head held high, Willa replied, "My loan is not due until October. We'll talk then."

She made as if to push around him. The banker put a hand on her arm, his fingers curling tight.

Something primal stirred in Gideon. He shouldn't be listening. But he didn't like Theodore Pierce, and in spite of himself, he admired Willa Malone.

Men like Pierce reminded him of another time, another place. Of men who took without giving. Of one particular man who cared for no one except himself.

His jaw tightened.

"August, not October," Pierce said, his tone cold.

A tiny sound of dismay escaped Willa. She was not, Gideon thought, as tough as she tried to appear. "But you extended the loan."

"Things have changed."

No surprise there. Men like Pierce knew how to manipulate forms and paperwork to their advantage.

Willa's small shoulders rose and fell, her breathing now fast and anxious.

Gideon's insides sparked, a match to dry kindling.

"But when Papa died, you said you'd give us extra time." Her fingers worried her skirt.

"Times are difficult for all of us. Too many like you have not paid their bank debts and, though I am a sympathetic man, I can no longer carry this town on my shoulders."

Gideon would have laughed had he not been so angry. Sympathetic, indeed. Pierce held townspeople hostage.

"I should have known I couldn't trust you." Willa jerked away from Pierce with that stubborn spunk Gideon could not help but respect. Her hat, that flat brimmed, ill-fitting man's hat, fell on a string to her back. A long thick braid tumbled down. "You will get your money, Mr. Pierce."

The banker's nostrils flared in distaste. "At the risk of being crass, I must inquire. Where will *you* get that much cash in such a short time?"

The spark, now a flame, moved into Gideon's chest. His pulse began a warning rhythm against his temple.

"That, sir, is my concern." Willa's voice was firm, but the fear was there, and Theodore Pierce, like a coyote smelling blood, pounced.

Cold gaze narrowing, the banker's fake smile dwindled to a long flat line. A mean line, like the one Gideon's father employed with his sharecroppers.

"No, Willa, it is *my* concern," Pierce snapped, relinquishing any pretense of civility. "I let your father have that money in a fair and legal loan. Now, he's dead, and my patience and altruism have grown thin. If you do not repay the full amount by the first day of August, you will forfeit your father's holdings, including the land claim on which you and your sisters reside. Is that clear?"

"I am perfectly aware, Mr. Pierce, of the original provisions of the loan even though you *did* agree to wait until October." Red-faced with humiliation, Willa stood her ground, head tilted high. Defeated, but proud. "Nonetheless, I will repay it on time."

Gideon's admiration edged up another notch. She was a fighter, but a fighter without a bit of ammunition against a man as powerful and wealthy as Theodore Pierce.

The banker barked a cruel laugh, his tiny mustache disappearing beneath his nose.

Mocking, he said, "Oh, yes, I've heard about the latest Malone escapade. *You're* to be the bounty hunter who brings your father's killer to justice."

Willa stiffened. "I *will* find him."

She would try. Gideon could hear it in her voice, see it in her stance. This determined woman would do whatever she must, even if that meant riding alone into the nation's most lethal territory to find a man who would shoot her on sight.

Stay out of it.

He tried to turn away, but his feet seemed nailed to the wood floor.

"*Tsk-tsk.* Impossible." Pierce casually flicked an imaginary bit of lint from his sleeve as if flicking Willa and her sisters off their land. "Surely, you're aware of the unspeakable horrors that await a woman alone in outlaw country."

Pierce's nostrils flared, his cruel smile tilted as though he enjoyed thinking of those horrors.

Willa skewered him with a glare, but her bottom lip, that pouting, delightful lip, quivered.

Gideon fought the urge to swoop in like a white knight and carry her as far away from Theodore Pierce as possible.

How absolutely bizarre.

But something in him burned, as inflamed as Willa's cheeks.

"Let me pass, please." She moved as if to edge around him. Pierce refused to budge.

"Do yourself a favor, Willa. Sell me the land today. I'll even forgive the interest and give you a small sum to tide you over. It will be mine soon anyway." He offered the ugliest of smiles.

"No. Now, please remove yourself before I make a scene."

The banker's face hardened. He grabbed her arm, yanked her up close, his voice low and lecherous. "Unless you or your pretty sisters want to work out some other more *personal* arrangements, I suggest you take my offer."

Willa gasped, her mouth open in shock. Gideon's steaming blood boiled over.

He stepped into sight. He had no plan, didn't know what he would say or do. But one glance at Willa's stricken face and all common sense fled.

He moved to her side. She glanced up at him, red-faced and as bewildered to see him as he was to be standing there.

"Why, Theodore, didn't Miss Malone tell you?" Gideon kept his tone light, easy and more than a touch condescending. "She's not going after her father's killer alone. She's hired the best tracker and guide in the West." He showed his teeth in a feral smile. "Me."

To Gideon's distinct pleasure, the banker dropped his hold on Willa. He took one step back, his eyes bulging. "You, Hartley? Folks say you retired."

"Tsk-tsk, Theodore." Gideon narrowed his eyes and imitated the banker's imperious treatment of Willa, his tone thick with sarcasm. "Have you been listening to idle gossip? I'd have thought better of a man of your *illustrious* station. As Miss Malone indicated, you will get your money, but you will not get her land."

Pierce's face mottled. His neck veins bulged. "Now see here, Hartley. This is not your business."

"I beg to differ." Turning his back on the sputtering peacock, Gideon offered an arm to Willa. "Miss Malone, shall we?"

She placed her tough little hand in the crook of his arm and smiled up at him.

For one infinitesimal second, Gideon remembered what it meant to feel worthwhile.

Chapter Five

They parted ways in the middle of the dirt-packed street.

Willa stared at Gideon's quickly retreating figure.

"Shouldn't we discuss the particulars?" she called after him.

He kept walking. "No."

Jerking her skirt above her ankles, she grabbed onto her hat and trotted to catch up.

"Mr. Hartley. Stop. Please."

One foot up on the boardwalk outside the saloon, Gideon cast a regretful look toward the swinging doors before slowly pivoting in her direction.

"'Arise, black vengeance, from thy hollow hell.'"

His habit of uttering sardonic phrases confused her. Most of the time she didn't know what he was talking about. This time she did, and she didn't like it.

"This isn't about revenge."

A black eyebrow shot up. "So you say."

An empty buckboard pulled by a team of mules rushed by too fast, stirring dust and scattering pedestrians. Willa stepped closer to Hartley and out of the street, her heart still thudding with the wonder of his words to the banker.

She waved a hand at the dust, coughed. "You said you'd guide me."

"To my great regret."

"Are you a man of your word or not?"

"What would you say if I said no? That my only intent was to rescue you from that supercilious, parasitic, posturing peacock."

Willa's mouth quivered at the apt description of Theodore Pierce. "I owe you my thanks."

"None needed. Now, if you'll pardon me." He turned once more to leave.

Willa followed him.

When his hand touched the top of the swinging doors, he cast a weary glance over the shoulder of his black vest. "You aren't coming in here."

"If this is the place you choose for our conversation, then yes, I am."

He sighed, and in a droll voice, muttered, "Perhaps I was under the wrong impression about our dear, *dear* friend, Mr. Pierce. Shall I fetch him?"

In spite of her reluctance at entering the saloon and her determination to convince this man to help her, Willa laughed.

And stood her ground.

"You are a most difficult woman, plain and simple Willa."

With a shake of his dark hatless head, Gideon retreated from the doorway, took her arm and aimed them away from the saloon.

In minutes, he'd marched them into the hotel's dining room where he ordered two cups of coffee.

Willa recalled their last preempted meeting in this establishment and hoped today proved more productive.

Hope, that delicate thread, wove through her.

From her skirt pocket, she produced Charlie Bangs's wrinkled, bloodstained wanted poster and spread it on the table. "The bounty hunter who came through Sweet Clover a few weeks ago was tracking Charlie Bangs into Indian Territory. He'd heard Bangs headquartered there."

"The bounty hunter who is now *dead*?" Gideon's look was pointed.

Willa's stomach twisted. "Yes."

"Knowing his way around the Nations didn't save his life."

His implication was clear. If a tough man got killed hunting outlaws, an inexperienced female didn't stand a chance.

His words terrified her, but condemning her sisters to the streets or a life above the saloon scared her spitless. "I have to try, Mr. Hartley. I can't lose my home, and this is the only way I know to get that much money before the due date."

"One hundred and sixty acres is worth your life?"

"My sisters are."

Unreadable azure eyes flashed up to hers and then back to the wanted poster spread before him.

"You do realize there is no guarantee you can find him. This Charlie Bangs."

"We'll find him."

"We. *Hmm.*"

He rubbed his fingers across the wanted poster over and over again as he studied the handlebar mustache, the soulless stare, and read the words written below.

Willa followed the movement of those manly hands. They looked strong, capable, the backs nicked and scratched from some recent labor. Or a brawl.

She refused to consider the latter. She needed Gideon Hartley. She was also still in shock, still reeling from his sudden, unexpected declaration that he would guide her search for her father's murderer.

"You won't back out on me, will you?"

She very much feared he would. His cynical attitude, laced with a good dose of reluctance, made her wary.

He stared at her, clear-eyed and a very different man from the one she'd encountered days ago at the hotel.

Had that first morning's inebriation been an anomaly, the result of an occasional night on the town?

His reputation and those strong hands said he could do the job.

It was the other reputation that worried her. The whiskey-soaked gambler.

Could he handle a firearm?

What army scout couldn't do that?

But she recalled the way his hands had trembled that day. An aberration? Or a warning?

To quell her doubts, she pulled her focus away from his contemplative, searching gaze to the words written at the bottom of the wanted poster. Savannah had read them to her. Wanted for murder, bank robbery and horse thieving. One thousand dollars, dead or alive.

A thousand dollars. More money than she'd ever seen in her life.

"Stubbornness and grit," Gideon said, drawing her attention back to his too-handsome, too-cynical face, "can only take you so far. What will you do with this man when you find him? Can you bring him to justice? How? Or will you shoot him and leave him for buzzard bait? That is, if you can get the jump on him. A man like Charlie Bangs will not be sitting demurely on his porch with his hands tied behind his back, waiting for you to escort him before the hanging judge."

"I don't expect it to be easy. That's why I'm hiring you."

"I am a guide, not a gunfighter."

"I can shoot."

"It's a fool's game you play, Willa. You're not a bounty hunter or a lawman. Nor are you a vigilante. You're a woman." His gaze drifted over her. "A small woman at that."

Her skin tingled under his assessment. The silly attraction she'd felt at their first encounter inside the saloon flared to life. It infuriated her.

"My gender has little to do with justice for my father."

"Ah, yes. Justice. Not revenge. Not plain and simple Willa with fire and brimstone shooting from her eyes."

She ignored his sarcasm. And his manly appeal. She needed him for one purpose only. To find the man who'd shot her father. She'd long since divested herself of any romantic notions about handsome men.

"I don't know any other way to get my hands on the money unless Savannah marries rich old Homer Baggley."

"Baggley?" He looked affronted. "He's a hundred years old!"

"Not quite, but close enough. Worse, he has the manners of a goat and smells like one, too. All he wants her for is a brood mare." Willa blushed, shocked that she'd said such an intimate thing to a strange man.

And there was no stranger man she'd ever met than this one.

He was dangerously disturbing—his looks, his propensity for random outbursts of educated language, his determination to appear as if he did not care about anything at all.

But he did in fact care. Otherwise, he wouldn't have come to her rescue in the mercantile. And he wouldn't be sitting at this table, contemplating what he termed *a fool's journey*.

These small bits of revelation about Gideon Hartley encouraged her.

Somewhere inside him was a gentleman, or once had been. She was counting on that.

He tilted back in his chair, those troubling, secretive eyes focused on her in a way that deepened the heat in her cheeks. "What about you? You could marry. Don't you have a beau eager to dance to your tune?"

"If I had a man, it certainly wouldn't be someone like Baggley. He'd have a backbone. He'd be ready and willing to go after the outlaw who killed my father." She slapped an infuriated hand onto the tabletop. "We'd already be saddled up and riding hard."

"I see." Gideon stroked his lower lip in thought. "What of your other sister, the Titian-haired healer? Surely, a woman of her beauty has admirers."

Mercy had admirers, all right. She shunned them with a coldness completely contrary to her caring nature.

"Neither of my sisters is for sale."

"Admirable."

If the worst happened, Savannah could return to her mother's aunt in St. Louis. Mercy would make her own way. Somehow.

She simply had to have that bounty.

Three feet away sat her only chance to make that happen.

While she grappled with her intractable situation, Gideon remained silent, alternately studying her and the poster of Charlie Bangs.

Tension tightened her shoulders, pulled a frown to her brow. Her pulse ticked like a timepiece in her ears.

She'd done her best, said her piece. The rest was up to him. And the Lord.

With studied grace, Gideon rose and refilled his coffee cup, lofting the pot and both eyebrows toward her. She shook her head. Coffee made her nervous. She was already nervous enough.

Finally, he asked, "You are certain of this?"

"I'm going, Mr. Hartley. With or without you. I'd much prefer with you."

His handsome mouth lifted in a sad little smile. "Then pray, dear lady, that you do not soon regret that questionable preference."

Sweat sluiced from Gideon's body as if he'd taken a dip in the creek.

With the Bakers' wagon and team parked nearby, he swung the ax into a felled hickory that would provide at least a cord of firewood. His eager and constant companion, the nine-year-old Matthew, gathered the dismembered limbs, stacking them on the wagon.

This much wood should last a few weeks, maybe the summer. It was next winter that worried him.

Hopefully, by then Isaiah would be able again. His progress was slow, the wound stubborn about healing, regardless of Mercy Malone's weekly visits and various ointments and herbs. But he was out of bed now, hobbling about, doing what he could, even though the leg pained him mightily.

A man to be admired.

Gideon paused to wipe sweat, his thoughts immediately running to the tracking journey that lay ahead of him and to the saddlebag he'd slung into the back of the wagon.

That he'd agreed to accompany Willa on her futile quest troubled him greatly. He couldn't guide, not until he knew he could do so without failure, though Willa did not know this. From hard experience, he knew better than to guide inebriated.

Yet, whiskey was the only way to silence the voices and get through the day.

He was a man imprisoned by his own folly and the false assumption that he was in control.

Gideon wiped the wet kerchief over his sweating face and watched the blond boy strain with the weight of the firewood.

"You're a good worker, Matthew."

The more he complimented the child, the faster and harder Matthew worked. He was a winsome youngster, a son any father would be proud of.

"Someday, this farm will be mine." The boy's chest puffed out. "If a man takes care of the land, it will take care of him."

"Your pa teach you that?"

Matthew's shoulder hitched. "I reckon."

The boy touched something tender inside him. Isaiah was a fortunate man.

An ache, a yearning, pulled at Gideon. Toward what, he couldn't say. Family, maybe. Children. Most men wanted those things.

Had he ever?

If he had, he didn't remember. He'd been on his own, riding the frontier in one way or the other, since his eighteenth birthday.

The yearning gathered under his breastbone and set up camp.

Likely, he'd never have a son. Didn't deserve one. But he knew how to appreciate someone else's.

Wood clattered against wood as the boy dumped his load in the wagon and went back for more.

Gideon watched the child from the corner of his eye as he balanced a log on end and sliced the ax through the middle.

"Mr. Hartley." Matthew held up a leafy stem of some sort. "Reckon Mama can make us a berry pie?"

Ax fisted in one hand, Gideon walked to where the boy was surrounded by low-growing shrubs and plants. The world was green and fruitful this time of year.

"What do you have there?" Already shaking his head, he took the stem. Clusters of white berries dangled from the plant. He gave the boy a sharp look. "Did you eat any?"

Matthew's eyes widened. "No. Are they bad?"

"They're poison. Most white or yellow berries are." A man could get deathly ill on white baneberry. A child could die. Gideon motioned toward the creek. "Go wash your hands."

Matthew raced to the creek. Gideon returned to the tree he'd felled.

When the boy returned, Gideon set the ax aside and hunkered to his boot toes. "Nature can teach you a lot, Matt. See this weed? Those are duckweed and good to eat. Over there is pokeweed."

"Ma makes poke salad."

"But she boils it first and gets the poison out. You can't do that with pokeberries. So leave them be. Plenty of plants are good to eat, but some aren't. Always ask before you taste."

The boy blinked at him, his pale lashes specked with wood chips. "Where'd you learn so much?"

Gideon picked up a stick, sailed it toward the kindling pile. "A man learns a great deal by listening and observing. Nature has much to say."

Matthew, ever the mimic, sailed a stick, too. "Pa said you was a tracker. When I grow up, I want to be a tracker like you and learn all about nature."

Gideon squeezed his eyes shut, pretending to wipe sawdust from his eyelids. He was no one to be admired or imitated.

"If you own this farm, who'll work it while you're traipsing around the country?"

"I reckon I ain't thought of that."

"Your pa's a fine man and an excellent farmer. You'd best stick to farming like him. I don't even have a place to call my own. Tracking is lonely."

He'd never thought that before.

Matthew considered, his little face screwed up like a wagon spring. "You ever done any farming?"

The question sailed through Gideon's mind like a frigid north wind, leaving him chilled, though sweat drenched him. "Yes."

Gideon. Help me.

Teeth clenched against the voices, against the boy's unmerited admiration, Gideon pointed to a spot a few yards away. "A fair amount of dead wood over there on the creek bank. Add it to the kindling pile."

Matthew pivoted on his boots to peer in that direction. Quick as a rabbit, he trotted toward the creek.

The boy would do about anything Gideon asked without complaint or question.

That kind of admiration should feel good. Instead, it rotted Gideon's bones.

He shot a glance toward the wagon. With the boy out of sight, he dropped the ax in favor of the saddlebag and the flask calling to him.

As he tipped the bottle to his lips, a small voice said, "I could use a drink, too."

Gideon gulped the burning liquor and quickly closed the flask, trying to keep a straight face, though a shudder rippled through him.

With a nonchalance he didn't feel, he motioned to the wagon's front. "Canteen's on the bench."

"Oh." Matthew's usually pert steps dragged as he retrieved the canteen. Staring at Gideon in thought, he drank, then backhanded his lips. "I seen you drink that before. Is it whiskey?"

"Medicinal." The lie tasted bitter on his tongue.

"Does it taste good? 'Cause you sure drink it a lot."

Gideon's heart thudded painfully against his ribs. "No."

The boy contemplated some more while Gideon felt as small as the wood flecks speckling the ground.

"Pa says spirits are bad. They make a man forget who God wants him to be."

Shamed, Gideon slid the flask back into the pouch and tossed the saddlebag onto the wagon seat.

He hadn't intended to bring the flask this time. Yet, he'd not been able to leave it behind.

"Your pa's a smart man. You listen to him. You hear?"

Aflame with a conscience he didn't know he had, Gideon grabbed the ax.

He'd promised to wean off the whiskey the way a baby weans off milk. He had to. Either that or ride as far away from Sweet Clover as he could. Far enough that he'd never have to guide Willa anywhere or look into her honey-colored eyes and see only disillusionment.

Chapter Six

As if the Malone sisters didn't have enough problems, Mr. Baggley came to call.

Willa was tempted to slam the door in his face. For once, the old man looked presentable. This, she decided, was not necessarily a positive occurrence.

A straw boater in hand, his pinstriped pants and vest were new and spotless, his white shirt shockingly pristine. Not a tobacco stain in sight.

Hair slicked back with pomade and his mustache waxed into little curlicues, he looked like an advertisement for the circus.

He'd spruced up, at least outwardly, for this impromptu call on his intended.

The fact that Savannah had no such intentions seemed not to deter Homer Baggley in the least.

Though his clothes were new, it was too much to hope that he'd had his yearly dip in the creek. His grimy hands probably hadn't touched water since Noah's flood, the nails darkened with dirt. The remains of this morning's or perhaps last week's corn bread lodged in his long graying beard.

"I'm come for Savannah," he proclaimed pompously, loud enough for the neighbors in the next field to hear him.

This was the way he went about town. Loud, boisterous, imperious, letting everyone know he was rich, and they weren't.

He'd even offered to donate money for a new church building if it was named after him. The Homer Baggley Church of Sweet Clover didn't sit too well with the good citizens, so Reverend Danforth had gently but firmly declined.

Blocking the doorway with her annoyingly small frame, Willa stuck a hand behind her back and signaled Savannah to remain out of sight.

"I am sorry to tell you this, Mr. Baggley—"

Before the outrageous lie claiming a sudden outbreak of smallpox could form on her tongue, Savannah appeared at her side.

Willa sighed.

"Mr. Baggley." Savannah's voice was strained. "How... kind of you to call."

"Kind?" Willa muttered under her breath and received a sharp glance from her baby sister.

Kindness was both Savannah's strength and weakness. As was her rigid training in the conventions necessary to a polite society. One simply did not turn away a well-meaning visitor.

Had Miss Pennington of the ladies' academy met Mr. Baggley, Willa dared to think she would change her mind.

Baggley shoved a bouquet of flowers at Savannah.

The fragrant blossoms looked suspiciously like the sweet peas growing in front of Belle Holbrook's house. Had he purloined them along the way?

Savannah caught the bouquet against her bodice. "How... lovely. Thank you."

"Ain't you gonna ask me in? I rode all the way out here to bring you posies and court you right and proper."

Willa pinched the back of her sister's arm.

Savannah stiffened, narrowed a sidelong glance in her direction and with genteel courtesy said, "Welcome to our home, Mr. Baggley."

While Willa fought not to shove the insistent old man, regardless of his reputed wealth, onto his backside and slam the door, her sister stepped to the side and made room for Mr. Baggley's entry.

As he passed, Willa almost swooned. Not from attraction. From the stench.

Though he'd doused himself with enough bay rum to perfume the West, nothing could cover the odor of a long unwashed body.

The smell wafted off him in near-visible waves. The stench, a cross between a polecat and a dead rat was strong enough to melt the red clay chinking from the cabin walls.

Sweet Savannah offered a strained but gentle smile, the cornflower eyes darting from Willa to the man. Like windswept butterflies, her dainty hands fluttered and wobbled, seeking rescue, finally gripping the flowers for all she was worth.

Savannah was too delicate to endure this strain.

Willa had a mind to shoot Baggley, drag his carcass outside and put them all out of their misery.

Her conscience pricked, the troublesome thing. As a Christian, she shouldn't think such things. Savannah wouldn't. But she wasn't Savannah. She was tough, practical Willa who did what was necessary.

At the moment, biting down on her teeth until her jaw

ached was necessary. Savannah had made herself clear on the matter. Willa must be polite.

Displaying courtesy to the ill-mannered old geezer was one thing. Letting him court her fragile sister was quite another.

Now that Gideon had agreed to track Charlie Bangs, Savannah no longer had to consider marrying anyone except for love.

Unfortunately, Willa had yet to convince her baby sister of this.

Some wise and wonderful man would someday come along and see past Savannah's lameness, past her delicate constitution and frequent illnesses and love her for all he was worth. And Savannah would have the joy of falling in love.

Willa still held on to those girlhood aspirations of romantic love, though they were no longer for herself. She dreamed for her sisters. She, an aging spinster as plain as pudding, had long since given up hope.

If Gideon Hartley flashed in her head, it was only because she needed his expertise. He was, after all, a disturbing man who frequented saloons and drank too much.

And quoted poetry.

Lips firmly pressed together, Willa set the coffee to boil but stayed nearby in case she needed to send Baggley scurrying back to his ranch.

She'd heard he'd punched cattle for Charles Goodnight and now ran a hundred longhorn cattle of his own. Some said he'd rustled them. Others said he'd jumped a gold claim in Nevada and gotten rich on someone else's efforts.

That rumor alone was enough reason to keep him away from her baby sister.

As Savannah's suitor expounded on some tall tale about his exploits in the War Between the States, he flapped his arms like a bird in flight. Skunk stink erupted.

Savannah stuck her nose in the sweet peas.

Willa eyed her rifle standing in a corner near the door.

She wouldn't have to waste much ammunition, which she'd need for the upcoming trip. One bullet. Then she'd bury Homer in the garden.

With these sinful, but satisfying, thoughts came the realization that Savannah might seriously contemplate marriage to this frightfully inappropriate suitor.

She prayed diligently and somewhat loudly every night that Willa would not undertake the dangerous expedition into Indian Territory.

Was Savannah willing to sacrifice herself on the altar of a horrible marriage to protect Willa?

The prospect broke Willa's heart. Savannah loved her enough to do it. Willa wouldn't allow it. Savannah would be no one's brood mare.

Willa set her mind to speak with Gideon today. He'd claimed business to attend to before he could leave, but time was wasting. If Baggley's increasingly frequent visits were any indication, he had every intention of dragging her sister to the altar sooner rather than later.

Willa slammed the coffeepot down hard. Savannah jumped. Baggley went right on rambling.

"What do ya think of my duds?" The scrawny little man stuck out his bird chest, his thumbs looped beneath his vest. "Fancy, ain't they? Ordered 'em from Chicago."

Savannah's cheeks tinged pink.

"Quite—" she searched for something kind to say "—cosmopolitan."

He beamed and patted his chest with both hands. "Hitch your wagon to me, honey, and you'll be wearing fancy duds, too. Won't nobody even notice that gimpy leg no more."

The pain in Savannah's expression ripped into Willa.

Willa glared at the thoughtless old goat. She needed to shoot him. Real bad.

"Coffee, Mr. Baggley?" *With a dose of arsenic.*

"Sounds mighty fine, Miss Willa. I'll take some refreshments, too. Afterward, me and my little woman are going for a buggy ride. Did you know a feller can rent one down at the livery off that Irish feller? Not that I cotton much to the Irish. Ignorant bogtrotters."

Willa bristled. Did the man not have the intellect to realize the woman he courted was half-Irish?

"Mr. O'Shea seems to be an honest Christian man," Savannah commented somewhere in between Baggley's threat of putting a stop to any Irish trying to take over their fine town and his braggadocious insistence that he was rich enough to buy the livery and all its trappings.

If fire and brimstone could shoot out of her eyes, the way Gideon had claimed, Homer Baggley would be smoldering ash. "Savannah will not ride in a buggy with you."

"Now, see here, Miss Willa, that's for Savannah to decide. Us being engaged and all."

The rosy color drained from Savannah's complexion. "Mr. Baggley, we are not engaged. Why, sir, I barely know you."

Willa's face hardened. "You're not courting, either."

Baggley fumbled in the pocket of his bib overalls and pulled out a wad of cash. She and Savannah both gasped at the sight.

"If you're thinking I cain't support her, here's the proof."

The man seemed incapable of comprehension.

"Mr. Baggley," Savannah said, "you shouldn't carry that much cash on your person. Ruffians pass through Sweet Clover."

"Now, don't you fret, pretty thing." Completely misinterpreting her concern, he reached out and patted Savannah's hand. "You won't be losing me to some scallywag. No, siree.

You'll have your man fit as a fiddle for our wedding day." He winked broadly. "If you get my drift."

Willa wanted to slap his filthy paws away. Savannah sat as stiff and pale as a marble statue, appalled at his forward behavior. Miss Pennington clearly never had any dealings with the likes of Homer Baggley.

He patted Savannah's hand again, then laced his fingers through hers. She stared down at the joining as if he'd injected typhus into her bloodstream.

"Heard someone in town say you was a right fine hand at sewing and was craving one of them fancy machines."

Savannah wiggled her fingers free. "Wherever did you hear such a thing?"

"I inquired at the mercantile about your preferences. Figured if we was getting hitched, I needed to know how expensive you'd be."

"Mr. Baggley," Willa started. Shooting was too good for this smelly, self-absorbed varmint.

He waved her away, his focus on Savannah. "I ordered you one."

"Sir, it wouldn't be appropriate. Surely, you understand. I cannot accept gifts from a man I hardly know."

A man she'd keep on *not* knowing if Willa had her say.

Baggley grappled for Savannah's hand again. Savannah skillfully avoided the touch by raising the flowers to her nose.

"I'm eager to get some young'uns started so getting acquainted won't take long. But I tell you right now, I ain't tending our brood. That's a woman's job 'til they get big enough to work the farm. I figure I need six or eight boys quick as we can make them."

Savannah's face turned crimson. She fanned herself. Her efforts stirred the intolerable smell. She stopped fanning and pushed the flowers closer to her heart-shaped face.

"I declare, you must not say such things. It isn't proper."

He sipped the coffee Willa had served him. The brown liquid dripped from his mustache onto his white shirt. If he noticed, he ignored it.

He continued his nonsensical insistence that Savannah was his bride-to-be, making outlandish promises alternately with shockingly inappropriate remarks until Willa's patience strained to the snapping point.

Finally, despairing of him ever departing, Willa grabbed her hat from the wall peg and shoved it on her head. "You'll have to excuse us, Mr. Baggley. Savannah and I have a previous engagement."

The fact that he was being dismissed slowly dawned on the man. Gripping his boater, which now bore dirty handprints, he rose to his feet.

And tainted the air.

Willa, breathing through her mouth, ushered him to the door.

To keep up proprieties, Savannah said, "Good day to you, sir."

He'd taken one step out the door when he turned, the glint in his eye a warning of more to come.

"I expect you're craving an invite to the Faragates' barn dance." As if a thought had actually crossed his mind, he waved his hat, erasing the left-handed invitation. "Aw, what am I thinking? A crip like you can't do no jigging."

A hand to her high-necked collar, Savannah's mouth worked like a fish out of water.

Willa slammed the door before her sister could faint dead away, fashion a polite reply or worse, agree to be courted by the outrageous man.

Twitching the window curtain to one side, she watched the

distasteful bag of humanity climb aboard a handsome one-horse buggy and turn toward town.

As soon as he disappeared from sight, she flung open the door and windows. There wasn't enough fresh air in Oklahoma Territory to undo the damage Baggley had perpetrated on her home.

"I would have shot him had he remained any longer. I reckon the milk's gone sour from the smell."

"Now, Willa, don't be cruel. The poor soul doesn't seem aware of his rather odiferous personage. His suit was—" she waved a dainty hand as if she could snatch the perfect kind word from the air "—clean."

Willa snorted. "It won't be for long. Don't go feeling sorry for him."

"There is good in everyone. Mr. Baggley included. He would be a good provider, and he is not put off too badly by my lameness. Both of those are good qualities."

"He calls you a gimp and expects you to produce babies like a rabbit."

Savannah flushed crimson. "Such talk."

"Generated by Baggley himself. Really, Savannah, how could you even consider him as suitable?"

"I don't." Her thin shoulders shuddered. "However, he seems eager to please even if he's a tad forceful and silly at times."

"Silly? The man doesn't have sense enough to pound sand in a rat hole."

Worry wrinkles formed between Savannah's eyebrows. "Were I to ask, I believe he'd absorb our debts."

"As well as our property!" The notion outraged Willa. Stinky Baggley was not taking her sister or her home. "*I* will resolve the loan."

Savannah fidgeted with her collar. "I don't want you to go after that criminal."

The tender plea stirred Willa's love for her younger sister. "I know, sweet girl, but I must. Stop considering Baggley as the answer to our prayers. We already have an answer."

"What if you're wrong? What if the Lord sent Mr. Baggley so you wouldn't have to go after that outlaw?"

"He didn't. He sent Gideon Hartley."

"Whom you know nothing about! Why, the man could be a scallywag or a—a—a." Savannah waved her dainty hands, apparently unable to think of anything worse than *a scallywag*.

A weary, but smiling, Mercy walked through the open door and plunked her medical bag onto the table. "Why did I pass Homer Baggley on the road? Don't tell me he was here again."

"He was." Willa's tone was as aggravated as a bug in a jar. "Can't you smell him?"

Mercy removed her bonnet and let the mahogany hair tumble to her shoulders, shaking it out as if her head couldn't hold up the heavy locks any longer.

She sniffed the air, wrinkling her nose. "Oh, my. Savannah. You poor child."

"I am not a child, Mercy, though you and Willa seem inclined to forget that. Securing our farm is as much my responsibility as Willa's. We must keep every option open."

"Baggley is not an option, Savannah," Willa insisted, "even if he's made up his mind to marry you."

Like an actor in a Greek tragedy, Savannah stared at the now-bedraggled bouquet.

With a sigh that broke Willa's heart, she murmured, "What if I have to?"

Willa knew what her sister was thinking.

What if Willa couldn't find Bangs? Or worse, what if she never returned to Sweet Clover?

Chapter Seven

Weaning off the liquor didn't work. Gideon tried for days and failed. Every single day.

To avoid the constant temptation of the saloon, he started spending more time on the Baker farm.

Today, the Baker children had headed to the creek with their mama while Gideon plowed another acre for planting corn. Isaiah kept him company from a nearby stump.

Hot, sweaty and craving whiskey, Gideon leaned against a wide tree next to his friend and sipped his canteen. He'd finally faced the truth. He wanted to quit. He'd tried to quit. He couldn't.

Several days a week, he awakened with both a head- and a heartache, the taste of the previous night's whiskey sour on his tongue. The shame of lost control was a dark truth from which he could no longer hide.

This morning had been one of those days. To cure the aches, he'd begun the day with a double shot, which had reminded him of Willa Malone's disappointed eyes.

She'd be even more disappointed to learn he could not, anytime soon, guide her anywhere.

The liquor owned him.

Shifting away a little, he hoped Isaiah couldn't smell this morning's libations.

Whittling on a stick, Isaiah said, "When I pray, I get the feeling you're battling more than a reluctance to take Willa Malone into outlaw territory."

"She's pressing to get on the trail."

"You're not ready?"

"No."

"Why not? It's what you do, what you're good at. You told me you missed the work. People talk about you as if you mapped the territories by yourself."

Gideon allowed a grin. The faded pride of those accomplishments lingered, and yet, without redemption, they were but a fragrance on the prairie wind.

"Got some business to do first." Which he had no idea how to handle.

Isaiah mulled that a bit, whittling away, flicking curls of wood into the grass. "What about your family? How do they feel about this journey?"

Gideon flinched, chest contracting. "No family. Home's where I hang my hat."

The whittling paused. Thoughtful eyes bored into the side of Gideon's face. "I see."

He probably did. Isaiah was the kind of perceptive soul who could see right into another man's head.

"Everyone's dead." Gideon tried to sound casual but failed. "All but one."

"And that one?"

Anger bubbled up, a vile fountain. Gideon clamped down on his molars hard enough to break iron, barely expelling the bitter words. "*That* one is to blame for their deaths."

A long silence ensued. Isaiah was either thinking or praying. A calm, patient soul, he never rushed headlong into any discussion.

Gideon took a kerchief from his pocket and wiped sweat. Sweat from the heat, from the anger, from the need for whiskey, which grew by the moment.

The sound of retching broke the uncomfortable silence.

Isaiah grabbed his crutch. "Who could that be? The children are with Mary."

Matthew wobbled into sight behind the house. He paused, hands to the knees of his gallused overalls and retched again.

"The boy's sick. I'll see to him."

With long strides, Gideon traversed the freshly plowed field. He felt Isaiah thumping along behind as fast as his crutch could carry him.

When he reached the child, Gideon went to his haunches. Immediately, the smell hit him. Mortification followed.

"Oh, Matt," he said quietly, "what have you done?"

"What is it, Gideon?" Isaiah limped up next to him. "What's wrong with him?"

Matt, barely able to focus, looked up at his father, his words garbled. "I'm sorry, Pa. You told me. Spirits are bad. I did wrong."

"Spirits! Where did you get—"

"You were right, Mr. Gideon." The boy sank to the loose dirt, his head in his hands. "It don't taste good."

Isaiah's gaze turned on Gideon. Terrible knowledge and deep, deep disappointment settled on him, pulling his shoulders and his mouth downward.

"From you, Gideon? From *you*?" The agony in his voice blasted a hole in Gideon as surely as if he'd shot him.

He wished he had.

Gideon rose with the boy in his arms. "I'll carry him to the house."

The short walk was the longest he could remember taking in a long time. He'd ruined his friendship with the Bakers, defiled himself even more than usual and hurt this endearing little boy who admired him in a way he had no right to be admired.

"Set him outside by the door in case he purges again." Isaiah's voice was curt, wounded, sad.

Gideon did as he was told, propping the boy in the shade of the house. The child's head lolled.

He wanted to say something, to apologize, ask forgiveness, *something*, but feared that nothing he said would matter now.

"I'll go."

Isaiah nodded once as he sat down beside his son and put an arm around the lad's shoulders. Here was a good father. One who would instruct, discipline and forgive.

Matthew's misdeed lay firmly at Gideon's door. It was his transgression, not the boy's. He should never have brought whiskey to this farm.

With heart heavier than an anvil, he went to his dependable horse, tied a few feet from the cabin door. Taken from his saddlebag, the telltale liquor bottle lay on the ground next to the animal, empty.

Gideon grabbed the shameful evidence and shoved it into the saddlebag. As bleak and hollow as the deepest cavern, he mounted Traveler and rode slowly toward town, vowing all the way to never touch another drop.

But God help him, what he wanted more than anything was to get stinking drunk and wipe away the vision of the sick boy and the crestfallen friend.

Belle Holbrook, Willa thought as she sat in the widow's parlor, was an intriguing woman. An enigma. A puzzle.

Belle was beautiful, certainly, with thick black hair swept

high above stormy gray eyes, regal bone structure, and a porcelain-over-roses complexion. Clad in the finest fashion, the thirty-something Belle had the rigid spine and perfect manners of one born to privilege.

Though men frequently popped their necks to watch her walk past, she paid them little mind. Other than a soft smile, a tip of a pretty parasol, a friendly "good day," she swept elegantly down the board sidewalk, comporting herself with the utmost propriety and dignity.

Yet, something about Belle stirred speculation. People wondered about her. In the mercantile, at church, on the streets and, rumor said, even in the saloon.

This predisposition to incur notice seemed completely unintentional, for Belle was as private as she was friendly.

Perhaps the speculation was fueled by the fact that she was the most unusual of creatures—an independent female of considerable wealth and a great deal of mystery.

It was the independence and perhaps a dab of the mystery that drew Willa to her friendship as surely and easily as a bee is drawn to hollyhock.

Though the woman must have come from money somewhere, she'd arrived in Sweet Clover the previous autumn accompanied only by a small child, and several large trunks. She'd paid cash for a homestead, hired a dozen workers to build and furnish a beautiful two-story house, and smilingly deflected any questions about her past or the husband who must have left her a generous inheritance.

Alone, except for four-year-old Pearl, Belle occasionally hired one of the Malone sisters to work in her home or garden. Belle understood about being a woman alone in the West.

While Belle had considerably more in common with Savannah, she'd enlisted Willa's aid in making quilt tops for the less fortunate.

Every Tuesday after supper, rain, shine, or often in the case of Oklahoma Territory, gale or drought, Willa walked the three miles to Belle's home on Oklahoma Avenue. The house boasted a picket fence and a cheerful burst of spiky sweet peas around the front porch.

The very sweet peas Homer Baggley had purloined for Savannah.

Whoever Belle was and wherever she'd come from, she'd brought a special brand of philanthropy and elegance to the fledgling town. She'd not, however, found occasion to attend church, a troubling aspect to the gossip mavens of Sweet Clover. If Belle was a believer, she kept her faith at home.

This particular Tuesday as they sewed patches of cloth together to make bigger squares, Willa told the other woman of the bounty on Charlie Bangs and of her plans to claim it.

Little Pearl, wearing ribbons, ringlets and ruffles, played quietly in the corner of the parlor with a large furnished dollhouse, the likes of which Willa had never seen. A quiet child, Pearl's hair was as dark as Belle's, her eyes the color of spring elm leaves.

"Don't try to talk me out of it," Willa said after explaining her decision to go after Charlie Bangs.

She fully expected Belle, like all the others, to be aghast at the temerity of a single woman chasing an outlaw.

Belle's pretty hands paused above a colorful mass of joined fabric blocks, needle and thread aloft. "Why would I do that?"

The response so shocked Willa she pricked her finger. Not that this was an uncommon occurrence, given her pathetic sewing skills. After learning about Maeve's precious quilt, Belle seemed bent on teaching Willa to quilt.

Willa couldn't refuse. The quilts were for a good cause. She also enjoyed the other woman's company, though she despaired at ever developing anything resembling expertise with a needle.

Despite Willa's ineptitude, Belle's merry laugh and bright company made the quilt top an adventure.

"I thought you'd object," Willa said. "Everyone else does."

"Fiddlesticks. You're smart and strong. It won't be easy, but if you feel compelled, then you should do it." Her pretty features hardened. "I've known men like Charlie Bangs. He needs to hang."

Willa wouldn't argue that. She sucked her pricked finger, buoyed by Belle's encouragement.

"You don't think it's inappropriate for a woman and a single man to be alone on the trail for weeks?"

Belle gave a nonchalant shrug. "Life is different here in the West. A woman is freer to forge her own path. There will still be talk. You must prepare yourself for that and determine beforehand that you will not let it bother you."

This summed up Belle Holbrook in a tidy thimbleful.

Gossip did not faze her.

Willa, too, cared as little about gossips as she did a swatted housefly. They'd already found her wanting, she, a plain spinster who worked like a man and didn't have a frilly bone in her body. She didn't begin to fit with the recently formed Territorial Ladies' Society.

"There's already gossip. I'm accused of everything from being a witless girl to committing the unpardonable sin."

One of Belle's eyebrows ticked upward. "Yet, you're set on doing this completely unconventional thing."

Willa set her jaw. "I have to."

"Who is the man who will accompany you? Not a relative, I take it?"

"I have no relatives in the Territory besides my sisters. I've hired a guide. He's reputed to be the best. His name is Gideon Hartley."

Belle's bow mouth opened the slightest amount. Something in her gray eyes sparked, a hint of banked lightning.

"Gideon," she said, softly, slowly, as if savoring the taste of the name on her lips. "That rascal. He didn't tell me."

A roar of unrecognized emotion, stunning in intensity, jolted Willa. "You know Mr. Hartley?"

Belle cocked her dark head, a hint of a smile lifting her mouth. "We're acquainted."

Willa braced to hear tales, as she did from the ladies at church, about Gideon's notorious saloon escapades. Or worse, that he was a despoiler of young ladies, a debauched and worthless scoundrel.

None were forthcoming.

Belle added a stack of colorful fabric squares to her lap and bent her head to the task.

Willa fidgeted. She wanted to inquire about how well the beautiful Belle knew the handsome tracker, though this was not Willa's business nor should it be her concern.

She could well imagine that Gideon would be as besotted with the mysterious beauty as any other man.

Did he strain his neck watching her walk past the hotel?

The stir of that unnamed feeling made her stomach hurt. Perhaps it was hunger. She'd not had a bite since the single biscuit this morning before chores.

"Do you know if he's a good tracker?" she asked.

"If you're asking if Gideon will do all in his power to help you find your outlaw, the answer is yes. If anyone can track Bangs, Gideon can."

Again, Belle used the familiar form of Gideon's name, intensifying Willa's curiosity. Neither Belle nor Gideon had made the land run. Had they known each other in another place?

Laying the sewing in her lap, Willa gripped her fingers together and spoke the worries that she dared not share with her sisters. Since Belle knew Gideon, she might have answers.

"I first encountered Mr. Hartley in the Red Diamond Saloon. A bounty hunter was shot and needed Mercy's doctoring skills." She added the last quickly, lest Belle think her a floozy who frequented dens of iniquity. "It was only nine in the morning but Mr. Hartley was already there, smelling of whiskey. He drinks. And gambles. When we meet, I often smell alcohol on his person." She twisted her fingers together. "I fear he's a drunk."

Belle's lovely hands paused in their work, her gray gaze holding Willa's with piercing intensity. "Are you asking me to talk you out of your decision?"

Willa took up the needle again and stabbed it into the cloth. "Absolutely not."

"Gideon promised to guide you, correct?"

"He did, though I'm not sure he meant to agree." She told Belle of the day Gideon had put Theodore Pierce to rout in the mercantile.

Belle's merry laugh filled the room. Little Pearl looked up from her curly-haired doll and smiled. The child was always so quiet and watchful. Willa wondered if she talked at all.

"Ah, Gideon. How like him. For all his dark cynicism and sarcastic wit, he's a tender heart. Rescuing damsels in distress seems to be his calling."

Willa nearly burst with the need to ask how Belle knew these things.

"I'm not a damsel in distress."

Without comment to Willa's assertion, Belle fitted a bright

yellow fabric square next to a brown one. "When are you going?"

"I don't know. Gideon said he had things to take care of before we could leave, but that was days ago. Whenever I see him on the streets, he makes excuses." She laughed ruefully, "Or spins on his shiny black heels and slithers into the saloon to avoid me."

Belle chuckled. "Gideon Hartley is a man of his word. He's said he'll accompany you. He will."

"We need to go now. Time is wasting."

"Then, my friend, you must press the advantage."

"I'm afraid I don't have one. He holds all the aces."

Mischief twitched Belle's lips. Her laugh was merry. "Oh, Willa. I think not."

Putting aside the growing quilt top, she leaned forward, lowering her voice. "Here's what you do."

Chapter Eight

Gideon sat on the side of the hotel bed, head in hands, craving sleep that wouldn't come and the drinks that would make it happen.

Neither was forthcoming.

He eyed the washstand. An empty glass sat next to the blue patterned pitcher and washbasin. A *water* glass. Nothing but clear spring water.

He rose, poured another drink, knowing full well water would do nothing but make the craving worse. Coffee, perhaps, would help, but he didn't dare leave this room. He'd lived on coffee and whiskey and little else for so long his body shook with the need.

If he left this room, he'd be doomed.

He checked his pocket watch lying on the dresser.

Two and a half days. He felt as though he'd struggled with his demons for weeks. His humiliation at the Baker farm remained fresh and sharp, a much needed reminder of why he'd locked himself inside this hotel room.

He did not trust himself. He, a man who'd been trusted by the military, the government and dozens of settlers, no longer believed in himself.

"Only two and a half days," he muttered in dismay. Less than three days without a taste or a drop.

Would the craving ever cease?

He'd emptied the ever-present stash of bottles in the back alley the moment he'd arrived at the hotel from the Bakers' farm.

How much longer until he felt normal again?

Would he ever?

He'd forgotten what normal felt like.

A knock sounded at the door. He startled, his nerves as jittery as a condemned man at a hanging.

Ignoring the sound, Gideon walked to the window, looked out.

A fine one-horse buggy trotted past, a pretty woman at the reins. If he had a smile left in him, he'd have waved and called her name.

Belle. The only person in this town he trusted. And only because he knew her secrets and she knew his.

The knock came again, more insistent.

"Go away!" he called, and the sound rattled his brain, took his breath.

His head pounded. His insides felt as if he'd been eviscerated except his guts had to be in there. They roared and raged, paining him something fierce.

He closed his eyes and tried to remember how to breathe. Tried to remember why he'd even want to.

In these few agonizing days, he'd paced, tossed and turned, slept not a wink and was attuned to every footfall, every murmur, every creak in the hotel.

"No rest for the wicked."

And the righteous don't need any. His mother's smiling voice came toward him from somewhere.

"Mama," he said, then shook his head. Mama was dead. She wasn't here.

But she'd seemed so real.

Would he fall prey to hallucinations? Would he lose his mind and become demented, tormented by the evils of his past and present?

Not much scared him. But that did. He'd always had a strong mind. Losing it would be the end of him.

He sank to the bed, thrust his pounding head into his hands. The basin rested at his feet in case he was sick again.

Yesterday had purged his stomach, though the nausea persisted.

For how much longer?

The vision of Matthew Baker invaded his pain. An admiring little boy sick on whiskey because of him.

Failure. You're a failure. A worthless drunk.

Gideon. Help me.

He pressed his hands to his temples, pleading for the voices to leave him alone.

Only the whiskey will silence them. You know that. You've tried going without. You can't. You'll fail. Go to the saloon. Peace awaits.

The voices came at him, swarming him, hounding him.

He wasn't sure if they were real or in his head. He wasn't sure of anything anymore.

The knock came again. *Real*, he thought.

Were the voices real, too?

He looked around the room. Alone. No one but him, the way he wanted. No one could know. The shame was too great.

"Gideon. Open this door. I know you're in there."

He moistened dry lips, heart hammering fast as a galloping horse. "Mama?"

Mother knew. She'd discovered her son's weakness, his failings. He'd let her down.

He pressed harder at his temples, tried to reason. Mama wasn't here. She was dead. Long dead.

Again, he frowned around the room, seeing no one.

"Gideon?"

Who was talking?

The knocking commenced, louder, harder, more insistent.

Someone at the door. A female someone. Not Mama. Not Emily.

Miss Hattie?

"Go away." The sound was feeble to his ears.

His humiliation already deep enough, Gideon had no desire to share the disgusting fact of his debauchery with another soul, no matter who pounded at his hotel door.

Couldn't a man die in peace?

"'There is no peace on earth, I said.'" With an automaticity that confounded Gideon, Longfellow's words rolled from him and echoed over and over again. *No peace on earth. No peace anywhere. No peace.*

He was basking in this deep melancholy, sorting the voices, assuring himself that he was completely, mercifully alone and fighting the desire to fling himself from the hotel window when the persistent soul at the door hammered harder, louder.

"Mr. Hartley." *Knock, knock, knock.* "Gideon. I know you're in there. Open up now, or I shall do something drastic."

More knocks, hard enough to rattle the wooden door. Hard enough to jar his aching brain.

He recognized that voice. The voice of a thousand tormentors. Willa. A reminder of who he'd been and what he'd become.

With a deep sigh, he stumbled to his feet, teeth bared, and, determined to send her running for the hills, yanked open the door.

"Get out." He slammed the door in her face.

"Mr. Hartley." *Knock. Knock. Knock.* "Open this door. We must talk."

Talk. The relentless termagant desired conversation. At a time when his conversational skills were devoid of intellect.

He wasn't even certain she existed.

Legs weak, sweating profusely, Gideon opened the door again, taking care to fill the gap with half his body lest his nightmare barge her way in, exactly as plain and simple Willa was inclined to do.

He slapped a hand on either side of the doorframe, as much to hold himself upright as to bar her entry.

He showed his teeth in a feral growl. "What is it?"

Dressed in her usual tiresome brown, she stood straight as an arrow, her whiskey-colored eyes boring into him with stormy intensity.

Whiskey. Ah, for a sip of that golden nectar.

He closed his eyes to block the thought, only to find the vision of a clear glass filled to the brim with that thirst-quenching, voice-silencing elixir.

A different voice—Willa's—jolted him into focus.

"We should be on the trail by now. Yet, I've not had a word from you in days, and here I find you hiding out in your hotel."

"I had business." If she didn't leave quickly, he might further diminish his reputation as a man by fainting.

"So you said, but Miss Hattie claims you've not left this hotel room for three days, not even for a meal."

Miss Hattie was a busybody, and he was a man in the throes of a great and mighty struggle, Lucifer on one side and the Lion of Judah on the other.

He, whose namesake was said to be a mighty warrior, was caught in the middle, his own predisposition straining toward the side of darkness.

Willa's presence did nothing but exacerbate the problem.

If he continued to stand in this doorway, knees weak and blood rushing through his brain in a dizzying pattern, he'd likely collapse on Willa's scuffed and dirty boots.

He glared at her. Was she real? Or a figment of his troubled imagination?

He wobbled. Wove. Struggled to stand upright. Sweat poured off him. He trembled until he feared he could no longer hide his weakness.

Sheer will, the companion who'd carried him for so long, was nowhere to be found.

"You'll have to pardon me." He started to close the door.

She stuck her boot in the way. "Gideon, are you ill?"

"Yes."

"I'll get Mercy."

Quicker than he thought he could move, he reopened the door and grabbed her arm, detaining her.

Mercy he desperately required but not the kind Willa had in mind. Not the Titian-haired sister with the healing hands. "No. I will recover."

She glared down at the hand gripping her elbow.

Could she feel his trembles? Would she suspect?

He released her.

"Please. Go." He was almost at the end of his strength. She must leave now.

True to Willa's stubborn refusal to do anything he asked, she stepped closer and touched a cool hand to his diaphoretic forehead.

He'd had no inkling that a man had this much liquid inside his body, but in the three days hence, he'd perspired an ocean.

Gideon backed away, letting that cool, comforting hand fall into thin air. He deserved no kindness, no help. This was his just punishment for too many sins, too many deaths, too much dependence on whiskey rather than God.

Yes, somewhere between the day he'd left San Antonio and now, he'd lost touch with the Almighty. Had abandoned that greatest of helpers, the God of his mother and, once, of himself.

He deserved to be desperately ill.

Too exhausted to remain standing, he backed into the room and sank to the edge of the bed. Willa remained in the doorway, quiet for once, a mercy in itself.

Although he'd dipped his head low in mortification, he felt her arresting eyes on him.

"Are you drunk?" Her quiet voice held only a hint of accusation.

A harsh laugh jolted his pounding headache. "No."

He heard her movement and looked up to find her at his washstand.

"For pity's sake, woman, can't you leave me alone? I'll come to you when I'm well enough."

She moved toward him, ugly brown skirt swishing, moistened cloth in hand, and gently wiped his brow. The kindness in that simple gesture burned at the back of Gideon's eyelids.

"Can you eat anything?"

"No." His stomach rolled.

Eyeing the nearby basin, he fought down the nausea. Moisture pooled in his mouth, threatening.

Willa followed his gaze.

If he had an ounce of pride left, he was in danger of losing it. Along with anything left in his belly. "I'm ill, Willa. Please. Leave."

"Are you contagious?"

"No."

She wet the cloth again and pressed the coolness to the back of his neck. He shivered, burning up and freezing at the same time.

"Can I get you anything? Anything at all?"

The biggest bottle of rotgut in the territory. "No. Just go home. I'll be better in a few days."

He hoped. He'd not gone three days without a drink in so long he couldn't recall the last time. Ridding his body of the poison would take time. How much, he didn't know for certain.

More than three days apparently, he thought with brutal sarcasm.

Being Willa, she didn't budge. "A hot toddy might soothe your stomach."

"No! No whiskey."

Her hand paused. A beat passed. Then another. He could practically hear the wheels turning in that sharp mind of hers.

He looked up into knowing eyes.

"I see," she said.

To his shame, he feared she did.

Willa fretted to understand Gideon's ailment. One thing was for certain, he could not travel in his current weakened condition. Though she itched to saddle up and ride, she couldn't leave without a guide. Which meant she had to get him well and get him on his feet. Somehow.

Having arrived at The Tarbridge Hotel armed with Belle's keen instructions, she'd fortified herself to manipulate the man into doing her bidding—she, who didn't have a single feminine wile. After one look at Gideon, she'd let Belle's instructions fly out the window.

Frankly, she was relieved. Not that he was ill. She needed

him too badly for that. Relieved not to carry out Belle's palm-sweating instructions.

Her guide was not in the throes of a vicious hangover as he'd been the first time she saw him and as she'd suspected the moment he opened the door. Nor did he appear to be suffering from any common illness she was aware of. So, what ailed the man?

He'd refused a hot toddy. Had practically shouted, *No whiskey*, as if he hated the stuff.

Odd, indeed.

She let her gaze drift around the hotel room. There was no sign of the whiskey decanter she'd seen before. Only water. Neither was there the scent of alcohol in the room or on Gideon's person.

No whiskey. She pondered this new occurrence, turned it over in her mind, worried it like a dog gnaws a strip of wet rawhide.

The absence of hard liquor meant something.

Gideon Hartley was a man who daily frequented the saloon as if it were his home. Could refraining from spirits make him sick?

Flummoxed, uncertain how to assist if assisting was even required, Willa considered the man before her.

Even in his pitiful state of illness, with his black hair mussed, his face unshaven, he was roguishly handsome. His white shirt was untucked and rumpled, his sleeves unfastened, baring strong wrists and forearms, all of which only added to his rakish appeal.

Not that Willa allowed herself more than a passing notice.

She and Gideon had a business deal. She was here only to protect her interests.

She'd cared for Papa in his cups. She could nurse Gideon until he was well enough to ride, although she had no experience with his current ailment, if indeed the lack of spirits was his trouble.

Frowning at the man, who also frowned, his eyes squeezed tight in a tortured face, Willa rubbed her hands up and down the sides of her skirt.

Papa had enjoyed his ale, usually on Saturday night after a week's hard toil, but the only whiskey in their home was for medicinal purposes. The same bottle had sat on the shelf since last year.

Would he recover if she left him alone? Did he need her help at all?

She really should get Mercy. Mercy would know what to do.

But if Mercy saw Gideon in this weakened condition, she'd ask questions. Depending on the answers, she'd likely suspect he drank too much and too often, and she'd begin her pleadings all over again that Willa not go in pursuit of Charlie Bangs.

Willa did not want to broach that argument again.

Furthermore, no man wanted to be seen as weak in the eyes of a beautiful woman like Mercy.

Since Willa had no thought that Gideon would ever find her attractive, and she only required his expertise, not his courtship, Gideon didn't need to pretend with her. She was also not a talebearer.

She set her jaw tight as a maiden's corset. Any man who allowed spirits to put him in such a lowly condition deserved to be ill.

But she needed him.

Gideon, who'd gone as silent and pale as death itself, tilted sideways.

His feet were bare, which gave her a funny flutter in her

belly. Nonetheless, she gripped his ankles and hoisted him onto the bed.

Many was the time she'd assisted Papa in this manner. Yet, the realization that Gideon was not her papa nor a relative was not lost on her. Had she a shred of concern about her reputation, she'd leave and not return.

If she remained in this hotel room with a man, she sealed her fate, compromised her virtue and ended any hope of ever finding a husband.

If the situation hadn't been dire, she'd have laughed. In a few days, she hoped to be riding into dangerous territory with this man. Being in his hotel room didn't begin to compare with weeks on the trail.

Just by planning the bounty-hunting expedition, the town already considered her compromised, and if a tiny seed of hope remained that a suitable man might someday marry her, she'd crushed it under the heel of common sense.

She was thirty years old. No one fell in love with an old maid. Practicality outweighed foolish dreams. She would nurse Gideon back to health, and they would find Charlie Bangs and collect that reward.

A little shiver ran through her, but she braced against it. She could not allow anxiety to enter in, regardless of the nights she'd jerked awake, heart thundering in the darkness.

The journey ahead was dangerous, foolish, considering the man she'd chosen as her companion and guide.

None of this changed her mind. Selling her baby sister to Homer Baggley was not to be considered, though if the old man had focused his lecherous gaze on Willa, who had no illusions about herself, she would have accepted faster than an eye-blink.

Desperation did that to a single woman in a man's world.

Gideon groaned and muttered, his voice trailing away into the intelligible. "'The thirst that from the soul doth rise...'"

More of his poetry, which she didn't recognize, that seemed to ooze out of him with the sweat, which was plentiful.

Taking the only chair in the room, a straight-backed wooden affair strung with his black vest and a rather elegant jacket she'd never seen him wear, Willa plopped down beside his bed to wait. Why, she did not know. She only understood that he needed her, whether he believed he did or not.

She most certainly needed him. *Required* him, or at least his expertise.

Determination infused her until her back was as straight as a wall and her mind raced, grasping for what little nursing knowledge she'd borrowed from Mercy along the way.

She *would* make him well. She *would* get him on his feet and on his horse.

He tossed, groaning, muttering. Willa pressed soothing fingers to the hand he'd flung in her direction. Reflexively, he curled his fingers through hers.

The heat of his skin stirred something in her. Pity, most likely. A dab of disgust laced with human concern.

Scooting the chair closer for comfort, she did not pull away. His hand was broad, the fingers thick and, unlike Homer Baggley, his nails were clean. Even in sleep, his touch was strong and masculine.

A shiver of awareness prickled the flesh on her arms. Other than her father, she'd never been completely alone with a sleeping man.

He opened his eyes and speared her with a fire-blue gaze. "Willa?" he cracked.

"I'm here."

"Go home." His eyes drifted shut, his face awash in sweat and distress.

Stubbornly, Willa kept her seat, clinging to that big firm hand.

"Shh," she said. "Sleep."

Sleep cured many ills.

"Can't," he muttered.

If the dark circles and reddened eyes were any indication, he hadn't been sleeping well, if at all. Sick people usually slept all the time. Which was additional evidence that Gideon was in the grip of more than a common illness.

Remaining quiet and still for some time, she regarded him, hoping to see him rally soon.

Suddenly, he jerked his hand away and cried out. "Emily. Tad. No. No!"

The guttural sound was drenched in grief, a sound so broken that Willa's eyelids burned.

He thrashed, cried out again. Was he in the throes of a nightmare?

Compassion welled in Willa's heart.

She patted his shoulder. "Gideon, wake up. You're dreaming."

He stirred, sat bolt upright, his eyes open but unseeing. "Get out. Get out now!"

Was he speaking to her? Or to someone in his nightmare?

Rising, Willa rewet the washcloth and placed it on his head, murmuring soothing nonsense, the way she'd done for her sisters when they were small.

At her voice, Gideon seemed to settle, though occasional tremors wracked his body. Whether he dreamed or was delusional, Willa didn't know.

She shuddered at the sight of his manly form so weakened by some unseen force.

What if he was dangerously ill and needed a doctor? What if he died? What if she was responsible for his demise?

Willa stroked the sides of her skirt over and over, her fingers clutching and releasing the rough fabric.

Anxiety pressed inside her rib cage. She rubbed at the spot, whispering prayers and hoping for mercy.

For the next several hours, she alternately wiped Gideon's drenched brow and paced the floor, pleading for God to do something, anything.

Every time Gideon struggled to his senses and clapped those haunted blue eyes on her, he'd rasp out two words. "Go home."

If he thought for one lucid second that she'd walk away and chance losing her only hope of tracking Papa's killer, he was not only sick in body, he was sick in the head.

Which was likely, anyway.

Clamping her jaw like a vise, she stubbornly remained at his side.

More than once, he bolted out of the bed and prowled the heart-pine floor like a big wounded cougar in search of something, growling at her, demanding she leave.

When he opened the chest of drawers and extracted a gun belt with a pearl-handled Colt .45, Willa thought her heart would stop. "What are you doing?"

Red-rimmed eyes glared at her. "Leave me."

She marched to him, stuck out one hand, the other on her hip, and tapped her foot. "Give me that."

He stood there staring at the weapon as if he couldn't remember why it was in his hand.

A bad sign.

With blood rushing in her ears, a wad of fear below her breastbone, Willa reached out, gripped the barrel, pushing it downward as she took the pistol from him.

He relinquished the weapon with little resistance.

Breathing a sigh of relief, she said, "I'm going downstairs for some food. You need to eat."

"Leave the gun."

Not in a million years.

"No."

Their gazes caught, tangled, wrestled before she spun on her worn boots and left him standing in his bare feet, looking both bereft and dangerous. She slid the pistol into her skirt pocket.

All the way down to the dining room and back, Willa gnawed at her bottom lip. She had no idea what she was doing, but she was in too deep to turn back now. She'd spent all afternoon in a man's hotel room.

The sisters would be worried. She needed to let them know where she was. But informing them of her current purpose was unacceptable. They would have a ring-tail hissy fit. And upon learning the truth about Gideon Hartley, they'd be terrified to let her go anywhere with him.

Going, she would, and he was going, too.

Pleasant smells rose from the kitchen as she entered the dining room and asked for a cup of broth. She was hungry, and the fragrance of apple pie nearly made her swoon.

Having only enough money for the broth, she willed away the growling, demanding hunger.

"Visiting someone, Willa?" Miss Hattie handed over the broth. The scent curled upward from the cup, warm and comforting. Willa was tempted to drink it herself.

"A sick friend."

"Oh?" Hattie perked up. "Who would that be?"

Willa fidgeted. The last thing she needed was for anyone to know about Gideon's illness or the fact that she was not leaving until he rallied.

While a fine woman who ran a good hotel, Miss Hattie was in a unique position to gather news like a reporter. Having found popularity from sharing the comings and goings of Sweet Clover's inhabitants, Hattie shared liberally. Gossip was entertainment in a settlement like Sweet Clover.

Somehow, Willa had to avoid being the topic of that entertainment.

"Now, Miss Hattie, some ladies prefer privacy during their ailments." That much was true, if misleading.

Hattie's wrinkled lips pouted in cheerful disappointment. "I see."

Willa fled toward the stairs, aware that Hattie's curious gaze followed her.

Back in Gideon's room, she found him sitting on the side of the bed, head in those manly attention-drawing hands. He looked up at her entry.

"I'm better. Go home."

He didn't look better, but he was, at least, lucid.

"As soon as you eat something." She set the cup of chicken broth on the seat of the chair in front of him.

He stared at it for the longest time, as if she'd offered him a dose of poison.

She lifted the cup and held it out. "Drink. It's broth, not arsenic."

With a weak huff of amusement, he took the white pottery mug. His hand shook, sloshing liquid. He hissed through his teeth, steadied his arm with the opposing hand and slowly brought the broth to his lips.

Everything in Willa wanted to hold it for him.

At one point in his piteous attempts, she reached out. His warning glare stopped her. Her hand fell to her lap.

In his rumpled white shirt and with his face set like granite, Gideon looked both pitiful and courageous. His determination resonated inside her. If he was this resolute about drinking a cup of broth without her interference, how much more determined would he be on the trail?

The notion encouraged Willa considerably.

He managed a few sips, then set the cup on the chair with an exhausted sigh. "Enough for now."

The ordeal had brought on the sweats again. He shivered

and lay back against the pillows, eyes open, chest heaving as if he'd run up and down Miss Hattie's staircase.

"You said you'd leave," he growled, glowering. "Go."

Since this must have been the hundredth time he'd issued the command, Willa did what she'd done the previous ninety-nine. She ignored him.

"Are you cold?" He'd vacillated between the two extremes, first freezing and then burning.

He nodded, his distraught expression almost grateful.

He needed her, as she needed him, though in quite different ways. Being of the male persuasion, he didn't want to admit it.

Stubborn souls, these men. Stubborn and irritatingly interesting.

Willa covered him with a blanket, then went to the nightstand to wet the cloth again.

"Do you know what ails you?"

"Yes."

Quietly, gently, so as not to offend, though she knew she would, Willa asked, "Is it the alcohol sickness?"

His eyelids slammed shut. His voice was rough as if he'd swallowed a corncob. "You're annoying me. Get out."

In that, she found both an answer and a very worrisome question.

Hoping he'd sleep, Willa waited until his breathing was slow and even before she unloaded the .45.

Quietly tiptoeing to the dresser, she replaced the holster and pistol but kept the bullets in her pocket.

The shadows on the wall warned of the waning day. The sisters would be worried if she didn't go home soon.

She glanced at her patient. A troubled frown pinched the muscles of his handsome face.

Her fingers fairly itched to smooth his brow and stroke his whiskered jaw. She reached out, caught herself and pulled back.

Gideon Hartley aroused all kinds of feelings inside her. Pity, worry, hope and that unnamed emotion that made her want to touch him.

She curled her fingers into her palms.

As if he'd felt her thoughts, he stirred.

"Emily." The words were hoarse and aching with emotion. "Emily."

Who was Emily? Had he a wife somewhere, waiting for him to leave behind his wanderings and his vices and come home to her?

The notion stuck in Willa's craw like a chicken bone.

His thrashing began again. He called out, muttering names and nonsense. Sometimes he spouted a line of poetry.

"Emily," he cried again, piteously.

"I'm here." Willa took his hand, willing him to believe the woman that he wanted was with him, hoping the knowledge would soothe his restlessness.

It didn't.

Caught in a new nightmare, Gideon flailed and struggled with some unseen force. His torment tore at her heart.

No wonder he didn't sleep.

In times past at the side of a sickbed, she'd often seen Mercy place her small sturdy hands on the patient and pray.

Willa didn't claim to have healing hands. Likely, God only heard Mercy.

Having no better idea, Willa touched the fingers of each hand to Gideon's shoulder and prayed.

Gideon knew he was dreaming and fought to wake up. He'd had this dream too often. Every time he didn't drink himself to sleep.

But he wouldn't do that anymore. Not after Matthew.

He'd promised...someone.

He couldn't remember. The nightmare closed in, drove out all other thought.

Fire roared around him, hot, so hot. He swung his head from side to side to avoid the flames. They scorched him. His face, his hands.

A child screamed. Gideon's horse reared, nearly dislodging him from the saddle.

"Jump," he begged, holding out his arms.

The horse plunged into the murky river. A snake rose from the dark churning waters, fangs bared. Someone laughed. He knew that voice. He turned toward the sound and water rushed over his head. He cried out, flailing to reach the surface.

From somewhere, another voice penetrated the nightmare. A woman prayed, pleading with the Almighty to help him, to heal him.

Yes, he thought. *Take away this terrible bondage.*

"Great is thy faithfulness, oh, God. No shadows," he muttered. "Take the shadows."

In a great cataclysmic heave, need and grief seized up inside him. "Oh, God. Almighty Father."

Verses and snatches of prayers his mother had taught him rambled through his muddled mind. He quoted them, not sure if he spoke aloud or in his head.

Hadn't God forsaken him? Hadn't God taken everything from him that mattered? His family, his reputation, his ability to guide and now his self-control?

Not God. His father. Thomas Hartley.

Hatred bubbled and steamed like a boiling cauldron.

A dark figure in his dream planted seeds of bitterness in his soul.

The seeds sprung up from the ground, stems dark, ugly and twisted.

"God," he pleaded again, not knowing if he still dreamed or if he'd awakened in the pits of Hades.

He bargained then, begging God, promising anything in exchange for a well body and for the peace he desperately longed to find.

Suddenly, as if someone had struck a match to a bonfire, light glowed all around him. The dark shadows receded.

At last, he slept.

Chapter Nine

Something stirred in the room. Gideon drifted to the surface. Bit by bit, awareness filtered in.

His body ached. He was as weak as dishwater. But he was alive and shocked to be glad of it.

The last thing he remembered was crying out to God.

He must have slept, something he'd craved to do for days, but the nightmares had forced him to remain awake, afraid of what he'd see.

Had God heard the feeble, distorted prayer and touched him?

He ruminated on the thought. For years, he'd pushed God further and further into the background of his life. He'd stopped reading his mother's precious note-lined Bible, the only thing he had left of hers. He never prayed anymore. Hadn't in years. Praying only brought on the weight of his sinfulness and the terrible bitterness he could not release, not even to God.

He would never forget nor forgive what Thomas Hartley had done. God had no right to ask it of him.

The urge for a glass of whiskey slammed into him like a fist. One small drink to wash away the sour taste, the awful memory and to quell the fury rising in him like a fire on the mountains.

With a weary sigh, he realized the battle wasn't over. His body felt better, but his mind still wanted what he knew he should not have.

He tugged a moist cloth from his forehead.

And became aware that someone touched him. The pressure was light and pleasant. Comforting.

He remembered then. Willa. That strong, pertinacious, spirited female who both intrigued and plagued him.

Turning his head, he glimpsed her, the little brown wren with the enchanting bottom lip and arresting brown eyes.

Slumped in the only chair in the room, she'd leaned her head on the edge of the mattress and fallen asleep, her fingers grazing his arm.

He couldn't see her face, only the top of her chestnut-colored hair and that long thick braid he found so captivating. Resisting an urge to touch it, he remained still, not wanting to wake her.

How long had she been there?

She looked small and vulnerable, the latter a word he didn't think independent Willa would appreciate.

He knew why she'd come to the hotel, but why had she stayed? Why did his heart thud and his breath quicken to know she'd been the one at his side?

Emotion surged in his chest, stunning in intensity. Gratitude, of course, but something more, something powerful and infinitely more alarming.

Feisty Willa Malone made him feel things that he'd long ago put aside. Made him want things he couldn't have.

That he felt some bizarre attachment to plain and simple Willa troubled him deeply.

She stirred then and sat up, leaning back against the latticed chair. Wisps of dark hair had come loose from her braid and danced around her face. She was sleep-drenched, one cheek indented by a long red mark where she'd rested her face on the mattress edge.

Their eyes met, and Gideon saw a tumble of thoughts and emotions flicker through her whiskey-brown eyes.

Whiskey.

Shame flooded him.

He never wanted to live through another time like this but wasn't confident he was strong enough to resist.

How had he fallen to such a state? He, a man who'd stood bravely against outlaws and renegades, against cheats and even his own father, had become a slave to his own vice.

He disgusted himself. Another reason to drink. Another reason not to.

"How are you?" That full bottom lip moved and drew his attention.

He glanced away from her sleepy face, chagrin washing through him in cold rivulets.

Willa had not only seen him at his lowest point, she knew the reason for his weakness.

"You shouldn't be here." His voice was a frog-croak, rusty and hoarse.

As if he hadn't spoken, Willa went to the pitcher and poured a glass of water. "Drink this."

Though weak and drained, he managed the glass without shaming himself further. But he recalled the humiliating incident with the broth and wondered how she could trust him to guide her anywhere.

Maybe she wouldn't after this. He was surprised at how disappointed he'd be if she turned him away.

Perhaps he needed this journey as much as she did.

If he could stay sober.

"What time is it?" he managed, his throat easier after the water.

Willa crossed to the dresser as if she knew exactly where he kept his timepiece. She seemed familiar with his room as though she'd been here longer than one afternoon.

He peered toward the window. It was open a few inches. The lace curtains waved with a slight breeze. Sunlight dappled the floor and hurt his eyes. But the air smelled fresh and clean.

Blinking against the glare, he glanced toward Willa. She was half in and half out of the sun, fuzzy to look upon.

"Two o'clock. On Friday."

"Friday!" He struggled to sit up. Having a woman in his room for an afternoon was inappropriate. Spending days on end sequestered with him had compromised her as surely as if they'd eloped.

The idea of eloping with Willa to spare her humiliation rumbled through him like a runaway stagecoach.

He almost laughed.

If Willa cared one bit for her reputation, she'd never have asked him to accompany her to Indian Territory.

She'd likely shoot him if he even suggested a hasty, convenient marriage to protect her reputation.

Still, his mother had taught him proprieties in his treatment of the fairer sex. He'd just forgotten how to use them.

"Have you been here the entire time?"

"For the most part, since Wednesday."

That strange emotion hit again. A mix of chagrin and a shockingly powerful desire to embrace her.

He reined in his thoughts, laying them at the feet of his weakened condition. He was grateful to plain and simple Willa, and once his body strengthened, he'd help her find Charlie Bangs. He would not, however, offer to marry her.

After seeing him in this state, she'd refuse anyway.

In the dining room, Willa ordered coffee while Gideon remained behind to make himself presentable. She'd wanted to stay, mostly to be certain he didn't sneak out the door and head to the saloon, but he'd insisted, dangling the lure of a real meal.

Since she hadn't eaten anything other than the corn bread she'd grabbed on a quick visit to her sisters, the lure had hooked her right in the belly.

The trip home had been awkward at best as she'd struggled not to lie, ending with a reassurance that she was visiting a friend and a promise to tell them more later.

Fortunately, Mercy, who would have seen right through her, was delivering a baby at the Denton farm, and Savannah was caught up in sewing lace on a bodice for Saturday night's barn dance.

Currently seated at one of Miss Hattie's plain square tables next to a wide window, Willa gazed out on the afternoon's activities. The saloon was busy as usual, cowhands and farmers roaming in and out through the swinging doors. Down the street, men hammered away at yet another saloon.

She sighed, fretting over the addition of another place where Gideon might imbibe. She needed him sober.

Men built saloons while the ladies of the area longed for a school. As yet, the town council had not even raised the funds for a teacher. Sweet Clover was fortunate to have a church, which could be used when and if a teacher was hired.

Willa mourned her lack of formal education. Would a regular school have been able to teach her to read? Or was she too dumb, as Savannah's mother had declared when Willa was nine years old?

A wagonload of lumber rumbled down the dusty street, followed by a small perky dog. A young boy in knee britches sat on the tailgate of the wagon, his bare legs swinging.

The sight made Willa smile.

Taking a tiny sip of scalding hot coffee, she wished Gideon would hurry. They needed to hammer out plans, but she also needed a hot bath and her tooth powder.

She touched a hand to her hair, felt the wayward sprigs.

No wonder Gideon had practically pushed her out the door.

Not that she cared what he thought. She knew she wasn't pretty. All the baths and tooth powder in Oklahoma Territory wouldn't change that.

When Gideon finally appeared in the opening between the dining area and the hotel lobby, fresh energy spurted into Willa. Definitely the stout coffee taking effect. Though she must admit, other than his reddened eyes, Gideon looked good, as if he'd never been indisposed. Hair damp and neatly combed, his face shaved, his clothes clean and without wrinkles, he drew the attention of the only other lone female diner in the room, Trudy Langston.

A pinch of jealousy surprised Willa.

Gideon gave a polite nod. His attention didn't linger, though lovely Trudy, in her feathered hat and plaid ruffled dress, was clearly interested.

Miss Hattie entered behind Gideon through the arched opening, her sharp gaze noting when he settled across from Willa.

"I could eat a horse," Willa blurted.

Gideon quirked one black eyebrow.

To Hattie, who now hovered over their table like a bee on a sunflower, he said, "One horse for the lady. I'll have the special."

Hattie tittered like a schoolgirl. "Oh, Mr. Hartley, you charmer."

If he hoped to deflect attention from his long absence, he failed. Hattie filled his coffee from the sidebar and said, "You're looking very chipper this afternoon. And here I thought you'd been ill." Like a sharpened knife, her gaze cut toward Willa. "Could a certain lady have anything to do with that?"

Gideon let a meaningful beat pass before he offered a cool smile. "You'll pardon us if we have business to discuss."

Hattie sucked in a little gasp, a hand to her white collar. "Of course. Business." Her nose practically twitched with the need to ask what kind of business. She wisely didn't. "Whatever the case may be, Mr. Hartley, I am delighted to see you hale and hearty."

He was neither of those things, but Willa kept her countenance.

If Gideon was the least discomfited by Hattie's suspicions, he didn't let on. The man was smooth as warm butter.

Willa ordered the special, too, and Hattie left.

Seeing no reason for polite conversation given their last three days together, albeit days in which Gideon was not the best conversationalist, Willa got right to the point. "Can we leave on Monday?"

Gideon began his irritating coffee preparations. She tried not to watch, or fidget, as he tasted, added sugar, cream and tasted some more.

"A few more days. Perhaps a week."

Even though she chaffed at the reply, she'd expected it. He was in a weakened condition. He'd need some time to regain his stamina, of which she hoped he had an abundance. In the meantime, she'd worry that he'd fall prey to the lure of the saloon. Make that two saloons. Short of hog-tying him, she didn't know what to do about it.

"The journey won't be an easy one," he said.

He did not, she noted, make mention of his illness nor of her presence at his side. Was he embarrassed? Unconcerned about her opinion? Or, she shuddered to think, was he often ill in this way, giving her even more reason to worry about his ability to abstain from strong drink?

Finding her way back to his statement, she said, "I understand that."

"I'm not sure you do." He added more sugar and sipped, grimaced. "Do you realize how many things could go wrong?"

Actually, she didn't. "How different can it be from traipsing from town to town with Papa? I've done that all my life."

"Papa's not here," he reminded her over the rim of his cup.

The words were a sharp sword through the heart. The back of her throat ached. She took a sip of coffee and let the hot liquid wash down the emotion.

As angry as she'd been at Papa for leaving, she missed him so much.

"I'm confident that I will do fine. *We'll* be fine."

Willa was not sure of any such thing but she'd eat green bugs before she'd admit how badly her nerves jangled whenever she let her imagination have free rein.

She refused to be afraid.

"The Indians are mostly friendly, but not all. You could drown crossing a river, get snake bit, or attacked by wolves or bears." He added another dollop of cream. "Most dangerous of all, are the humans. The outlaws, one of whom you seek, will not take kindly to your company."

He seemed set on frightening her. He was succeeding, though the words only straightened her spine.

"If those things don't bother you, why should they bother me?"

"Oh, they bother me plenty." His spoon clattered against the saucer. Willa jumped.

"Tracking a man into Indian Territory isn't a Sunday social, Willa. It's going to be long, difficult and dangerous."

"How long?"

"Three, four weeks, maybe more. I've made some inquiries and have an idea of where your outlaw may be. That doesn't mean he's there. We could be gone a month or more and still come up empty. Are you prepared for that?"

No, she was not. They had to succeed.

"If you are trying to discourage me, you are failing."

He tilted his head back, looked at the hammered tin ceiling, his sigh weary.

"Ever been shot at?"

She gulped. Her belly jittered. "No."

Folding his arms on the tabletop, Gideon leaned in, voice soft as velvet. "Ever *killed* a man, Willa?"

Willa's blood chilled at the dispassionate tone and even more at the thought of shooting someone.

"No." She tilted her chin. "But I've killed plenty of wild game. I know how to shoot."

Anger turned his eyes to blue flames. "You think it's the same? You think watching a man bleed and die, knowing it was your bullet that killed him, is the same as shooting a deer?"

"Of course not," she snapped, though the question sent a jolt through her as cold as a Kansas snowstorm. "But he killed my papa and he deserves to die. I'll do what I must."

Gideon had a way of stirring her up, as if he knew her hidden fears and wanted to make her admit them. She wouldn't.

The troublesome man rubbed his bottom lip, pulling it between his index finger and thumb, his gaze lingering on her face until she blushed.

She was spared from further argument when Miss Hattie bustled out of the kitchen with their plates in hand.

"This looks delicious, Miss Hattie." Willa smiled, trying not to drool on the food. She was that hungry.

The hotel proprietor preened a little, refilling Gideon's coffee and fussing over him, apparently a favored guest, before heading back to the kitchen.

Willa bowed her head, hands clasped beneath her chin. "Lord, thank you for this food. I'm counting on You to help me find that outlaw. Amen."

She glanced up to see Gideon watching her.

Flustered, she waved a hand at his plate. "Eat."

A sardonic smirk, the kind she'd rarely seen him without until his illness, appeared. To be honest, she'd missed that annoying attitude of his. His cynical confidence gave her hope that he could get the job done.

"Afraid I'll die on you?"

"I won't let you." It was more sass than confidence.

Gideon chuckled softly and picked up his fork.

He was the most confounded human being she'd ever encountered.

Willa eagerly dove into a thick slice of savory ham surrounded by potatoes, carrots and a chunk of freshly baked bread.

Gideon settled a napkin in his lap and sliced neatly into the meat.

He should be hungry, but he picked at the delicious food and pushed it around on his plate without eating much. How could he get his strength back if he didn't eat?

Finally, as if giving up the effort, he put his fork aside, took up his cup, and downed the liquid in three quick gulps.

"I could use more coffee. You?" He rose for a refill. The woodsy masculine scent of shaving lotion rose with him, as did her gaze.

Her pulse tripped oddly. Though his secretive eyes appeared tired and rimmed in red, he was still too handsome. Neither of which should make any difference to Willa.

"More coffee, yes, thanks." Food was far more important than a man's appearance. She stabbed a buttery potato.

Gideon refilled their cups, then sat down, pushed his plate away and began his strange coffee ritual.

"Why aren't you eating? The food is delicious."

"Not much appetite."

She put her fork aside, dabbed her lips with a napkin and sought for the easiest way to ask the next question. "What are you planning to do for the next few days? Before we start our journey?"

"Why?"

"I was thinking. You probably shouldn't be alone. Having been so sick and all." She flushed, knowing he'd see right through her feeble attempts to keep an eye on him.

One diabolical eyebrow shot to the ceiling. "Are you moving into my room with me?"

The hot flush deepened. "I am not! I thought, perhaps, under the circumstance, you'd agree to spend your days on my farm. Savannah's a good cook."

She said the last feebly, hoping he'd believe she had his recovery in mind.

Carefully, slowly, he set his cup on the table.

"Why, Willa plain and simple," he said in that wry, sarcastic way of his, "don't you trust me?"

She squirmed, fidgeted, pleated the folds of her skirt.

Finally, she hitched her chin and blurted the truth. "Not one bit."

Chapter Ten

Saturday morning, Gideon awoke from a restless night in which the dreams had plagued him. Regardless, he felt better than he had in a while. He didn't even have a headache.

The desire for a glass of forgetfulness tugged at him, the imp on his shoulder insisting that one glass wouldn't hurt anything.

Fortunately, his hotel room was void of any beverage but water. Going to the stand, he drank deeply and stared at his reflection in the mirror. Weak and shaky, he'd lost weight. Getting strong again would take a few days. If he could stay away from the saloon.

Events of the past week rolled in like tumbleweeds across the Texas plains. Willa, with her tenderness, her rough little hands and her dogged determination loomed large in those foggy snatches of memory.

That she didn't trust him soured in his gut like milk left out in the July sun. He knew she was right, but he didn't have to like it.

He didn't even trust himself, especially after the misstep at the Baker farm. Why should she?

This morning, she expected him at the farm.

He hoped she didn't come looking for him with her lever-action Winchester. He grinned a little at the thought of her ferocity. Feisty, spirited, tenacious.

Willa desired revenge against Charlie Bangs whether she admitted it or not. Revenge and money. He sighed. Two of the greatest deceivers of mankind.

After morning ablutions, he had his usual pot of Miss Hattie's powerful coffee, but the egg she served him turned his stomach. He still wasn't well, but he managed to down a pair of buttermilk biscuits and took the rest of his breakfast out back to the spotted dog.

On return, he passed the hotel desk where Earl, the long-faced clerk with a tic in his cheek, handed him a folded note. "A lady left this for you, Mr. Hartley."

Expecting a note from either Willa or Belle, Gideon's stomach dropped when he saw Isaiah Baker's signature at the bottom.

We need to talk, was all the letter said. It was signed, *In Christ, Isaiah Baker.*

Carefully folding the paper, Gideon slid the missive inside his vest and wrestled with what this could mean.

Exiting the hotel, he turned right to avoid passing the saloon, though his mouth pooled at the thought of going inside. He headed toward the livery, saddled up Traveler and directed the horse away from town.

A confrontation was in store, though he wished he could put off facing Isaiah Baker for the rest of his life.

Now that his head was clear, his conscience bothered him something fierce. The note had been an impetus to handle the situation once and for all. Last week, he'd not been in shape to ride down the street, much less the distance to the Baker farm.

He was not a coward. Nor did he like trouble looming over his head like a black cloud. He'd face Isaiah and take whatever damage the other man wanted to dole out, aware he had it coming.

By the time he rode into the Bakers' yard, sweat beaded on his face and dread filled his belly. He didn't know if it was the dread of what Isaiah might say or the remnants of his battle with the bottle.

Chickens scattered, squawking and flapping around Traveler's feet. The steady bay didn't react.

A fat spotted pig grunted at him from the small enclosure he and Matthew had erected to keep the animal from destroying Mary's garden.

Matthew.

Shame burned through his veins like rattlesnake venom.

This was the first time he'd paid a call anywhere in nearly a year without a flask full of poison. He could sure use it now.

Reining Traveler to a halt, Gideon dismounted. Blood rushed in his ears. His pulse thudded hard enough to come through his skin.

The only good thing his father had ever taught him was to face punishment head-on and take it like a man.

Isaiah appeared in the doorway of the unpainted cabin, leaning on his walking stick. The children and Mary were nowhere to be seen.

"Gideon." Isaiah's face was serious.

Gideon nodded, sick and ashamed. "I got your note."

"Figured. I woulda come to town last week instead of sending that note, but this leg's got me hobbled."

Last week. Isaiah had waited a week for him to apologize.

The older man hitched his chin toward the chairs set up in the shade of the house. "Let's sit. The weather's fine today."

Sit? He'd expected to be shot. Or, at least, get a fist in the face.

As they settled in the cane-bottom chairs lined up outside the Baker cabin, Gideon saw the Bible in Isaiah's hand.

He had no objections to a sermon if that's what the man intended. The ills of strong drink, the damnation that awaited the drunkard, fire and brimstone from above.

"See this book, Gideon," Isaiah began. "I try to live by it. Try to raise my family by it."

"You have a fine family." Gideon gripped his hat in his hands, turning the band in circles. He admired Isaiah more than anyone he knew. Yet, he'd destroyed their friendship. "I broke your trust. I don't expect you to—"

Isaiah held up a hand to silence him. He flipped the Bible open to a marked page as if he'd prepared for this moment.

"Proverbs Seventeen. 'He that covereth a transgression seeketh love; but he that repeateth a matter separateth very friends.'"

Gideon frowned. "I don't understand."

"That right there, Gideon. Repeating a transgression separates friends. You've been a good friend to us. One transgression won't change that. A second one could."

Gideon sat frozen, stunned to his soul. He had no words as he grappled with the kindness the farmer offered like a gift.

"We knew about the drinking, Gideon. You can't hide that with all the perfume in France."

"I don't deserve—"

"Deserve has nothing to do with it. Matthew knows he did wrong. He knows you did, too. So do you, or you wouldn't be here. My boy will learn from this and be better for it."

"He's a good boy."

"He is." A slight smile tipped Isaiah's mouth. "And you're a good man. Mary and me, we want to put this incident behind us and keep you as our friend."

He was no more a good man than Isaiah was an evil one.

"I don't know what to say." He deserved to be hated, forced out, beaten to bloody mush.

"Say you'll never bring strong drink on my property again. Never repeat that transgression. Be the friend, the man, we believe you to be, the man my boy admires."

A sorrowful throb of regret pulsed through his veins. Regret and gratitude strong enough to choke him.

"You have my word," Gideon managed. He twisted his hat brim, stared at it. "Such as it is."

"Oh, your word is good." Isaiah placed a firm hand on his shoulder. "I've seen it in action around here on this farm while I've been laid up."

Isaiah's absolution made him feel worse than if the man had hit him in the face with a fireplace poker.

He raised sorrowful eyes to his friend. "Just doing what neighbors should."

The softest of smiles, gentle as a rainbow after a storm, parted Isaiah's whiskers. "Don't see any other neighbors working out here from dawn to dark. I'll tell you what I do see. I see a man with an aching soul. What troubles you, son?"

Son. "I'm all right."

"Tell me about the family you have left. The one you hate so much."

Gideon wasn't surprised that the perceptive friend had picked up on his feelings for his father.

"My pa. Thomas Hartley." He spat the distasteful words.

"And your mother?"

The furious stew of emotions boiled up in his chest hotter than a blacksmith's forge.

"She was a fine Christian woman. I don't know how she put up with him."

"Love covers a multitude of sins."

Gideon rose and paced across the expanse of grass. Chickens clucked and flapped.

He didn't want to talk about this. Couldn't.

Memories flooded in like the first rain on Noah's ark. Memories that made him want a drink worse than he wanted his next breath.

He'd spent years drowning the past, and all it took was a single mention of Thomas Hartley to stir it up again.

After a long tense silence, Isaiah's kind voice forced its way in. "I'd sure like to get that lean-to finished before winter."

Gideon slowly turned to look at his friend. A friend who forgave without reason and backed away when he perceived he'd intruded too far. A true friend.

"Thank you, Isaiah," he choked out. "I'll get to work."

Shading her eyes with a cupped hand, Willa fought a spurt of anger when Gideon rode down the trail leading from the beaten path to her door. He was finally here. She didn't know whether to be relieved or to hit him with the hoe she was using to dispatch the weeds choking out the seeds she and her sisters had planted.

All of yesterday, she'd waited for Gideon to arrive. He hadn't, and she'd fretted, hoping he wasn't ill again. Or worse, that he had returned to old habits. By this morning, she was just plain mad and fixing to go into town and drag him out of the saloon at gunpoint if necessary.

Savannah and Mercy were already aghast that she'd spent the night at his bedside. When she'd explained that he was ill, leaving out the reasons for that illness, and reminding them that without Gideon Hartley she'd be riding into outlaw territory alone, they'd hushed. They had not, however, been pleased.

Tossing aside the hoe, Willa tromped toward him, her boots heavy with dirt clots.

She gave his appearance the once-over.

"You look better," she declared as he met her halfway.

His lips tilted upward. "Than what?"

In spite of her annoyance, Willa grinned. "Perhaps I should ask, how are you feeling?"

"Right as rain."

"Liar." She gentled her tone to soften the truth.

If Gideon noticed her aggravation, he ignored it. He led his horse to a shade tree and left him to graze on the abundant grass.

Mercy, ever alert in case someone arrived to seek her medical assistance, came to the door.

"Oh, hello, Mr. Hartley." There was a noticeable coolness in her tone.

Like a gentleman, he doffed his black hat. "Miss Mercy."

Mercy tilted her head in courteous, if strained, acknowledgment. Her hair was down this morning and shining like burnished copper in the sunlight. Gideon was a man. He'd certainly noticed her beautiful sister, and if that bothered Willa, she'd keep her thoughts to herself.

"Willa tells me you've been under the weather," Mercy said. "I'm glad to see you out and about."

Gideon cut a sharp glance toward Willa.

Willa widened her eyes at him, breath held, fearful Gideon would somehow relate exactly what his illness had been.

"Thank you," was all he said.

She exhaled in a breathy gust. Fur would fly if either sister suspected Willa's guide was a dissipated drunk.

Willa couldn't say she'd blame them, either. In this particularly important case, silence was the better part of wisdom.

"Well," she said brightly, pivoting toward Gideon. "Thank you for offering to help on our claim today."

Mercy looked from Gideon to Willa and back, speculation brimming. "Do you know much of farming, Mr. Hartley?"

"A little." Wry amusement lit his expression. "I'm sure Willa will be happy to teach me what I don't know."

Mercy's stiff shoulders relaxed. Her lips curved at the reference to Willa's bulldog tenacity. "She *can* be bossy when she wants something, can't she?"

That smirky little smile that both annoyed and appealed appeared on his face. "A regular harridan."

Willa puffed up like a toad. "I'm standing right here, you two. I can hear every word you're saying."

"Begging your pardon, madam." Gideon's teeth flashed, his eyes dancing. The rogue. He was not sorry at all.

He was, however, incredibly charming when he teased like this.

He made her mad. He made her uncomfortable. He made her *feel* the most confusing things. She wasn't quite sure what to do with him now that he was here and looked so...capable.

Resorting to practicality, she jerked her thumb toward the garden. "I'm chopping weeds. Mercy and Savannah are about to do laundry. There's plenty of work."

Though she wondered why, if he was able-bodied enough to work a farm, he continued to delay their departure.

Lower lip between finger and thumb, Gideon gazed over land that spread flat as a quilt top, most of it yet uncultivated.

"Tell me your farming plan," he said.

Willa blinked. "Our plan?"

They had no plan other than to keep control of what belonged to them and to survive day to day.

"I suppose we'll gradually clear more acres and do something profitable with it."

He squatted to take a handful of garden soil and weigh it in his hand as if he knew what he was doing. "One hundred and sixty acres of good land. Where's your water source?"

"A little creek runs through that copse of trees." She pointed toward the south woods. "And we have a cold spring behind the cabin. We hope to put in a pump."

Someday.

He nodded. "Are you running cattle or planting crops?"

"All we have is our milk cow. Papa cleared a few acres for corn before he left."

Tossing the dirt aside, Gideon stood and wiped his hand down his britches leg. "Corn is good. What about the rest of the land? What's planted there?"

"Nothing. It's too late now."

"In the fall, you could plant winter wheat," he said. "If you buy a few head of cattle, they can fatten on a portion of the wheat during winter, and you'll have two salable products in summer."

Willa stared at him in amazement. "Where did you learn so much about farming?"

He shrugged, his gaze sliding away.

"I was raised on a farm." He made the statement as though it pained him.

Curious.

Though Willa wanted to press for details, considering she knew next to nothing about his past, Savannah came around the side of the house, dragging a washtub. They'd been hard at work since sunrise and Savannah was already tiring, her limp pronounced.

Gideon noticed, too. He started toward the youngest sister.

Willa bristled, daring him to say anything that might poke fun at Savannah's disability. If he did, she'd see the back of him, even if he headed straight to the saloon.

From this distance, she could only hear snatches of the conversation. The need to protect her sister kicked in. Jerking her hat string tight beneath her chin, Willa marched toward them.

Suddenly, Savannah's dimples flashed, her smile bright as she gazed up at Gideon. Willa's tension seeped away.

Whatever he'd said, Savannah had not taken offense.

Gideon hoisted the washtub, slowed his steps to match Savannah's painstaking ones and followed her around to the side of the house, charming her with light conversation.

A funny feeling skittered through Willa's chest. The man was a curiosity that rattled her brain and ignited a vexatious yearning to be pretty like her sisters.

She grabbed the hoe and stomped back to the garden where she whacked viciously at a weed.

Gideon Hartley was a gambler, a drunk and the trail guide she'd hired. She could check her silly feelings at the door and get on with business.

He was supposed to be here yesterday. Where had he been? Why hadn't he come?

Furiously thrashing at the weeds while she fumed and fretted, Willa slowly became aware of another sound. A rhythmic chop and sweep coming from somewhere behind her.

She whirled around to find Gideon methodically hoeing another row.

The corner of his mouth slid upward. "No weed goes unpunished?"

"You make me mad."

He dispatched another weed. "I wonder why that is."

"I don't know," she mumbled. "Where were you yesterday?"

With the hoe in front of him, he rested one wrist on top of the handle. "You missed me?"

"I was concerned about your health."

"No, Willa, be honest. You were concerned that I spent my day in the Red Diamond."

"Did you?" she asked, almost piteously.

A pained expression flickered and was gone. "No. Nor did I imbibe. If you must know, I visited a friend."

A vision of beautiful Belle Holbrook flashed through Willa's head. Followed closely by the name Gideon had called during his nightmares. *Emily.* Who was she? Why did it suddenly matter so much?

A thousand feelings swirled through Willa that she neither understood nor wanted.

"Belle?" she blurted before she could stop herself.

"Why, Willa, do you think I have a sweetheart?" Tone mocking, he asked, "Are you jealous?"

He was laughing at her. And she didn't like it one bit. The arrogant rogue. "Don't be ludicrous. Belle is my friend."

His teeth flashed, eyes twinkling. "Mine, too."

Strangling the hoe handle, she turned her back on him and assailed a stubborn weed with enough energy to build a house. So what if he had a woman. None of her business. Once they captured Charlie Bangs and collected the reward, she'd never have to see him again.

The thought opened a cold place inside her, left her bereft. Confounded man. He caused no little amount of consternation.

"A friend of mine is in town," he said quietly.

She spun back toward him. "I don't want to hear about your conquests."

That smile again, that mocking, irritating grin. She wanted to slap it off his face.

"His name is Frisco Burgess. Ever heard of him?"

"No," she snapped.

"That's good."

"Why?"

"If he heard you describe him as my conquest, he'd shoot us both. Frisco's not a man you'd invite home to Sunday dinner."

Willa huffed. "Savannah would."

Gideon chuckled softly, his attention drifting toward the two sisters bent over the washtubs. "I believe she would."

Willa followed his admiring gaze.

Savannah stood over a galvanized washtub, scrubbing vigorously on the washboard, while Mercy manned yet another tub where she rinsed, wrung and hung the items on a droopy wire they'd tied between two oaks. The fronts of their dresses were dark with water spots.

Naturally, Gideon admired Savannah. Any sensible man would, though she was reluctant to call Gideon sensible. Savannah was all the feminine, delightful things that Willa wasn't.

"I didn't tell them the real reason for your illness," she offered, remembering that he had no way of knowing if she had or not.

"I gathered as much. Thank you."

"I didn't do it for you. They'd try to stop me from going if they knew you...overindulged."

His face closed up. "As they should."

He dropped the hoe then and walked to the shade tree, leaned his back against the bark and slowly slid to the ground where he tilted his head back and closed his eyes.

The handsome bay horse, grazing nearby, ambled over to snuffle his master's shoulder. Gideon grasped the stirrup and pulled himself to a stand long enough to retrieve his canteen before slithering once more down the tree.

Willa glared. What was in the canteen?

He tipped it up and drank deeply.

Hoe clattering to the dirt, she started toward him, suspicious.

He looked fatigued, washed out. His color had faded from a rich tan to a pasty shade.

Remorse struck her. He was still recovering. In her snit, she'd let that little truth escape her common sense.

As she lowered herself to her knees in front of him, her skirt pooled against the cool grass. Gideon opened his eyes and must have read her expression because he sighed and closed them again.

"It's water, Willa. Only water."

So he knew she suspected the worst of him. She couldn't be blamed for being suspicious, not after the three awful days at his bedside.

Following a long quiet spell, while birds twittered in the leafy canopy above and a squirrel darted down the rough bark and away into the woods, Gideon seemed to gather himself.

"Frisco knew where we might find Charlie Bangs."

A spurt of energy shot through Willa. "He did? Where?"

"Your outlaw," he said with that droll twist of his handsome mouth, "was last spotted in Keokuk Falls."

"I don't know where that is." She didn't know where much of anything was in this vast open territory.

"It borders Indian Territory, along the North Canadian River. About three days' ride, maybe four."

She leaped up, grass flecks tumbling from her skirt. "If we leave tomorrow, we can catch him."

Using hands to his knees for leverage, Gideon slowly rose while keeping his back against the oak.

"Look at me, Willa," he said in irritation. "After an hour in the sun, I barely made it to this shade tree. You think I can ride a horse for days?"

"If we wait too long, he'll be gone."

"He likely already is. He's a criminal. He's either finding a new place to rob or holing up somewhere remote until the dust clears. Frisco thinks he's heading deeper into the Nations."

Willa's burst of energy flagged. This was taking too long. At the current rate, she'd never claim that bounty and pay off the loan.

"Keokuk Falls is too dangerous anyway," Gideon went on. "Unless you're looking to get your throat slit or a nail hammered into your temple while you sleep, you'll steer clear of that town."

She shivered. "You're trying to scare me."

He gripped her upper arms. "I'm trying to keep you alive."

His fingers held her lightly, but she felt their strength, their warmth through her cotton sleeves. For an unwell man, his hands exuded more power than she had in her whole body.

She liked his touch, liked having his hands on her this way. A flush rose into her cheeks.

Finding Gideon Hartley attractive was unconscionable. It simply would not do.

Furious at herself and at him for reasons she didn't want to consider, she fumed. "Are you? Or are you trying to put me off until it's too late and the bank takes this farm?"

His eyes narrowed. "I wouldn't do that."

"Then when can we leave?" She knew she was being unfair. But his weakened condition was his own fault, not hers.

He dropped his hold. Instantly, she missed his touch.

"Four days," he murmured. "Give me four or five more days."

Chapter Eleven

Gideon discovered, quite to his surprise, that he enjoyed the handful of days spent on the Malone land claim, particularly the time he battled wits with the entertaining, unpredictable Willa.

Miss Savannah was as sweet and tender as the honey cake she'd baked the day they'd discovered a beehive and robbed a good amount of honey. Her guileless blue eyes and refined nature made him wonder about the brains of the town's single males, though he'd lived long enough to understand the more unfair workings of nature. A chick that was different was forced out of the nest or pecked to death by the others.

Savannah's crippled leg made her different and therefore an unacceptable mate.

Mercy, the Titian-haired healer, kept him at arm's length, proving to be more suspicious, more aloof, than the other two. She worked alongside her older sister in the fields he tried to help cultivate as long as his body would hold up, though she frequently hurried away to tend the sick or injured.

Then there was Willa. He tried not to think about her too much, but he did anyway. He'd never met anyone quite like her. She challenged him, aggravated him and appealed to him in a curiously elemental way.

That she nagged him worse than any fishwife was understandable. He only hoped the extra days he'd requested were enough.

He'd need every bit of stamina he could muster to keep them both safe and well on this hazardous quest of hers.

After the second day of working on the Malone farm and sweating more poison from his system, he'd fallen into his bed so exhausted that if he'd had a nightmare, he didn't remember it.

Exhaustion, he decided, was a better sleep potion than rotgut whiskey.

So, when he arrived once more at the Malone farm, he felt strong and alive.

As he settled Traveler for the day, Willa greeted him in the yard. She braced both ugly boots in front of him as if they were about to engage in fisticuffs. The notion of the small brown wren making war on a man his size made him smile.

Willa took offense, fluffing up like a mad cat. No surprise. He'd come to expect it.

"I never asked you to do all this work."

"My working makes you mad?"

"It's not necessary. You're still recovering. I need you well." Her attitude stirred him. As usual.

He perched both hands on his hips. "What did you think, Willa? That I'd sit in the shade, sipping lemonade while three women break their backs to make a farm out of this place? You think I'm that much of a scoundrel?"

"We take care of our own business."

"I have no doubt that you can. But is it so wrong to accept help from a friend?"

Her bottom lip quivered. "You won't always be here. We can't depend on you."

Gideon softened his stance, willed his racing pulse to settle and fought off the insane urge to take her in his arms.

"I'm here now, Willa. I owe you a favor, considering the three days you kept me from jumping out the hotel window." He let the corner of his mouth tip up the slightest bit, though he wasn't teasing.

"You wouldn't have." She, too, softened her belligerent posture. "You'd have survived without me."

"Would I?" He recalled the scary moment when she'd taken the pistol away from him. He'd been in the throes of a terrible nightmare when he'd come to himself, holding the loaded Colt. Temptation had flitted through his troubled mind.

Thank God she'd been there. He meant that with all his heart. God must have heard his prayers because he was alive and feeling better than he had in a long time.

Plain and simple Willa had a lot to do with that.

A disturbing truth.

Abruptly, he turned away from the uncomfortable conversation and went to his horse.

"Are you leaving?" Willa asked.

"Do you want me to?" With one hand on his saddlebags, he stared over his shoulder.

Willa fidgeted with the folds of her ugly brown skirt, finally admitting, "No."

He laughed, a sound as rusty as his conscience. "Was that so hard? To admit you need me?"

"I need you as a guide," she huffed. "Getting you strong is more important than farm work."

He heard what she didn't say. It wasn't his company she desired. Or even an extra hand on the farm. It was his sobriety.

He didn't know why that hurt, but it did.

Gideon stuck a boot in the stirrup and swung onto Traveler's back. "Be saddled up and ready to leave on Monday. Daybreak."

Willa's brown eyes widened. "You're still leaving?"

"I am."

"Aren't you coming back before then?"

"Why would I?"

Before he could examine why her attitude upset him, he spun his horse and rode away.

"I don't want to go."

Saturday evening, Willa was still upset, still wondering why she felt the uncontrollable need to provoke the only man willing to ride off into Indian Territory with her.

Now, as if she didn't have enough to fret over, her sisters expected her to attend the Faragates' barn dance.

She, a tomboy in her papa's boots, at a barn dance was like inviting a Jersey cow to tea.

"Willa, please. If you don't go, I won't, and I deeply yearn for the pleasantries of social interaction."

Her round blue eyes pleading, Savannah's dainty little hands fussed and fidgeted with the new layer of lace she'd sewed onto each of her dress's bell sleeves for this very occasion.

The blue cotton print, which enhanced her stunning eyes, was only one of the dresses Savannah had brought with her from St. Louis. Mercy and Willa didn't have the luxury of such nice garments. Willa preferred her riding skirt to frilly ruffles and lace anyway, but Savannah loved pretty things and was generous about sharing hers, including the green dress she wanted Willa to wear.

"Church is enough society for me," Willa insisted, knowing she was being stubborn. "I don't fit at parties and dances."

"Don't be silly. Of course you do. Everyone does. Billy Reins is bringing his fiddle, and if you've a mind, you could take Papa's penny whistle to play so you won't have to dance."

What Savannah was really saying was that no one would *ask* Willa to dance. The penny whistle would give her an excuse not to be humiliated. She would be anyway.

"I'm not as good as Papa. Besides, no one wants to dance to an Irish musical instrument except an Irishman."

"Nobody thinks that but you." Savannah spun toward Mercy, who sat in front of a grainy mirror, dressing her long cinnamon hair. "Isn't that right, Mercy?"

In the mirror, Mercy's green gaze connected with Willa's. "Playing for the enjoyment of others is an act of unselfish generosity."

When she put it that way, Willa would feel guilty if she didn't take along *the wee pipe*, as Papa had called it. Although some in Sweet Clover would grumble about a woman playing music for a dance.

Some would grumble anyway because there *was* a dance.

You couldn't please everyone.

But, a little voice whispered, she could please her little sister.

Moving behind Mercy, Willa took up the brush and began to stroke her middle sister's shining copper locks. "You should wear your hair down, Mercy. A crowning glory like yours should be seen."

"I have no desire to be noticed, Willa." Mercy confiscated the brush and put it on the dressing table. With agile fingers, she twisted and wove her hair into a severe knot behind her head. The style was intentionally unattractive.

Willa caught her bottom lip with her teeth, mulling over Mercy's coolness toward other people. She hadn't always been this way. She'd once laughed and danced and flirted with the best of them. Now, except for her medical calls and a few select lady friends, she kept to herself.

"If not to socialize and dance," Willa demanded, "why do you want to attend?"

"Because Savannah wants to." Mercy gave Willa a pointed look. "The dance is important to her."

"Please, Willa." Savannah's dainty hands clasped beneath her chin in a prayer-like gesture. "Dancing with other girls at Miss Pennington's School is not the same as a real dance."

Willa sighed. Mercy had exposed the obvious truth. Willa was being selfish. "I'll go."

Savannah chirped happily and danced a wobbly jig. "And you'll wear the green dress? Please. The color is delightful on you."

Willa eyed the dress Savannah had pressed and laid out on the bed. With its light green underskirt and darker green bodice and overskirt, the gown was too fancy. Willa had never worn anything so elegant. "You can't make a silk purse out of a sow's ear, Savannah."

Savannah's merry laugh rang out, her cheeks pink with pleasure. "You are not a sow's ear. You're lovely, even if you do try to hide under Papa's old hat."

Willa took offense. She didn't hide the way Mercy did. She simply was who she was. But to appease her baby sister, she acquiesced. "I'll wear the dress."

The Faragate barn was packed with people, some Willa knew, but many she did not. Apparently, everyone for miles around had come into town for the social event.

Billy Reins stood on a barrel, merrily sawing out a tune on his fiddle as the crowded mass shuffled around the wooden floor, a luxury Sadie Faragate had insisted upon for the explicit purpose of hosting parties. The fact that her husband owned the lumber company meant they could afford such extravagances.

Willa and her two sisters settled on wooden straight-back chairs arranged against one wall of the massive barn. The punch bowl rested on a table nearby with easy access from the chairs whenever they needed to appear busy instead of pitiful.

Though she'd slid the penny whistle into her skirt pocket, Willa had no intention of making a spectacle of herself by removing the instrument. As it was, she sat, back stiff as a tree trunk, and felt like the sow's ear she'd alluded to earlier. Once a wallflower, always a wallflower.

Every muscle in her body was tense.

As Savannah was taller, the borrowed green dress was two inches too long and Willa figured she'd trip on it if she moved around too much. Nevertheless, the longer hem covered Papa's ugly boots, the only shoes she owned.

None of this mattered because, as she knew would happen, not one person had asked her to dance.

Mercy busied herself in a conversation with one of the local ladies who'd recently given birth, doting over the white-gowned infant in the woman's arms. It was always this way with Mercy in social settings. She gravitated toward her patients and the children.

A woman like Mercy should be married with her own babies.

Yet, it was her youngest sister who made Willa's chest ache. Savannah had been beyond excited about the gathering and now she sat with Willa the wallflower, sipping punch from the nearby table, making polite conversation with others who paused for a refreshing drink.

The dainty toe of Savannah's buttoned shoe tapped to the

music, her smile bright, as she eagerly watched the swirl of dancers and waited for someone to invite her to dance.

Willa didn't know if this was a good thing or a bad one. Savannah could waltz, but would she be able to keep up with the faster steps?

Thank goodness Homer Baggley was not yet present to make some horrid comment. She hoped he didn't come at all.

Couples swept around the floor to the jaunty likes of "Buffalo Gals" and "Camptown Races," slowing for a waltz or two, then speeding up for a lively schottische.

Though families and children made up the largest contingent of partygoers, single cowboys and farmers had gussied up and come to town, too. There were plenty of spare partners, but folks in Sweet Clover knew that Savannah was lame.

With the barn door open, the night breeze flowed in with the arriving guests.

Aware that she was watching the door, though she couldn't say why other than escape, Willa noticed when a group of boisterous cowboys tumbled in, laughing and talking loudly.

They had, she suspected by their rowdy exuberance, visited the Red Diamond before coming to the Faragates' barn.

The four made their way along the perimeter, bumping into dancers and drawing attention with their noisy behavior. The loudest pair each grabbed a partner and pulled her onto the dance floor.

The remaining two approached the ladies sitting against the wall.

Willa braced herself. She wanted to dance, to be noticed, to be chosen, if only to avoid the humiliation of being a wallflower, but she wasn't sure she wanted the attention of either of these fellows.

Giving a sweeping flourish of his hat, a thin cowboy in dungarees held up by red suspenders bowed toward Savannah.

Blond hair neatly combed, his mustache trimmed and waxed, he was young and not bad-looking. At least, he didn't stink!

"Hello, pretty lady," he drawled in a strong southern accent. "Would you do me the honor?"

Savannah dimpled prettily. "Why, sir, we've not yet been introduced."

The cowboy punched an elbow into his friend's side. "Introduce us, Jack."

"Ma'am," the beak-nosed Jack responded. "This here is my friend, Walt Hammond. And you would be?"

"Miss Savannah Malone, late of St. Louis," she said. "I'm pleased to make your acquaintance, Mr. Hammond."

Jack guffawed. "Well, look at that, Walt. Ain't she sweet and proper? You picked a good one."

Walt, who seemed more mannerly than his friend, said, "Miss Malone, would you care to waltz?"

Sure enough, the fiddler had slid into a slow one-two-three rhythm.

Some of the tension in Willa's shoulders abated. The cowboy seemed all right.

In her polished School for Young Ladies manner, Savannah held her hand toward the blond Walt. "I would be delighted, Mr. Hammond."

As her partner led her onto the floor, Savannah flashed a happy smile at Willa, lifted her slender arms in the proper Miss Pennington's waltz form and began to follow Walt's movements with grace and ease. Her dimples flashed repeatedly.

Willa's mood lifted as her baby sister sailed slowly around the dance floor, barely a sign of her crippled limb. Savannah was happy. So Willa was happy.

Tapping her boot toe, Willa gazed around the large barn, amusing herself by silently naming the people she knew. Liam O'Shea and his young son danced with sweet, timid Tilly

Wasserman. The church elders and their wives talked in a clutch, probably about the schoolmaster they hoped to hire soon. Next to the▪ was Theodore Pierce whose greedy eyes gleamed when they met hers.

Willa quickly turned away, spotting the beautiful Belle Holbrook in a full multi-layered dress of burgundy silk that shimmered as she swayed to the romantic music with her partner.

Willa's heart lurched. Gideon, in a gold brocade vest and starched white shirt, his arm around Belle's waist and one hand holding hers, smiled affectionately into the face of the stunning brunette.

Willa hadn't known he would be here. Considering his easily taxed stamina, she hadn't expected him to be. He'd said nothing about the dance.

She sniffed and looked away.

His personal life was nothing to her.

Yet, a void opened up inside Willa. Though reluctant to admit it, she longed to be pretty and desirable like her sisters and Belle.

But she'd been on the shelf too long. She was too old for such wishes. Men wanted a young lady of manners and grace like Savannah. Or a stunning, wealthy widow like Belle.

Not a tough old spinster who'd never been kissed.

Fighting the ache that wouldn't go away, she went to the punch bowl for yet another cup and sipped the sweet ginger liquid, forcing her attention away from Gideon.

He and Belle apparently were a couple.

When the waltz ended, the fiddler kicked into an exuberant polka. Willa looked for her baby sister.

Savannah stepped away from her partner, but he laughed, grabbed her hands and pulled her back.

Willa tensed. Could Savannah dance a polka?

The cowboy started off in a feisty trot.

Willa set the punch cup aside, unease gathering like vultures as she watched.

Too soon, Savannah struggled to keep pace with the speedy dance. Her limp became obvious. She stumbled. The cowboy caught her and whirled her in a circle.

The spin was too much. She lost her balance and stumbled again, throwing both arms out to keep from falling.

Not wanting to further embarrass Savannah, Willa fought the urge to rush onto the floor and escort her sister to a chair.

"Please be kind," she whispered, helpless to stop what she feared was about to happen.

Valiantly, Savannah danced on, striving to keep up. When she stumbled yet a third time, her partner stopped dancing. Right there in the middle of everyone, he stopped, backed away as though Savannah had broken out in smallpox and stared down at her feet.

"What's wrong with you? Are you drunk?" His exasperated voice carried to Willa, which meant this side of the barn had heard his rude question.

Walt's half-drunk friend, Jack, who hadn't the sense God gave a rock, danced alongside and hollered, "Looks like a hobbled mare to me. Is she a cripple?"

A mortified Savannah gasped as dancers near them paused to stare.

Willa leaped to her feet.

For a fraction of time, Savannah stood frozen, and then, face flaming, she grabbed the sides of her full skirt and fled. As she pushed through the gawking crowd, murmurs followed.

She ran, as she had as a child, to Willa. Willa wrapped an arm over her shoulders, wishing she could protect her sister from the world. "Shh. They're drunk. Pay them no mind."

Savannah trembled with humiliation. Fat tears shimmered on her upswept eyelashes, teetering, ready to fall.

Suddenly, a dark figure in a gold brocade vest placed himself between Savannah and the gawkers.

"Miss Savannah," Gideon said quietly, "would you care for punch?"

She shook her head, cheeks aflame. "I want to go home."

Gideon glanced at Willa, and she saw the compassion there, completely unexpected from a cynic such as him.

His next words, directed to Savannah were gentle steel. "And let those rotters have the last laugh? You're made of stronger stuff than that."

Holding her hands to her cheeks, big blue eyes liquid with emotion, Savannah whispered, "What should I do? I'm so embarrassed."

"Dance with me. I'd be honored." He offered a hand that was part challenge and part kindness.

She shook her head. "I can't. I'm—"

"Yes, you can. I watched you. You waltz with the grace of a ballerina. I have no doubt that your problem was that graceless cowpoke, not the slight inconvenience of tight shoes."

The white lie garnered a tentative smile from the mortified woman. Gideon well knew from his days at the farm that Savannah was lame.

Tight shoes, indeed.

His kindness melted a thick patch of ice around Willa's heart.

Gideon Hartley confused her, but he pleased her, too. He was such a contradiction. She never knew which man he'd be, the inebriated cynic or the educated courtier.

Willa gave her baby sister's shoulder a light push. "Go on. Dance. Hold your head up. You're a Malone. I'll shoot anyone who says another cross word."

Savannah's giggle was small and tentative, but it was there. "You wouldn't."

One eyebrow cocked in amusement, Gideon allowed a droll smile. "She might. As would I."

Pink flames on her cheekbones, Savannah put her small hand in Gideon's and allowed him to lead her in a gentle, swaying waltz that clogged Willa's throat and caused her to like Gideon Hartley more than she should.

When the slow dance ended, he whispered something to Savannah and she nodded, head up, pink pleasure returning to her porcelain cheeks. Though the next music moved more quickly, Savannah somehow kept pace. Willa could only credit Gideon's expert timing and his ability to know exactly when to gently lift his partner off her feet and set her down again. The effort must have been tiring, but he guided her through not one but two lively dances until Savannah's smile was full blown.

If, Willa thought with single-minded purpose, he was recovered enough to dance so magnificently, he was recovered enough to travel.

And she'd tell him so.

After returning Savannah to her chair, Gideon somehow managed to coax Mercy onto the floor, and then returned for Willa.

"It's not necessary," she said when he reached out his hand.

"Yes, it is." The stubborn man waited, resolute, that half-amused expression on his too-handsome face.

Not wanting to spoil the much improved mood and deeply touched by his benevolence toward her sisters, Willa gave in, her pulse jumping a little too much, which was ridiculous. She was far beyond the age to go all twittery over a man.

As Gideon slid an arm around her waist and clasped her work-roughened hand in his increasingly strong one, Willa forgot all about her age, her unsuitable boots and the too-long hem.

The night was warm, the lilting music clear and sweet above the conversation and shuffling feet, and the strange feelings in her chest felt too good to waste. Just for this dance, she'd let herself pretend the impossible.

Gideon tugged her closer, his blue eyes suddenly serious, though the amused tilt of his lips never faltered. "You look lovely tonight. Green becomes you."

She should argue the fact, confident that no dress could make her lovely, but his unfamiliar words soothed a bruised place on her heart.

"Thank you. I'm grateful for what you did for Savannah."

He responded with quiet sarcasm. "Dancing with beautiful women is never an imposition."

As he whirled her around the wooden floor, she almost believed she was one of those beautiful women.

Breathing in Gideon's warm spicy cologne, she closed her eyes and swayed with the melody.

Naturally musical, following Gideon's surprisingly accomplished lead proved easy, but she was glad for the times she and her sisters had danced together while Papa played the fiddle and sang in his merry Irish lilt.

She wondered where a trail guide had learned to dance with such polish and flair.

"Are you still angry with me?" He grinned down at her.

"I don't even remember why I was mad in the first place." Tonight, she didn't want to remember.

"Nor do I. Truce then, fair maiden?" he lightly teased, his eyes twinkling.

Willa laughed. "Truce. I'd rather dance than fight." No point in adding that this was the first time in her life she'd danced with a man other than Papa.

"A stunning proclamation." He pretended shock. "So, then, 'if music be the food of love, play on!'"

As if to accent his dramatic declaration, Gideon swung her into a dizzying spin and then dipped her steeply to one side. He laughed down at her, azure eyes sparkling with mischief. She couldn't help but laugh in return.

She had not known a dance could be such delightful entertainment.

Or was it the company?

When they straightened from the exhilarating dip, Gideon had somehow rotated them so that his cheek rested against hers, his breath warm against her ear.

The resulting effect was a closeness that made her heart rattle against her ribs and her breathing increase, though she could blame both of those on the lively exercise.

A thrilling shiver sent goose bumps down her spine.

Other couples flowed rhythmically around them, the ladies' skirts swirling wide, while Willa felt like a butterfly in a cocoon, nestled safe in Gideon's arms.

It was ludicrous. It was foolish. It was insane.

They were two people who barely tolerated each other.

Except that wasn't exactly true.

He confused her and made her feel things that might break her heart. When he'd stepped in to shield and rescue Savannah that same heart had almost come out of her chest.

"'She was a phantom of delight,'" Gideon whispered against her ear. "'A lovely apparition, sent to be a moment's ornament.'"

He was teasing. She knew he was. Yet, she could not control the rush of heat to her cheeks, the rattle in her pulse or the soar of pleasure winging through her like fresh air through a window suddenly opened into a stale, empty room.

Just for tonight, she'd relish the feelings. Tomorrow was soon enough for practicality.

Chapter Twelve

The dance ended somewhere near midnight. Partygoers said their goodbyes and started off into the star-filled darkness, the Malone sisters among them.

A near giddy happiness permeated their conversation, and there was nothing Willa could do but credit Gideon for their mood.

Willa cast a glance at her baby sister. Dancing had meant so much to her, but now she limped badly, and Willa regretted the decision to walk to the dance rather than bring the wagon. She'd erringly considered the well-being of the tired plow horse rather than her sister.

The Faragate home was on the north end of town behind the lumber mill and the Malone farm to the south. They had a long walk ahead of them.

As they passed through town, raucous music and laughter poured from the saloon. Bright lantern light spilled out onto the boardwalk and onto the dirt street like melting butter. A cowboy in spurs and a hat stumbled through the batwing doors and fell onto the wooden walkway, making all manner of clattering noise. Another man emerged, helped the first one to his feet and with arms around each other, went singing toward the horses tied at the railing.

Crossing to the other side of the street, the sisters hurried past. Fights and gunshots frequently broke out in the saloon, particularly on Saturday night when cowboys left the ranches and rode into town to spend their week's pay.

Willa couldn't help thinking of the many nights Gideon had frequented the establishment. Was he there now? Had he gone straight from the dance to quench his thirst on something stronger than ginger ale?

As the business district faded behind them, Willa held the lantern so that it cast a wide circle around her and her sisters. The moon was bright and stars were out but the lantern guided their footsteps. She did not want Savannah to stumble and fall.

At the clip-clop of approaching hoofbeats, the sisters moved to one side to let the rider pass.

The big bay gelding plodded around them and stopped.

Willa lifted the lantern to see the rider's face. A wiggle of pleasure found its way through her bloodstream.

Gideon dismounted. "Evening, ladies."

He tugged his hat brim.

Savannah giggled. "Mr. Hartley, what a surprise. I haven't seen you in ages."

His smile flashed white in the lantern's golden glow. "I was out for a stroll and saw three lovely ladies walking alone. Perhaps you'd allow me to walk with you."

Willa snorted. "Why would you walk? You have a horse."

Though her tone was matter-of-fact, she couldn't deny being amused by his ruse.

"Well, look at that. He must have followed me." Gideon blinked at the bay as if he'd never seen it before. "And here

I wanted a pleasant evening stroll." He turned to Savannah with a tilt of his mouth. "Could I impose upon you to ride this big fellow? I'd consider it a great favor."

Something sweet and undeniable curled in Willa's belly.

While Gideon kept up his charming, amusing chatter, Savannah gratefully accepted his assistance onto the saddle. Voluminous skirt spread around her, she clung sidesaddle to the horn with Gideon leading the animal.

The three sisters had no need of an escort—they were accustomed to walking alone—but the horse was a blessing for the lame sister.

They plodded onward, talking, mostly about the dance, reliving the hilarious moment when an angry red rooster flapped down from the rafters and chased the dancers from the floor.

A bright moon and stars canopied overhead, lighting the two miles of beaten path.

Other partygoers, some on horseback, some in wagons and others like them on foot, journeyed the same direction, dropping off as they reached their homes.

Conversation was merry, the energy from the dance still piping through their tired but happy bodies.

When they reached the cabin, they stood outside in the cool night, talking quietly and listening to the whip-poor-wills calling back and forth in the woods.

Gideon seemed in no hurry to rush away. Perhaps the temptation of the saloon pulled at him and he stayed as a reminder of what he should not do. She couldn't think of any other reason for him to linger.

Mercy soon went inside, followed by a limping Savannah, who no longer tried to hide the pain. Before she closed the door, Savannah graciously thanked Gideon for the ride and the dance. Her dimples flashed a few extra times and Willa was determined to have a stern talk with her innocent little sister. Gideon was as unsuitable as Homer Baggley.

Reluctant to end the evening, Willa remained in the pleasant darkness with Gideon and his horse. Probably, she told herself, to keep him out of the saloon. Only when he was with her could she be sure he wasn't drinking. Even then, he was a man. He could do what he pleased. He didn't have to listen to her.

But he had.

So far.

"Is there anything to be done for Savannah?" he asked quietly, taking up residence with one shoulder against the side of the cabin, his hat held in both hands.

Was he inquiring because he wanted to court her younger sister? Or out of friendly concern?

Willa didn't ask, but she was even more determined to have that conversation with Savannah.

She shook her head. The pins in her hair had loosened during the lively dances. She plucked them out, dropped the pins in her pocket, and let her braid fall over one shoulder. "The doctors in St. Louis didn't think so."

"A pity." His gaze had followed Willa's movements, landing on the long braid. "Did you enjoy the Faragates' social?"

"Yes, did you?"

"More, perhaps, than I should have." His self-mocking grin indicated his previously weakened state.

She did not think, given the rigorous exercise he'd received lifting Savannah and then squiring Mercy and her around the dance floor, that he was quite as weak as he let on.

Was he delaying the start of their journey for another reason?

"Papa always said to take pleasure where pleasure was found

because there 'twas never a bad thing that couldn't get worse." She dredged up her father's Irish lilt for good measure.

Gideon's white teeth flashed in the faint light. "A wise man, your papa."

"I miss him." The familiar stab of grief opened a hole in Willa's chest. "He was filled with stories and laughter and bonny music, even if he was a rambler looking for the pot of gold." She smiled, though the action was fond sadness. "Which always seemed to be somewhere over the next horizon."

"Your family moved around a great deal?"

She leaned her back against the side of the cabin, palms braced behind her on the rough unpainted logs, logs she'd helped fell and hone and put in place during the short months when Papa was still excited about the prospect of their new homestead.

"Wherever the next opportunity might be. The coal mines in Kentucky, then the railroads across the country to Kansas. Then to free land in Oklahoma Territory and finally to the gold field that killed him."

"You're as well traveled as I," he said softly. "Though I've not been to Kentucky."

"Where do you come from, Gideon?"

He was silent for a moment and because she'd put out the lantern to save fuel, she could barely discern his shadowy expression.

"Texas," he said finally, "but I've guided from Missouri all across the west."

"So, you are not too far from home."

"Home is where I hang my hat."

"But you come from Texas originally."

"That was a long time ago."

He grew pensive, and she discerned his memories of Texas were not happy ones.

To cheer him and because she was reluctant to go inside, though common sense said she should, Willa asked, "Where did you learn to dance so magnificently?"

"Magnificently, you say?" He chuckled, a warm and gentle sound that caused a flutter of butterflies in her middle. "Why, Willa plain and simple, you flatter me."

He fell into that half-amused tone that seemed his way of dissembling.

"Don't deny the obvious, me lad," she said lightly, teasing as she lapsed again into Papa's lilt. "We Irish appreciate a fair, musical step such as yours."

"Well, then, madam, shall we?"

Before she knew what he was about, Willa was in Gideon's arms, moving beneath the moonlight. He had to be tired, but the strength flowing from his muscled body into hers sent a little thrill through Willa.

The troublesome man confounded and invigorated her. She didn't know if she could trust him, didn't know if he'd let her down, but somehow they'd formed a budding friendship that gave her hope.

He danced better than any Irishman, a mark in his favor. Papa would approve. But then he'd approve of Gideon's propensity for the saloon and copious bottles of rotgut, as well.

For this moment under the stars, Willa put those concerns as far away as she could push them and remembered Papa's adage to take pleasure where pleasure could be found.

With grace and ease, Gideon moved her across the green grass, around the yard and near the garden where the fragrant scents of Mercy's herbs carried on the night air.

It was magical, it was beautiful, and Willa almost cried from the pure indulgence of Gideon's light and tender embrace.

When at last they stopped, Gideon did not release his hold, but gazed into her face, his expression soft and unreadable.

Willa's pulse ticked up, thudding against her collarbone. The smallest smile lifted at the corners of Gideon's mouth. He stared down at her for the longest time.

When finally, he released her and stepped back, looking perplexed, she felt the loss of his touch and wondered what was happening to her.

As if to distract them both from the strange mood circling the yard as sure as the impromptu waltz, Gideon pointed toward the sky. "A shooting star."

By the time she followed the direction of his arm, made visible by his shirt's white color, the star had disappeared.

"I missed it." She sighed, sad.

"'Bright star, would I were steadfast as thou art,'" he murmured softly, rubbing a hand over the back of his neck as he looked away into the darkness.

"Shakespeare?" she asked.

"Keats." Then he lapsed silent again, and she wondered where he'd gone in his thoughts.

When he spoke, his manly voice was low and serious. Gone was the charming, teasing dancer.

"There'll be plenty of stars on our journey."

Her heart lurched. "The journey."

Gideon had skillfully switched topics on her again, and Willa struggled to rein in the bevy of emotions racing through her veins.

At times, the concept of riding into the wilderness with this man in pursuit of an outlaw seemed as foreign to her as Africa. Weeks had passed since the bounty hunter's death and her decision to go after Charlie Bangs. Weeks since she'd accosted Gideon in his hotel room, only to discover her one hope of finding the man who'd killed her father was a drunk.

Was he still? She prayed not. In fact, she'd taken to praying more lately than she had in years. About him. About the home she could not bear to lose. About the dangerous journey ahead.

"Do you have everything ready to go?" She was relieved, if confounded, to return to safer ground. Dancing with Gideon had gone to her head in the strangest way and established a mood she did not understand. Did he feel it, too?

His shoulder lifted, fell, the gold brocade catching the moonlight. "All I'll need. We'll travel light."

"Shouldn't we take a pack mule?"

He huffed, a soft puff of breath. "Not unless you want your outlaw to see you coming from a mile away." His tone deepened, hard as steel. "In that territory, we have to be able to move fast."

Though the night was warm, Willa rubbed her arms, suddenly chilled. She understood his meaning. If trouble came, as it surely would, they'd need horses with wings.

Jasper was the only horse she owned. He was a big, dependable draft horse, not a fleet-footed steed.

Gideon stepped closer, closed his hands around her upper arms as he had that day in the garden.

"Want to change your mind about this?"

Her chin went up. "No."

She couldn't, no matter how afraid she might be.

Chapter Thirteen

"*Gideon, help me.*"

"*Tad,*" he groaned. "*Jump. I'll catch you.*"

Flames shot from the boy's arms, from his hair. He stretched his fiery hands toward Gideon.

Then they were falling, falling, falling.

A hoarse scream ripped through the mist of his nightmare. Gideon jerked awake, chest heaving, heart thundering. Someone had screamed.

He sat up and surveyed the hotel room that had become his home. He was alone. Had someone screamed in a nearby room? Or below his window on the street?

The nightmare flooded in as real as it had been that day on his father's San Antonio cotton plantation. Tad's screams. He could still hear them in his ears.

"Tad," he whispered, followed by the fury he always felt when he thought of his lost family.

Except for one man, they'd still be alive.

Hatred curled in his belly like a viper.

He sat up, scrubbed his hands over his face, trying to erase the dream. A weak sun overshadowed by gray clouds penetrated through the lace curtain.

The dark tortuous images remained in the room, circling through his brain like wolves on the hunt.

Only the whiskey had kept them at bay.

He wished for a drink more than he wished to keep breathing.

But he'd promised. God, Willa, Isaiah. A promise he had to keep or die trying.

He scrubbed both hands over his face.

Why hadn't he dreamed of last night's dance? Of the moonlight moments with Willa that should not have happened but that were entirely too pleasant to regret?

Why were the nightmares back to haunt him?

But he knew. The anger never faded. Now that he was sober, without stupor to block them, the memories of his past had free rein.

No amount of dancing with beautiful women could silence them.

Only the whiskey had that power.

While he dressed for the day, his pulse still erratic, he forced himself to think of last night's pleasantries.

Willa, the plucky warrior woman, had always intrigued him a little more than was prudent, but last night, in that green dress, with her full mouth laughing as he teased and quoted poetry she claimed never to have heard, she'd captivated him as surely as if she were a siren from the pages of *The Odyssey*.

Outside her cabin beneath a star-glittered sky, he'd been sorely tempted to kiss her. Had yearned for her touch with such power he'd almost lost his head.

"What madness was that?"

He had no right to think of her as anything but half the promised bounty.

He had a job to do. Wisdom earned through disaster reminded him of that. Do his job and keep his thoughts away from women and drink.

He wanted to see her but knew he shouldn't. Not today when she disturbed him almost as much as the nightmare.

Gideon paced to the window and stared out. Across the way, a spotted dog sniffed around the front of the hotel, tail low, eyes watchful. Rob Jacobs passed by and kicked at the animal. The dog was quick—*experienced*, Gideon thought grimly—and received only a graze against his hind leg. The poor mutt didn't even yelp.

Ire rose in Gideon's gullet, struggling to get out. The dog, with ribs as prominent as bed slats, was hungry. Had the man no compassion?

His fist tightened. He was tempted to find Rob Jacobs and beat him to the ground.

He knew his fury was aimed at more than a dog abuser. He was angry at his father, at himself.

Today was Sunday. The pious would be in church, worshipping God, as they should be. As *he* should be, after his promises.

Yet, God expected something from him that he could not give.

Leaving his shave for another day, he bought a thick slice of Miss Hattie's breakfast ham for the dog, fed him in the alley behind the hotel, then retrieved Traveler from the livery and rode out to the Baker farm.

Mary and the children were likely heading to church by now. He doubted Isaiah was up to the rough wagon ride, and he desired a conversation with the farmer one last time before he and Willa rode out. He wasn't sure why. Isaiah couldn't promise that God would protect them on the trail. He couldn't promise that Gideon wouldn't fail again.

And he certainly couldn't erase his past or his nightmares.

Yet, something about the farmer's confident faith gave Gideon a hope he couldn't explain. A hope that redemption was still possible for a man like him.

He just didn't know how to get there.

Isaiah Baker sat in his usual spot outside his cabin, bad leg propped on an upturned log. When he saw Gideon ride in, he lifted a hand. A Bible rested on his lap. He could not get to the church meeting, but he and God would have their time together.

He offered Gideon coffee, and considering his empty stomach, Gideon was pleased to accept. This morning, the stray dog was better fed than he was.

Fetching the brew from inside the house to save his friend the effort, he carried out a still-warm cup for each of them.

Mary had made her man comfortable before she'd left.

He rolled that over in his head. A good wife, like Mary, was a treasure.

For the first fifteen minutes, the conversation was light and casual. Talk of the crops, Matthew's lost tooth, the healing leg. Gideon told Isaiah about the stray dog and received permission to bring him out as a gift for the children.

"He looks to be part hound," Gideon said. "He may prove to be a hunter."

"We could use him. Rabbits are about to take over the garden no matter how many we eat."

Something settled in Gideon. The spotted dog would be part of a family the way he needed to be.

Family, a topic he tried not to think about, but the reason, he realized, that he frequented the Baker farm. They filled a missing place in him.

Like most settlers, Isaiah was eager for news, so Gideon

told him about the Faragates' barn dance and the rooster that took offense.

The older man slapped his good leg and laughed until Gideon thought he might tumble off the chair.

"I'm sure sorry I missed that. What a sight! I hear the Faragates' barn has a wooden floor."

"That's a fact."

"I reckon a handsome young swain such as yourself danced with all the pretty girls."

Gideon fiddled with his hat, grinning. "I tried."

"Anyone in particular?"

Couldn't be. "Mostly danced with an old friend and the Malone sisters."

"Ah, now there are some beauties. Fine ladies, too."

"Can't argue."

"Guess you're still set on this crazy idea of leading Miss Willa into outlaw territory."

"She's set on going. I can't let her go alone."

"You think she would?"

"I know she would. She's an indomitable force, Isaiah. All fire and gumption. If she sets her mind to do something, she'll do it."

He thought of the way she'd stuck her ugly boots to the ground and refused to leave him alone and sick in his hotel room. What other woman would have risked her reputation and a female's delicate sensibilities to see him through the torturous hours?

But, he reminded himself sternly, Willa had only done those things because she needed him on the trail, not because she cared about him.

Except he wondered if maybe she did.

Not that he'd let her get too close. He wasn't worth one hair in her beautiful braid.

"You sweet on her?"

Last night in the cool darkness outside her cabin, he'd wanted to kiss her.

It must have been the moonlight and the pleasant euphoria of the dance.

"I admire her pluck, but I'm not looking for a woman."

"Why is that, son? Why not find a good woman like Willa Malone or one of her sisters and settle down on a nice plot of land? Have a few children? Is it the trouble with the liquor?"

Gideon flinched at Isaiah's blunt question. He'd never let on that he had a *problem*. But the older man knew. He had ample evidence after the fiasco with Matthew.

"My life is on the trail. No place for a woman."

"Yet, you're taking Willa."

Setting his untouched coffee aside, Gideon pulled a handful of grass. "That's different."

"Is it?"

Letting the green blades sift through his fingers, Gideon wiped a hand down the side of his pants, watching as the grass sailed away in the wind.

"What if something happens to her, Isaiah? What if I fail her?"

"Will you?"

"I don't know," he said honestly. "I haven't guided in nearly a year." It wasn't the guiding that worried him.

As if Isaiah knew that, he said, "Whiskey's a cruel master."

"I've quit." Except he wasn't sure he had.

"Treating the symptoms isn't the same as curing the disease."

Gideon cocked his head. "Meaning?"

"You ever consider going back to Texas, settling things with your pa?"

The need to purge Thomas Hartley from his soul pressed

at Gideon. He inhaled a long summer-scented breath and let it out as slowly as he could. It did not ease the turbulence.

When he spoke, his tone was quiet but cut from tempered steel. "If I ever see him again, I'll kill him."

Isaiah fastened a thoughtful, compassionate gaze on his. Compassion, not the judgment Gideon expected.

A pair of red hens pecked at the grassy yard. Pecked, digging up worms, the way his mind kept digging at old wounds that wouldn't heal.

As if he'd heard Gideon's thoughts, Isaiah said, "Hate's a poison to the soul. Sooner or later, it festers and busts open."

Isaiah reached forward to rub at his healing leg, well knowing what he spoke of. Because of good care, he'd healed from the festering infection that could have cost him a limb. A good nurse in Mercy, a doting wife, a loving family.

"You're an educated man," Isaiah went on. "You probably know this Good Book better than I do." He lofted the well-worn Bible. "The Great Physician is the only One Who can heal a soul."

A helpless darkness crept over Gideon, a shadow he could not shake. "He doesn't seem to be answering."

"Oh, He's answering, all right. Maybe you're not listening. Or maybe you're not willing to do what He's telling you."

Gideon rose and paced the well-trodden yard. The chickens moved on to greener grass. Still digging up worms.

His head started to pound, pressure building until he feared where it would end.

"I can't go back to San Antonio." He wouldn't.

"Didn't say you have to go back, though it might do you good." The farmer flipped open the Bible, the pages whispering as he searched for a Scripture. "Right here in the book of Mark, Jesus says, 'And when ye stand praying, forgive, if ye have ought against any, that your Father also which is in heaven may forgive you your trespasses.'"

A man needed to be sorry to be forgiven, didn't he?

Thomas Hartley had never expressed one hint of shame or guilt. He'd never asked for pardon.

How could Isaiah expect him to forgive a man like that? How could God?

Gideon retrieved his coffee cup. The brew had gone as cold as his insides. He tossed the dregs onto the ground. "More coffee, Isaiah?"

His friend gave him a look that said he knew Gideon did not want to hear what he had to say.

He guided the conversation to safer ground but soon made his excuses and rode away more bitter and angry than when he'd come.

The streets of Sweet Clover were quiet as Willa left her sisters visiting in the churchyard and walked from Sunday morning service to The Tarbridge Hotel where she hoped to find Gideon.

As she stepped upon the recently swept boardwalk outside the two-story hotel, she cast a furtive glance down the street to the saloon, which was blessedly closed on Sunday morning following a rowdy Saturday night. Wherever Gideon was, he wasn't in the saloon.

Holding up the hem of the overly long skirt, she thought about last night's dance. Gideon's admiring looks and pretty words had hummed in her blood all through church until she realized she'd not heard a word of Reverend Danforth's sermon.

She'd whispered a prayer for forgiveness and promised to do better next week.

Now, as she entered the hotel, Miss Hattie came down the stairs to the left.

"My, don't you look pretty this morning, Willa."

Willa couldn't help the thrill that passed through her. She seldom received compliments and, still glowing from Gideon's attentions, she'd worn the green dress to church. She'd even had Savannah dress her hair in a becoming upswept style.

"Thank you, Miss Hattie. Have you seen Mr. Hartley today? We have some business." She'd added the last to avoid Hattie's speculative looks.

"Business, is it? On the Lord's Day?"

So much for avoiding speculation.

Willa tugged at the high neck of her bodice, the lace a bit scratchy. She'd hardly noticed last night.

"Yes, business."

Hattie's bun wobbled as she shook her head. "He left out early. Fed that spotted mutt a piece of my good ham first, though. Good ham like that to a stray dog. Can you imagine?"

After last night, yes, she could believe it of him. "Did he indicate his destination?"

"Can't say he did. Shall I give him a message for you?"

"Tell him he's expected at the farm. We've work to do."

"Ah, work, yes. On the Lord's Day."

Fearful of rolling her eyes at the woman, Willa made her escape.

She was disappointed by Gideon's absence. Not because she'd gussied up a little, but to protect her interest in his sobriety. At least, that's what she told herself.

A wagon loaded with churchgoers rumbled past, children waving from the back where their feet dangled over the edge.

Behind them a few horses and a clutch of people on foot headed toward their homes and Sunday dinner. Their voices carried on the humid air.

Willa's belly growled at the thought of dinner.

She gazed up at the cloudy sky, wondering if it would rain today.

Hoping to avoid ruining Savannah's dress in a downpour, she turned toward home.

She'd only taken a few steps when a familiar horse and rider cantered into town. Gideon dismounted, tying the bay at the railing outside the hotel.

Willa changed directions and hurried to catch up with him. "Gideon."

He stilled, one hand on his saddlebags. A deep scowl plowed across his brow. "Your timing is impeccable."

Confused, she stepped up next to him. "What?"

With a gusty exhale, he said, "I am not in the mood for conversation."

"I thought I'd see—"

"If I'm drunk?" Irritation shot from him like cannon fire. "I'm not." He held his arms out to each side. "See? I'm fine. I do not require a keeper."

She jerked her chin up, pulse clattering like a rock in a tin cup. Gideon was in a horrible temper for some reason.

"That wasn't it, at all." Well, maybe in part.

"Then what is it? Why do you insist on trailing me like a bloodhound?"

Willa gasped. A flush of humiliation heated her face.

With as much dignity as she could muster, she spun around, caught the hem of her too-long dress on her boot heel and almost tripped, then righted herself and marched away.

Hot tears pressed at the backs of her eyelids, but she dashed them away in anger.

Whatever burr had gotten into Gideon's saddle had proved one thing. She'd been foolish to romanticize last night's time together. Gideon did not share her fond remembrances. He hadn't found her attractive as she'd let herself imagine after that lovely moonlit dance.

All well and good. She had no use for romance. She had a bounty to collect.

Chapter Fourteen

Guilt was an interesting emotion. It either compelled or repelled. Today, Gideon's guilt had done both.

He stalked up the hotel staircase, angry with himself, and shut the door with a too-firm hand. The wood vibrated.

Isaiah's calm, probing talk of forgiveness stuck in his craw worse than a chicken bone.

And now he'd offended Willa.

Yes, she was a gnat in his gravy, but she'd done nothing to earn his ire.

He'd seen the hurt in her brown eyes, the way she'd withdrawn almost like the kicked spotted dog. She'd turned her back on him and walked away, nearly stumbling. He'd reached out to catch her, but she'd cold-eyed him so that he'd suffered momentary frostbite. Her tough-girl expression, he thought, had been nothing but a cover of how much his words had stung.

"What a gallant friend you are, Gideon Hartley," he murmured.

He should ride out to her beloved farm and apologize.

She might shoot him, he thought with grim humor, knowing she wouldn't. But her ferocity touched him in an oddly endearing manner.

The saloon would open soon. He could spend his afternoon there and forget about his father, Isaiah and Willa Malone.

He could also forget about returning to his former occupation.

With a growl, he battled the urge, and instead of doing the one thing that would assuage his ever-pecking conscience, he pocketed a peppermint stick from the bowl on his bureau, left the hotel and rode Traveler the short distance to Belle's house. She'd promised him a home-cooked dinner, an offer which both distracted him and made him smile. Cooking was a new pursuit for Belle Holbrook.

He patted Traveler's muscled neck. "Should be interesting."

Belle's cooking, unlike that of the Malone sisters, might not please the palate, but the child, Pearl, would improve his disposition.

Belle met him at the door, looking, as she always did, elegant, beautiful and proper. No one would ever guess who she'd once been. Who she still was when the mood suited her.

Next to her, tiny Pearl, in dark ringlets and red ribbons, hopped up and down chanting his name. "Gideon, Gideon, Gideon."

Ignoring the fact that Pearl was dressed like an untouchable princess, he hoisted the four-year-old high into the air. "Pearl of great price, jewel of my heart."

The little girl's giggle was his reward. She threw her arms around his neck and pressed her soft cheek to his.

"I smell peppermint," she said pertly, leaning back to look him over as if the candy would be hanging from his ear.

He gave a mock scowl. "Peppermint will rot your teeth."

Pearl set her mouth in a giant fake smile, showing her tiny perfect teeth. "I have pretty teeth. See?"

He laughed. "Check my vest pocket."

"I knew it!" she exclaimed with delight. She fished the candy from his vest, and he set her on her feet.

"Gideon, you spoil the child." Belle's hands rested on the skirt of her fashionable blue-and-white frock as she fondly observed the exchange.

He shrugged. "She's not spoiled, are you, Pearl? She's a jewel."

Pearl poked the peppermint in her mouth and grinned around it.

He and Belle had this argument often, and he always won.

"Are you going to feed me?" he asked of Belle. "I need cheering up."

Belle laughed merrily, perhaps a bit louder and more robust than most ladies would dare to allow. Belle carved her own path. Like Willa, in a way, though he'd never considered their similarities before.

"Courageous man that you are, I baked meat loaf for the first time, and there is plenty left on the sideboard."

"Am I in danger?" Gideon glanced at Pearl. The little darling pressed her lips together in an effort not to laugh.

Gideon clutched his chest in a pretend groan. "Then I shall go to my death with a full belly."

Both females laughed at his teasing, and he followed Belle through the elegantly furnished parlor into the kitchen where the scent of baked meat filled the air.

His dark temper began to lift as surely as if a curtain had parted and the sun had decided to shine. The merry duo of Pearl and Belle had that effect.

There remained, however, the problem of Willa.

When he'd finished the meal, which was better than he'd

expected, he read a story to Pearl and then assisted Belle in rearranging the furniture to make room for a new chair she'd ordered.

"Frisco was in town," he said at one point.

"I know. He came to see us."

They both looked to little Pearl, playing quietly with her dolls.

"Did he say why he was in Sweet Clover?"

Belle shook her head, expression darkening. "Not this time."

Gideon let the subject drop. His friend Frisco, like Belle, carved his own path. No one could tame him, and now that he'd developed a reputation as a gunfighter, he could not remain in one place very long. Some young pup always thought he was faster.

"Are you making me rich yet?" he asked.

Belle tilted her pretty head, whether to acknowledge his swift conversational shift or because she was, indeed, making him rich.

From a tall bureau, she took out a pair of ledgers, and they sat at the kitchen table to go over the figures.

Belle, most people would be surprised to know, excelled at business, and Gideon trusted her with his money more than he did the suspiciously conniving Theodore Pierce. He'd urged her to go into the banking business, but she'd declined, and he understood her reluctance.

"Your shares have increased in value." She slid a finger along a row of increasingly large numbers, a lily-white finger as smooth as Pearl's.

Belle was meticulous about her skin, unlike Willa, who didn't seem to care if she baked as brown as the hard-packed earth.

Unusual women, these two friends of his.

And there was Willa, back in his thoughts. Along with the nagging need to make amends.

"Reinvest," he said.

"All of it?"

Considering, he scraped a hand over his whiskered jaw. "Every penny."

"I'm thinking about buying more myself."

The railroad continued to expand across the country. Gideon counted himself fortunate to have been in the right place at the right time to buy shares.

"You're already a rich woman, Belle." When she'd left her business in Tucson, she'd invested the proceeds in the railroad, receiving a fat profit in return.

"A woman alone can never be rich enough."

The statement put him in mind of his greedy father, which made him think about his earlier horrible treatment of Willa. She was a woman alone.

"Is there anything you or Pearl need before I leave town?"

"We take care of ourselves, Gideon. Always. You know that."

He did. Belle's independence was one of the qualities he admired about her.

"Alas, chivalry is dead if the fair maid has no need of a knight," he lamented with a smile, and Belle laughed, rising with him as he readied to take his leave.

"You will be careful."

"Always. You know that." He repeated her words with a gently mocking smile.

"Take care of Willa. She's a good girl."

He became solemn then. "You have my word."

Her eyes held his until he could almost read her thoughts. *Don't let what happened before happen again.*

She wouldn't say the words, wouldn't bring up the subject, but the past hovered there, a bee waiting to sting.

"Is there more to this trip than meets the eye?" she asked. "As far as Willa and you are concerned? I saw the way you danced with her."

"If you're asking if I'm courting Willa, the answer is no."

"Do you want to?"

That was the way of things with him and Belle. They were brutally honest with one another.

"I can't allow it." But he remembered the way Willa had felt in his arms, her smile, her lavender fragrance.

"Ah. I see." Belle touched his arm, her gaze soft. "Take care, my friend."

He heard all the things she didn't say. Both of them knew that personal lives had no place on the trail or in business. Too much was at stake.

Gideon nodded. "You'll keep an ear to the ground while I'm gone?"

"Yes, though without entering the saloon, which would cause no amount of furor, all I can do is pump Agnes Pierce and the other wives for information during our Ladies' Society meetings."

Gideon didn't dare enter the saloon at all, at least not now. Not until Willa had her bounty in hand.

"It will have to do until I return." He pressed his hat into place, adjusting the black brim.

"I can handle anything that arises during your absence."

She could. She didn't need him. But they'd once made a good team.

Pearl left her dollies and hurried over to cling to his leg. "Will you bring me a present?"

"Pearl," Belle admonished. "You shouldn't ask Gideon for things."

Gideon tweaked one of the child's ringlets. "I will, indeed. Now, you be a good girl for your mother and say a prayer for Uncle Gideon."

"I will. Every single night." She crossed her heart.

Gideon bent for Pearl's innocent, adoring hug and then headed in the direction that he should have gone in the first place.

Mercy, who'd been gathering herbs in the garden, stepped inside the cabin. Her medicine bag needed replenishing after a bevy of summer flu and new babies.

"We have a caller."

Savannah, in Papa's wooden rocking chair, froze, her nimble fingers paused on the hem Willa had ripped when she'd stumbled outside the hotel. "Not Mr. Baggley, I hope."

Mercy shook her head. Her mahogany hair hung down her back, shining and beautiful, free from the severe style she usually wore. "You are spared that indignity for today. Mr. Hartley is here."

"Oh, how lovely." Savannah cast aside her sewing. "He was so kind last evening. I don't think I could have borne it had he not intervened."

At the mention of Gideon's name, Willa's stomach leaped, which was foolish, considering how rude he'd been to her after church.

"He's here to work, Savannah, not to pay a social call." She sounded gruff and was instantly ashamed. Touching her sister's arm, she said, "We all enjoyed last night, and I'm glad you convinced us to attend."

"You and Mr. Hartley certainly stood outside for a long time after we came home." Mercy slanted Willa a questioning look.

Visions of Gideon's face so close Willa could feel him breathe drifted through her thoughts.

"We're leaving in two days. There's much to discuss."

Before her sisters could tease or speculate, she hurried out the door. There was nothing between her and the trail guide but a business deal and a tentative friendship that waffled with each meeting.

After the ugly scene outside the hotel, she didn't like him in the least.

Whatever he had to say, he could just say it and leave.

Under the sprawling sycamore, Gideon dismounted, patted Traveler's neck and left the horse ground tied. The docile bay dropped his head and began to graze.

"Today is Sunday," she said as if that explained her inability to say anything more intelligent.

The truth was she felt awkward after his cruel comment and sour mood.

He dipped his head in acknowledgment. "I brought you something."

He had? Why? "What is it? Bloodhound repellent?"

If she seemed belligerent, he had it coming.

Dark amusement lit his eyes. "You have my permission to shoot me if that gives you recompense."

Her lips quivered. She supposed this was the closest to an apology she would get, if this was indeed an attempt at making amends for his churlish behavior.

"As much as that appeals, I refuse to disable my trail guide. You're necessary."

"As one always wishes to be." He reached inside his vest and removed a tiny pistol. "For your boot."

She drew back. "My rifle will do."

"No, Willa, it will not do. Every precaution is required for a journey such as this."

Goose bumps prickled on her arms. The ominous words reminded her of exactly how serious this task would be.

"I've never fired a pistol."

"How good are you with the rifle?"

Her chin went up. "Good enough to keep my family in venison and rabbit. Is a pistol the same?"

"No. We'll need to practice."

He took her hand, turned it up and placed the small firearm on her palm. It weighed little, and she could see how something so small could slide easily into her oversize boot.

He went to his horse and removed several weapons and a box of ammunition. A gun belt containing a pair of pistols, a rifle and a double-barrel shotgun.

Willa stared wide-eyed at the arsenal. "You said you couldn't shoot."

Gideon strapped on the gun belt. "I said I was no gunfighter. The ability to shoot is a requirement on the trail."

Holsters riding low on his hips, he busied himself with tying a leather string around his thighs. He certainly *looked* like a gunfighter.

The sight gave her a strange buzz of energy.

"What are you doing?" she asked.

Nimble fingers tied off the opposite string before he glanced up. "We're going to practice."

"With that many guns?"

"I'm rusty." The corner of his mouth hitched up. There it was, the grin that caused all sorts of untoward reactions.

"I'll warn the sisters and get my rifle."

He paused, one hip lower than the other, looking incredibly dangerous. "The derringer, Willa. Practice with the pistol."

Of course. She already knew how to use the Winchester.

They set up targets away from the cabin, and Gideon fired first, both scaring and reassuring her with his accuracy. Pistols turned backward in the holsters, he drew and shot quickly, moving from target to target in rapid succession.

He was quite impressive, and Willa was relieved to notice that his hands no longer trembled.

Finally satisfied that he was not as rusty as he feared, he holstered the Peacemakers. "Your turn."

While explaining the operation of pistols in general, Gideon let her heft the heavy weapon he kept on his hip. It was like her rifle, only shorter.

Certain she could shoot almost as well as he, Willa took aim with the derringer as she would have the Winchester and fired. A frown pinched her face.

"Try again, focus down. The smaller barrel rises with the recoil."

She did as he instructed and still missed.

"What am I doing wrong?" The words croaked out like trapped bullfrogs. She hated admitting she couldn't do something as well as a man.

Without poking fun as she'd feared he would, Gideon stepped behind her, close enough that she felt his warmth. Their shadows stretched out before her, his head next to hers so that they blended together as one.

The image was disconcerting.

"Raise your hand and aim, as if to fire. But don't." His words were a murmur against her hair.

Awareness of him, of his masculine scent, his strength, his nearness tingled her skin. It made her mad, this—this attraction!

Setting her jaw, Willa raised the pistol and closed one eye.

"Both eyes open. You need to see everything around you and be able to switch targets quickly."

Targets. As in outlaws.

Don't think about that. Just shoot.

Nodding her acknowledgment, and shoulders tight with determination, Willa forced both eyes to stare at the target.

Gideon's fingers slid along her arm until his hand rested beneath hers. His chest touched her back, his cheek close enough for her to feel the unshaven scruff. His woodsy peppermint scent flowed around her, distractingly pleasant.

Last night's moonlit dance floated through her mind.

Stop it, Willa.

Gideon had made his feelings as clear as spring water. Last night's dance was a frolic, a moment out of time, not a courtship. He was her guide, not her beau.

They had a long dangerous journey ahead. A clear head and a steady hand were essential. She could not allow old-maid silliness to endanger their lives.

Chapter Fifteen

Willa hated walking past the saloon where rinky-dink piano music and loud laughter flowed out onto the boardwalk like the whiskey inside flowed into men. Papa was no longer nearby with his wit and pistol to scare away inebriated, leering faces.

She hadn't even brought her rifle.

Tonight, she'd stayed too long at Belle's house. They'd planted tomatoes and then worked on the quilt, chatting until both of them were shocked when Belle's daughter began to rub her eyes and ask for a bedtime story.

Truth was she'd gone to Belle's to keep her mind away from the journey that would begin first thing tomorrow. She was both eager to begin and afraid of what the coming weeks might hold.

Would they be able to find Charlie Bangs? If they did, could they capture him?

Yesterday's target practice with Gideon had soothed some of her fears. He could and would assist if the need arose.

He'd smelled good, not of whiskey.

By now, the sun had long disappeared and Willa scurried along the back of the unpainted clapboard businesses, the moon and window lanterns her only light. Willa squinted into the darkness, annoyed with herself. She should have borrowed a lantern from Belle.

As she passed the rear of the saloon, the raucous piano player belted out a bawdy tune that made her blush, even in the darkness. Considering the extra layer of noise ricocheting through the thin walls, some of the local cowboys must be in town tonight. Cowboys or outlaws. They'd be shooting up the place, fighting and riding their horses down the boardwalk before daybreak.

Merchants would have a mess to clean up in the morning.

The raucous piano stopped for a brief breath-releasing moment.

Soft weeping broke the silence. Willa froze, alert, listening.

"Hello?" she turned toward the sound. "Is someone there?"

The sobs abruptly stopped. A small shadowy form rose from the backstairs of the saloon.

"Wait."

The small figure paused, one foot on the next step as if to flee at any moment.

Willa hurried to the staircase, concerned that someone was in need.

Her foot bumped something soft and alive. She jerked her boot away. The form moved, and in the shadowy darkness, she saw a dog gazing up the staircase at the human figure.

Willa made out a small female above her. Was this a child? Behind a saloon?

A snubbing sound, as if she was trying not to cry, came from the child on the steps.

"Are you hurt?" Willa peered hard into the shadows. "Do you need help?"

"No." But the girl didn't move, nor did she stop crying.

Without thought of danger, Willa climbed the steps. The child averted her face, but not before Willa saw, by the light from the upper windows, a white handkerchief held to her mouth and nose.

"You're bleeding." She gently tugged the child around.

With a start, Willa realized this was no child at all, but a young woman. Very young. And exotically beautiful.

Richly scented perfume emanated from her colorful red-and-yellow robe.

Please don't let this teenager be a saloon girl.

"Must go." The tremulous accented voice was soft as a whisper.

"Not until you stop bleeding," Willa insisted. "Sit."

As if accustomed to taking orders, the young woman complied.

Willa took the handkerchief, tilted the girl's head back and inspected the bleeding nose.

The scent of blood assailed Willa. Sweat beaded on her upper lip. Her stomach threatened. Blood was Mercy's domain, not hers. Yet, Mercy was not here and this girl needed a kind hand.

"I'm Willa. What's your name?"

The girl tried to stand. She swayed. "Must go. He get mad."

Willa steadied the girl with a hand on her slender silk-covered arm. "Did he hit you?"

The girl shook her head, though the denial didn't convince Willa. Something was very wrong. "Please. Must go."

A whiskey-soaked voice, as rough as corncobs and louder than a fog horn, ripped above the incessant piano music.

"Coy Ling!"

The girl jerked as if she'd been shot and leaped to her feet.

"Stop." Willa grappled to hold the woman's arm. "Come with me. I'll take you somewhere safe."

Coy Ling frantically shook her head, the silken robe rustling.

Before Willa could say more, she rushed up the stairs and disappeared. A door slammed behind her.

Willa stared up at the saloon's second story, wondering and worrying about the teenager, shocked that someone so young could work for Madam Frenchy.

She considered following, demanding that Coy Ling be released, but knew the futility in such action. Bordellos were a sad fact of life for many women, and no law protected them, especially here in the mostly lawless territories.

Outrage rose in Willa like a sickness. She banged a frustrated hand against the stair railing and resumed her homeward trek.

The man with the whiskey-soaked voice had hit Coy Ling, made her bleed. She had no doubt of that. Were the girls inside the saloon frequently abused?

Until tonight, she'd never given them much thought.

Now, she could not get them out of her mind, especially the young Chinese girl.

Something should be done. But what?

"God, please protect her." A prayer felt so useless, but she didn't know what else to do.

If Sweet Clover had a town marshal, she'd insist he investigate.

Mind whirling with the incident, she forgot about the darkness and paid little attention to her surroundings. The town, even the alleyway she'd cut through on her way from Belle's, was familiar.

Suddenly, someone grabbed her from behind. A man. A

strong man. A hand clapped over her mouth. A filthy tasting, hard-as-stone hand. Her head jerked backward. Her boots lifted from the solid safety of the earth.

A lightning bolt, part fear and part energy, jacked through Willa's bloodstream. She struggled, kicked backward, slung her elbows, but he held her so tightly against his stronger body that resistance proved futile.

A whisper pressed hot and foul against her ear. "Don't go borrowing trouble like your daddy did. Look what it got him. Let sleeping dogs lie or pay the price."

The shock of his words ricocheted through Willa.

What did he mean? Who was he? She struggled to turn even the slightest bit, hoping for a glance of his face.

He shoved her head downward, hard. Her neck popped.

Alarm raced along her nerve endings.

What did he know of her father?

What had he meant by the cryptic message?

Instinctively, she fought the only way she could. She sunk her teeth into the nasty flesh pressed against her lips.

The man yelped. Cursed. Let go.

Willa jerked in a breath and screamed.

A beefy fist swung, struck her cheek and knocked her to the hard-packed dirt. Her back slammed against the corner of a nearby building. Breath flew from her lungs in a whoosh.

Back and cheek burning with pain, she scrambled for both breath and purchase, crab-crawling to escape another blow.

Footsteps pounded from somewhere and another shadowy figure emerged. In the darkness, she couldn't identify anyone.

Desperate, Willa felt the ground for a weapon. Finding a rock, but woozy from the blow, her back throbbing, she tried to stand.

Her knees wobbled. She thrust a hand toward the nearby building for support.

The two shadowy forms scuffled, fought, grunted. Blows landed.

One of the dark figures tore loose and raced away, footsteps thundering down the alley.

Strong hands gripped Willa's arms and lifted her to a stand. She fought, kicked, swung the pitifully small rock.

"Willa." He shook her lightly. "Stop. It's Gideon."

"Gideon?" All the fight went out of her. She wilted.

"Are you all right?" His powerful hands gentled against her shoulders. His voice, solicitous and concerned, buoyed her.

"I—I—" Willa sucked in a steadying breath. She could not have him thinking of her as a vaporous female unable to take care of herself on the trail. He might back out of their deal. "I had the situation in hand."

"Ah, yes, of course." Suddenly, he was Gideon again, the ironic tone back in place. "A suitor, no doubt, enamored by your charms, awaited you in the darkness. Behind the saloon. How romantic."

"There was nothing romantic about it." She bit out the words. "He attacked me. Grabbed me from behind."

Gideon turned coldly serious. "Did you recognize him?"

"No. Did you?"

"No." He huffed a frustrated breath.

"He mentioned my papa. Told me to let sleeping dogs lie if I knew what was good for me."

Gideon stilled. "What else? Anything."

She wracked her brain for the exact words. "Something about my daddy knowing too much. No, that's not it. I can't think right now."

She wobbled and Gideon noticed. He stepped closer, slid an arm around her waist and led her down the alley away from the noise of the saloon.

In the light from the overhead hotel rooms, he inspected

her face. A muscle jerked in his jaw. His tone hardened to iron. "He hurt you."

"I'll mend." But she didn't turn away from his tender touch.

"Are you hurt anywhere else?"

"I'll mend, I said." She wanted to press a hand to her aching back, but if she did, he might use her injury as another excuse to delay their journey.

His fingers gently probed the burning spot on her cheek. "Nothing broken. But he hit you." With a dangerous sort of stillness, as lethal and pointed as a bayonet, he murmured, "That will not do."

Willa quavered at the ferocity of his outrage against the man who'd attacked her.

Gideon moved his hand to her hair and then to her shoulder. He seemed unable to stop touching her, to stop assuring himself that she was safe. "What were you doing out here at this time of night?"

"I was visiting Belle and let the time get away from me. Cutting through the alley gets me home faster, though I hadn't tried it in the dark before." She shuddered, her voice trembling.

"Come. I'll see you home."

"No need. I'm perfectly capable of—"

"Arguing with a rock." He took her hand, placed it inside his elbow and started walking. She either had to trot along or cause another ruckus.

One ruckus per night was enough.

Regardless of her bluster, she did not want to walk home alone.

Chapter Sixteen

Willa slept little that night. Her brain was wrought with thoughts of the journey ahead, of the strange warning she'd received in the alley and of the young Chinese girl she'd been too shaken to mention to Gideon. What was the use? If a girl chose that life, no one could or would stand in the way.

Another thought, this one just as sinister, floated through her overactive mind. What was Gideon doing outside the saloon? Was he visiting the brothel? A girl like Coy Ling? Was he there to drink and gamble the night away?

Willa frowned into the darkness.

He hadn't smelled like liquor. That, at least, was a relief.

"God, make him stay sober. We have to find Bangs and collect that bounty."

Eventually, she prayed herself to sleep, only to awaken with a start when someone knocked on the cabin door.

The room was still dark. Morning yet to dawn.

She flung aside Maeve's quilt.

Mercy was frequently called out in the night to tend the

sick, but, just the same, Willa approached the door with her rifle in hand. Plenty of rogues roamed these territories.

"Who is it?" Her sleepy voice was rusty as an old hinge.

"Gideon."

Gideon?

Had she overslept?

By now, her sisters had bounded out of bed, tossing blankets over their bedclothes. Mercy lit a lantern. Light chased the shadows into the corners of the cabin.

Unbolting the heavy wooden door, Willa stepped outside in the cool predawn. The birds hadn't even begun their morning praise song.

Dressed for the trail in leather chaps and vest, a shadowy Gideon held the reins of two horses.

Traveler's saddlebags bulged with supplies, and a fat bedroll was secured to the back of his trail-worn saddle. The other horse was saddled but unburdened.

"What's this?" She eyed the extra animal.

"Leave Jasper for your sisters. Freckles is better suited to the trail."

Freckles. A fitting name for the muscular brown Appaloosa bearing white speckles across his rump. "Where did you get him?"

"Does it matter?"

"Only if you stole him."

Gideon laughed, interestingly chipper this early in the morning. "Get dressed and pack up. We ride at daybreak."

By now, the smell of coffee perked through the open door and the sisters moved around inside, making last-minute preparations.

The day had finally arrived.

Willa's nerve endings tingled. She was wide-awake now.

Mercy insisted she take a pouch of medicinal herbs, along

with written instructions for their use. These she handed, without comment, to Gideon, who stuffed them inside his leather vest.

Savannah brought coffee outside, promising a hearty breakfast in a few minutes.

Taking occasional sips from the cup, Gideon remained outdoors where he secured Willa's bedroll onto the new horse.

Irritated at herself for oversleeping, she hurried back inside and dressed, braided her hair and splashed water on her face. The smell of Savannah's fried eggs and pancakes made her belly growl.

By the time they'd eaten breakfast, the rising sun painted red and gold radiants across the eastern sky.

"Mount up," Gideon said.

For once, Willa didn't take umbrage at his bossy tone.

With Mercy and Savannah standing in the yard, faces wreathed in concern, offering prayers and admonitions to come back safely, Willa tossed an unladylike leg over the unfamiliar horse and followed Gideon toward the sun.

At first, nervous, she chattered like a squirrel but eventually they settled into a companionable rhythm of occasional spurts of conversation followed by miles of silence.

By nightfall, when they stopped to camp, Willa's back ached and her legs trembled from the unaccustomed hours in the saddle. Gideon appeared unaffected as he gathered wood and built a fire. Though the weather was warm, the evening had cooled. Additionally, a fire served as a deterrent to wild animals.

There were bears and mountain lions in this country.

They camped by a shallow, trickling creek and Willa got busy refilling canteens and preparing a pot of coffee to go with the bacon and biscuits left from breakfast.

"How far did we travel today?" she asked more to break the silence than for conversation.

Gideon pulled the bedroll from his saddle. "Maybe fifteen miles. The going was easy."

It was?

He untied her bedroll and tossed it to her. She caught it with a grunt, her lower back twinging.

Gideon scowled. "What's wrong?"

"Nothing." She turned her back to him and began untying the rope binding her bedroll and all the supplies layered inside.

"We can slow down and rest more often if you need. Sitting a saddle all day takes some getting used to."

Willa stiffened her very tender spine. Anything he could do, she could do. Even if it meant suffering with an aching back. "This isn't a picnic. I'll be fine."

"And the Lord said unto Moses, I have seen this people, and, behold, it is a stiffnecked people.'"

In spite of her aching body, Willa laughed.

They ate their meal and Gideon tended the horses, giving them both a good rubdown while Willa rinsed out their tin dishes and placed a bedroll on either side of the small campfire.

As she removed her boots and set them beside her blankets, she realized this would be the first time in her life she'd been alone all night with a man other than her papa, not counting the nights she sat at Gideon's sick bed. He'd been weak then, and sick. Now, he wasn't.

For a moment, she considered the awkward situation, the complete compromise of a spinster alone with an unrelated man.

Across the flickering flames, Gideon faced her as he, too, prepared for sleep.

If he felt the least bit awkward, he didn't let on. He'd likely slept beside a member of the opposite sex before. She hadn't.

A shadowy outline of the day's whiskers gave him a rugged, dangerously appealing look.

That he was a handsome man, she could not deny. Nor could she deny that he, with his random bursts of poetry, deep intellect and unexpected kindness at exactly the right moments, caused a stirring below her heart that she neither understood nor wanted.

Yet, she still wasn't confident she could trust him. Not completely.

They talked in low tones about this and that, random bits of conversation to pass the time. He told her about a new invention called the gramophone that he'd seen demonstrated in some far-off place he'd visited. A machine that played music.

So enthralled was Willa that she shyly removed the penny whistle from her bedroll and played a jaunty Irish tune that made him smile.

He wasn't, he claimed, surprised that she was musical. Not after dancing with her. He was, however, impressed because he could not play a single note of music.

This so pleased Willa that her cheeks heated as hot as the fire crackling between them.

She laid the pipe in her lap and asked for more wonderful things he'd seen and done.

This led to talk of inventors and painters and of a man named da Vinci, whom Gideon greatly admired.

She'd known he was as educated as she wasn't, but today he'd impressed her with his knowledge of nature and the signs he'd read to find the right trails. A pile of rocks here. A tree carving there. A handful of animal tracks or tree markings.

She knew a smidgen about traveling in unfamiliar territory but not nearly so much as Gideon.

"Where did you learn all these things?" she asked, fighting not to rub her lower back.

He honed a hunter's knife against a flint rock. "Books, mostly, and experience."

Which made her feel even more ignorant. She wished with all her strength that she could read. Wishes were useless as she'd learned long, long ago. Only the things she wrestled into submission came to pass. An unyielding will and a strong hand, these were the tools she'd been dealt in life.

God made Gideon smart. He'd made her practical.

They were, she thought with some bemusement, a good team.

"I think I'll say good-night."

"Play one more tune to sleep on."

Pleased that he'd asked, she took up the flute and played a slow, lilting melody that ached with the longing she felt inside but could not name.

"'Music, when soft voices die, vibrates in the memory,'" he murmured, and though Willa didn't recognize the line, she knew he quoted another of his poems.

"It's true, isn't it? We match music to a memory and it lasts forever."

"What memories do you have, Willa plain and simple, that stir so fine a melody?" he asked in a lazy, ironic voice.

From the campfire, a log snapped, tumbled, shot sparks into the night above. Gideon's face was half shadow and firelight, and though his voice was light, his eyes were serious.

So she told him a bit about her younger days, about the mother she didn't remember and of the two stepmothers who hadn't stayed, one through death, the other through choice. She told of the constant moves to chase Papa's dreams and a little about the jolly Irishman who sang and danced and entertained his daughters whenever they had little else to enjoy.

"I never got to have much schooling," she admitted, and

immediately wished the words back. She didn't want him thinking she was stupid. "I reckon you had plenty."

"I suppose." He returned the sharpened knife to a thin leather scabbard he wore on his belt. "My mother loved learning. She wanted to send me back east to college."

"Did you go?"

"My father wouldn't hear of it." His tone had changed, darkened, almost angry. "You should get some rest, Willa. Good night."

His father was not a happy topic.

"You don't like to talk about him. Your father."

"He isn't worth the breath it takes."

"Who is Emily?"

He tossed another log on the fire and stirred it with a stick. Sparks and yellow-blue flames shot upward.

"She was my sister."

"Was?"

"She's dead." He dusted his hands together. "Go to sleep, Willa."

He'd told her more tonight than she'd ever known about his past. He'd loved his mother, his sister and hated his father. Though she wondered why, she didn't ask. Not because she wasn't bold, but because she heard the pain in his words and didn't want to hurt him further.

She stretched her arms to either side in a great wide yawn, her mind full of her companion, and then slid beneath her blanket.

Overhead the stars sprinkled the heavens in silver twinkles. She found the North Star and from it the Big Dipper. The eternal vastness of God's universe settled around her.

"'Let the stars and the moon pour their healing light on you,'" she whispered, thinking of Gideon.

"I beg your pardon?" Gideon's manly voice came from the other side of the smoke.

"An Irish blessing Papa used to say. There's a healing tranquility in gazing at the stars and moon. In knowing that all is right in God's kingdom."

"Indeed, there is." His voice sounded pensive in a way that made Willa ache. In those soft yearning words, she heard more of what he didn't say than of what he did.

God's kingdom was at peace. Gideon Hartley was not.

Gideon awakened with a start, heart thudding. Someone had touched him. He grappled for the pistol beneath his head and sat up, cocking the gun as he moved.

"Gideon." Willa spoke softly. "Wake up."

Willa. Willa touched him, her small hand rested against his shoulder.

Breathing easier, he quickly surveyed the campsite. The fire had burned to red embers. Nothing moved. No twigs snapped. No wild animal threatened, neither man nor beast.

Once he'd assured himself that they were alone, he murmured, "What's wrong?"

"You were having a bad dream," her tender voice whispered. "Are you all right?"

So that's why his face was wet with sweat. "Yes."

The dregs of the familiar nightmare returned then, gauzy cobwebs of the past.

Slowly, he released the hammer on the pistol and laid it aside to wipe a tired hand over his eyes. "Sleep's impossible."

Without the whiskey to addle his brain and render him unconscious, sleep was fitful at best. He'd hoped hitting the trail again would make a difference. Apparently, it hadn't.

Willa's unexpected mention of his father was the likely provocation.

"Why is that, Gideon? What causes the nightmares? What haunts you?"

He sighed, a gusty, heavy, weary exhale of defeat. "Go back to bed, Willa."

She hesitated, her fingers still resting with light concern against his shoulder.

Willa. He sighed. She touched him with far more than her hand, though he dared not let her know.

Gideon moved away, causing her arm to fall to her side, and lay with his back to her and to the slowly dying fire.

After a long moment, he heard her steps crunch softly against the grass and then the rustle as she settled again.

Willa was a perceptive woman, a smart woman. He admired her strength, found her easy to be with, a danger because if she knew everything, she wouldn't be here with him now.

She already knew too many of his secrets.

The next few days were long, hot and uneventful. Days of endless riding, vast prairies and hardwood forests, and of short stops to eat and water the horses before more endless miles of riding.

Creek crossings, always a concern when traveling in uncharted lands, were many and, so far, easy. The new horse, Freckles, did his job without complaint or balking.

On the third night, drums from the nearby tribal lands kept Willa awake. Gideon assured her that these natives were peaceful.

Nonetheless, Willa slept with one hand on the rifle beside her bedroll. The memory of the Plains Indian raids and of the burned homesteads across Kansas remained vivid in her mind even though they'd happened when she was younger.

One day, they stopped in a small settlement and the next, at a trading post where Gideon asked questions about Charlie

Bangs and showed the photo on the wanted poster. If anyone knew his whereabouts, they refused to reveal it to two strangers.

Each night, they made camp alongside a creek or river where the horses could water, and forage grew lush and green.

Gideon was a perplexing companion who recited poetry as they rode through grass as high the horse's bellies and read from a slender book whenever they stopped to rest. At times, he lapsed into silence for miles and miles only to stop and point out a nest of bluebird fledglings or a red-tailed hawk making lazy circles overhead.

At the latter, he'd spout some bit of philosophy or verse before lapsing into loose-limbed watchfulness all over again.

And every night, she'd awaken to hear him moan and thrash against the relentless dreams.

"What are you reading?" Willa asked one hot afternoon, as they ate their noon meal beneath an enormous cottonwood's shade.

She perched on one elbow with her side against the soft grass while he leaned his back on the thickly ridged tree bark.

Even soft bark would have been too much for Willa. Her back still ached with bruises from the encounter in the alley. The bruise on her cheek was fading, though every time she touched it, Gideon's expression darkened, and she recalled the tenderness in his hands and voice that night in the alley.

He flipped the book cover closed and held it up for her to see the title. She couldn't read it, so she said, "Is it interesting?"

"Wordsworth stirs the imagination. Would you like to borrow it? I have another book or two in my saddlebag."

"Is that how you memorized so many verses? Reading on the trail?"

"That and my mother—" He didn't finish the sentence,

rather handed the book across the short space between them. He'd already told her about his educated mother.

"I'm not much for books." How could she be if she didn't know what they said? "You can do all the reading we need."

A flush of humiliation heated her neck. Would he notice? Would he ask questions?

His gaze pinned her for a silent moment as if he read her mind and knew her shameful secret.

Willa hopped up, wiped crumbs from her riding skirt and scurried to the creek to rinse out their tin dishes.

"We'll reach a bigger settlement tonight," Gideon said when she returned. "Not a place we want to linger, but I know the saloon keeper. If he has information about your outlaw, he'll tell us."

Willa hesitated. They were going to a saloon. Would Gideon be tempted to drink?

"We haven't learned much so far." A truth that gnawed at her like a rat on hard cheese. "You still think the information you collected from your friend Frisco holds true?"

"Maybe. A gang of outlaws robbed a train at Wharton Station a week ago. Rumor says Bangs was with them. Unless I miss my guess, they'll lay low for a while."

Before they'd left Sweet Clover, he'd ridden up to Horsethief Canyon, a surprising turn of events she hadn't expected, an action that made her wonder. Why was he welcome in an outlaw hideout? How had he gained information from a bunch of criminals?

She hadn't asked because he'd returned with hints of where Charlie Bangs and his companions might be. Such valuable information was all that mattered.

"Where do you think they'll go?"

A shoulder lifted. "Plenty of places to hide in Indian Territory."

Clouds moved in later that afternoon and with them came the blessing of a breeze to cool their ride. Gideon frequently rotated in the saddle to stare toward the western horizon. Dark clouds began to build.

By midafternoon, the prairie breeze became a whipping, whistling wind. They hunkered low in the saddle, heads down. The horses, too, bowed their necks against the powerful wind.

Leaves and small branches sailed overhead and tumbled across the tall grass. The grass itself swayed and twirled, slender green-clad dancers in a frenetic ballet.

Gideon's horse moved close to hers. Above the wind, Gideon called, "Be looking for somewhere to shelter."

"What about the nearby town?"

He hitched a chin toward the southwest.

"Storm's coming," he shouted, and his next words chilled her bones. "We can't make it to town."

May was the month of wild and dangerous thunderstorms on the plains. Gideon knew this, had considered the fact before agreeing to Willa's job offer. From long experience, he also knew that the coming storm deserved respect and attention.

He pondered their choices.

To their east, lay the hardscrabble town of Woodman's Post. Behind them, a day's ride was Clower Camp. Ahead, loomed the river with the disturbing promise of floodwaters if a storm dumped enough rain.

Pressure mounted in Gideon's head. He should have planned better, should have taken a route that assured known shelter rather than depending on the occasional trading post or rare settlement.

Instead, he'd chosen the easiest route. Though she'd traveled across the country in a wagon, gritty though she might be, Willa had never sat a saddle for days on end through rugged wilderness.

The harder days would come soon enough when they reached the mountains.

Yet making the right choices was his job, and he wasn't sure he had.

Had his skills diminished during the year since he'd guided that final hapless family across the Arkansas?

His stomach tightened against the ugly memory. Though he wished for the relief found only in the golden nectar of his most hated and most desired beverage, he'd vowed not to drink while guiding. He hoped he could keep that promise.

He hadn't even brought along medicinal whiskey. At times, late at night when sleep seemed impossible, he wished he had.

"There!" Willa's sudden shout broke his dangerous reverie.

Following the aim of her pointing finger, Gideon nodded. Ahead, a stand of trees bowed low over what appeared to be a rock outcropping. "Go."

They urged their mounts into a lope.

Before they reached their destination, the sky opened. Rain hammered them like sharp cold nails. Steam rose from the heated earth. A mist formed around them.

As they reached the trees, leafy limbs slapped at their bodies, tormenting the horses, but provided a slight break from the driving rain. Quickly reining to a halt and dismounting, Gideon hurried to survey the rocks. A shallow indentation with minimal overhang, probably a fox den, but in this downpour, they couldn't be particular.

Again, his fault. He should have been better prepared.

"Grab the fish slickers," he shouted.

Falling to his knees, he scraped nature's debris from beneath the rocks until he hollowed out enough room for the two of them. Willa joined him to shove their bedrolls as far back against the stone wall as possible and spread the oiled rain slickers to hang over the opening. Smart woman.

They worked in silent tandem, preparing a shelter for themselves and securing the horses, unloading what they'd need if this proved to be their only cover for the night.

With a distant hope that God was listening, Gideon prayed against the danger of a cyclone.

Blue jagged lightning crackled across the dark sky. The sun had fled, scared away by thunder so near and so loud the earth trembled.

A twister was a possibility.

The horses moved, restless. Freckles whinnied, backed up, straining against the lead rope tied to a nearby tree. Traveler's eyes widened with fear, the whites showing. His large body trembled.

Willa and Gideon nestled close to each other beneath the narrow overhang. Rain poured a waterfall over the edge and ran downhill beneath the slickers and into their puny excuse of a shelter. Willa shoved the side of her boot into the soil and pushed outward.

Seeing her intent to create a ridge, Gideon joined her. Side by side, they dug and kicked at the growing mud wall until the rain stopped trickling inside.

Lightning became constant now. Flickers and flares, jagged, blinding bolts that turned the air blue. Wind whipped and howled and the fear of a cyclone thickened in Gideon's chest.

In his years on the trail, he'd ridden out two of the violent whirlwinds, but he'd seen the destruction they could leave in their wake, seen the death of livestock and settlers.

Their rudimentary shelter would not protect them from a twister.

"Are the horses safe enough?" Willa turned her rain-dampened face toward his. Worry wrinkled her brow, pulled her full bottom lip into an interesting pout.

Not if a cyclone twisted out of those black clouds.

"It's the best we can do," he answered. "Riding farther in hopes of finding a better place could be lethal in this lightning."

Willa nodded her agreement. Her lips moved in quiet prayer that he could hear, mostly for the horses. His respect for his stalwart traveling companion, already strong, grew deeper.

Every trail rider knew his horse must come first. Animals depended on humans, especially animals tethered to a tree.

A thunderbolt, so intense his ears rang, struck nearby. Willa jumped, gasped.

They sat with shoulders and sides touching, knees drawn in. He was acutely aware of Willa's petite size and the fact that she was female to his male.

The buzz of her nearness hummed in his veins.

The fact that he was attracted to Willa bothered him to no end. She was a Christian, a good woman, as Belle had carefully reminded him, as innocent as he was jaded. He was a trail-hardened drunk with blood on his hands.

With stern control, he quieted the buzzing and vowed to keep any hint of attraction firmly to himself.

Protecting her, however, was his job. This reminded him of the yellowing bruise on her cheek and another he suspected resided on her back. He'd seen her rub the offending spot when she thought he wasn't looking, saw the way she gingerly dismounted or bent to wash in the creeks.

When he returned to Sweet Clover, he'd find the man who hurt her, and he'd make him pay.

Willa shivered, and Gideon slipped an arm over her shoulders, drew her closer into his warmth. He could not allow a woman in his charge to take a chill.

They were both soaked to the skin. The night, if they spent it here, would prove long and miserable. If he'd been alone, he wouldn't have cared.

"This is cozy." Willa snuggled her head against his shoulder.

Considering his recent thoughts, Gideon laughed. "You are a most unusual woman."

"It's only rain."

As if to put the lie to her brave statement, a stunning bolt of lightning directly outside their shelter left them momentarily awestruck and silent. Freckles reared, screamed.

Gideon's heart slammed against his ribs. That was close. Too close.

Removing his arm from Willa's shoulder, he peered toward the horses. The curtain of rain made seeing impossible.

"Is he hit?" Willa started to crawl toward the opening.

Gideon grabbed her arm. "Nothing you can do if he is."

She leaned out anyway. "Freckles is loose."

Shaking off his hand, Willa charged into the storm.

"Willa, stop! Come back!"

But she disappeared into the blinding rainstorm.

A quick check told him Traveler remained tied but Freckles had bolted. There was no telling how far or how fast a terrified horse might run.

Willa couldn't stop him even if she had wings.

Struggling against the wind, Gideon raced into the storm calling Willa's name. Each shout was snatched away.

Crazy woman. Prairie lightning was deadly. She would get herself killed.

He could not let that happen.

Holding his hat against his head, he swiped water from his eyes and spotted movement to his left. Lightning split the air, raised the hair on his neck and arms. Gideon tensed, waited for the electrical impulse to rip him in half.

In the shock of light, Willa emerged from the rain curtain, dripping water like a leaky roof.

"I can't find him," she cried.

"We'll find him when this lets up," he shouted into her face, hoping he didn't lie. Riding double would slow them down and exhaust Traveler. Finding Charlie Bangs without another horse would be next to impossible.

"Let's get you to safety." With a determined grip on an equally recalcitrant Willa, Gideon led them back to the shelter.

Their mud wall had collapsed when they'd stepped on it and water puddled underneath the rocks where they'd previously sat.

With a sigh, Gideon settled into the puddle next to Willa. "We won't be dry, but we should be safe from the lightning."

"Freckles—"

"Can fend for himself." The words were intentionally terse. He valued the horse as much as anyone, but Willa's life came first.

Warrior woman, he thought with surprising amusement. Not once had she complained, and though her action bordered on suicide, she'd braved the elements for a horse.

The storm didn't let up until after nightfall and still spurts of occasional rain splattered the rocks overhead.

Unable to build a fire, they supped on jerky from the saddlebags and then tried to sleep.

Tomorrow, they had to cross the river. A raging, rolling river nearing flood stage.

Chapter Seventeen

The next morning, the sun glared down at the earth as if in defiance of last night's storm. In the rain-washed morning, with leaves and limbs strewn across the land, birds fluttered about, warbling in joyous consolation at surviving the night.

Gideon awakened from a fitful sleep with Willa curled against him, one small hand on his chest, her face snuggled into the bend of his neck. At some point in sleep, he'd turned inward toward her and slung his left arm protectively across her, an action he didn't recall.

He gazed down at the top of her hair, at the curve of her cheek and felt something tremble inside him, something soft and melting in a vacancy where nothing had lived in years.

Though their shelter was damp, he was reluctant to disturb her. Reluctant to let her go.

The trail ahead would grow progressively more difficult.

A stirring outside the shelter spurred him into action. Footfalls, movement.

Gently, a finger to her soft lips, he woke Willa. Her brown eyes sprang open but, at his silent warning, she remained still.

She was a magnificent trail companion.

Easing the Colt .45 from his holster, he nudged the rain slicker aside and peered out.

A relieved sigh seeped from him.

"Your horse is back."

Freckles stood calmly next to Traveler, his teeth yanking on wet bluestem as if he'd never had so much as a jittery nerve.

Though they were both damp, a day in the sun would dry them, so they eschewed the impossibility of building another fire, mounted up and headed toward the rugged town of Woodman's Post.

Near midmorning, they rode into a settlement about the size of Sweet Clover, with roughly as many businesses, though, here, most were saloons.

"Why so many saloons?" Willa turned her head from left to right, a frown tugging her dark eyebrows together.

"We're nearing the border to Indian Territory." The damp saddle creaked as Gideon stood in the stirrups and stretched his legs, looking in all directions, ever-watchful. In a liquor town, a man couldn't be too vigilant. "Fire water is legal on this side but not there."

"So they cross the border into towns like this to buy whiskey?"

Gideon met her troubled gaze, saw the questions there, knew he and his desire for liquor were responsible for her concern. "Don't worry about me, Willa."

Let him do the worrying. A saloon was a temptation he'd heretofore avoided. However, if he wanted information, his best chance was in saloons and towns like this one where outlaws and vagabonds were either ignored or protected by the townspeople.

Woodman's Post was quiet this morning, an anomaly, he knew from previous visits. He hoped it remained that way until he had Willa farther down the road.

Traveling with a woman through the territories was perilous anytime, but in a lawless liquor town, having her along could prove fatal. Women were scarce and in high demand.

Surreptitiously scanning the streets and doorways, Gideon directed the horses to the hitching rail outside the three-story Rusty Spur Saloon.

He looped Traveler's reins over the rail. "You can remain outside if you prefer, but keep your rifle handy."

Without looking at him, Willa yanked the Winchester from the saddle holster. "No."

The simple terse response reminded him that she did not trust him inside a saloon. And for very good reason.

He wasn't confident he could trust himself.

God, if you're listening, don't let me fail.

"This early in the day, business is slow." His damp boots thudded, rubbing the inside of his heels, as he stepped up on the boardwalk, every instinct on high alert. "But this is a place we don't want to be for long. Watch your back."

The inside of the Rusty Spur Saloon smelled like a dozen others Willa had entered in search of her father. The sharp, piercing smell of whiskey, the stale body odor and the nastiness of spittoons not yet emptied of last night's tobacco permeated a lingering haze of cigar smoke.

Something about the place, benign though it appeared, felt sinister, as if the walls had seen evil and absorbed it.

A liquor town, Gideon had said.

The hairs at the back of her neck tingled.

She gripped her rifle tighter.

A white-aproned barkeep swept sawdust and cigar butts into

small piles. The only person in the place, he scooted chairs and aligned tables as he worked.

As the batwing doors flapped shut behind them, the man looked up. Balding, a dozen dark hairs folded over the top of his round pale head. The hair missing from his head was found on his bulging forearms.

If Gideon's description of the town was correct, a burly bartender was a necessity for keeping some semblance of order.

The man leaned his broom against a round table and squinted toward the newcomers.

Suddenly, a smile split the fleshy jowls. He stormed across the room.

"Hartley, you varmint, is that you?"

"Ward." Gideon removed his hat, which, like hers, was still damp from last night's drenching. He shook Ward's hand. "Long time."

"I'll say. Thought you'd quit us." Going behind the bar, Ward rummaged under the counter, clinking glass against glass, and produced a bottle of amber-colored spirits.

"Got some fine whiskey here."

Gideon laughed, a strained sound that worried her. "Coffin varnish, Ward. I know about that moonshine still you've got in back."

"Best around. Won't kill you, but sure will make you drunk."

The two men grinned at each other with the look of men who'd known each other long enough to have been through some trouble and come out on the other side, with, if not trust, then respect.

Ward plunked two glasses on the bar and reached for the bottle.

Willa's breath went shallow. What would she do if Gideon decided to drink himself stupid?

Gideon held up a hand. "None for me. I'm working."

Narrow eyes blinked. "Never stopped you before."

Gideon leaned an elbow on the bar, casual as could be, but Willa felt his tension. "Things are different now."

Ward reached across the space and clapped a beefy hand on his shoulder. "You got to let that go, friend. Weren't your fault. Tragedies happen."

Gideon flushed, deep and dark. Frowning, he shook his head at the barkeep. A silent message to which she was not privy was exchanged. Gideon refused to meet her stare, though she held on, curious to know what Ward knew.

What wasn't Gideon's fault? Did it have anything to do with his bad dreams?

As if he understood Gideon's warning, Ward put the whiskey bottle on a shelf behind him and produced two cups of coffee and a small plate of corn bread and pickles.

Easier now, if not relaxed, Willa waited for Gideon to make the first move.

He'd refused the whiskey. Would he refuse the food, as well?

He nudged his chin toward her and then to the plate.

Belly grumbling, she accepted a slice of the yellow corn bread.

The barkeep jerked a thumb toward Willa. "This your woman?"

"Yes." Gideon spoke without hesitation, as if expecting the question.

Willa tried not to react to his statement, understanding that in a place like this, an unattached woman would be seen as fair game. Nonetheless, a tingle of energy pulsed through her. What would it be like to be someone's woman? To love, and to share a life with a man who loved her, too?

The image of a sober Gideon Hartley intruded into that

imaginary space, a remnant perhaps of waking this morning snuggled against his strong, sturdy chest, his arms around her, his heartbeat steady in her ear.

Ward guffawed and slapped a fat hand onto the bar. Willa's ears rang. "Never figured you for the type to settle down with one woman. Good ones are hard to find out here in the territories."

Cool as last night's rain, Gideon kept up the pretense. "Indeed, they are. Worth more than rubies."

Another little thrill, completely inappropriate, danced through Willa.

"What brings you to Woodman's Post if you ain't here to drink? You selling whiskey to the Indians now? I got plenty you can take with you at a fair price."

"Now, Ward, you know that's not legal." Gideon doctored the steaming coffee in his slow methodical manner, his movements intentionally laid-back. Willa saw him glance repeatedly into the dingy wide mirror spread behind the bar. He was watching the door, surveying the entire room.

She knew him well enough to know that regardless of his easygoing appearance, this bar made Gideon apprehensive.

Ward laughed again. "A man's got to make a living."

Taking the wanted poster from inside his leather vest, along with a coin, Gideon pushed them across the shiny bar. "Looking for information."

"Charlie Bangs," the barkeep said softly, pocketing the money. "Bad hombre. Shoot you between the eyes for looking at him funny."

"A good reason to bring him in."

"You bounty hunting now?"

"In a manner of speaking. He killed my woman's pa."

The bartender's speculative gaze returned to Willa. "Right sorry about that, ma'am."

"Thank you."

The barkeep tore off a piece of the corn bread and dabbed it with a honey spoon. "Bangs came through here four days ago, spent the night, did some drinking and gambling, then stocked up on enough whiskey to supply half of Indian Territory."

"You think he's selling it to the tribes?"

"I know he is. Carrying a wad of cash, too, but I didn't ask no questions. Like I said, Bangs ain't a man to cross."

"Was he alone?"

Corn bread crumbs tumbled to Ward's apron front. He swiped a paw at them. "Riding with a skinny pock-faced fella I never seen before. Pock-face couldn't hold his liquor and flapped his jaw good and plenty. Got in a tussle with one of the cowboys."

The barkeep poured himself a cup of coffee and laced it heavily from the whisky bottle.

Willa watched Gideon carefully, saw the sweat bead on his forehead. He flicked another glance into the mirror.

Was he fighting temptation? Or concerned about the criminal element present in this town?

Ward seemed friendly enough, but his saloon, and this town, spooked her. Gideon, too, she thought.

Still watchful of the mirror, Gideon took a long sip of coffee. "Any idea where Bangs and his pal were headed?"

Willa's hopeful heart thudded once, hard, and then sped up.

"Into Indian Territory for sure, with that much whiskey. I overheard Pock-face mention a woman over in McAlester, so they might be headed there. Not sure. Might have been the whiskey talking." His burly shoulders shrugged. "Money or not, my girls don't like Charlie Bangs. And they don't cull much." Walt laughed softly as though the shameful acts in the upstairs brothel amused him. "I was glad to see him go."

The men continued to talk in a leisurely way, sip coffee and eat until the corn bread and pickles had disappeared, though tension emanated from the place on the bar where Gideon's muscled arm touched hers.

Willa remained silent but watchful. Occasionally, she heard movement overhead. Voices drifted in from the street. Men passed by the swinging doors.

The air seemed to be holding its breath, waiting for something.

When a pair of cowboys ambled inside the saloon, Gideon quickly pocketed the poster, tossed more coins onto the bar and, with a quiet word to Walt, gripped Willa's elbow and exited the building with such stunning speed Willa knew something was wrong.

Normally, she'd take umbrage to being led around like a horse. But when the two men had walked in, boots scuffling, they'd both immediately turned their attention toward Willa with a hard-eyed glare at Gideon. She'd seen their reaction in the mirror and shuddered.

"Take it slow to the edge of town and then ride hard," Gideon murmured as he handed her Freckles's reins. "Talk later."

Fingers of fear gripped the back of Willa's neck. He must have recognized the two men. Or maybe, they'd recognized him.

Two miles out of Woodman's Post, Gideon slowed Traveler to a walk, leaned forward and patted his neck. Willa came alongside him on Freckles.

"What was that about?" she asked.

He turned in the saddle and squinted into the distance behind them, studying the sky.

She followed his gaze. No dust. No sign of being followed.

Some of the anxiety she'd felt in him for the last hour seemed to ebb. He removed his hat, wiped a hand over his forehead. "Had a run-in with those two last year. Didn't want a repeat with you along."

"I can handle myself."

He looked skyward and sighed. "Tom Becker is an evil man, Willa. He traffics in anything. Guns, whiskey, women."

A chill prickled her skin. "Women? They sell women?"

He gave a short hard nod, mouth set in a grim line. "They don't take kindly to interference, either."

Which meant Gideon had interfered. "I never heard of such a thing."

"As well you shouldn't. Buying and selling young girls isn't exactly Sunday dinner conversation for fine ladies."

"It's evil. Like slavery."

"Yes." His jaw hardened. "Evil men will always take advantage of the desperate."

The young Chinese girl flashed in Willa's head. Was she a victim of men like Becker?

"Remember that night in the alley behind the saloon when that man attacked me?"

A muscle twitched below his eye. His gaze went to the faded yellow bruise on her cheek. "How could I forget?"

"I saw a young girl on the back stairs. Very young, Gideon. Maybe fourteen. She was crying, her face bleeding. When some man yelled her name, she skittered away, terrified."

Gideon's expression darkened. Something dangerous moved through him. "Why didn't you mention this before?"

"I thought it was her choice to be there. Now, I wonder."

"I've suspected—" He shook his head.

"Suspected what? That the saloon girls aren't there by choice?"

"Maybe. Not certain yet. Something is amiss upstairs at the Red Diamond. But evidence is hard to find."

"Coy Ling. Her name was Coy Ling."

His head snapped toward Willa. "Chinese?"

"Yes. Does that matter?"

"Very much so." His soft voice was as cold as winter. "Men like Becker and Flack prefer girls who don't understand the law, the language, the culture. They can lie to them and their families with the promise of good jobs. To desperately poor immigrants, the lure is too good to refuse. Money exchanges hands and the girls disappear into brothels across the west."

"That's unspeakable. I never knew. I feel so ashamed that I judged them all as bad women."

"Maybe some are, Willa. But not all."

Gideon ruminated on Willa's tale of the young Chinese girl as they approached the violently churning river through soggy grass and horse-high brush. The current ran swift and swollen from the heavy rains.

Pulling their horses to a stop on a high bank, he searched for an easy place to cross. On a dry summer day, the red muddy water here was shallow. Not today.

"Becket's Ferry is a day's ride back in the opposite direction," he said, weighing options.

Willa frowned at him. "Going back will slow us down. If Bangs was headed to McAlester, as that bartender thought, we can still catch him."

"Drowning is preferable?" he asked.

Backtracking, though, was not the best idea. Becker had recognized him in the saloon. A man of Becker's ilk might come gunning for him, if not out of hatred for Gideon, out of a desire for Willa. A woman with her sass and wholesome beauty would fetch a pretty penny.

Unease had plagued him from the moment they'd ridden into Woodman's Post. At first, he'd thought it was the temptation to drink, which had been powerful enough to shake him. Now, he knew something else was in the wind. What, he didn't know. Yet. But the meeting with Becker gnawed at him.

Rotating in his saddle, he scanned the landscape as far as he could see, contemplating.

Nothing but waving grass, butterflies and birds. The scenery should have felt peaceful. It didn't.

While he considered, Willa dismounted and walked down the riverbank where she measured the depth with a tall stick. "It's shallow along here. A sandbar or something."

"Willa, wait. It might be—" Before the warning words were out of his mouth, she stepped into the benign-appearing water.

And began to sink.

Shock widened the whiskey-colored eyes. She held a hand out to each side and stared down at the swirling water. "Quicksand. Gideon, it's quicksand!"

She began the fruitless effort to escape, straining toward the shore, but sinking more with each movement.

Gideon thought his heart would come out of his chest. In one quick leap, he left the saddle and hit the ground running, tearing away his vest and boots.

Many a man and horse had lost his life to quicksand.

The sucking mud reached Willa's knees.

She fought bravely, a soldier battling a more powerful enemy, arms stretched toward the shore and her horse's reins. They dangled so near and yet just out of reach. Sensing her growing fear, Freckles backed farther away.

"Stop struggling," Gideon shouted. He fell to his knees on the muddy bank and strained toward her, one arm outstretched.

She leaned as far forward as she dared, her chin touching the water, her legs trapped. "It's no use. I can't reach you."

The quicksand below the surface forced her upright.

She was waist deep now.

Terror blasting through him like last night's lightning, Gideon raced to Traveler for his rope, tied it to the saddle horn and launched the loop toward Willa.

She caught the lariat, slid it around her waist. Gideon breathed a temporary sigh of relief. He had her. Now, to get her out.

"This may hurt," he warned.

Mouth set with her usual resolve, Willa nodded. "Whatever it takes."

Gideon motioned toward the horse. Traveler slowly began to back away.

Willa gripped the rope with both hands and locked her eyes on his.

From the strain on her face, the pressure around her middle must have been excruciating, but she kept her focus on his, trusting him with her life.

Trusting him.

Something shifted below his thundering heart, something as dangerous and sinking as the quicksand.

Time seemed to tick slowly. The hot sun scorched his neck. Muddy red water slapped and swirled, striving to hold onto its victim.

If he moved too quickly, the powerful horse could snap her in half. If he moved too slowly, she'd sink farther and faster until she disappeared from sight.

"Tell me if the pressure is too great," he said.

"I can handle it."

Inch by slow inch, Willa rose from the churning liquid, a sea goddess covered in mud, fighting for her life.

Everything in him wanted to rush into the river and carry her to safety. He steeled himself against the temptation until the moment she struggled free from the quicksand's hold and fell forward onto the shore.

Gideon swept her into his arms and carried her higher on the bank.

His mud-covered boots slipped, and he went to his knees, cradling her close as they tumbled onto the grass, exhausted, lying close, wet, muddy, but alive.

"You could have been killed," he groused, more scared than mad.

"I had the situation in hand," she said, and then snickered because she clearly had not.

He stared into her tawny eyes, thinking she was the most intriguing woman he'd ever known.

He'd been scared out of his mind, afraid of causing another death, but most all, he'd been afraid of losing Willa.

A most disconcerting discovery.

What was happening to him?

Breath puffing fast and hard, Willa's fingers fumbled against the rope at her waist, her face pinched with discomfort. Gently, Gideon pushed her icy fingers aside, loosened the rope and pulled it over her head.

They were side by side on the grass, facing one another, breath slowly returning to normal.

He couldn't make himself move away.

"Are you hurt?" He barely resisted the temptation to run his hands over every inch of her body to be sure.

"No."

"Would you admit it if you were?"

A semblance of a grin tweaked her lips, and he had his answer.

"Let me see your hands."

She curled her fingers into fists. "They're fine."

He grabbed a hand and turned it palm up. As he suspected, rope burns had peeled away the skin.

Regret pinched him. He scowled at the wounds and then at her. "We'll set up camp across the river and make use of Mercy's herbs."

"Not on my account. We still have plenty of daylight. Where will we cross?" Returning his scowl, she used his shoulder as leverage and pushed to her feet.

She took one step toward her horse and stopped as quickly as she'd begun.

With a stunned expression, her mouth dropped open. "My legs—"

"Won't hold you yet." Gideon caught her before she fell, sweeping her into his arms. "Hardheaded female. One of your ancestors must have been a mule. You can't even walk."

She sniffed, that mulish chin poked toward the sky. "But I can ride."

Chapter Eighteen

Willa didn't know whether to be grateful or insulted. No man in her entire life had *handled* her as much as Gideon Hartley. The fact that she felt as safe and comfortable snuggled against his chest as a baby in her mother's arms was simply ridiculous. She was an old maid. She was not supposed to have this rush of gushy feelings. They made her…itchy.

Especially after she'd humiliated herself by plunging into quicksand like a greenhorn who didn't have enough sense to know better.

"Anyone could get into quicksand on this river," Gideon said as if he'd read her mind.

"Lying will not soothe my wounded pride."

His reply was a smirky little grin.

And there was that itchy feeling again.

They'd reached Freckles, and Gideon assisted her into the saddle. "Do I need to tie you on?"

She squinted at him in mock annoyance. "Try it, and I'll push *you* into the quicksand. Without a rope."

Chuckling, he held up both hands and backed away to mount Traveler.

Willa gathered the reins in still shaky and weak fingers. Her palms burned. Some of Mercy's yarrow salve would feel good. But not now, not when they were getting closer by the minute.

The quicksand had frightened her, but she suspected the episode had frightened Gideon more. He tried to pretend he didn't care. Tried to tease away the seriousness of the event.

His amusement, she realized with a start, like his bursts of poetry, was a cover for his deeper feelings.

For several more miles of riding, he refused to cross the river and Willa wasn't certain if he was taking them out of the way or not. Tired from her ordeal, her legs heavy as felled logs, she rode at his side without complaint.

Eventually, he found a quieter stretch of river that suited him, and though the crossing left them soaked yet again and the horses had to swim for it, they managed the crossing easier than she'd expected.

They were also cleaner, the mud washed away.

By the time they made camp that evening in thick hilly woods, Willa was bone weary and eager for rest. They'd traveled miles from the river, far from anything or anyone, having passed within sight of an Indian settlement hours ago.

Gideon gathered wood and built a fire, and then went to tend the horses.

Willa rummaged in the saddlebags for their meager food supplies.

A gunshot silenced the birdsong. She grabbed her rifle, turning slowly in a circle.

"Gideon?" She heard the tremor in her voice.

He emerged from a stand of trees, holding a large jackrabbit aloft. "Supper."

Willa fisted a hand on each hip. "You scared me."

"Want me to toss it back?" If he'd shouted a warning, he'd have scared the rabbit away.

"No." Her mouth watered at the notion of fresh meat for supper. "I'm tired of beans and jerky."

"We shall dine like kings."

He prepared the rabbit and soon the delicious smell of smoked meat saturated the air.

Gideon crouched on his haunches, feeding the fire and turning the rabbit on the spit while Willa made coffee and fresh biscuits, the latter a treat in which they'd not yet indulged.

"Gideon?"

He tilted his hat back, eyebrows raised in silent question.

"This morning at the saloon, the bartender said something I didn't understand."

Wariness sprang into his expression.

"What tragedy was he talking about? What happened that wasn't your fault?"

He shoved a stick at the fire. Sparks crackled skyward. "Ward's wrong. It *was* my fault."

Pain pulsed in the silence. He didn't want to talk about it, but Willa, being Willa, pushed on. "What happened?"

He stared into the fire and sighed, long and deep as if the question took away all his energy.

When Willa despaired of getting an answer, he spoke, the words hard and matter-of-fact. "A boy died. I was drunk."

And you are tormented because of it, she thought.

"Is that why you have bad dreams?" she asked gently.

Gideon stood, tossed the stick onto the logs, watched it catch fire. "Keep an eye on the meat. I'll see to the horses."

The horses were already settled for the night. Gideon, clearly, was not.

Gideon knew he wouldn't sleep that night, for more reasons than the dreams that were bound to come after Willa's probing inquiries.

They'd eaten their supper without much conversation and when dusk descended, Willa had settled into her bedroll, exhausted from the day's misadventures.

Assured that she had the loaded Winchester at her side, Gideon took his rifle and made a wide circle around the camp. His instinct nagged him tonight. All seemed quiet, but he couldn't shake the feeling that trouble was coming.

He ventured back to the campfire and added a thick log. Yellow-and-blue flames lit the circle of grass and dirt, driving away animal predators. He paused next to Willa. Her breathing was slow and even, an enviable thing, and her dark eyelashes fanned beneath her closed eyes.

She didn't know she was beautiful. He'd never known a woman like her, a woman without artifice, a tough little smidgen of strength and grit, and yet very much a woman.

A woman to be reckoned with.

His lips moved without sound, quoting Whitman, as he watched her sleep. "'I wander all night in my vision, stepping with light feet, swiftly and noiselessly stepping and stopping, bending with open eyes over the shut eyes of sleepers, wandering and confused, lost to myself, ill-assorted, contradictory.'"

Lost to himself. Contradictory. That was him, all right.

He tilted his head toward the star-sprinkled heavens, aware that Willa's faith and his both matched and conflicted. How he wanted to believe that God could forgive his wrongs, could take away the hatred and the constant, gnawing desire for strong drink. Neither ever seemed to go away, especially on nights like this when he could not sleep and dead faces rolled through his thoughts.

"Lord God," he whispered, "this woman deserves better than me, but I'm all she has at the moment. Help me to remain both diligent and sober. Failing again would be the end of me."

Nothing stirred except the night sounds of snapping logs

and a mournful hoot owl. The Creek, on whose land he camped, believed owls to be harbingers of death. He hoped they were wrong.

He scanned the sky in search of a sign, a signal of some kind that God had heard and cared.

Nothing changed. He wondered if the long abuse of alcohol had destroyed his soul.

A twig snapped. Gideon spun toward the sound, rifle ready.

A pair of red eyes glowed from the woods' edge. A young doe stepped into sight, her black nose twitching. He expected her to see him and bolt, but she didn't. Perhaps the fire mesmerized her. Perhaps his ability to remain completely still fooled her.

He could easily take the deer, but preserving the meat would take a day or more and slow them down. She might have a fawn nearby.

Lowering his rifle, he murmured, "Go on, little mama."

At his whisper, her tawny head jerked up, and she bolted into the woods from whence she'd come.

Gideon's gaze drifted to Willa. She hadn't stirred.

Tenderness moved over him.

He knew then, as sure as he knew his name, he'd protect Willa Malone with his life.

Pressing his back against an ancient birch, he slid to a sit with the rifle across his knees. To pass the time, he mentally quoted all the Scripture and poetry he could remember, which was considerable, something he'd done as a boy when learning a new poem to surprise and please his mother.

Remembering had always come easy. Forgetting was the hard part.

At some point after the Twenty-third Psalm, he must have dozed.

He jerked to alertness. Something had moved. The atmosphere had changed.

With barely a motion, he slid his finger to the rifle trigger.

The leaves rustled. A tall skinny man stepped into the firelight. Gideon rose, bringing the rifle up with him.

The stranger led a horse with one hand, but the other rose into the air. "Howdy, mister. I come in peace."

"State your business."

"Passing through. Saw your fire and wanted some company. Hoping for a bite of grub or some coffee."

"Little late, isn't it?"

The conversation woke Willa. She stirred.

Gideon willed her to remain quiet and unnoticed.

He put a hand to his side and motioned her to stay down. She went still.

"Got lost," the stranger said. "Sure could use some grub."

His tone was friendly, maybe too friendly. In this country, a man couldn't be too careful. Unexpected strangers were more often than not men on the run, bushwhackers looking to steal horses or money or anything else they came upon. Like women.

A man riding in alone often had companions waiting in the woods while he scouted the number of men and guns in the camp.

Gideon had been ambushed before. He couldn't let that happen again, not with Willa present.

Gideon motioned toward the leftovers they'd saved for breakfast. "Help yourself to the biscuits. The coffee's cold."

"Won't matter none." The thin stranger produced a tin cup from his saddlebag, an action that had Gideon's rifle leveled at his back. When he turned toward the fire, the man said, casual-like, "Now, mister, you don't need that firearm. I mean no harm."

Gideon allowed a cool smile. "I'll have to beg your pardon, but a man traveling in this territory must be cautious."

Sly eyes cut toward Willa's inert bedroll. "Especially traveling with a gal."

Gideon ignored the comment, but his suspicions shot up a notch. The man was scouting, all right, taking in everything in the camp.

The question remained. Was he alone?

"What's your name, stranger?"

The man squatted by the fire and poured himself a cup of coffee. Firelight bathed him in flickering shadows. "Jess Brown. Yours?"

Nothing familiar in the name, unless it was false, which it likely was. "Hartley. I'd be obliged if you'd finish your coffee and be on your way."

"Now, that ain't too neighborly of you, Hartley."

Gideon shrugged. "As neighborly as I get. I trust you understand."

"Hartley." Brown brought the tin cup to his lips and slurped loudly. "I've heard the name."

The hair on Gideon's arms tingled, but he kept his council. Let the fellow talk. Perhaps he'd reveal more than he intended.

Brown chugged down the remaining coffee, stuffed a pair of biscuits inside his vest and another into his mouth.

"Good biscuits." The sound was muffled around the full mouth. "I'm obliged."

Gideon waited, watching, while the man fiddled around the campfire a little too long before swinging onto his paint horse.

Leaning forward on the pommel, Jess Brown settled hard eyes on Gideon. The fire danced evil shadows across his face.

"Heard a rumor about you, Hartley. Heard you and your gal are hunting Charlie Bangs. A word of caution. Don't."

With a jerk of the reins, he spun the horse and disappeared into the trees.

The words hung in the air. Jess Brown hadn't been lost. He'd known exactly whose camp he'd ridden into.

And he'd come with a warning.

Gideon hunkered next to Willa, a hand to her shoulder. "Willa."

"I'm awake. Is he gone?"

"Yes. Maybe not for long. We need to break camp."

"Now?"

"Now."

Night riding was slow and dangerous with only the light of the moon and stars and instinct to guide them.

Willa had heard Jess Brown. They must be close to finding Charlie Bangs. They did not, however, want to encounter him in the middle of the night with him having the advantage.

"He knows we're after him." Willa's body rocked with each step, still too tired to do much more than remain in the saddle. "We've lost the element of surprise."

"An outlaw like Bangs always has someone after him. He won't expect us to know where he's hiding."

"We don't."

"Not yet. But we will."

Though buoyed by his confidence, Willa kept a careful watch, her Winchester across the pommel. Gideon did as well, the six-shooters on his hips occasionally glinting in the moonlight.

It was going to be a long, long night.

By the time dawn broke in streaks of purple, Willa sagged in the saddle, happier to see morning than she could express. At least now they could see who or what approached.

They were in hilly, forested country, as pretty and green as Papa's tales of the Old Sod. Indian villages dotted the territory along with a few trading posts, squatters and the sparse town. Late in the night, they'd passed shadowy teepees that Gideon identified as belonging to the Seminoles.

Coming over a rise, they spotted a covered wagon nestled in a grove of trees. No one stirred around the white-ashed campfire.

"They must still be asleep."

Though his face was gray with fatigue, Gideon's back straightened as he squinted toward the camp. He placed a hand on his rifle.

"Something's not right."

"Why do you say that?"

"Too quiet. Travelers don't linger. They rise early and move on." He pointed upward.

A shiver slithered down Willa's spine.

Buzzards circled overhead.

Slowing the horses with orders for Willa to remain behind him, rifle ready, they rode into the camp and stopped. Nothing stirred.

"Hello, the camp," Gideon called. "How do you fare?"

When no response came, he dismounted and carefully approached the back of the canvas-covered wagon.

"Hello?"

Suddenly, he whipped around. "Willa, bring Mercy's medicines."

Jumping to her feet, Willa hurried to do as he asked.

Gideon climbed inside the wagon and, when she followed suit, he knelt next to a woman, his fingers to her neck.

A child of perhaps two or three lay waxy white and stiff beneath her limp arm.

The stench and evidence of illness emanated from the wagon, ripe and overwhelming.

"Gideon?" Willa whispered. "What's happened?"

He shook his head and moved to the man beside the dead woman and child. He touched the man's neck. Hope flared in his face. "Sir. Mister. Can you hear me?"

A weak and raspy voice replied, "Maudie?"

Gideon and Willa exchanged glances. Maudie must be the dead woman. While Gideon held the man's head, Willa tried to no avail to get some water into him.

He closed his eyes and went limp.

Gideon laid him down with care. "I've seen this before."

So had she, though Mercy was the one who fought the grim reaper. "Cholera? Ptomaine poison?"

"Could be contaminated water, but most likely food poisoning."

"I wonder how long they've been like this. Can we save him?"

He shook his head but didn't say the words that were visible in his expression. "What's in Mercy's bag?"

She handed over the pouch. As Gideon read through Mercy's instructions, the sick man mumbled something and grabbed Gideon's arm, his eyes wide and staring.

"Help. Save...family." Struggling to say more, his mouth opened and closed and opened again before he fell back, motionless.

Gideon leaned his ear against the man's chest, then sighed, long and tired. "He's gone."

And with him the family he'd begged Gideon to save.

Willa climbed out of the wagon, gulping in the fresh air, fighting not to gag and make things worse. As if they could be. She was fighting, too, the desire to cry for the sad little family on their way to somewhere in search of the promised land. And all they'd found was death.

She didn't hear his approach, but Gideon's strong hands

gripped her shoulders. He pulled her back against his sturdy chest. "Nothing we could do, Willa."

"I know. I know." Knowing didn't make the tragedy any less.

Needing comfort, she turned into his embrace. He gathered her in, his chin resting on top of her head, his heart thudding beneath her ear. "They're so young," she whispered. "We can't leave them."

She heard him swallow, clearly as upset as she.

"Make camp," he said. "Everyone deserves a decent burial."

Lips pressed together, Willa nodded.

Taking time to dig graves would slow them down. They risked losing Bangs's trail. But she couldn't live with herself if she left the family to the buzzards.

Willa reluctantly stepped away from Gideon's comforting touch. They had work to do. Sad, terrible work.

In the wagon, Gideon found farming implements and began digging in the rain-softened earth. Willa walked deeper into the trees to gather fallen limbs and dead wood for a campfire.

Coffee would drive away the heavy fatigue, though she'd be careful to make it with the water they carried with them, just in case water had killed the little family.

A flash of red caught her eye. Going closer, she saw a small form huddled in a blanket next to a tree. A child.

Dread pulled at her belly. Was he dead, too? A child who'd stumbled from the wagon of sick people only to die alone in the woods?

Twigs snapped as she crouched beside the child. His eyes fluttered open. "Mama?"

A relieved breath seeped from her. "I'm Willa. What's your name?"

"Gwady."

"Grady, are you sick? Does your belly ache?"

His little head swung back and forth against the blanket. "No. Mama and Daddy's sick. They won't get up. Daddy said they ate something bad."

They ate something bad. So Gideon was correct. They'd poisoned themselves with their own food.

The boy's little lip quivered. Tears flooded his eyes. Bravely, he tried to blink them away.

Willa knew next to nothing about children, but this one twisted around her heart like a sweet, sad vine.

"Didn't you eat it, too?"

He wrinkled his nose. "Hu-uh. I don't like sausage. It smells funny."

Sausage. Food brought to sustain life had taken it instead. "You must be hungry."

He nodded.

"Let's get you back to the wagon."

Willa scooped him into her arms. Slight and thin, the boy didn't weigh much more than a pail of fresh milk. He clung to her, his small body trembling.

As she walked into camp, carrying the child, Gideon dropped the shovel. "Dear God. Another one?"

"He's alive. He said he didn't eat the sausage. It smelled funny."

"The sausage."

Expression grim, features set against the desolate emotions pulsing through the sorrowful camp, he reached them in a few long strides and took the child from her arms.

Clearly pained, Gideon closed his eyes for the briefest moment, and then opened them to gaze tenderly down at the boy.

"How old are you, son?" His voice throbbed with kindness.

"I five." Grady held up a full hand of fingers.

"Five." Gideon's eyes shut again. His Adam's apple convulsed.

"His name is Grady," Willa said, "and he's hungry."

"Where's Mama and Daddy and Baby Joe?" the boy asked.

"Let's get you fed, and then we'll talk. Okay?" Gideon's voice was so gentle and stricken Willa ached to hear it.

This innocent child had lost everyone, every single member of his family. Now, all that stood between him and death were two strangers who could not take him with them.

Chapter Nineteen

Standing the boy on his feet, Gideon kept him occupied away from the death wagon and the family now wrapped in blankets and awaiting a shallow grave far away from everything they'd known and everyone who cared about them.

While Willa rummaged in her supplies for a meal, Gideon, the boy hovering close at his side, completed the sad task of grave-digging. The child dug, too, and the sight stuck in Gideon's chest like a swallowed brick. Grady didn't know. He was too young to understand.

Talking softly to Grady as they worked side by side, Gideon throbbed with worry and with the desire to shield the child from the harsh reality that he was now an orphan. A smart little fellow with big gray eyes and a sweet demeanor, Grady reminded Gideon of Tad, though Tad had been seven when he'd died.

Memories of the little brother swamped him with each shovel of dirt. He'd dug Tad's grave, too.

Tad, the lively, sweet-natured boy who would ride with

Gideon across the cotton fields, waving to friends among the sharecroppers. Tad had made friends everywhere he went. He'd had Mother's innate kindness.

"Mister." Using a spoon, the boy flung dirt onto the body-shaped mound. "Why are we digging these holes?"

The graves were deep enough. Gideon tossed one last scoop onto the pile, set the shovel aside and crouched beside the child, one hand on Grady's slender shoulder.

"Grady, I need to tell you something. It's going to be hard. You're going to feel deeply saddened." The horrid words stuck inside his chest, clogged his heart until it threatened to explode.

Grady heard the seriousness in Gideon's voice and grew still as a frightened rabbit. "Is it about Mama and Daddy and Baby Joe?"

"Yes."

Wide gray eyes locked on his. Gideon could see the intellect in them and wondered how much he'd figured out on his own.

"Your daddy, mama and brother were very, very sick. They tried hard to get better but they couldn't."

"It was the sausage, wasn't it?"

"I believe so."

"I don't like sausage." Grady's lips quivered and he blinked rapidly as if he suspected what was to come.

Gideon gathered him into the vee of his knees, holding him sideways against his chest so he could meet the boy's eyes. "You won't understand this completely until you're older, but your family isn't going to get well, Grady. They won't ever wake up anymore. Not on this earth."

For a long painful moment, the child looked more stunned than sad, his skin as pale as those of his dead family. A single tear trickled down each cheek.

In a shattered whisper Gideon knew he would never forget, Grady said, "I don't want them to be died."

"I know. I know." Gideon clutched the boy close, holding him tight as if to block out the harshness while understanding far better than he wanted to the devastation Grady would carry with him all the days of his life.

They ate their breakfast in strained silence, the job ahead pulsing between them like a fresh wound. Grady gobbled his food, but neither Gideon nor Willa had much appetite for anything but strong, hot coffee.

"I could take him for a walk in the woods while you—" Willa couldn't finish the sentence.

"He knows, Willa. He should be there."

"And afterward? What then? What will we do with him?"

Gideon flashed a glance toward the boy and then back to her. "We'll talk later. Alone."

He was right. The boy didn't yet need to hear a conversation concerning his future, especially when there were no good choices to be made.

Gideon finished his coffee and set the cup aside, pushing to a stand. Weariness hung on his shoulders as he went to the wagon and carried the wrapped forms to the graves.

They were both too tired to move, and yet they had three people to bury and a child to care for.

God, give us strength. Show us the right path for this boy.

For someone who believed God helped those who helped themselves, this time Willa didn't know how.

She rose, dusted her skirt and held a hand toward Grady. "You are a very brave boy. Your mama and daddy would be proud."

He put his small hand in hers and followed her to the gravesites.

Heartsick and somber, they completed the grim task. She was only mildly surprised when Gideon produced a small Bible from his saddlebag and read the comforting words of John 14.

"Are they in Heaven now?" Grady raised his head from the graves to the sky.

"Yes," Gideon said simply, for what other comfort could they give?

As they walked back to the campsite, Willa said, "He must have people somewhere."

"We might find information among their belongings." Gideon hitched his chin toward the wagon. "Look for letters, maps, anything that identifies who they were, their origins or their destination. Grady and I will finish up back there."

Willa didn't argue. She could search for the items he mentioned. She just couldn't read them.

Together, Gideon and the boy piled as many stones as they could gather onto the graves.

Heat beat down on them. Gideon's body ached with fatigue, but Grady's bravery kept him moving. The child was made of hardy substance, finding and toting rocks far larger than he should have been able to carry.

Someday, he'd remember this and understand that he'd done his part, done his best, for his family.

Once satisfied that predators would be hard-pressed to rob the graves, Gideon broke a board from the side of the wagon and, using the dead father's building supplies, showed Grady how to fashion three simple cross markers, two large and one small.

Willa exited the back of the wagon with something in her hands.

Gideon squinted against the blazing sun as she came toward them.

"I found some letters," she said.

"Any addresses or names we can contact for Grady?"

An odd expression came and went on Willa's face. She held out the stack of envelopes.

He was tired, heartsick, in the middle of digging his knife into a makeshift grave marker. He also battled a raging desire for the biggest jug of moonshine in Indian Territory.

Couldn't she see he was busy?

The words snapped out before he could stop them. "Just tell me what you found, will you?"

Hurt flashed through her eyes. She turned her head away. "I can't."

Gideon's hands paused on the thick board. That she couldn't read had crossed his thoughts a time or two, but he'd dismissed them. Her sisters were educated. He'd thought Willa was, as well. They were all intelligent women.

"Why?"

She looked at him in surprise, as if she'd expected him to sneer.

"I can't read. I'm too stupid to learn."

He laughed, a tired bark of disbelief.

Willa ruffled up like a brown wren fluffing her feathers in a rain puddle. "I'm delighted that my ignorance can bring you such amusement."

"Willa." Gideon put the cross aside and went to her, gripping her upper arms. "You are one of the most intelligent women I have ever known. Your lack of reading skill indicates poor teachers, not an inadequate student."

She bit down on that enchanting lip and kept her head turned away. Two spots of pink colored the crests of her cheeks.

"Papa moved us around so often I never went to regular school, but Savannah's mother tried and failed. She said I was dull-witted."

Gently, he squeezed her arms, tugging slightly to make her look at him. She didn't. "Your stepmother was wrong."

Willa sniffed. "Apparently not. I can't read a lick."

"Then *I* shall teach you."

Her head snapped up, her brown eyes round as saucers. "Why?"

He stared at her pretty face, that fascinating lip, for too long. Her blush deepened, and Gideon again contemplated a most troublesome stir beneath his dead heart.

"I am a man who appreciates a challenge." He lifted an eyebrow. "You are not a coward, are you, Willa?"

She bristled, glaring a hole right through him.

Willa was anything but a coward, but goading her was the best he could do. Better an angry Willa than a hurt and humiliated one.

The truth was far deeper than the need to prove that she could learn. The woman had fascinated him from the start. She was a worthy companion and a charming one, though her charms were the most unique he'd ever encountered. He was, he feared, growing emotionally attached to this woman who had dragged him back from the brink of destruction.

This disturbing attachment could not be allowed, of course.

Willa plain and simple deserved better, for he did not know how long he could hold out against the whiskey. Ultimately, he would fail her in the ways that mattered most.

Yes, he would teach her to read. He would give her that because she had, quite literally, saved his life, but he could not give her his heart.

The day was painful, hot and long, and they were worn slick as a flat rock in an ice storm, so they mutually agreed to camp where they were for the night. Tomorrow was soon enough to tear the boy away from everything he'd known and take him into an uncertain future.

Willa thought her heart would shatter when Grady sat at the end of the graves until long shadows drove him to the firelight. Now, he sat cross-legged in front of the fire and stared into the flames.

Willa served him a plate of food and sat down beside him, putting an arm around his thin shoulders.

Gideon joined them, taking the opposite side, as if two strangers could buffer the boy from the tragedy of an outside world.

Night noises, first the crickets and then the whip-poor-wills, added sound to the crackling fire and the silent humans. Woodsmoke filled Willa's nostrils, a welcome respite from the smell of sickness and death.

Yawning, the child sagged against Willa. Gently, she repositioned him so that his head lay in her lap. Gideon lifted the small booted feet onto his knees and covered Grady with the red blanket.

Grady stirred, turned his face up toward Willa. "Mama read us stories at night."

Willa winced, her gaze going to Gideon.

Oh, how she wished could read to this heart-shattered child. How she wished she had children of her own, a boy like this one, and the gift of books to share the way Gideon did.

"Gideon has some books." She stroked her fingers over Grady's soft hair. "Would you like him to read to you?"

The boy considered for a moment. "I guess that would be all right."

Rising from his makeshift bed of laps, the boy waited until Gideon fetched the book, then rearranged himself with his head on Gideon's thighs.

Gideon opened the small Bible. *Interesting choice*, Willa thought.

"Do you know the story of a very brave boy who faced a mean giant?" Gideon's manly voice rumbled in the semidarkness. Shadows and flames wove a tapestry across his handsome face. Light and dark. Good and evil, as we all are. But Gideon had changed since the first time she'd met him. She saw more good than evil. Especially now, with the child.

"Is it scary? I don't like scary."

"No. God took care of David. He'll take care of you, too."

Grady snuggled in closer and sighed. "Okay."

Gideon read the story, embellishing here and there to make the child smile and ending in a way that both comforted and taught a lesson about God's love and provision, even in the face of disaster.

Gideon Hartley was a complicated man, and, as she watched his tender ways with the hurting boy, Willa very much feared she was falling in love with him. Love made a woman dependent and vulnerable, and she was too old and obstinate to give up her independence.

Being a woman in this world was hard, but she'd stood on her own two feet all her life. Trusting Gideon to guide her and remain sober was difficult enough. Trusting him with her heart was impossible.

But his tenderness with Grady melted her and made her wish she were different.

When the sleepy boy yawned again, Gideon gathered him up like an infant. "Let's get you bedded down."

"Can I sleep with you? I won't wiggle or wet the bed."

At the plaintive request, Gideon only nodded, as touched by Grady's situation as she.

Willa took more blankets from the wagon, finding them

thankfully clean, and made a pallet for Grady next to Gideon's bedroll.

With a glance of gratitude, Gideon put the boy down and covered him to his chin. "There now. I'll join you soon. You rest."

Grady touched a spot on his forehead. "Daddy kissed me right here."

Gideon bent low and touched his lips to the spot. "Sleep well, little man."

Willa thought her heart would burst.

Chapter Twenty

Early the next morning, they gathered a few of Grady's belongings, all the documents they could find—though they were few—and other keepsakes the boy would one day treasure, and started on their way.

Gideon led the team of oxen tied to the back of his saddle, figuring he could sell or trade them in exchange for Grady's care until his extended family could be found. According to three of the letters tied with string, Grady's family had come from Tennessee. Hopefully, someone there would send for the boy.

"What if they don't?" Willa had fretted last night after Grady slept. "What if no one comes for him?"

The same worry had crossed Gideon's mind. They couldn't take a child on a bounty hunt into perilous outlaw country. But leaving Grady with more strangers didn't sit well, either. What if no one wanted him? What if no family existed or none came to his rescue?

He'd wrestled the worry half the night and come up empty.

"Buffalo Gap is located near a railroad line and still has a few businesses and homes." Though most had disappeared after the coal mining disaster a few years ago. "It's the best we can do."

"How far away is Buffalo Gap?"

"With the oxen and child along, two, maybe three, days."

He knew what she was thinking. Bangs might take a notion to leave the territory. Unless the outlaw ran out of money, Gideon doubted he'd go far. He was safer here in outlaw country than anywhere.

With Grady riding double on first Gideon's horse and then Willa's, they stopped more frequently. A man and woman at a farm shared a meal of eggs and spring-cooled milk while they watered the horses and rested a bit.

At a trading post, Gideon picked up useful information about Bangs. He was in the area, all right.

By sundown, they made camp near a natural water hole, still several hours from Buffalo Gap.

Their journey of a few weeks threatened to stretch considerably longer. Couldn't be helped. The little boy was more important than Willa's outlaw.

Taking two strings and hooks from his saddlebag, Gideon guided Grady to the pond, grabbing grasshoppers as they went.

"Did your papa ever take you fishing?"

"Yep. But I never catched nothing."

"Never caught anything?" Gideon gently, automatically corrected the child's grammar, though why he tried, he didn't know. It wasn't as if he'd have any say in Grady's education.

"Nope. Papa did the catching. I watched."

"I think maybe you're big enough to catch one by yourself now, don't you?"

"I guess I'll have to if I want to eat. Papa's not here no more."

Gideon blanched at the stark reality of Grady's dilemma. He squatted beside the small boy.

"Listen to me, Grady. Miss Willa and I will see to it that you have someone to look after you. You're a brave boy, but you have some growing to do before you'll be on your own."

The sweet face brightened. "I can stay with you and Miss Willa?"

He'd dug this hole. Now he had to get out of it. "Miss Willa and I are on a journey to find a very bad man, and there are other bad men where we're going. It's too dangerous to take a little boy."

The big gray eyes clouded up. "But I want to stay with you."

Even if he wasn't in danger of being shot and killed, Gideon wasn't fit to take charge of an orphaned boy. He'd long ago distanced himself from the decent life Grady deserved.

As much as he wished things were different, they weren't. This was the reality of who he'd become. He'd make a worthless father.

The thought cramped in his gut.

"You've got kin back in Tennessee. It's only right that we contact them. They'll want you with them." He hoped he wasn't lying.

To leave the sticky conversation, he showed Grady how to set up a fishing pole with a long stick, string, hook and bait, then directed while the boy tied a double knot and dropped the hook into the water.

"Think we'll get one?"

"If we're patient enough."

"Papa said Jesus liked to fish."

"He did, indeed." Before he knew what he was about, Gideon relayed the story of the disciples fishing all night without a catch until Jesus came along and told them where to cast their nets.

Funny how those childhood Bible stories kept surfacing now that his head was clear and he was back on the trail.

He pointed. "You're getting a bite."

Hunkering down next to Grady, he whispered encouragement and direction.

After a brief battle, a pan-sized bass flopped on the bank at Grady's feet.

"I got one. I got one!" Grady danced around, laughing in childish delight. For that one moment, heartache fled as the boy basked in the delight of his first fish.

Grady grabbed for the slippery bass and when it slid from his hands, once, twice, his giggle rang out loud enough to catch Willa's attention.

She spun toward them, smiling, backlit by the campfire. Gold and red highlights glowed like a halo around her dark hair.

Something turned over in Gideon's chest. Willa, the boy, a fish for supper and the gathering dusk. Somehow all of it felt right and good, as if God Himself looked down and smiled.

"Flights of fancy," he murmured to himself.

The contentment, as inappropriate as it seemed, didn't go away. That night, he slept with Grady snuggled close to his side, one arm around the small boy, praying, not for himself or the usual plea for dreamless sleep, but a prayer for Grady and his future.

If Gideon dreamed at all, he didn't remember.

As they rode the final miles into Buffalo Gap, Grady sat in the saddle in front of Willa, holding on to the saddle horn. The trail was rough with numerous inclines and rocky creek crossings, an excuse Willa used to keep one arm wrapped around the little boy's waist.

Sweet and accepting, he touched her in a deep place she'd

never explored before. She wanted to shield him from the cruelty of life, to take his pain on herself, and she wondered if this was what it felt like to be a mother.

To pass the time and keep his mind away from tragedy, she sang silly Irish ditties and told him the stories her papa had told her. Stories of Irish fairies and poet kings.

When she mentioned the poet kings, Gideon rattled off a poem that made them laugh.

Gideon had changed during their travels, or perhaps she'd come to know him better. He still slept fitfully and experienced nightmares. He'd also occasionally fall into a dark silence and withdraw, pensive and aloof, especially when the subject of his family in Texas arose.

Nevertheless, his protectiveness of her and Grady spoke volumes about who he really was beneath the cynical smile.

The problem was the better she knew him, the more she wished she were the kind of woman a man could love.

Though he appeared relaxed and easy in the saddle, Gideon's watchful attention to the surrounding woods and bluffs told a different story. He was anxious.

Getting ambushed, he'd told her away from the boy's hearing, was a possibility. Now that word had gone out that he was traveling with a woman that likelihood had increased.

Simply by being female, she endangered them all. Even this precious child.

She snugged Grady a tiny bit closer. He tipped his head back to look at her and smile.

What would it be like to have a child of her own?

The yearning stretched in her chest, both painful and wonderful.

"Tobucksy County, Choctaw Nation," Gideon said, his horse's hooves crunching on granite ballast as they rode next to a cinder-lined railroad track.

Willa observed the verdant hilly land, glad to have her thoughts diverted. Pondering these odd feelings for Grady and Gideon left bruises on her heart.

High above them, caves drilled black holes in the mountainsides, perfect hiding places for those on the run. Someone could be watching them now and they wouldn't know.

A general sense of disquiet had ridden with them since the night in camp when the stranger had threatened them. The wrong people knew they were here.

"Up ahead." Gideon hitched his chin toward a slight clearing in the trees. Chimney smoke rose over a small settlement that had scratched out a place for itself in the woods.

Beneath her arm, Grady tensed and pressed his back against her. He dreaded the parting. So did she. In four days together, Willa had tasted motherhood. And she would never forget how good it felt.

The town of Buffalo Gap was smaller than she'd hoped, many of the buildings abandoned, but a railroad depot remained open next to a handful of businesses. A mixture of tired-looking farmers and Choctaw Indians moved about the once-bustling mining town. At one end of the dirt street, facing the business district, a white church shot a steeple into the sky.

They stopped first at the general store, where Gideon asked her and Grady to remain outside and keep watch. He wanted to talk to the merchant in private about a safe place to leave the orphaned boy.

He returned with a Choctaw man in a flat-brimmed hat and beaded moccasins, black braids hanging over his shoulders.

Regardless of Gideon's assurances that the Choctaws were a peaceable people, she placed one hand on her rifle butt.

When the stranger approached Grady, Willa would have

slid the weapon from the saddle had Gideon not given her a swift hard shake of his head.

Speaking softly in a language she didn't understand, the Choctaw slipped a leather strip of beads over Grady's head and placed something in the boy's hand.

Grady unfurled his fingers, his eyes widening. "Candy! Thank you, Mister."

Grinning, he popped the lemon drop into his mouth.

Willa relaxed, ashamed of her suspicions. This man had shown compassion to a hurting boy even as she'd misjudged him by his skin.

Gideon untied the oxen from Traveler's saddle, handing the ropes to Jacob Anotubi, the Choctaw whose quiet friendship had never failed him over the years. Jacob would make good use of the strong team, and Gideon had obtained supplies, information and a little cash in exchange.

Information from the Choctaws was, he knew, reliable and insightful. A hospitable people whose observation skills were second to none, the Indians knew who was on their land at any given time, knew where a man might hole up, knew who to trust and who to watch.

Gideon was grateful they trusted him. From Jacob and his family, he'd learned a smattering of native languages and enough of their customs to be made welcome in many homes. Travel through their territorial lands was much easier when the only enemies were nature and criminals from US justice.

With the white church at the end of the street their destination, they swung into their saddles and bid the dignified Choctaw farewell.

As Gideon rode the short distance, Grady rode with him. Gideon pulled the boy close, holding him with one arm and sorry for what was to come. Although Willa questioned him with her eyes, words couldn't get past the painful tightness in his chest.

They'd discussed this moment, had even explained to Grady what had to happen, though none of them were happy about it.

The stalwart little boy had made his desires clear. Clinging to the only anchors in his heartbreaking storm, he preferred to remain with Gideon and Willa, an impossibility that tore a strip from Gideon's hide and left him raw and bleeding.

"According to Jacob," he finally managed, "Reverend Larssen will be home this time of day." He tried for a grin that fell short. "The preacher favors his wife's cooking."

Willa tilted her head, eyes sorrowful. "Do you think he'll—"

"Jacob thinks so. Claims the minister is a good man, trustworthy. From Jacob that's high praise."

"I see." She looked away, her chest rising and falling as if she battled tears. He'd never seen her cry, but he could tell she dreaded the parting as much as he did.

He'd watched her with Grady since the awful discovery. Neither of them knew how long the child had been alone with his dying family, but his sad, endearing acceptance of something he could not change had torn both of them apart.

And yet, somehow, the tragedy had bonded them all together.

Each time Willa cuddled the boy close or stroked his hair or lay beside his bedroll, one arm protectively circling his shoulders, to tell him a story and hear his nighttime prayers, Gideon had seen the kind of mother she'd make. The kind of mother he'd had as a boy. The kind of mother every child should have.

Grady had no one at all.

If he fell a little in love with the tender warrior woman each day, Gideon would keep that nonsense to himself. A man with so much hate and guilt had no room for love.

The Reverend Matthias Larssen met them at the door, a napkin tucked into his red-plaid collar. Broad and tall, the preacher with the white-blond shock of hair looked more like an aging lumberjack than a minister of the gospel.

"Welcome. Welcome." Larssen tugged the napkin from his collar as he eyed the riders in his front yard, his gaze settling on Grady, who innocently fiddled with the beads around his neck.

"Finish your meal, Reverend. Our business can wait."

"Come in and eat with us. Mrs. Larssen cooks plenty." A sparkle lit gentle blue eyes. "And she is a very good cook."

When he saw Gideon's hesitancy, the preacher added, "'Be not forgetful to entertain strangers: for thereby some have entertained angels unawares.' You wouldn't have us miss the opportunity, would you, stranger?"

Gideon chuckled, though his heart was heavier than a wagonload of feed. "You won't find any angels here, but we'd be obliged. The boy could use a hearty meal."

After tying the horses, they followed the man inside the small parsonage.

A plump middle-aged woman with blond braids circling her head like a crown bustled around a square table, adding plates and utensils for the newcomers. She smiled as they entered, and Gideon felt a little better about what he had to do here.

Had there been a sheriff or a marshal, he'd have taken the child to him. A lawman would have more extensive contacts, but a preacher could be trusted to send letters and watch over Grady until relatives could be found.

The reverend and his wife seemed hospitable and kind.

While they dined on sliced ham, fresh garden peas and hot bread with creamy yellow butter, Gideon explained Grady's situation.

As he spoke, leaving out Willa's quest to find Charlie Bangs, two pair of gentle blue eyes moved back and forth between Gideon and the boy.

Though he'd hesitated to speak bluntly in front of Grady, Gideon had told him of the plan and wanted him to understand that this was not an easy decision.

"Trying to find his family is the right thing to do. They should know what happened to their kin and to raise the boy the way they see fit. He belongs with them."

Gideon put aside his slice of soft buttery bread and looked toward Grady, who now sat motionless, not eating, his eyes wide and worried.

Another stab against Gideon's conscience.

"He's an exceptional boy. He'll give you no trouble."

"We are charitable people, Mr. Hartley, and the child has my sympathies." The preacher turned up his large palms. "But a congregation in this territory is small with little to support a minister. I am frequently gone from home, riding a circuit to carry the gospel or conduct weddings or funerals in other settlements. This is a hard land."

Was the man going to turn him down? What would they do if he did? Ride on to McAlester? Hope to find a sympathetic soul there?

"Will you refuse, then?"

"Mr. Larssen," the blonde woman spoke, hands quietly folded on the table. "Religion that God our Father accepts as pure and faultless is this—to look after orphans and widows. God will provide."

The pastor's eyes crinkled as he put his fork down. "A wife is a fine thing, a worthy helpmate to keep a man in line." He glanced toward Willa. "I suspect you know that."

Letting the man believe Willa and he were married was

preferable to revealing the real reason for their being together. A man of the cloth wouldn't approve of bounty hunting.

"Every day on the trail is added danger, especially for a small child," Gideon said. "I can pay you for his keep until his relatives arrive."

"As my wife reminds me, it is our duty to do so. You can rest assured any offering you give will be used for his care."

Though the situation with the reverend wasn't as enthusiastic as Gideon had hoped, the decision was made. Grady would remain here until his people came for him.

While Willa and Mrs. Larssen stayed inside to wash the dishes and engage in quiet conversation, the preacher and Gideon stepped outside to get the letters from the saddlebags. Grady clung to Gideon's leg with the tenacity of a blood leech, his desperate grip conveying his anxiety.

"I'll have a word alone with Grady," Gideon said after handing over the letters and pointing out the names and addresses for the man to contact.

"I understand." Giving Grady's shoulder a reassuring squeeze, the minister went inside the house.

Gideon waited until the screen door snapped shut before going to a crouch on the thick green grass.

"Grady," he said, "Reverend and Mrs. Larssen will look after you until your relatives can be contacted to come and take you home with them. Do you understand?"

"Will you and Miss Willa stay here with me?"

"We can't." A knot formed in Gideon's chest.

"I don't want to stay here. I want to go with you. I want you to be my daddy now." Grady's little face twisted as he bravely fought back tears.

Gideon thought his chest would crack open and spill his heart onto the ground. "I know, little man. If I could take you, I would. But it isn't safe. And you likely have family back in Tennessee who love you."

"You love me, too, don't you?"

God, help me. Help this child.

He dragged the boy into a fierce hug. "I do. I do."

Suddenly, Willa was on her knees beside them. Gideon looked up into damp brown eyes and opened an arm, inviting her into the embrace.

For long painful moments, while Grady's hot tears soaked his shirt and Willa trembled with leashed emotion, Gideon held them, these two people who had come to mean too much to him in such a short time.

Shakespeare was correct.

Parting was, indeed, such sweet, sweet sorrow.

Chapter Twenty-One

Heavy silence hung over the two riders as Willa and Gideon left Buffalo Gap. If he lived to be a million, Gideon believed he'd forever remember the betrayed, bereft expression on Grady's face.

Another face to haunt his dreams. Another failure, though this was not of his making.

The boy had lost so much already, and now he was losing them.

Willa, who was normally as strong as an oak, had clung to Grady—and to him—until he'd almost lost his composure, which would not have helped the child.

Still, he understood Willa's grief. Grady had woven his sweet, bright personality around both their hearts.

Ruefully, Gideon shook his head.

Feelings had deluged him of late, a result, he was sure, of not drowning them in whiskey.

He was not sure he completely appreciated sobriety, even

though it had allowed him to get back on the trail and to feel worthwhile again.

Those things he credited to the woman riding at his side.

Plain and simple Willa both captivated and disturbed him.

They'd ridden a good mile, veering off the timeworn trail when she broke the silence.

"What if no family comes for him? What if there is no one who cares?"

He'd wrestled that worry until his mind was frayed. "The reverend and his wife are good people. They'll do right by him."

"He's such a dear little boy. I'm going to miss him. So much."

"I cannot argue that."

She lapsed into another melancholy silence and Gideon turned his attention to the trail. While he shared her sadness, a guide with a distracted mind could get into serious trouble fast.

Twice he stopped and dismounted to read trail signs. A whittled stick discarded beside the trail. A swirl of hoof prints. Three riders had stopped here. Something had spooked them, made them spin and turn south.

"We aren't going to McAlester," he said.

Her head snapped toward him. "But Bangs is there!"

"Not anymore."

A pretty little frown wrinkled her brow. He had the most irrational need to touch it, to smooth away anything that perturbed her.

"Then where is he?"

"Of that I'm not certain. But not McAlester."

Jacob Anotubi's information would push them farther east, deep into the Ouachitas. If they were fortunate enough to find their quarry there, the ride to a jail in Fort Smith would not be as long and grueling.

"Where are we headed?"

He pointed at the ground. "We'll know soon enough."

She fluffed up in that brown sparrow way he found so appealing. Better an annoyed Willa than a sad one, grieving for the boy.

"Riders." With a dip of his head, he turned his attention and hers toward two horsemen approaching from the woods to his left.

He braced himself, wary, ready.

They'd met a handful of travelers in the last week, all of them peaceable, except for that one night in camp. Gideon expected the faces would grow less friendly the deeper into the wilderness they rode. This northeastern corner of outlaw territory was infamous for aiding and abetting unsavory types who'd put a bullet in your back for the sport of it.

He'd prefer not to share that frightening fact with Willa, though he suspected she knew.

Feeling for the pistols riding against his thighs, he saw Willa slide the rifle from its holster. Even though she could hold her own, he didn't like the prospect of Willa in a gunfight.

She was his charge, his to defend.

The riders neared. A dark, unusually tall figure in a brown vest and black hat who rode a horse with ease was trailed by a smaller man slouched low and tied to his saddle.

Dappled rays of sun obscured their faces but glinted on a silver star pinned to the tall man's chest.

"US marshal and maybe a prisoner," Gideon murmured. "Keep the rifle handy."

The US Marshal Service out of Fort Smith was the only American law with jurisdiction in Indian Territory.

Gideon raised his hand in welcome as the pair came within speaking distance.

"Bass Reeves, US Deputy Marshal," the dark man said, tapping the silver star.

"Reeves?" Some of Gideon's tension eased. "It's Gideon Hartley. We met a time or two in Fort Smith."

"Hartley, you say?" Reeves reined a big gray horse to a stop, squinting at Gideon through shining black eyes. With an amused twist of his mouth, he said, "You still owe me two dollars."

Gideon laughed. "You have an exceptional memory."

The indomitable marshal, Reeves, was renowned for his toughness. Put a warrant in his hand and no circumstance could make him deviate until he had his man in custody.

"I never forget. Just ask this fella. Been tracking him for months. Now, he's going to pay a visit to the judge in Fort Smith."

The hanging judge, Isaac Parker.

"What did he do?"

"Plenty to earn a noose necktie." Reeves shifted, ever-alert to the man tied a few feet away. "Hear you're tracking Charlie Bangs."

Gideon had learned never to be surprised by anything on the trail. News traveled, especially if you didn't want it to.

"Do you have information?"

Bass rubbed a finger and thumb over his bushy black mustache. "He's not running solo."

"Coyotes seldom do. Who's he with?"

"Idaho Tom and Les Newton, rumor says."

Willa's saddle creaked as she leaned toward the lawman. "Do you know where?"

Gideon had hoped she'd keep quiet and let him do the talking. With a prisoner present, even though he was unlikely to escape from Reeves, Gideon didn't want any loose information.

"Willa," he said, "meet Bass Reeves, the best lawman this territory has ever seen."

Eyeing her with benign interest, Reeves touched the brim of his hat. "Ma'am. Bangs may be holed up on a farm about three miles north. Ben Crawford's place. *You're* not going in there after him, are you?"

She bristled, her stubborn pride showing. "He killed my papa, and I aim to bring him in."

Reeves's attention drifted from her to Gideon. "You got a warrant?"

"Don't need one. There's no law in Indian Territory. A wanted poster serves just as well."

"You know what I'm saying. You get yourself or your woman killed, you got no law to come looking for you."

"If we're dead, it won't matter anyway." But the worry for Willa ruminated in his guts, hot and acidic. He offered the lawman a cynical half smile. "You want to deputize me, Bass?"

Reeves considered longer and more seriously than Gideon had expected. "I will if you've a mind."

"I don't." He was no lawman. Didn't have it in him. Didn't want it.

Gideon dug in his vest pocket and pulled out two silver dollars, passing the coins across the space between his horse and the lawman. "Paid in full."

"Good thing. If you stay after Bangs, you're liable to get killed, and I'd never get my money." Reeves laughed, his mustache quivering like a squirrel's tail above white teeth.

"We'll get him." Willa's insistence almost made Gideon smile.

Bass jerked a thumb toward the hard-eyed outlaw slumped low in the saddle. "I'd join your party except for this feller. We best be getting on. Judge Parker is waiting."

"Good to see you, Bass. Safe travels."

"You folks take care."

With that, Reeves clicked his tongue and the two horses started forward again.

Gideon stared after the deputy marshal, considering how very much he'd like to have the lawman along on this quest to bring Charlie Bangs to justice. Another experienced hand could be the difference between life and death.

Willa was tough, but she was not experienced.

"Let's go." Willa tapped her heels to Freckles and turned toward the north. Over her shoulder, she said, "We can make the farmhouse before dark."

Her impatience didn't surprise him. She didn't know what she was getting into.

He did.

Urging Traveler to a trot, he caught up with her and slowed to a walk. As they traveled, they formulated various plans and discussed the problem of more than one outlaw. He'd expected that, had planned for it, though it worried him more than if Bangs were alone.

"One man's fairly easy to get the drop on," he told her. "Several can be a war."

Willa nodded and fell silent. She had to be scared, but she kept her fears inside.

The going was hard, the wilderness thick and brushy, and the rocky hills grew steeper by the minute. They were somewhere in the San Bois, as lethal a place as any he'd ever been. The few homes they'd encounter likely harbored men running from the law.

Criminals knew the best places to hide.

They would not, Gideon figured, get the drop on anyone tonight.

"Remain alert," he advised, peering through the thick forest and heavy underbrush for signs of life or of a homestead.

She touched the rifle as if reassuring herself that it was still there.

Like him, she also had a derringer and a knife in her boots. He hoped she didn't have to use them.

Overhead, bluffs and cliffs jutted from the low mountains. Sun glinted off the rocks. Gideon squinted toward them.

Though he spotted no one, a lookout man was likely.

They needed better cover.

Giving a slight squeeze of his legs, he swung Traveler off the trail and deeper into the woods.

Willa's head snapped toward him.

"Why aren't we sticking to the trail?"

"Because everyone else does." He drew a finger to his lips, then aimed the same finger toward the cliffs. "Let's find a place to camp."

Her eyes widened in understanding as she gazed upward. She nodded, whispering, "I thought we were—"

He raised a hand to stop the coming argument. He knew what she'd thought. Voice low, he said, "Charging in like the cavalry would be suicide."

He saw the rise and fall of her throat. Knew she was anxious.

So was he. For her. If anything happened to this lion-hearted woman, he'd go mad.

"Okay," she whispered, and he barely heard her above the sound of brush rubbing against saddles.

She was trusting him, believing in him.

The knowledge curled in Gideon's belly, both fulfilling and unsettling.

"First, we find the farmhouse," he said. "Then we determine if your man is there and how many people we're dealing with. We need to catch Bangs alone. We'll be dead if we aren't strategic."

"Strategic," she murmured, and he wondered if she knew the meaning.

Willa was bright. She'd figure it out, though he was still amazed that someone of her intellect had not learned to read. She would. He'd see to it.

But that was for another day.

Today, he was worried sick. Not for himself. His life didn't matter that much to anyone.

Willa's did.

She was a liability. Whether she liked it or not, a female faced greater peril than a man alone. Riding with Willa was different than traveling with Belle. Belle could hold her own.

Could Willa?

They didn't talk about it, but it weighed on him.

Near sunset, beneath a sky streaked with orange, Gideon smelled smoke.

Smoke. Thick, heavy smoke.

A shudder of dread rippled through his body.

He realized he was praying again.

Praying that the smoke was a campfire or a settler's chimney.

He hated fire as much as he hated his father, a hatred that must somehow come to a reckoning lest he die of it.

Isaiah had assured him God could heal the hurt and take the anger. His friend, so far, was mistaken. No healing. No reckoning. His father was the debtor, the sinner, the man to blame. Even death was too good for Thomas Hartley.

Shoulders tense, Gideon surveyed the horizon. The smoke thickened, spiraling high into the sky like a gray snake.

"Something's burning," Willa said.

"Already burned from the looks of it." His nostrils flared

with the acrid smell. He recognized the signs of a smoldering building, just as he recognized signs on a trail.

The worst of the flames had happened days ago, leaving behind the infernal smoke and ash to foul the air and haunt survivors.

If there were any.

With a foreboding stronger than any in recent days, he considered riding in the other direction.

A coward's way. Avoid the place.

What if there were survivors in need?

He was not, would not be, a coward. No matter the personal cost.

Head thick with the smell, belly rolling with nausea, he aimed Traveler toward the spiraling smoke.

They passed through a shallow willow-lined creek where the horses wanted to linger. He wouldn't allow it.

As they broke through the trees, Willa gasped.

"Oh, Gideon. It's a cabin. A cabin has burned."

As he'd suspected.

"Nothing we can do." *Nothing.* Like before. He'd arrived too late.

Though smoke curled and swayed like cobras above the desolation, the fire had died and only gray ashes and the remnants of someone's home remained. A fallen fireplace. A blackened stove.

Three chickens pecked around an unburned shanty.

"Maybe someone's inside that shed." Willa pointed. "They could be hurt."

Memories rose in his head. Flashes of a burning shirt, the smell of roasting flesh.

Dismounting, he turned his back to the destruction and took deep breaths. Sickness pressed for release.

Death he could handle. But not death by fire.

If he discovered a burned body, he'd lose his mind.

"Gideon." A small hand touched his back. "Are you all right?"

"I'll check the shanty." He had to get away from the ashes, from the smell, from the terrifying notion that they might find a charred body.

Yet, a human being, burned or not, dead or alive, could have taken shelter inside the remaining building.

Willa would flog him if he said so, but he would not allow her to see the kind of horror she would never be able to forget. Not if he could shield her.

"I'll go with you."

"No." His tone was intentionally harsh. "Keep your rifle ready and watch my back. We don't know what, or who, we'll find in there."

Realization made her blink. "Do you think this is the farm where Bangs was staying? Ben Crawford's place?"

"Yes." It had to be. They'd ridden three miles and this was the only farmhouse.

What had happened here?

Leaving Willa with the horses next to a stand of black-jack oaks, he rounded the destroyed house and approached the shanty. The door was bolted from outside, a sign that the building was either empty or someone was locked in.

Pistol in one hand, he slowly turned the lock and, standing to one side, pushed the door open with the flat of his hand.

In the dim interior, something moved.

Gideon swung his Colt toward the shadow. A raccoon shot out between his feet.

He jumped back and then shook his head, mocking himself as his eyes adjusted and he peered inside a storage shed. Farm implements, a few canned goods, a trunk, and the odds and ends of life that wouldn't fit inside the small house.

On a shelf next to jars of green beans were two jugs he'd recognize anywhere. Moonshine jugs.

The gnawing desire flared.

A breeze stirred the acrid scent of smoke into his nostrils. Ash dusted his pant legs.

Mental flashes of fire and death pushed through his brain.

Like a man in a dream, he went to the shelf and took down a jug, uncorked it and sniffed the contents.

The powerful fumes of alcohol made his eyes—and his mouth—water.

Fighting a battle he didn't think he'd ever win, he slid to the dirt floor, his back against the shanty wall, the opened jug between his upraised knees.

A few drinks, the imp on his shoulder whispered. Only one or two swallows, and he could ignore the destruction around him, the memories of the people he didn't save.

Drink half the jug and forget everything. For a while.

He sniffed the contents again, long and deep, and then he shuddered.

A shadow darkened the light from the opened door.

"Gideon?"

He raised his eyes. Willa stood over him.

"Ah, the avenging angel."

She hefted the rifle. He wanted to laugh. She wouldn't shoot him. She needed him.

But she needed him sober.

He clenched his teeth, fighting hard. The scent teased him, the promise of forgetfulness.

"What are you doing?" Her voice was small and anxious.

"'The thirst that from the soul doth rise, doth ask a drink divine.'"

"Why?" She slammed the butt of the rifle against the hard-packed ground, jarring him. "Why now? You haven't been tempted before, not even in the saloons."

"Oh, do not be deceived, plain and simple Willa, I was tempted."

He tilted his head back against the wooden shanty wall. Shards of fading daylight shot beneath the loose boards.

"What stopped you?"

He lowered his head and met her fiery gaze. Warrior woman. All grit and vinegar and vulnerability.

"You."

She blinked, her full bottom lip dropping open as though the answer surprised her. He hadn't meant to let her know that she, with her prayers and her spunk, had made him want to be a better man.

Still did.

Slowly, he corked the jug, ashamed of the temptation, ashamed of who he'd become and that the alcohol still had its hooks deep into his flesh. Into his very soul.

He was a hopeless man, made useful only by the opportunity to give Willa the one thing she wanted.

Willa had won his devotion and his loyalty, but even she could not bring him redemption.

Chapter Twenty-Two

Willa thought she'd faint when she walked into the shanty and saw Gideon with the open liquor bottle. Faint or whack him over the head.

She meant to stop him any way possible, even if she had to tie him at gunpoint while she emptied every bottle she could find.

Up until now, he'd remained focused and solid. Grady's dead family had shaken him. Leaving Grady behind had upset him, too. But instead of faltering, he'd held her hand and kept them both strong.

What was it about this burned farm that sorely tempted him to drink again?

Leaning the rifle against a row of shelves, she slid to the dirt floor beside him and took his hand. "Thank you."

His head swiveled toward her. In his eyes, she saw raw, stark pain and more than a little chagrin.

"I must apologize. It was quite ungentlemanly of me to behave in such a manner."

His formal talk was a shield she'd come to recognize. Gideon hid behind his intellect, his poetry, his vocabulary.

"What *is* it, Gideon? What's happened?"

He looked away, focused on some distant time and place. "Nothing for you to worry about."

This time, he was not getting away with an evasive answer. "The nightmares are real, aren't they?"

"Yes." His sigh rushed out. She didn't smell a single drop of whiskey on his breath. "You, plain and simple Willa, are a persistent nag to my conscience."

"At least you have one. A strong one or you wouldn't be this tormented."

A soft mocking sound rumbled from him. "More's the pity."

"Tell me."

He sighed again, laced his fingers with hers and bounced them lightly against his thigh. "You will not let me rest until I do, will you?"

"No. And you won't rest until you let it go."

"Let it go?" His snort was short and cynical. "I think not. My family is dead, Willa, burned alive. That is something a man can never let go."

Burned alive. No. Please no.

Willa closed her eyes, envisioning the horror and loss Gideon had endured. No wonder the burned farmhouse had sent him reeling.

Chest hot with sympathy, she asked, "What happened?"

He was silent for a while and she thought he might not tell her, but she waited, patient, praying he would purge his soul of whatever canker ate at him.

The musty smell of dust and old wood filled her nostrils, overriding the ash and smoke.

In the quiet waiting, Gideon's breathing sounded loud and distressed.

Finally, he scraped a hand over his unshaven face and began to speak.

"We argued that day, my father and I, and nearly came to blows. Lest I raise my fist to my own father and break my mother's heart, I left the farm, rode into town."

"The fire happened while you were gone?"

"Yes. And he was too drunk to save them." As if he'd tasted poison, Gideon spat the accusation. "By the time I returned, the house was in flames. I tried to get inside, but I was too late. If I'd come earlier, if I'd never left—"

He stopped talking and tilted his head back. A throb of sorrow, deep and dark, pulsed inside the dim dirt-floor shanty.

Willa hurt for him, longing to give comfort, not as she'd done during those days in the hotel when she'd barely known him and was furious to discover she'd hired a drunk. This was different. *They* were different.

Regardless of today's temptation, Gideon was no longer a drunk.

And they were no longer strangers.

Whatever they'd become to each other, regardless of what happened after this, she wanted to be the one he confided in, the one he leaned on. The one he turned to in times of need, believing he'd do the same for her.

What in the world had happened to her?

But she knew. Oh, she knew.

"Tad was seven," Gideon said. "I was his hero. He was mine. I loved him."

"Your brother?" She rubbed a soothing thumb over the top of his hand.

He nodded grimly. "He'd run upstairs, I supposed, believing I could save him. He was screaming my name from my bedroom window."

Gideon's eyes dropped shut, his face drawn and desolate.

"I'll never forget those agonized screams. Or the sight of my brother on fire. Burning. That gentle little boy aflame. His clothes, his hair, all of him, Willa, a ball of fire."

Dear Lord.

A sob pressed at the back of Willa's throat. She put a hand to her lips to keep from crying out.

"I yelled for him to jump. I didn't know what else to do."

Willa's lungs felt crushed, too painful to breathe.

"Did he?"

"Yes." Gideon shifted, turning his body, drawing her close as if desperate for comfort. The saddest smile she'd ever seen lifted the corners of his mouth. "If I'd told Tad he could fly to the sun, he would have believed me."

"He sounds like a wonderful little boy. Like Grady."

"Yes. Very much like Grady." He sighed, a heavy, throbbing sound. "I rolled him in the grass. Crying, praying, pleading with God to save him. He didn't."

He stopped again, took a breath and blew it out. She could feel him tremble, the emotion powerful enough to break him. Yet, he didn't break. He fought to survive.

Willa touched his rock-hard jaw, wishing there was something she could say or do that would change what had happened that day. Knowing there was nothing that could.

"Have you ever," he whispered, almost to himself, "smelled burning flesh?"

The question was too horrible to contemplate. Willa's stomach churned. "No."

She wanted to weep and wail. For him. For his lost family.

Like a relentless wind, another thought blew through and left her cold. If she felt bereft, how much worse was the burden on Gideon?

"He died in my arms, Willa. And I couldn't do anything."

She understood then the horror he'd lived through, the

horror that had shattered him. Gideon had lived his life running from a grief that haunted him at night and still threatened to consume him.

With every fiber of her being, she yearned to help Gideon come to grips with the tragedy, this man who'd shown her in a thousand ways that he was far more than a drunken trail guide. That he cared about much more than himself and his whiskey.

In that tender, devastating moment, Willa accepted with a tremulous heart that she, too, cared more than she'd thought possible. She loved Gideon Hartley.

As she stared into his handsome face, mind and heart filled with a hundred tangled emotions, Gideon's expression changed, softened. Something tender moved over him.

He brushed his thumbs across her cheeks. "Don't cry. I didn't mean to make you cry."

Was she?

She raised a hand, felt the moisture and, unused to displays of tears, tried to turn her head away. Gideon wouldn't let her.

"Willa," he whispered, gently cupping her cheek. "Dear Willa. Miracle of women, oh, noble heart, whatever shall I do about you?"

While she tried to grasp his poetry, he drew her against his chest. She rested her head over his heart, flummoxed but strangely thrilled. His broken heart thudded, strong and valiant, against her ear.

And she was almost certain he touched his lips to her hair, not once but twice.

He'd held her before, but this was different. This felt romantic, like a man embracing a woman he loved.

Foolish thoughts, perhaps. But the mood had changed from tragic to tender. And she welcomed it.

Perhaps Gideon cared for her, too.

Did she want that, considering all the darkness in him?

Yes. Yes, she did. For there was light and good in Gideon, as well.

She longed to look into his face, to raise her lips for his kiss.

She did not, for she had no experience in the ways of romance. Only a distant hope she'd all but relinquished.

Willa settled against him, wishing, yearning.

Gideon's arms tightened around her. His broad hand stroked her back in delicious circles, his fingers lingering at the nape of her neck, raising gooseflesh.

She shivered in delight, amazed to feel this way.

Gideon caused her to feel things she'd never felt before.

Womanly things that she'd considered unimportant, feelings she'd brushed aside, convinced they were not intended for a plain tomboy like her.

She wanted to remain forever in his arms, listening to his heartbeat, giving and receiving something more than comfort.

For these few moments, she could forget the frightful thoughts of the dangers they were about to face.

And maybe, just maybe, he could put aside thoughts of his tragic past.

She wanted badly to do that for him, to give him the peace he'd sought for too long in a bottle.

Slowly, Gideon untangled them and pulled away. His hands slid down to grip hers, his gaze intense but so tender that tears stung the backs of her eyelids.

"You're an extraordinary woman, Willa. I—" He stopped, shook his head. "Thank you."

Thank you seemed a cold comment, considering the way her blood still rushed and her pulse pounded.

Had she imagined the kiss against her hair?

With a bravery she didn't feel, she said, "Thank you for telling me about your family. I'm so sorry."

"As am I."

Yes, he was. Every day of his life, he punished himself for something he could not change.

"Did your father survive?"

His nostrils flared. "Nary a singed hair. Didn't even know his family was dead until he sobered up the next day."

He withdrew a little more, and Willa regretted her question.

Why did she always have to plunge in? A gentlewoman like Savannah would have sidestepped any further painful conversation, but not Willa.

Now that she'd begun again, she didn't know what else to say.

No words on earth would erase what he'd gone through.

"He could have saved them, Willa, but he was too drunk to bother. It was my eighteenth birthday and every person in my family except me was dead because of him."

His birthday. A date that no longer held joy.

"So your father is still alive?"

"I wouldn't know. I haven't seen him since the funeral."

"Why?"

"Because I hate him. I can't forgive what he did. He doesn't deserve forgiveness. Not mine. Not God's. I'm afraid if I ever see him again, I'll kill him." His words were quiet and resigned but made of iron. "He deserves to die alone with only his whiskey and his money to keep him company."

"While you're filled with hate and liquor to cover the pain? Just like him?"

Gideon jerked away.

Tension emanated from him. Tension and anger. She'd touched a nerve.

He pushed to a stand and stalked to the doorway where he leaned a hand on each side of the frame.

Willa rose and started toward him, but stopped halfway across the dirt floor.

Gideon's rough breathing mingled with the cluck of chickens in search of a roost.

A hen passed between him and the door, pecking the ground. Pecking, as she'd done, against his open wounds.

"Gideon?" she said when the silence lasted too long.

"I am *not*," he said through clenched teeth, "*anything* like my father."

Before she could respond, he walked away from the shanty to kick through the burned rubble.

Willa stood in the doorway, grieving for him, but angry with herself.

For one brief shining moment, she'd imagined how it felt to be a woman in love, a woman loved. For those few minutes in Gideon's arms, with his trail-hardened hands touching her face in tenderness, she'd believed he had feelings for her.

Clearly, he did not. Even more clearly, she was a fool for thinking romantic thoughts.

Once this journey was complete, he'd take his money and move on. He'd leave her behind, as surely as her father and all three mothers had done.

Kicking through the burned clutter in search of clues to the home's recent occupants, Gideon wrestled with Willa's accusation that he resembled his father. He didn't. He couldn't bear to be anything like the man responsible for everything terrible in his life.

Yet, that impish voice he normally buried in strong drink whispered that maybe he was.

If he looked in a mirror, would he see himself? Or Thomas Hartley?

He'd never compared his need for a few drinks to help him sleep with his father's frequent drunken rages.

They weren't the same.

Were they?

Willa scuttled around the perimeter of the ash heap to unsaddle the horses and set up camp for the night. They didn't speak. He couldn't. Not yet.

When he looked her way, she avoided his eyes. He wished he could erase the wounded expression she tried to hide but, knowing if he spoke, he'd say something he shouldn't the way he almost had in the shanty.

Willa moved him. Tormented him. Like the liquor.

He felt as low and worthless as a worm. Yet, like a man obsessed, he thought about the release waiting in a jug inside the shanty.

Had Thomas Hartley had the same thoughts? Release? From what? He was a rich man with a good family and everything a man could desire.

Shaking off the thoughts of his father and of the moonshine he would not allow himself to touch again, if only to prove he was nothing like his despised parent, he rummaged through the ashes.

Near the blackened cook stove, he discovered what he'd been looking for. A clue. Four tin cups piled together with the smoky remains of a pottery jug exactly like the ones in the shanty.

He picked up the moonshine container, shook it. Empty.

Four drinkers had gathered around this pile of ashes that had probably been a table. They'd gotten drunk enough to cause a fire.

Bangs and his companions? If so, they were close. Maybe too close.

He had to get his mind off Willa, the liquor and his family, and he had to do it fast.

While Willa carried their bedrolls inside the shanty, he left the rubble to brush down the horses and tote the saddles inside, too.

If things were easier between them, he'd have chosen another place to camp. Here, with the stench of smoke reminding him of death, he'd sleep little. A good thing, perhaps, considering that criminals might be nearby.

Willa, though, would be safe and snug inside the shanty, a thin salve to his smarting conscience.

Long into the cool, quiet night, Gideon leaned on the outside wall of the shanty, keeping watch. Willa didn't know. She thought he'd bedded down on the opposite side of the hut. He had but only until she'd fallen asleep.

Sleep would not come for him. Not even outside away from her stiff turned back and the reminders that his sharp words had cut her.

Wishing he could retract the argument, he accepted that the anger had, as Isaiah once warned, festered inside him until putrification spewed from his soul, out-of-control, shaming him and soiling others.

Including Willa, this woman who meant more to him than he could allow.

He turned his gaze heavenward to the sprinkle of diamonds surrounding a yellow slice of moonlight. Melancholy thoughts flitted through his head, so that he was mildly surprised when the words from his mouth were a poetic Psalm he'd long forgotten until now.

"'When I consider thy heavens, the work of thy fingers, the moon and the stars, which thou hast ordained; what is man, that thou art mindful of him?'"

Indeed, what was man that God paid him any attention whatsoever?

He sighed into the gray darkness where the shadows of trees and the farm's debris hulked like monsters. He had no fear of the dark, never had. Night birds and rustling leaves high in the trees overhead soothed him, gave him hope that God was awake and on duty.

He hadn't thought this much about God in years.

Because of Isaiah? Or had Willa and her interesting mix of self-reliance and faith stirred his sleeping soul as surely as she'd warmed his chilled heart?

Traveler nickered. Gideon swung his attention to the two horses tied next to the shanty. And then to the darkness beyond.

Nothing moved. All appeared calm.

He settled back against the rough wood.

For so long, he'd felt abandoned by the Almighty. In a sense, he'd blamed God for the loss of his family.

Isaiah Baker's words came back to him. God had not abandoned him. *He* had abandoned God. He'd replaced God with whiskey, a very poor substitute that had only caused him greater sorrow.

Traveler nickered again. Willa's Appaloosa responded, moving restlessly.

Gideon rolled to his feet.

He glanced inside the shack to be sure Willa still slept and then decided to patrol the clearing and stretch his legs. The horses were restless for a reason. Big cats roamed Indian Territory, and Traveler had always alerted him to their presence.

Sometimes the predators were human.

Without a campfire, the pale shaft of moonlight guided his footsteps.

After reassuring Traveler and Freckles with a soft word and

a pat, he stepped into the tree line, rifle ready, alert for activity or glowing eyes.

Though stealthy, Gideon's movements through the underbrush released the scents of sweet blackberry blossoms and pungent pine. He breathed them in, grateful to smell something besides smoke.

Cicadas pulsed around him like millions of tiny heartbeats. Lightning bugs flickered in the underbrush.

Quiet. Peaceful.

A scream ripped the night.

"Gideon!"

Willa.

His heart stopped. Fear shot shards of glass into his bloodstream.

Whirling toward the shanty, he broke into a run, heart chugging like a locomotive. Low-hanging limbs and brushy briars grabbed at him, slowed his progress.

Willa had been asleep. She'd been safe. She had a rifle at her side.

But the fear in her voice had been real.

Though he hadn't strayed far from the camp, the distance seemed miles away. His legs felt like dead logs.

He crashed into the clearing and skidded to a stop. Even in the moonlit darkness, his eyes had adjusted enough to see figures. One large male and one small female. Willa.

A gun cocked. "Don't come any closer."

He wouldn't. Not with a shadowy man holding a pistol to Willa's head.

A tremor of rage blinded him, and it took a second to ride it out, rein it in, clear his thoughts.

"Toss the rifle aside," the man commanded. "Drop the gun belt."

Reluctantly, Gideon did as he was told, but kept his attention on Willa and the gun at her temple.

"Are you all right?" His soft, easy tone belied the fury roaring through his bloodstream.

Her head moved in a barely perceptible nod. "Yes. I'm sorry."

Sorry? For what? He was the one who should be sorry. He was supposed to be guarding her.

As he lowered the gun belt to the ground, the metal barrel caught the moonlight. He planted a foot close to the weapons, hoping for a chance.

"Who are you?" he asked, though he was confident he knew. "What do you want? If it's money, I have a little. Take it and go."

The man laughed, a cold harsh bark that held no mirth at all. "Got what I want right here. Heard she wants me, too. So here I am."

Gideon's stomach twisted. "Charlie Bangs." He ground out the despised name.

"The man of her dreams." Bangs jerked Willa's arm, pulling her up to his hard mustachioed face. "Hello, darlin'. I hear you been looking for me."

"Let me go." She kicked out, part mule, and let him have a boot to the shin.

Bangs yelped.

"You little wild cat. I'll teach you." He twisted her arms behind her.

She sucked in a pained gasp.

Savage rage spurted through Gideon.

Fists tight, he started forward.

To his left, a pistol cylinder rolled, clicked. "Don't try it, Hartley. Charlie ain't alone."

Gideon stopped and shifted his attention from the man holding Willa at gunpoint to the corner of the shanty.

Two other men stood in the shadows near the horses, guns aimed at him.

"How do you know me?" Information. He needed to know who and what he was dealing with and how much they knew.

Someone hawked and spat.

A skinny pock-faced man eased from the shadows. "Everyone knows about the drunk trail guide who drowned that kid in the Arkansas. Heard you're trying to dry out. A pity. The kid'll still be dead."

Guffaws burst from the three outlaws.

Gideon steeled himself against the accusation. This was no time for self-recriminations. The past was gone. He could not fix it. Willa was here and now, and she was in trouble.

They both were.

"Let the woman go. I have money in the bank in Fort Smith. You can have it all. Take me there now, but let the woman go."

Again, the drunken laughter from Pock-face. "We don't need your money, Hartley. We're rich. Bangs stole us a silver mine. What we need is a woman."

"Shut up, Les," Bangs said.

Even in the scant light, Gideon saw Willa's eyes widen. She had to be afraid, but she didn't show it. She was smart. Like him, she hung on every word, searching for a way out of this mess.

He tried to reassure her with a slight nod, hoping she got the message, though he didn't know what to do other than bargain.

"A man never has too much money, Bangs. Leave the woman. Take me."

"Tell you what we're gonna do, Mr. Poetry Man, being

as how you're so generous and all. We're taking the woman, but we're gonna leave you a present." Bangs nudged his chin toward the shanty. "Get the moonshine, Tom."

Idaho Tom. A vicious killer.

"All of it?"

"All we can carry. Except for one jug. We'll have a little fun first." Bangs's feral teeth gleamed. "Tie Hartley to yonder tree, and so's he don't suffer too much, give him a few drinks. Then leave the jug real close to him. I've heard a wolf will gnaw off his own leg to get free. I figure Hartley will pert near do anything to get to that whiskey once he's had a taste or two."

"You go get the 'shine, Les. I'll take care of Hartley." Idaho Tom pulled a rope from one of their horses and came at Gideon.

Every instinct screamed fight. Gideon eyed his pistols. If he moved fast enough—

Bangs's voice stopped him. "Don't try anything funny, Hartley, or this gal of yours gets a kneecap removed."

"Don't listen to him, Gideon. They'll kill us anyway."

Willa's words went straight to Gideon's heart. She had more grit than a sand hill. What she didn't understand was the cruelty of men like Idaho Tom and Charlie Bangs. They'd hurt her just to enjoy her screams. Dying would come later.

Which bought them some time. Not much, but maybe enough.

"Sit down there, boy." Idaho Tom kicked at the back of Gideon's knee. "Sit."

Gideon raised both hands and complied.

Charlie Bangs snorted. "Well, ain't that sweet? Poetry Man don't want his woman hurt."

Gideon kept his eyes on Willa, telegraphing a confidence and reassurance he did not feel.

Idaho Tom squatted next to him. His breath reeked of whiskey and onions. Gideon sucked in a lungful of air, pushed out his chest and held his breath.

With a vicious little grin, the outlaw strapped Gideon to the tree, yanking the ropes tight around his chest. With sadistic pleasure, Tom looped a piggin' string around Gideon's neck.

Fighting the bonds would cut off his air and choke him to death. Slowly.

If he didn't think fast, he was as good as dead.

And Willa faced a fate worse than death.

God, if you're listening. Take care of her.

Chapter Twenty-Three

Willa's heart chugged louder than a freight train. She squirmed against the man who'd killed her father, who'd likely kill her. And whose evil friend was slowly, surely strangling Gideon.

Fury and fear mingled together with such ferocity her vision clouded.

Think, Willa. Think.

Hadn't Gideon warned her of the dangers? Hadn't everyone tried to stop her?

If Gideon died, it would be her fault.

She could not let that happen. She couldn't lose him.

But what could she do? The men had grabbed her while she slept, before she'd had a chance to go for her rifle.

She regretted the scream. If she'd let them put her on the horse as they'd planned, she'd have been gone before Gideon returned. He'd be safe.

But even more full of guilt than before.

The way she saw it, she had nothing to lose by fighting. As Bass Reeves had warned, no one was coming to their rescue.

Her life and Gideon's depended on them...and a merciful God.

Keep the outlaws talking? Pray for a chance to escape?

With both of them trussed up like turkeys, what chance would they have?

The moment Les had mentioned a silver mine, suspicion had sprouted that Finn Malone had, as the man in the dark alley had hinted, discovered more than a pocket full of gold dust. There was silver in the hills of Colorado.

Buying time, she took a chance. "Was there silver on my father's claim? Is that what Les meant?"

Bangs tensed. "Shut up, girlie. Sticking your nose where it don't belong can get you hurt. Like it did your pa."

Anger fought with fear. "You killed him."

Bangs shrugged, as if her papa had been nothing but a bug to stomp. "Had to."

"Why? He was a good man, kind enough to share his campfire, but you stole what he'd worked for. Didn't you? You low-down, dirty—"

A thick, filthy, whiskey-soaked hand clamped over her mouth. Willa sank her teeth into his flesh.

Bangs spun her sideways and slapped her. She fell.

Gideon shouted something. She heard a grunt, saw him fighting against the ropes, saw Idaho Tom slam a gun butt against his temple. Once. Twice.

"Stop! Don't hit him. Stop!"

Her plea came too late. Gideon slumped to one side, dark liquid trickling from his head.

Bangs loomed above her, dark and menacing. She crab-crawled backward, seeking escape.

The outlaw aimed a gun at her face. "Behave yourself now,

girlie, lessen you want your beau to die before he's had something to ease the pain."

Willa stilled. Her cheek stung from the slap. Her shoulder throbbed. She'd hit something on the way down.

Hoping Bangs didn't notice, she slid her hand behind her, searching for the object, hoping for a weapon.

Just as her fingers made contact with a sharp stone, Bangs grabbed her elbows and forced her to sit up.

Hope drained away. Her knees went weak.

"Reckon that took a little feistiness out of you." He tied her hands behind her back. "See, boys, you got to knock 'em around a little, let 'em know who's boss."

He ran a dirty finger down her cheek. "I like my women fancier than you, but you'll do. You got some sass in you. Makes things funner."

He grinned. Below the handlebar mustache, a bottom tooth was missing. She hoped it had given him lots of pain.

The pock-faced Les exited the shanty, dragging the trunk neither she nor Gideon had bothered to open. It was full of moonshine jugs.

He uncorked a bottle, took a swig and passed the jug around.

"Want a drink, girlie?" Bangs sat down next to her on the ground, too close, his breath hot and rank against the side of her face.

"No." She turned her head away.

He chortled. "Your sweetheart does. Hold his head, Tom, so Les can give him a swig. I reckon he's real thirsty by now."

"Stop!" Willa tried to stand. Bangs yanked her backward. She fell onto her side. "He's unconscious. You'll drown him."

"He's gonna be dead anyway." Bangs gestured with his gun. "Go ahead, Les. Let's hear him gurgle."

Gideon's awareness returned, but he kept his eyes closed, listening. His head throbbed. His thoughts were fuzzy. He wanted to shake the cobwebs out of his brain, but some instinct warned him to remain still, to pretend to be unconscious.

He heard the voices and remembered. Bangs and his friends had ambushed them. They had Willa.

He listened harder, heard her talking, bargaining with Bangs. She was alive and seemed unhurt. So far.

She had to remain that way, no matter what it cost him.

A rough hand grabbed his hair and wrenched his head back against the rough tree trunk.

"Wake up, sleeping beauty." With a drunken chortle, someone else shoved a bottle against his mouth.

Fiery liquid burned his nose and pooled in his mouth. He let it trickle out, fighting not to strangle. The piggin' string stretched tight against his windpipe.

A hand grabbed his cheeks and squeezed, forcing the alcohol between his lips.

He coughed, sputtered, blew the whiskey back on the men. One of them slammed his head against the tree trunk. He let his head loll, feigning unconsciousness.

"Come on, Charlie," Les whined. "We're wasting good whiskey. Let's take the woman and get back to the hideout before the sun comes up and someone sees us with her."

"What about Hartley?" Idaho Tom kicked Gideon's side. His breath whooshed out.

"I'll take care of him." Bangs's cold tone prickled the hair on Gideon's neck. "Get the woman on her horse and get ready to ride."

"What if he comes to?" Les worried. "Ain't you skeered he'll follow us?"

The ugly laugh came again. "He ain't going nowhere."

Gideon tensed. If they took Willa, he could track them. He had to stay alive.

He heard the explosion. Felt the burn. The last thing he heard was Willa screaming his name.

★ ★ ★

She would not break down. Hysterics served no purpose. Crying would not save Gideon. It would only display weakness.

These outlaws were like wild animals, alert to any sign of vulnerability.

Yet, Willa hurt in ways she couldn't express. Physical, emotional. Her world had shattered with the report from Charlie Bang's pistol.

He'd shot Gideon. Just as he'd shot Papa.

Was Gideon dead, too?

She did not think she could bear it if he was.

Willa forced away the terrible image and focused on the here and now.

She wasn't certain where she was. They'd ridden for miles into the wilderness, much of it uphill, and stopped somewhere in the mountains in a dugout nestled beneath a cliff and hidden in underbrush.

She stared around the space, taking in details, committing everything she could to memory, thinking, always thinking.

Someone had gone to great lengths to build a cozy hideout. The front portion, built of weathered wood and sod, blended into the landscape, while the back space pushed inside a dark cave. The center was braced with rough-hewn logs and crammed with a table, chairs and supplies. A gang could hole up in this place for weeks.

The thought of being here for weeks with these men sent fear spearing through her.

Bound hand and foot, there was little she could do about it. She was at their mercy...and they had none.

She pressed as deep into the shadows as she could, though Bangs seemed intent on settling too close.

From atop the rickety table, a rusty kerosene lantern cast

long shadows, filling the space with harsh fumes. Her eyes stung. She longed to be back on the horse in the fresh air.

Everything about this hideout stank.

The trash of former occupants littered the floor along with the gang's saddlebags and jugs of whiskey. Near a sooty black spot in one corner were a pan and a blue-speckled coffeepot.

Idaho Tom tossed two of Gideon's books at her feet.

She jumped, startled.

"Something to remember him by." His grin was as evil as Lucifer himself. "You can read us some of his favorite poems."

Willa stifled the cry that threatened to erupt from the depths of her soul. They'd taken Gideon's books. Did that mean...?

Lips pressed tight, she tried not to react. Tom seemed to enjoy terrorizing her.

The ride from the burned farm to this dugout had been rough. The horses had strained and stumbled over the rocky terrain.

During the ride, she'd looked for the trail signs Gideon had taught her, committing to memory how Bangs had led her to this place so she could find her way out. With only the moon as light, she hadn't seen enough.

If she somehow managed to escape, she could wander lost and alone in this massive wilderness forever.

Hands tied to the saddle horn, she'd managed only to snag and bend a few branches with her extended boot. Which mattered little. No one would come looking for her.

They'd shot Gideon. Even if he'd survived, he was injured and tied to a tree.

And likely drunk from all the whiskey Idaho Tom had dumped down his throat.

She shuddered. He'd be helpless against wild animals.

Maybe the bullet had been a mercy.

"You taking her with us to Colorado?" The skinny pock-faced Les lounged against one rock-and-sod wall, a jug between his knees, his long legs stretched out.

Idaho Tom came and went from the tiny dwelling, apparently on guard duty. He'd been the one to drag her off the Appaloosa and dump her like a sack of flour inside the cave. He didn't say much, but his eyes were the emptiest she'd ever seen.

He scared her even more than Bangs did.

Her father's killer looped a finger through his jug, propped it on his shoulder and swigged long and deep.

As he backhanded his mouth, he stared at Willa.

She fought down a shiver.

"Don't know. Maybe. Depends on how much trouble she is. Might leave her for the wolves like we did that rummy guide of hers." He snorted, slapped his knee, though his aim was off and he smacked the filthy floor. "Bet he's not spouting fancy words now."

Willa's eyes fell shut. She forced them open.

Think. Don't mourn. Do that later. Think.

"Seems a shame to leave her to the wolves, considering how her pa made us rich." Les laughed. "Stupid Mick."

Bangs growled. "That claim is mine, Les. I'm the one who shot him. I'm rich. You're not."

Pock-face sat up straighter, weaving. "I earned my share, same as you."

Bangs smirked. "We'll see."

The skinny outlaw slumped against the wall, glaring as he continued to drink in sullen silence. Dirt and dried grass from the dugout walls sifted onto him. He didn't even notice.

Idaho Tom stumbled through the narrow doorway. "All clear. Let's get some shut-eye."

His cold gaze moved from Charlie Bangs, who was drunker by the minute, to Willa, who'd scooted as far into a dark corner as she could. Bangs lolled against her side, sniffing at her, making disgusting noises that turned her stomach.

Idaho Tom walked close to them, crouched down and tipped up her chin. "Pretty thing."

The voice, the smell. She recognized him now. Idaho Tom had been the man in the alley. The man who'd warned her not to pursue her father's death.

Why hadn't she listened?

She refused to meet his eyes, afraid of the evil she'd find there. She held her breath, praying for him to leave her alone.

Bangs roused himself enough to kick the other man's boot. "Mine."

"You're too drunk to appreciate her."

"So are you. She ain't going nowhere."

Idaho Tom's lascivious gaze roamed over her. He wobbled, barely upright.

"Glad we finally got one. Tired of Pierce taking all the merchandise."

Pierce? Theodore Pierce? But that didn't make any sense. How would these outlaws know Sweet Clover's banker?

Mind racing, certain she must have misunderstood, she prayed for Idaho Tom to leave her be.

After a long moment, the drunk outlaw staggered away, taking a jug to sit near the entrance where he'd placed his saddle in case of a quick exit. With an inebriated sigh, he slumped against the saddle and chugged the whiskey.

Willa's breath oozed out. She never thought she'd appreciate drunkenness. Tonight, she did.

Bangs raised his bottle for another drink. The liquid slid down his chin and onto his shirt. The jug tumbled from his hand, spilling the moonshine across the floor. The pungent smell mixed with the man's stench.

His heavy body sagged against her, his breath slow, long and deep. He was too drunk to drink anymore.

Across the room, Les was already passed out, mouth open, snoring.

That left only Idaho Tom. He scared her the most.

With her hands and feet tied, she couldn't get to her knife or the derringer.

She slid a look toward the lantern, gauging the distance.

Closing her eyes, she feigned sleep. She could hear the glug-glug each time Tom raised the jug.

Then she waited.

The abundance of moonshine must have been the reason the men had returned to the farm. From their drunken conversations, she'd learned they were celebrating a successful robbery, which provided the money to travel in style to Colorado.

Had Papa really owned a silver claim?

Long moments passed. Moments in which she prayed for Gideon, prayed for herself. Prayed for the courage to do the only thing she could think of.

She could literally die trying. But she would not die without a fight.

When at last she heard the clink of Tom's pottery jug against the rocky floor, she opened her eyes a slit.

The hawk-nosed Idaho Tom was out. Like Bangs, his jug was tipped onto the side, spilling his precious moonshine onto the piles of filth and trash.

Willa waited a few more minutes. Drunken snores and heavy breathing convinced her that the time had come.

Her hands and ankles fettered, she gently, slowly eased away from Charlie Bangs, using her knees to shift him to the floor and onto the saddle blanket he'd tossed there for her.

He grumbled once. His eyes flew open.

Willa froze and waited.

He smacked his lips, mumbled something. The heavy lids dropped shut.

She waited again, letting sleep and liquor take him deeper.

Once she was confident the men were all unconscious, Willa began the slow, arduous process of scooting an inch at a time toward the lantern.

One inch. Then stop to listen and look. Another inch. Tom muttered something. She froze. He flopped over onto his side, went still again.

Inch by inch, she moved closer.

She had one chance before the noise woke them.

The table leg was inches away.

Lying on her back, she drew her knees up and kicked with all her strength.

The table scraped, wobbled, tilted.

The lantern crashed onto the floor. Kerosene and fire exploded. Trash ignited. Flames licked across the debris, hungry for the spilled whiskey.

In seconds, smoke and fire saturated the small space.

Willa coughed, choked, nose filled with smoke. With her hands bound behind her, she couldn't even protect her face.

Idaho Tom leaped to his feet.

"Fire!" he screamed, shaking his burning pants leg in a macabre dance. "Get out!"

Flames blocked the way between him and his companions.

Idaho Tom didn't hesitate. Not once.

He left them.

Willa's skirt ignited. To smother the flames, she rolled to one side and tried not to think of the coming agony as she shoved her bound wrists into the inferno.

Gideon heard the screams.

Hair prickled on the back of his neck.

A figure burst from the entrance of the robber's hidey-hole and raced toward the horses corralled below the rocks, his clothes on fire.

Clothes on fire. Like Tad.

Smoke belched out of the cave. Grass and shrubs combusted.

Horror washed through Gideon. Memories swamped him. He smelled burning flesh. Heard the screams. His brother's terror ricocheted inside him, echoing off the walls of his heart, his soul.

Not Tad. Willa.

Willa was in there.

He pressed a hand to his throbbing, sticky shoulder, then scrambled up the rocks like a mountain goat to the cleverly hidden cliffside dugout. His legs trembled with the effort.

Sweat poured from his forehead. Or was that blood? In the dark, he couldn't tell.

If not for Traveler and Willa's broken branches, he'd never have found his way here. Clever Willa. Smart Willa. She'd led him to her.

The drunken outlaws had made one crucial mistake. They hadn't made sure he was dead.

He was close, though.

His head swam, his eyes blurred.

Darkness threatened. He fought it. Prayed. Like Samson in the Old Testament, he pled for strength one last time.

Hurry. Hurry.

He clenched his jaw against the knife-like pain in his shoulder.

Left arm nearly useless, his right arm trembling, he pulled himself up the last outcropping. Smoke and heat belched from the dugout. Flames licked up the hillside.

A second man stumbled out. Smoke circled him. He stumbled, fell, rose again to race to the horses below.

That made two. Where was the third? Where was Willa?

A dread worse than death overtook him. Willa was in there. The place was on fire.

Was he too late?

He swayed. Sprinkles of gray floated in front of his eyes.

His family was in there. Tad. Emily. Mother.

He shook confusion from his brain. Not his family. Willa. History would not repeat itself. Even if it cost him his life.

Warm, sticky liquid clouded his vision. He brushed it away with his good hand and crawled over rocks and shrubs toward the opening. The smell of smoke and kerosene made it easy to find.

"Willa!"

God, please save her. Help me find her. Don't let me fail again.

A faint voice, maybe his imagination, beckoned from the inferno. "Gideon? Gideon?"

Aware he was entering hell, he threw his damaged arm over his nose and rushed inside.

Chapter Twenty-Four

Willa crawled through the darkness, blinded by the black smoke. Her eyes burned, watered.

Her wrists burned even more, but her hands were free, the ropes burned away in the flames.

She fumbled for the bindings at her ankles, but her hands hurt too much.

She coughed. Each breath hurt more and did less to fill her lungs. Time was running out.

Using her knees and bound feet to push herself, she continued the worm-like crawl in pitch-black darkness toward what she hoped was the entrance.

Fire chased her, a dragon blowing his breath at her legs, licking at her skirt.

Exhausted and fighting for air, she paused, rested her cheek against the floor. Her breath came short. Lungs exploding. Couldn't breathe. Too much smoke.

She closed her eyes, waiting for death. Tears leaked from the edges.

Suddenly, strong arms, trembling arms, scooped her up, began to run. She had no time to reason out the identity of her rescuer. Didn't matter. She was dying.

Her head swam. Blackness threatened to overtake her.

Just as she was going under, cool, clean air swept over her face. She sucked in a breath, coughed, dragged in another breath.

Air, clean, precious air.

She almost wept from the pleasure of it.

"Willa. Willa."

Gideon, his voice agonized, crushed her to his chest. His heart thundered, clattering like a runaway train over loose railroad ties.

Oh, beautiful heartbeat.

Gideon was alive! *Thank God. Thank God.*

He stumbled and went down on the uneven boulders, cradling her in his lap as carefully and tenderly as a baby in his arms. Brushy limbs scratched at her. She winced and protectively drew her hands close to her body.

"Willa." He repeated her name over and over as if he couldn't say it enough. "My valiant, precious jewel. Joy of my desiring. Willa, Willa."

Gideon continued to ramble, murmuring soft words and snatches of beautiful poetry that went straight to Willa's heart.

"You're alive," Willa managed, her throat achingly raw, voice raspy.

Smoky tears wept from her stinging eyes.

In spite of his injuries, Gideon had somehow found her. He'd faced his horror of fire. He was here. He was alive.

Though the pain in her hands was excruciating, she touched his face, felt for the head wound. "Gideon, they shot you. You're hurt."

As if a bullet was nothing, he shook her off. Her hand fell to his chest. She felt the stickiness, knew it was blood.

"Oh, Gideon."

"I thought I'd lost you. I thought—" He brushed a knuckle down her cheek, his tender touch shaky. "Did they hurt you? Are you hurt? I'll tear their throats out if they hurt you."

His heart pounded. A weak, rapid pounding beneath her palm.

She shook her head. "They were too drunk to—"

Realization struck her with a force that made her forget Gideon's heady, touching words. Almost.

Two of the men had escaped the fire before her. Bangs was still inside. Passed out cold from the moonshine and smoke.

Let him die.

The ugly words flashed like lightning in her head.

He deserved to die. He'd killed Papa.

Maybe he was dead already. It wouldn't be her fault or her doing.

Wouldn't it? She'd kicked over the lantern. She'd set the blaze in the tinderbox of a dwelling.

The inward battle lasted only a second. She wanted justice. Justice belonged to the law.

Vengeance belonged to God.

Willa pulled away from the loving solace of Gideon's embrace and struggled to her feet. Her lungs ached. Her wrists and palms screamed.

She'd deal with those later.

"Bangs," she rasped. "He's still inside."

A weary sigh escaped Gideon. "And you mean to save him."

Even in the scarce ribbon of moonlight, she saw the awful, seeping wound on his temple. Saw the damage that Bangs and Idaho had done.

Breathing labored, Gideon tried to stand with her. His legs

gave way. With a grunt of determination, he braced against the rocks and rose.

He wobbled, then straightened, jaw tight and determined.

He was badly injured. Probably worse than he let on. Far worse than she was. The outlaws had beat him, choked him, shot him.

Gideon, this man she loved, should be dead. Yet, he'd tracked her. He'd pulled her from the inferno.

Now, his injuries were catching up with him fast.

"I have to try, Gideon. If I don't, I'm no better than him. You're wounded. You stay here."

She suspected his answer before he spoke.

With a grim look on his handsome, battered face, he motioned toward the belching cave. "Let's do this."

With Charlie Bangs slung over his saddle and tied securely to the horse and pommel, Gideon led the riders through the growing daylight toward a stream a half hour's ride through the mountain wilderness.

He was in rough shape, barely hanging on, but he grit his teeth and rode, resolved to get as far away from the hideout as possible before he gave in.

He knew the area, and now that the pink of morning pushed back the darkness, he wanted to move as fast as possible. Which wouldn't be all that fast given his condition and the volatile prisoner wrapped and trussed to his horse and saddle like a side of pork.

Bangs, stinking like smoke, cursed and ranted between raspy coughs.

"I'll kill you, Hartley. Shoulda finished you off last night."

He nearly had. Still might.

"If you had, you'd be dead," Willa told him, her tone cold. "I couldn't pull you out of the fire by myself."

Gideon turned his attention to her. His courageous warrior woman.

Her quick thinking and trail marks had given him the chance to track her to the cave.

What if he hadn't arrived in time?

He knew the answer.

By God's grace, he'd made it. He'd saved her from the flaming dugout. In a different manner, she'd saved him. From the liquor. From his darkly troubled thoughts. From the men who'd tried to kill them both.

They seemed to have a habit of rescuing each other.

A man could get used to having a woman like Willa in his camp.

Truth was he'd grown accustomed to the little brown wren with an eagle's heart.

More than accustomed. With startling clarity, given his physical condition and the rantings of a mad desperado, his brain sorted through the emotions and settled on one.

As soon as he did, it blew away like dry leaves in a whirlwind and left him hollow.

He was not, it seemed, in his right mind, after all.

Bangs's curse ripped the air again. "Just you wait 'til nightfall. Les and Idaho will hunt you down like a dog. Idaho's good with a knife. Likes to use it. Carves his initials in your hide."

Willa glared at the man as if to silence him. But like Gideon, she was also worried about the other two outlaws.

If Bangs didn't shut up, Willa might change her mind and shoot him.

Gideon allowed a sparse little smile at the prospect, though he knew she wouldn't. A solid core of integrity drove Willa. Her faith, he supposed, drove her to do the right thing, even when it wasn't easy.

"You're bleeding again, Poetry Man," Bangs sneered. "I hope you die."

He knew it. Knew he was quickly moving toward real trouble from the injuries.

Although he'd washed out the gunshot with moonshine the robbers had left behind and stuffed his bandanna in the empty bullet hole—a loathsome task—the wound bled from both sides of his shoulder.

More blood seeped into his eyes. He swiped at it with his equally bloodied shirtsleeve. His head pounded, but the bullet wound pained him something fierce, kept his teeth on edge.

Bangs ripped out another blast of vitriol.

Gideon suffered a few regrets about braving the smoke and flames to drag Bangs's sorry carcass to safety.

"'The wicked are like the tossing sea when it cannot rest,'" he quoted, "'whose waters cast up mire and dirt.'"

Willa snickered, giddy with exhaustion and relief.

Relief for him wouldn't come until Bangs was locked in Judge Parker's dungeon of a jail and Willa was out of this lawless land.

The threat of Bangs's friends hung over their heads like Judge Parker's best hemp noose.

Gideon's great consolation lay in the knowledge that there was little loyalty among murderers. Idaho Tom and his skinny compatriot had probably hightailed it in the other direction.

Though the farther he and Willa rode today, the safer Gideon would feel.

He felt Willa's gaze on him as she guided Freckles close to Traveler. "We need to stop and see to your injuries."

Sticky blood congealed on the skin under his shirt. "Soon."

He didn't want her—or Bangs—to know how weak he was.

Her hands concerned him more.

Without a word about her own pain, she'd gritted her teeth

and done what was necessary to help him drag an unconscious Bangs from the cave. If he'd known she was hurt, he would have stopped her.

Afterward, when she'd poured the contents of her canteen carefully over the blistered skin, he'd heard her sharp hiss.

They were both in rough shape, but they were alive. Bangs was captured. Willa would soon be able to repay her father's bank loan and secure a home for her sisters the way she'd dreamed.

He wanted that for her.

If they made it alive to Fort Smith.

With their injuries and a prisoner along, the city was another two days' ride, another two nights under the stars, in the wilds, where one of them would have to guard Charlie Bangs.

More days for him to remain vigilant, to provide safe passage to this woman whose strength and character moved him to words best kept tucked under his heart.

Soon, their hard, dangerous journey would be over. Willa would return to Sweet Clover, to her sisters.

He should have been pleased to see the end so near.

He wasn't.

He tried to rotate his shoulder. A lightning bolt of pain stabbed upward into his jaw. His head pounded harder.

Bangs had aimed for his heart. In his drunkenness, he'd hit the shoulder, a blessing, of sorts, but Gideon had lost a lot of blood.

The possibility of infection nagged him.

With every jounce of the horse, his shirt grew wetter, stickier.

He set his back jaw.

The heat and humidity rising from the forest floor made his vision blur.

Squinting, he tried to read the trail signs. Where was the stream?

The trees and brush wavered. He blinked, lifting his chin toward the bluffs. Where was Chimney Rock, the chimney-shaped structure guides used as a marker?

Was he lost?

He'd never been lost. Not once.

He started to shake his head, but the action made him dizzy. He couldn't quite corral his thoughts.

They'd have to stop soon.

"Gideon, are you all right?"

Willa's voice came from far away. He lifted a hand to wave off her concern…and tumbled from his horse.

Willa did what she had to do. Keeping her rifle at the ready, and though it hurt her scorched hands, she lashed the already bound Bangs to a tree and made camp right where Gideon landed.

Regardless of his toughness, her guide needed rest and tending.

And he called her obstinate.

"Mule-headed man," she muttered under her breath as she cradled his bloodied head in her lap and trickled water into his mouth.

He turned his face away. "I'm fine."

She snorted, though the sound held no amusement. Tenderness just about choked her. "I'm Queen Victoria."

One side of that handsome scruff-rimmed mouth tipped up. "Yes, you are."

"Drink this. All of it. Mercy says a patient needs lots of water after a bleeding."

Struggling to sit up, he took the canteen and gulped most of the contents. "Let's get moving."

"You need rest. We both do. The horses, too. We're camping for the night. Let me see that shoulder."

Letting her take charge, he sank back to the ground, weak as blue John milk and about the same color, his normally tanned skin faded. His eyes drifted closed.

With a grunt, his lips moved. "It could use a little cleaning."

A little? In the daylight, she saw the blood saturating the front of his shirt and leather vest. The wound on his head wasn't much better.

No wonder he'd passed out.

Briskly, she removed his vest and uncovered his shoulder, willing herself not to gag.

"Blood," she said, keeping up the spunk so she didn't join him in a dead faint, "is intended to remain on the inside."

He grunted again. "I'll keep that in mind next time someone shoots me."

"You do that." Stomach threatening, she gently, slowly removed the saturated bandanna and dabbed at the gaping hole.

Oh, my.

Bile rose in the back of her mouth.

She drew in a sharp breath. The coppery scent of blood spun through her senses.

Gideon's eyes flickered open. He squinted. She must have been as pale as sun-bleached sheets because he asked, "Are you going to faint?"

She harrumphed, all bravado and determination. "I am not given to histrionics."

"Says the woman who nearly lost her breakfast in the saloon."

He would have to remind her of that. She did so hate the smell of blood. But he goaded her, she knew, to help her through this moment.

"I do not faint," she said again, this time with emphasis.

"Your man's gonna die," Charlie Bangs shouted, straining against the ropes. "He's gonna die, girlie. Then it will just be me and you."

She and Gideon exchanged glances. Though her pulse clattered, she gave Gideon her sternest no-nonsense order. "You will not die. Do you hear me?"

Gideon's pale lips curved. "I have begun to think living is most beneficial to my health."

Bolstered by his efforts to tease, Willa rummaged in the medicine kit. She didn't need the written instructions to know which herbs would stop blood from oozing out of Gideon and fend off infection.

She set out the supplies, sent up a heartfelt prayer and said, "This will hurt."

He took a breath. "Do it."

She hesitated. "I have never wished so much for a bottle of whiskey."

"Nor have I."

She held the powdery wad of yarrow leaves an inch from the seeping wound, dreading what she had to do. "Talk to me. Recite a poem. Quote Shakespeare. Anything."

They locked eyes. He knew what she was doing.

"A poem the lady wishes," he murmured. "So be it. 'I met a lady in the meads, full beautiful—a faery's child.'"

Willa's fingers trembled. She hated this. Hated hurting him. Hated the smell of blood. Especially his.

She looked from the wound to Gideon.

"'Her hair was long,'" he said quietly, "'her foot was light, and her eyes were wild.'" So softly his lips hardly moved, he said, "Did you know your eyes are wild, Willa?"

With a start, she realized the poem was about her.

She shoved the medicine into the bullet hole.

Gideon's head went back, his teeth bared.

"Wild, indeed," he groaned.

Quickly, she bandaged the wound and repeated the less arduous process on his head wound.

When she'd finished, she sat back on her boot heels and took a deep breath. She shook all over. Her stomach refused to settle.

She wanted desperately to run into the woods and retch.

She did not.

If he could endure the agonizing treatment, she could keep her stomach under control.

"Does your head hurt?" She touched a fingertip to his bloodied hair.

Eyes closed, he leaned against a tree trunk, a reminder to her of how he'd gotten injured in the first place.

"Only when I think."

"Oh, Gideon. What shall I do with you?"

"I was thinking the same thing about you."

Her heart fluttered, preparing to take wing and fly right out of her chest.

"Get some rest," she said, not knowing what else to say. The man was delirious from loss of blood. "Try to sleep. I'll rustle up some grub and keep an eye on him."

She jerked her thumb toward Charlie Bangs who spewed a never-ending supply of hatred.

Gideon's good hand came up to cup her face. Blue eyes tender, he said softly, "I know that wasn't easy for you. You're a special lady."

Her pulse bumped up a notch. How she longed to be his someone special, but she suspected the words were only meant as a thank-you.

Briskly, pragmatic as always and afraid to believe he meant more than gratitude, she said, "Just doing what I had to."

Feeling flummoxed and sad and happy all at once, Willa stood, turning her back to move away.

Gideon caught the scorched, blackened hem of her skirt.

Willa stopped, waiting, her heart tethered to the wounded man by the merest touch of his hand to her garment.

"Willa," Gideon barely murmured, so that he seemed to be talking to himself. "Never in my life have I met anyone like you. If I were a different man—"

She held her breath, hoping, wishing, dreaming.

When he didn't say more, she shifted, peering over her shoulder.

Gideon's eyes were closed. His breathing slowed and his body relaxed.

He'd fallen asleep.

She'd never know what he was about to say.

Charlie Bangs laughed his ugly laugh.

Fort Smith bustled with activity. Steamboats powered up and down the wide silvery water of the Arkansas River, puffing their black steam into a gray, overcast sky.

Wagons filled with goods and people, riders and horses, and women in fancy dresses or prairie bonnets bustled about the crowded streets. A stagecoach rumbled into town.

Taking in the busy sights, Willa breathed deeply for the first time in days. They'd taken longer to get here than either she or Gideon liked, but it couldn't have been helped. Gideon needed rest.

For the past three fretful nights while he regained enough strength to travel, they'd watched over the evil, vitriolic outlaw. His malice was a living thing, writhing in the darkness, eager to devour them.

Bangs frightened her. Still did. How had her merry-hearted father ever come to trust such a man?

But they were here, in Fort Smith. The journey would soon be over.

She slid a glance toward Gideon, riding at her side, still pale and weak and in need of a doctor. His arm held protectively in the sling she'd made for him from his bloody shirt, he sat tall in the saddle, sheer force of will holding him there. The strain around his eyes and mouth betrayed his discomfort.

Even in his weakened state, he had insisted on taking his turn at night watching over Bangs so she could sleep.

Knowing he would protect them with his life, she'd slept like the dead, a thought that made her shudder.

He, a trail guide with a drunken reputation, a man who'd told her not to depend on him, had proven himself to be a man to trust.

After his sweet words the night of the fire and the tender moments when she'd dressed his wounds, she believed he felt something for her other than friendship.

She wouldn't ask, of course. She was not fond of humiliation.

They'd reached Fort Smith with Bangs alive, and that was the only thing she would allow to matter.

Gideon could, at last, see a doctor for the gunshot wound. Although she'd daily done her best to clean and medicate the wounds, she worried about infection. If gangrene set in, he'd lose the arm...or die.

Last night, when she'd come at him with the last bit of Mercy's healing salve, he'd shrugged her away, insisting she use the medicine on her blistered wrists.

If she hadn't loved him before, she'd have fallen hard during these last three difficult days.

"How are the hands?" he asked for the tenth time.

She held the reins with her fingertips, avoiding the harsh

rasp of leather against her blistered skin. "Stop fretting. A few blisters never killed anyone."

On the other hand, a gunshot wound had killed plenty.

They rode through the gates surrounding the fort and across the grounds to the redbrick courthouse and jail.

Inside, they turned Charlie Bangs over to a tin-starred marshal. Not unexpectedly, the outlaw shot his final volley of contempt.

With a defiant sneer she'd long remember, Bangs mocked, "Your old man died squealing like a pig."

Gideon grabbed his shirt collar and jerked him to his toes. "So will you." He thrust Bangs toward the lawman. "He's all yours. Make the noose tight."

Then, as cool as if the incident hadn't occurred, Gideon pivoted away and offered Willa his elbow. "My lady, I believe you have a reward to collect."

Chapter Twenty-Five

Willa locked the hotel room door, pushed a chair against it and spread her share of the reward money on the sumptuous four-poster feather bed. Five hundred dollars. She could scarce believe it. Just as she could scarce believe the luxury of this fancy hotel Gideon had secured.

Fancy in ways she'd never seen in her life. Rose-print wallpaper, a gold horsehair chair with curving arms, long gold-fringed curtains and an elegant oak wardrobe on polished heart-pine floors fairly took her breath away.

And a bathtub! Right there in the bedroom.

At a tap from the hallway, she scooped the money into a pile and stashed it under the mattress.

"Yes?" She opened the door a crack.

A dark-haired woman in a lacy maid's cap and apron peered at her with friendly eyes.

"Hot water for your bath, miss. Mr. Hartley ordered it sent up."

"He did?" Another reason to love him.

The man had no idea how wonderful a hot bath sounded after days on the trail.

Or perhaps he did.

She opened the door wider and let the white-aproned maid inside. She was followed by a stout, toothsome youth toting two buckets of steaming water, which he dumped into the curved claw-footed tub.

She knew some folks had a bathtub in their homes, but she'd never seen one. For the Malone sisters, a bath was a galvanized washtub dragged from outside and temporarily placed next to the stove.

"Do you need help, miss?" the woman asked. "Mr. Hartley mentioned your burns. He sent this packet from the doctor."

Willa took the brown-paper-wrapped bundle, her lips pressed together while her heart ballooned in her chest, as warm as the bath water. He'd thought of her. Again.

The silly notion that he might be courting her came and went. Silly, indeed.

They'd endured an arduous journey together. He was a kind man. She'd known that before they left Sweet Clover, though he tried to hide his kindness behind off-hand random poems and sarcasm.

"Thank you. I'll manage."

When the servants left, she luxuriated in the steam and scrubbed her hair with the fragrant soap.

The bath felt so good she remained until the water cooled and her fingers pruned, letting her mind wander through the weeks on the trail. If her thoughts lingered on her trail guide for too long, she let them.

She, who'd long since blocked any romantic dreams in exchange for scratching out a life for her sisters, had allowed herself to fall in love.

When she began to chill, she got out and dressed, wrinkled

toes curled into the plush hotel rug, wishing she had something fresh and clean to wear.

She brushed at her extra skirt, a garment that had seen many days on the trail. It, too, needed washing. Dust and grass filtered to the fancy patterned rug. The heavy broadcloth was only mildly cleaner than her remaining garment, the scorched riding skirt stained with Gideon's blood.

She removed the bloodied clothing from her saddlebags and pushed them into the bath water.

Someone rapped on the door.

Holding a towel to her heavy dripping hair, Willa called, "Who is it?"

"Me." That's all she needed, one word, to recognize his voice.

She opened the door.

Gideon stood before her, clean, well-dressed and too handsome for words, almost a stranger. Gone was the trail-weary guide, the bloodied companion, replaced by the suave gambler she'd met long ago. A gambler who caused butterflies to dance in her stomach.

She felt awkward in his company, as if she hadn't spent weeks alone in his company. As if they were strangers.

"You shaved." It was a silly thing to say, when her heart was full of so much more.

But oh, he looked handsome.

Eyes a twinkle, mouth curved in that mocking way of his, he stroked his jaw and chin between finger and thumb. "I hardly recognized myself."

"What did the doctor say?"

As if he wasn't breathtaking enough, a pristine white sling draped from his neck to his wrist, giving him a roguish appearance.

She was practical Willa in her dusty brown riding skirt,

and he was the man about town whom women followed with their eyes.

No one had ever followed her with their eyes.

"He claims I must have had a good doctor on the trail for he declared me well enough to escort a certain lady to dinner."

While she'd luxuriated in the bath, he'd been busy. From somewhere, he'd procured a clean white shirt and black trousers. His boots were as shiny as a pocket watch in a sunbeam and his black hat had been steamed clean.

Feeling like a beggar on the side of the road in her ordinary, dusty, trail-worn clothes, she shook her head.

"Your shoulder. You should rest." Her pulse clattered in her ears. Clattered like carriage wheels on a wooden bridge. "We both should."

His eyes narrowed slightly, blue slits of light that heard more than she said.

"You haven't eaten since this morning."

The last of the beans and bacon.

"I'll eat later." She waved a restless, guilty hand toward the room. "I prefer to rest."

She preferred no such thing.

Something flickered through Gideon's expression before he straightened to his full height.

Receding behind extreme courtesy, he touched the brim of his hat. "As you please."

As he walked away, his gleaming boots tapping lightly against the plank floor, Willa had the ridiculous notion that she'd hurt his feelings.

She hadn't. A man like Gideon had no need of a woman like her. He would not long be without companionship. Likely, a beautiful, stylish woman in a gorgeous dress, her hair swept up with sparkling combs, had already cast her eye upon the handsome tracker.

Gideon would smile and flirt in his southern way, spouting pretty poetry to make the beauty blush. She'd wave a dainty lace-edged fan and laugh into his eyes.

The problem with imagination was that Willa saw herself as that woman. Yet, she was neither beautiful nor feminine, and the finest dress she'd ever worn was too long and belonged to her sister back in Sweet Clover. All she had was a brown dusty skirt, a smoke-scented blouse, and her father's scuffed and worn boots.

No man wanted to be seen with a woman like her.

Going to the window, she threw up the sash to let the pleasant breeze flow in and to gaze out in wonder at the teeming city. Anything to take her mind off Gideon.

The hotel was in the heart of the city. A train whistle signaled. Steamboat horns bellowed. A sea of humanity bustled on the streets, in and out of storefronts, calling out to one another. Carriages jaunted past. A barking dog raced along behind one. Somewhere, a hammer clanged against metal.

Across the alleyway, piano music drifted upward from a public house, tinny and off tune.

Again, her imagination, as fertile as the Irish Sea, focused on Gideon. Did he dine alone? Had he heard the music of the saloon, calling to him like a siren's song?

Alone, perhaps lonely, was he tempted to drift across the street for company and refreshment?

Gripping the windowsill, she fought the urge to race down the stairs and stop him.

His business. Their deal was complete. He had his share of the reward and she had hers.

But a small, sneaky voice said inside her head, they still had to make the journey home.

She did not want an inebriated companion. Not now nor on the trip back to Sweet Clover.

Going to the tall cheval mirror, its mahogany frame glossy with beeswax, she brushed out her damp hair and quickly plaited the strands into one long over-the-shoulder braid.

Staring hard at the image before her, Willa put on her hat. Took it off. Using a rag from her bath, she wiped the dust from her boots and stared at her image again.

She was never going to look like anything except who she was. Willa, plain and simple.

She harrumphed. Sniffed. Made a decision.

"A person has to eat."

With that, she left the room, careful to lock the door, and started down the wide oak staircase.

Gideon ordered the biggest steak on the hotel menu and sat back in his chair to enjoy the luxury. It had been a while and it felt good.

He wished Willa had come.

She was tired, physically, of course, but also of him, he surmised. She had what she wanted. Now that her father's killer had been captured, Willa no longer required his expertise.

He pressed two fingers over his breastbone and rubbed the sore spot.

At the next table, a couple held hands and gazed lovingly at each other. He watched for a moment and then glanced away, aching deep in his belly for something he'd never wanted before.

A man staggered from the bar attached to the hotel. Gideon considered going in for one celebratory drink while his steak cooked.

Better not, a voice whispered. One meant many.

The voice was no longer his mother's or Isaiah Baker's. It belonged to Willa.

He did not want to disappoint Willa or compromise the

fledgling faith that budded in his soul. A faith that demanded something from a sober man. Something he battled against with all his might and yet, he found himself at a crossroads.

A blue-eyed waitress in white over black, her blond hair puffed high on her head, refilled his coffee cup. Good, strong, smooth coffee with cream and sugar, the way he liked it. He'd missed this luxury, had perhaps grown accustomed to an easier life than days on the trail and wild frontier campsites.

He smiled his thanks, took up the thick cream pitcher and returned to his ruminations.

His breath had clogged in his lungs when Willa opened the door of her hotel room. There she'd stood, scrubbed clean and pink, the floral scent of French soap rich in his nose, her stunning brown hair damp and hanging to her waist. He'd been sorely tempted to wrap his good hand in the glorious locks, to sift the soft waves through his fingers. To pull her to him and hold her, just hold her.

She probably would have stomped his foot with those ugly boots of hers.

Or not.

He was not a naive boy. He knew she favored him.

"I pray you, do not fall in love with me, for I am falser than vows made in wine."

Was he, as Shakespeare seemed to believe, too false for love? Too jaded, too damaged?

Could a woman like Willa plain and simple, but deep and true, as true of a heart as he'd ever met, pluck the strings of love's fair music that had long since gone silent inside him?

Mocking his poetic fantasies, he sipped at his perfectly pale coffee and watched the people coming and going. From his table, he had a good view of the entire place, a habit he'd developed to avoid being ambushed.

Feeling movement on the staircase, he glanced up.

His heart stilled, stuttered, beat again.

Willa, clinging to the banister, took the steps tentatively as if she feared coming into the dining room with so many people.

He could not help himself. He rose and went to her.

"I hope you've changed your mind about dinner."

Her chin came up. "I'm hungry."

There was something more than belly hunger in her small, fierce stance that touched him in the middle of his soul.

Offering his elbow, he guided her to his table and ordered her the best steak in the house.

"You look lovely," he said.

If she were his, he'd buy her beautiful dresses if she wanted, but he'd always remember her this way, the way she truly was. Willa, unpretentious, and as fresh as a summer rain.

With stern discipline, Gideon reminded himself that Willa was not his and could never be as long as his father stood in the way.

He stashed the problem of his father for later. Tonight, maybe for the last time, he'd enjoy this remarkable woman.

Even after they were replete, stuffed with succulent steak and garden green beans with new potatoes and slabs of hot buttery yeast bread, they lingered over coffee and conversation.

After all the days together on the trip, they still found things to talk about. The only subject Gideon resisted was discussion of his father.

He should tell her, and perhaps he would. Tonight, when he said good-night for the last time, a balm to ease the leaving.

They talked until shadows stretched like gray fingers across the streets and black-and-white clad maids moved around the hotel, lighting gas lamps. The lights cast a warm golden glow through the dining room and onto the staircase.

By mutual agreement, they left the hotel and began to walk along the boardwalk. A gaslight here and there and lamps from second-story dwellings illuminated their stroll. Unlike Sweet Clover, the raw dirt streets had long since hard packed and spewed no dust.

"Do you ever think about Grady?" Willa's small hand looped lightly inside his sling—where he'd placed it—her wrists bandaged white as if she'd slashed them.

Keeping his gun hand free, Gideon walked on the outside toward the street.

Willa was a strong woman, independent as America, but Fort Smith remained a rugged town, and he wouldn't take a chance of anything happening to her.

"I think about him often," he answered, for indeed, the boy played in his head like a violin, tender and yearning. He heard Grady's laughter, saw his face alight at the caught fish. He also remembered the look in his big, sad eyes the day they'd left him with the preacher.

"I miss him."

Gideon rubbed the center of his chest. "As do I. Hopefully, the reverend made contact with his family."

"I pray for that every night. And that they'll want him. Some folks already have all the mouths they can feed."

"A sad truth. Even the reverend was reluctant because of his financial straits."

"The reverend," she said in her determined, practical manner, "should not complain. You left a lot of money."

When he gave her a sharp look, she shrugged. "Mrs. Larssen told me."

Gideon said nothing. He was prickly about his good deeds being broadcast, as if they wouldn't count if anyone knew.

As it was wont to do, a Scripture flashed into place…*"and thy Father which seeth in secret himself shall reward thee openly."*

He didn't care about an open reward other than the one in his pocket, but he liked the idea of pleasing God.

He turned that over in his thoughts, and found it shiny like a new copper penny.

"I wish we could have brought him with us," Willa said. "I would have taken him home. A little boy would be a lively addition to three spinster sisters."

Gideon gnawed on the picture of Willa and the child together. A beautiful concept that heated a spot somewhere beneath his ribs and left a deep longing behind.

He said the only thing he could, "Impossible."

If Gideon had done one thing right, it was to leave Grady behind hours before encountering a group of men who surely would have killed them all. The child had already endured too much by watching his family die.

"I know," Willa said, her voice sad and small.

Even though they moved on to other topics, thoughts of the little boy hovered between them. They'd both grown attached.

Belle had warned him this could happen. This heart change. His lips curved at the notion. She seemed always to be right.

"Gideon?" Willa stopped in the middle of the boardwalk as if to question his sudden silence.

He shook his head to free it from the things he could not change and refocused on his charming companion.

Enjoy her while he could. One last time.

The smell of the river permeated the city. Shops such as Willa had rarely seen lined each side of the street. Dress shops and shoe shops displayed fashionable items that widened her eyes and made her gasp.

Gideon teased her lightly when she mooned over a pair of button-up boots with as much zest as Savannah mooned over the sewing machine in the mail order catalog.

Savannah would get her machine.

"No use buying boots when Papa's are perfectly serviceable," she said with a sniff, though she didn't believe her own words. Her five-hundred-dollar share of the reward was a lot of money, but other than the sewing machine, the farm would require every penny.

A mule-drawn streetcar rattled along beside them, its gas-lights brightening their path.

Gideon suddenly veered toward the street.

"Let's ride. See the town." Laughing, she raced with him to the corner where the trolley car belched out a handful of passengers.

And see the town they did.

Gideon teased and flirted with such cheer and charm that Willa found herself responding in kind. She'd never expected such behavior from herself, but found it quite refreshing to laugh and flirt and forget her worries.

If she fell more and more in love with Gideon, she'd deal with her foolish emotions later.

By the time they returned to the hotel, the weariness of the past weeks had caught up with both of them. Gideon was once again as pale as whitewashed walls. She shouldn't have agreed to all this activity.

But oh, tonight had been wonderful.

Stopping at the hotel desk, Gideon picked up an envelope that he slipped inside his black vest. Then he escorted her up the stairs.

His own room was next door but he paused in front of hers.

"Thank you for a delightful evening." For once, he was neither cynical nor mocking.

"The pleasure was all mine." Willa almost giggled at her fancy words. Gideon was rubbing off on her. Maybe she'd learn to read, after all.

She expected him to turn toward his own room next door but he hesitated instead. "Willa."

He lifted his good hand as if to touch her but changed his mind and let it fall to his side.

She waited, breath stuck like unchewed steak in her gullet, wishing for a perfect ending to a perfect day.

Just this once. Just this once, she wanted to feel pretty and desirable to someone who mattered.

Gideon mattered.

He moved close so that her back touched the wooden door and his face was endearingly near.

Her pulse trilled in her neck.

As only Gideon could, he whispered the prettiest words. "As Shelley would say, 'What is all this sweet work worth if thou kiss not me?'"

Then, his lips touched hers and his good arm found her braid and tugged her ever closer until she stood on tiptoes and slid her arms around his neck.

For that bright and glowing moment, plain and simple Willa felt beautiful.

Chapter Twenty-Six

Gideon punched the pillow and flopped to his good side, careful of the injured shoulder, restless, overthinking.

He shouldn't have kissed Willa. It made the leaving that much harder.

He'd planned to tell her tonight, to give her the ticket and the envelope, but he'd fallen into her innocent kiss and lost his mind.

He had no choice now. He'd have to face the morning and her disappointment.

From down below his second-story hotel room, a jaunty piano drew paying customers to the saloon.

Gideon blocked the thoughts, trying to weasel through his resistance and, amazingly, found them too weak to gain entrance.

For the first time in memory, he knew what he wanted, and it was not a bottle of whiskey.

Because of Willa, he'd gotten sober. Because of her, he was clear-minded, even though the doc claimed he'd suffered a

concussive disorder from Idaho Tom's gun butt. The headache had eased and he could see straight again.

More than that, the ache of loss and hate had eased. Search
though he might, he could not muster the rage.

How had that happened? Was it God, as Isaiah would say,
healing the grief?

He still despised his father, never wanted to lay eyes on him
again, but something inside him had changed.

He slowly repositioned onto his back, bad arm cradled
across his chest, and stared up at the dark ceiling, sleepless,
not because of the steady throb in his shoulder, nor of the
dreams he usually suffered. But because of what was to come
tomorrow. What *had* to come.

A reckoning was building. He'd known it since the early
days of sobriety. A reckoning to which Willa could not be
privy.

Willa awoke refreshed, her first thoughts of Gideon and
his tender, poetic kiss.

Her fingers went to her lips where she relived the lingering moment, his scent in her nostrils, his warm breath on her
cheek.

She stretched, wanting to linger in the sumptuous feather
bed, but longing more to see Gideon.

Dressing quickly, she rushed, her heart light and excited,
to the room next door.

A maid exited as Willa arrived. "Mr. Hartley's gone, ma'am.
Most likely in the dining room."

Of course. The dining room. He did so enjoy his coffee.

Light as an airborne feather, she floated down the stairs and
into the dining room.

Gideon sat at the same white linen-covered table as if waiting for her. He signaled to the waitress, who brought coffee and hot biscuits.

He looked tired. She knew how he battled sleep and how the nightmares plagued him, though he'd not called out in his sleep since the night of the fire.

"Didn't you rest well?"

"Well enough." He turned his attention to the coffee, going through his ritual of cream, taste, cream, taste and then a dollop of sugar and more tasting.

Something troubled him. "What's wrong?"

"Eat your breakfast, Willa."

She nibbled at a biscuit, sipped at the steaming brew.

Around the dining room, forks and knives clinked against china plates and modulated voices carried on quiet conversations.

But Gideon said little.

Did he regret the kiss that had changed her whole world?

She wanted to ask, but for once her boldness fled like a mouse in a roomful of cats.

Slowly, her good mood faded. Anxiety trailed in, an unwanted guest. She choked down what was likely a delicious breakfast, though she barely tasted the hearty fare.

Her gaze returned again and again to Gideon, but he focused on his dratted coffee and left her to stew.

Something was amiss.

When breakfast ended and more coffee poured, Gideon leaned forward, took her hand and turned it over to stare at the white bandages.

"Willa, we must talk."

"I knew something was wrong. Was it the—" a hot blush heated her cheeks "—kiss? Are you sorry it happened? Is that it?"

His gaze lifted to hers, burning blue and intense. "No."

Willa's heart began to pound, pushing against her rib cage, trying to escape.

"What, then?"

He loosened his hold, reached into a pocket and took out a ticket of some sort.

The thunder in her chest grew louder. A storm was coming. She could feel it in the air.

Gideon scooted the ticket across the table. "The morning stage will take you home to Sweet Clover."

"The stage?" Gathering up the slip of paper, she stared at the time stamp, bewildered. The coach pulled out in half an hour. "What about Freckles and Traveler? You can't leave your horses."

Those tired eyes seared her again. "The horses travel with me."

Like a bucket of icy spring water, realization washed over Willa, cold and final. "You aren't going back to Sweet Clover."

"No."

"Ever?" The hope in her voice should have shamed her.

"I don't know. There are things I must see to, things I must do."

"I'll go with you." Her cheeks heated to the point of combustion. She was humiliating herself.

"As fine and desirable a companion as you are, my lady, there are things a man must face alone. That I must face alone."

He reached for her hand again, but she pulled it back, clutching the horrid ticket that she did not want.

A flicker of hurt crossed Gideon's features, quickly masked. Or was that her imagination, the one that had dreamed last night that he loved her?

"I have one favor to ask of you," he said.

A favor. When he was sending her away?

Holding to her pride, she dipped her head in agreement,

though her eyes ached with unshed tears and her insides felt ripped and shredded.

She could not be angry, she reminded herself. She could not let him see how much his rejection grieved her. He'd kept his promises. She should be grateful.

Because of him, she had plenty of money to secure the land claim for her and the sisters.

This morning that did not seem to be enough.

From inside that rakishly handsome vest he withdrew a thick sealed envelope and handed it to her. Her hand shook as she accepted it.

One name scrawled in perfect manly script across the front.

"Please give this to Belle. She'll know what to do."

Belle Holbrook, her beautiful, elegant friend, a perfect match for a man like Gideon.

Hadn't she suspected all along that Belle was the one who owned Gideon's heart?

Now, she knew for certain.

It was Belle he thought about, Belle he wrote to, knowing that Willa could not eavesdrop on the romantic words written within.

Gideon loved Belle, not her.

That was the only thing that mattered.

"Of course." Willa battled the tears rising like a phoenix from the ashes of her broken heart. She nodded, one hard teeth-gritted nod. "I understand."

But she did not.

In his wild, adventurous life, Gideon had done some difficult things, but putting Willa on that stagecoach was among the hardest and, perhaps, the bravest.

He'd never forget the way she looked as he stood in the opened door of the coach, saying goodbye, making sure she and her money were secure. Making sure she knew Walker Ramos rode shotgun on the seat above and would see her safely to Sweet Clover. Walker, a good friend, a trusted gunman.

Bandaged hands curled in the lap of her brown skirt, her small calloused fingers had gripped Mercy's brown medicine bag. Brown, a color he would always think of as belonging to Willa.

Hidden inside the pouch was his letter to Belle as well as Willa's newly acquired fortune.

Perhaps he should have told her everything that was in his heart. But he could not be sure of what would happen during the next days and weeks of his life, and he was not one to give false hope.

Belle would handle the other issues if he didn't return. Belle could handle anything, though she'd understandably kept a low profile since Pearl's birth.

He rubbed a hand over his sore shoulder only to discover the ache was lower, nearer to his heart.

Willa wasn't even out of sight and already he missed her, as if a part of him was on that stagecoach.

Perhaps it was.

He sucked in a long breath and exhaled a deep yearning sigh.

The old Gideon would never have turned her loose.

But Willa deserved better than the man he was at the moment. He'd seen her disappointment, even more ripe and poignant than he'd expected.

She loved him. Perhaps he'd known for a while, just as he'd known that he could not accept her pure and holy love. Not as long as loathing and unforgiveness resided in the place meant for better things.

He stood alone on the edge of the street, watching the stage rumble away, watched until the dust settled and the carriage was swallowed up by distance and other conveyances.

Watched until his eyes burned with wanting to see her.

"'Love bade me welcome,'" he muttered. "'Yet my soul drew back, guilty of dust and sin.'"

Indeed, as Herbert's poem accused, he was guilty of too much.

The journey to Sweet Clover was tiring but uneventful and stunningly short compared to the weeks on horseback. As Gideon had promised, the darkly handsome Walker Ramos kept a sharp and watchful eye on everyone, though Willa had her rifle and wasn't the least bit afraid.

Not after all she and Gideon had been through together.

Gideon. She sighed and squirmed to get comfortable, the rough roads bouncing her and the other three passengers like babies on a daddy's knee.

She loved him. She missed him.

Dashing foolish tears, she glared out the window at the passing scenery.

Though she'd never ridden in a stagecoach before, Indian Territory was beautiful to gaze upon, and she suffered a moment of regret when the hills and woods gave way to Oklahoma Territory's flatter plains and tall grass prairie.

When the stage rumbled into Sweet Clover, Walker Ramos hopped down from the driver's box to open the door, his smile white and confident in his dark face.

"Ma'am." He took her hand to assist her.

Though another woman and a child rode in the coach as well, Walker's attention was on her, a woman who could quite handily jump from the carriage and run all the way to the farm.

She allowed him the courtesy and stood in the dusty, hot

street, gazing at Sweet Clover. New construction rose next to the barbershop, the sounds of hammers and men's voices on the wind. The weary little village seemed as determined as she to thrive.

The guard handed down her saddlebags and bedroll, placing them on the boardwalk next to the stage.

"Thank you, Mr. Ramos. You've been more than kind, and I felt perfectly safe knowing a friend of Gideon's rode along."

It pained her to say Gideon's name, to even think of him, but he was always on her mind.

Green eyes flashed with warmth. Ramos doffed his hat. "It was a pleasure to escort Gideon's woman. He is a man of exceptional taste."

Willa wanted to laugh at the man's exaggeration. If she was Gideon's woman and if she was so wonderful, why had Gideon chosen to part company?

Hoisting her baggage, she said her farewell and marched toward the bank. She would not wait one day longer.

Today, Theodore Pierce received his comeuppance.

The next day, Willa was still smiling at the shock on the banker's face, though even as she had plunked down the money to repay the loan, Charlie Bangs's mumblings about someone named Pierce slithered through her mind like a serpent. She'd put the thoughts aside, too busy enjoying the ruffle in the banker's dandified feathers. Pierce, after all, was not an unusual name.

Today, she had one final errand, this one not so pleasant.

Belle. And Gideon's letter.

Resolute, she marched the two miles to Oklahoma Avenue and knocked on Belle's door, a march that left her hot and sweaty.

When Belle, as regal as a queen in lavender and white,

opened the door, Willa was reminded of why Gideon had chosen Belle instead of her.

Bearing a delighted smile, the other woman reached out and drew Willa forward. "I heard you were back. Come inside and have some lemonade. You look scorched."

Thank you for noticing, Willa thought with grim humor.

"That sounds wonderful."

With Pearl quietly playing tea party with her dolls, Willa followed Belle into the sunny kitchen.

"So tell me of the trip. You found Bangs, I hear."

It seemed Belle had already heard everything, but Willa took a chair across the flower-decked table and filled her in on the rest, leaving out the uncomfortable truth that she'd fallen in love with Belle's sweetheart.

If she'd expected the tale of outlaws and gunshots to shock the beautiful widow, she was in for a disappointment. Belle's eyes sparkled with interest. "My, what an adventure."

"One I don't plan to repeat, I assure you." Willa set aside the drink glass and placed the thick envelope on the table. Get it over with, so she could get this elephant off her chest. "Gideon sent this."

Curious, a soft smile playing on her bow lips, Belle opened the thick letter. Green bills tumbled to the table.

Willa gasped. "What in the world—"

Belle glanced up, smiled, read the letter and laughed, loud and robust. "Oh, that Gideon. Such a gallant soul. Did he tell you what's in this letter?"

"No. I didn't read it." She hurried to add the latter, assuring Belle she had not read Gideon's personal, loving words.

Belle pushed the money toward her. Five hundred dollars. "He sent his share of the reward for you and says for you to buy yourself a new pair of boots."

Five hundred dollars would buy more than boots!

"I don't understand. I can't take that."

Belle's merry laugh rang out. "He knew you'd argue, so he sent it via me. Don't refuse, Willa. Give Gideon that much."

"But this is crazy. He worked for that money."

"Oh, Willa, Gideon doesn't need money. He needed the one thing that you gave him." She tapped the letter. "You gave him back his faith. His self-respect, too."

"He says that?" Hope rose that Gideon cared for her, after all.

"Yes, and he also says to tell you that he's looking into the silver mine situation."

Willa's heart leaped. Her fingers tightened on the edge of the table. "How could he possibly do that?"

Belle looked at the letter again and then back to Willa, and when she spoke, her words seemed intentionally vague. "He knows people. Just trust him. If the silver mine has anything to do with your father, he'll let us know."

Us. As in Belle.

"What else does he say?"

Again, Belle's expression receded as if she were hiding something.

"He says you are a hardy companion and much more, but some of it is only for my eyes, at least for now." The lovely widow reached across the table and squeezed the top of Willa's hand. "I'll tell you more when I can."

For Belle's eyes only.

A hardy companion.

With those two phrases, hope, that fickle thing, tumbled to the shiny wood floor and died.

Acres and acres of cotton whitened the Texas flatlands like snow. Sun hot enough to fry a thick steak beat down on the sharecroppers, backs bent to the hoe amid weeds that ever threatened the crop.

The barns and cotton gin remained standing, though in dire need of paint. The gin was quiet now, waiting for harvest, another backbreaking job.

A small cabin had been built near the old tree swing where Gideon and his siblings had once played. The big two-story house was gone, of course, and Gideon was not surprised to see that Thomas Hartley had made no attempt to clear away the rubble, though nearly fifteen years had passed.

He was surprised, however, that the memories flooding him like waters from a broken dam, though painful, no longer gripped him with rage.

He felt only a kind of quiet sadness.

His father did not yet know he was here, so he took the time to survey all he'd left behind.

Traveler shook his head, jingling the reins held too tightly in Gideon's grip. The horse had been eager to stretch his legs after the long ride in a train car across the Territory and deep into Texas.

He went nowhere without Traveler, but he'd left Freckles with a friend.

Dismounting, Gideon left the reins to dangle and let Traveler graze on the summer grass next to a windmill while he walked a short distance to the trio of graves.

Removing his hat, he read the names. His mother, sister and brother rested beneath carved stones, put there, he supposed, by his father after he'd ridden away.

A chasm dark with grief opened inside him. For his dead loved ones. For the broken relationship with his father. So many years. So many regrets.

The click of a pistol cylinder, somewhere behind his back, froze him in his tracks and stopped his reminiscence.

"State your business, mister." The hard voice was as cold as January.

Gideon raised his hands. The left one, holding his hat, rose only half way, though he'd chucked the sling two days ago.

He still had some healing to do. Inside and out.

Slowly, he pivoted on his boots and faced the devil.

"Hello, Pa."

"You!" Thomas Hartley recoiled as if his own flesh-and-blood son was a rattlesnake. The once-handsome face, now laced with time, showed the ravages of too much whiskey too often.

It occurred to Gideon that this was what alcohol would do to him in a few years' time if he let it.

Willa's fierce efforts to rid him of the poison flashed in his head. She'd accused him of being like his father. He wouldn't be. Not anymore, especially now that he'd seen Thomas Hartley again.

"You got no right showing up here after all this time."

Gideon held back a sigh. So much for a nostalgic reunion.

Had he for even one second hoped that Thomas would race down the lane in exuberant welcome like the father in the Prodigal Son story?

Perhaps not, but after all these years, Gideon had hoped for civility.

Gideon allowed a smirk, though his chest hurt something powerful. "I take it you won't be killing the fatted calf."

"Always the smart-mouth, weren't you?" Thomas waved the pistol, unwilling to put it away, though his only surviving child stood in front of him. "Get off my land."

Shoulder protesting, Gideon lowered his arms. "Mother's land, too, as I recall."

Thomas's eyes, as blue as his own, narrowed. "Is that what

you came for? Thinking you'd sneak in here and take what I've worked myself to the bone to get?"

Dander rising, Gideon goaded the old man, "She intended me to have her share."

Two thousand acres of prime cotton farm.

"Spoiled sissy, mama's boy with your books and fancy words, you don't have the backbone to run a farm like this. Never did."

Gideon tilted his head. "I would treat my sharecroppers fairly."

As if remembering that long ago argument, Thomas's face mottled. "They get what they need. What they agree to when they hire on."

"When you don't cheat them." He kept his voice soft and calm, but the anger started to rise, the same anger that had driven him away years ago when he'd caught his father cheating his workers out of half their annual share.

Thomas's lip curled. "If you've come here, broke and begging, expecting me to feel sorry and take you in, you've come to the wrong place, boy."

For a frozen moment, fury swirled in Gideon, a tornado of emotion threatening to send a fist into his father's face.

For the last several hundred miles, he'd thought and prayed and studied the Bible he carried in his saddlebags, hearing Willa's and Isaiah's words ringing in his head. He wanted to do this correctly, but already the old man had riled the hornets' nest within.

Clenching his hat in restrained fingers, Gideon reminded himself of why he'd come. Though loathing was easier than forgiveness, the ravages of hate had stolen fifteen years of his life.

He couldn't get them back, but he wanted a better future. He wanted something and someone he'd never imagined wanting.

To get them, he had to come here and lay the past to rest, not at the bottom of a whiskey glass, but at the foot of the Cross.

Drawing on reserves he didn't know he had, Gideon tamped down the vitriolic words he could easily spew on his father. Words he'd later regret.

"I didn't come for the land or to fight with you," he said softly, with a respect that surprised even him, and clearly stunned his father. "You can keep my share."

"Then what do you want? I'm not giving you money."

Gideon shook his head, pitying a man who thought of nothing else but earthly possessions. "I want you to know I forgive you."

Thomas glared, his shoulders jerked back as if insulted. Indeed, he was. "I did nothing wrong for you to forgive. You're the one who ran off and left a brokenhearted man alone."

Though the words threatened to stick in his craw, Gideon got them out. "If I caused you grief, I ask your forgiveness."

Suspicion clouded his father's expression. He squinted, face hard as iron. "You're wanting something. No man grovels unless he's after something. Not even a sissy one."

"I want nothing other than forgiveness and the peace with God it brings me. I hope someday you'll find the same."

If his heartfelt words had any effect on Thomas Hartley, the old man didn't show it. He waved his pistol.

"You've said your piece. Get back on your horse and get gone. I got work to do."

His father turned his back and stalked toward the small cabin that Gideon reckoned was his home now.

He never looked back.

Gideon gathered Traveler's reins and swung into the saddle.

He'd prepared for this moment, had known the likelihood of his father's rejection.

Still, it stung.

A boy needs a father. Even when that boy is a man.

"A father of the fatherless…is God in His holy habitation."

The random bit of verse settled over Gideon, a solace.

He'd done all he could. The rest lay at Thomas Hartley's door.

Aiming his horse toward the north and Indian Territory, he rode away from Hartley Plantation, a free man.

Chapter Twenty-Seven

The weeks following her homecoming were days of happiness as well as despair for Willa. Happiness, because the Malone sisters now owned one hundred and sixty acres and the cabin they'd built. Despair, because a piece of land felt empty without the man she loved.

When her sisters asked about Gideon, Willa could only tell them the truth. She did not know where he'd gone. She did not know when he'd return.

She was, however, certain that Gideon *would* someday come back to Sweet Clover. Belle was here. When that happened, Willa would stay strong and pretend to be happy for them.

They were wonderful people, good friends to her. She could do nothing less than wish them well.

She would, however, pine for a long time. Maybe forever. A heartache she kept to herself. Her sisters had their own troubles, and they could do nothing to ease her longing.

Every night, she prayed. Prayed that Gideon was safe, that he wasn't killing himself with whiskey, that he'd somehow found his way to peace. If the letter he'd sent to Belle was an indicator, perhaps he had.

Oh, how she missed him.

Not a woman given to emotional fits, Willa sought relief in practicality.

This particular afternoon when the days had begun to shorten and summer's heat relented enough that a body could breathe, Mercy found her in the garden viciously yanking weeds.

The gentle sister knelt at her side, burnished copper hair gleaming. "Willa, there's barely a weed left on this acreage. Three weeks, and you're out here every day, exhausting yourself. It's because of Gideon, isn't it? Something happened you haven't told us about."

Something had happened all right. She'd fallen in love with a most unsuitable, most wonderful, most complicated man. That wasn't supposed to happen. She was an old maid!

"He promised to teach me to read," she blurted. It was a silly thing to say, but it covered her real feelings.

Mercy touched the top of her hand, staying her frenetic weed-pulling. "It's more than that. He hurt you."

"Not his fault."

"Isn't it?" Mercy's turbulent green gaze probed into Willa. "Did he do anything—?"

"No, Mercy, no. Gideon was a perfect gentleman to the end."

"Men can be deceptive. I was worried…" She let the rest disappear unsaid.

"I know." Willa wondered again what had caused her middle sister to distrust people with such vehemence.

She could not help Mercy. She couldn't even help herself. Not when it came to matters of the heart.

"Savannah says you're in love with him."

Blowing a gusty breath, Willa dragged a sleeve across her eyes and tipped her head back to gaze at the single white cloud passing, mercifully, over the sun. "I'm not the kind of woman men fall in love with. I have you and Savannah and this farm. That's enough."

Except it wasn't. She wanted to be loved by the right man, to have children and watch them grow. She wanted Gideon.

After a long, aching moment that gave away the lie to Willa's words, Mercy spoke in a voice as tender as if Willa were the younger and Mercy the older.

"Savannah left us a few ginger cookies before heading to town. Come on. I'll make tea."

Cookies and tea, Mercy's cures for a broken heart.

Willa pushed up from the peas and dusted her skirt.

Savannah had mended the ugly burn hole, though the patch reminded Willa of Gideon, the way he'd rescued her, the beautiful words he'd whispered that awful night when they'd both nearly died.

As they walked the short distance, Mercy deftly changed the subject. Bless her.

"I told Savannah I would go to town for supplies after I called at the Stotz house." She was treating Marty Stotz for an abscess. "I don't know why she insists on taxing her strength. You and I can do the heavy errands."

Willa touched her arm. "Mercy, Savannah is perfectly capable of driving the wagon. Let her do what she's able. We can't protect her from everything."

"She's too young to be in town alone with riffraff and wild cowboys."

"Fret no more. There she comes."

Sure enough, their faithful horse, Jasper, plodded down the short drive and into the yard, pulling the wagon with Savannah in a jaunty yellow hat at the reins.

Willa had started toward her to unload the wagon when Savannah gripped the side rail and swung to the ground, limping toward her sisters as fast as her stricken limb would carry her.

"The banker's been arrested," she said without preliminary, breathless with the news. "US Marshals, a whole passel of them, rode into town while I was at the bank, marched in, took Mr. Pierce into custody and shut the bank down."

Mercy's hand went to her heart. "You were there? You saw this? Why would they arrest Mr. Pierce?"

Willa gave a very unladylike snort. "He's cheated everyone in town."

"That's not the reason." Savannah's usually pale complexion was as pink as a summer rose. "They arrested Madam Frenchy, too. The two of them were in cahoots with a band of outlaws. Some of the same outlaws that tried to kill Willa and Gideon." Her slender shoulders shuddered. "They were forcing young girls to work in the brothel!"

Aghast, Mercy looked left and right as if she thought the whole town could hear them from this distance. "How is that possible? No one would do that."

Willa put a hand on her middle sister's arm. "I thought the same thing, Mercy, but Savannah is right. Some women don't have a choice. They're forced into that life."

She told them about the young Chinese girl and the men she and Gideon had encountered in a saloon. The same men Gideon had been afraid might kidnap Willa, though she didn't share that last bit of apoplectic information with her sisters.

"Gideon suspected Coy Ling was being held against her will," she said.

Savannah's blue eyes widened. She splayed a hand across her yellow bodice. "Do you think Gideon had something to do with the Marshals coming to Sweet Clover? That he sent them from Fort Smith?"

Willa hadn't thought of it before, but now that she did, she nodded. "It's exactly the thing he'd do."

The man alluded to by the outlaws the night of the fire was, indeed, Theodore Pierce, and brilliant Gideon had put all the pieces together.

Admiration deepened for the man, broken in so many ways, but still caring and decent and determined to do the right thing, even for a young girl and others like her who he'd never met.

Turning this stunning news over in her mind, Willa and her sisters began unloading the wagon.

Savannah went inside the cabin but returned immediately. "Willa, get in the house. Hurry."

Alarmed, Willa dropped a sack of flour. "What's wrong?"

"Just do as I ask. Go in the house, wash your face and comb your hair. And put on my green dress, the one you wore to Faragate's barn dance."

So stunned was she by Savannah's bizarre behavior, Willa didn't move. "What on earth has come over you?"

Savannah stomped a dainty little foot, puffing up summer dust. "Oh, fiddlesticks. I'm too late."

While Willa gaped in consternation, the delicate sister, who didn't seem so delicate today, spun away and stormed into the house, leaving the wagonload of goods and dragging Mercy with her.

The plod and clomp of horse hooves drew Willa's open-mouthed stare from her sisters to the road.

Making an awning of her hand, she squinted at two riders in the distance.

Her heart, which had been thudding along right nicely, suddenly stopped and fell all the way to her dusty boots.

Two riders. A man and a boy.

"What—?"

Claiming Her Legacy

Afraid to believe her eyes, she remained where she was. In truth, she couldn't have moved if a cyclone swept past.

Gideon, dusty and road-weary, his blue eyes dancing, rode Traveler right up to her and dismounted.

She caught the familiar horse's bridle and stroked a hand over his velvety nose. Mostly, she held on lest her knees give way and she make a further fool of herself.

He was here. Gideon had returned.

"You're here." At her house. Not at Belle's. Why hadn't he gone there first?

"I brought someone with me."

Little Grady, eyes wide and mouth grinning, slid from Freckles's back. Shyly, he stood beside the animal and stared at her.

Squishy, motherly feelings as warm and sweet as Savannah's chocolate gravy made Willa's head light.

Seeing that Grady held himself apart, as if uncertain of her welcome, Willa went to the boy and crouched before him.

"I'm so happy to see you again," she said. "I missed you."

The boy flung his thin arms around her neck. "Gideon said you would. He said you wanted me."

Gideon had remembered how much she'd wanted to bring the child home with her. Tears sprang to her eyes. "Yes, oh, yes, Grady. I want you."

With the boy in her arms, she raised a wet face to the man standing at her shoulder, watching her with powerful emotion on his handsome whisker-scruffed face.

What happened? she mouthed to him.

"No one answered the preacher's telegraphs or letters."

"You rode all the way back to Buffalo Gap to learn that?" she asked, touched that he would do such a thing.

Gideon placed a wide hand on Grady's small back, the

other holding his black hat. Something about him was different, more settled.

"I did. After a trip to Texas."

She sucked in a breath, knowing how difficult such a trip would have been, aware of all that Texas meant to the man she loved.

"You made peace with your father?" she asked, hopeful for his sake.

"No." Gideon's tone was soft and accepting. "He refused. But I made peace with me. And with God."

Tears, those pests, curdled in the corners of Willa's eyes. Slowly, she loosened her hold on Grady and rose, keeping one reassuring hand on the boy's shoulder.

"I'm pleased for you, Gideon. Thank you for fetching Grady. I would be delighted to be his new mama, if that's what he wants."

Grady tugged her hand, his upturned face earnest and filled with a desperate longing that pinched her heart.

"I do, Miss Willa. Mr. Gideon—" he stopped, cast a shy grin at Gideon "—says he'll be my new papa if it's okay with you."

She smiled a tremulous smile at the child, afraid to look at Gideon, knowing if she did that her love was there for anyone to see. But he was Belle's. "I'm afraid that's not the way it works, Grady."

"Grady is getting ahead of himself." Gideon placed his hat on Grady's head with a smile and a wink. "Allow me to explain."

He took both of her hands, turned them up for inspection, and seeing the new pink skin, lifted each wrist to his lips, his gaze locked on hers.

Delight shivered through Willa, raising gooseflesh.

What was happening here?

"Your shoulder," she said.

"Is better." He tossed off the concern as if he'd never been shot. "Stop interrupting."

She clamped her mouth shut, her pulse taking a sudden notion to race like the wind.

"What our young friend is trying to say is that a boy needs both a mother and father. I have agreed to be his father, and we'd like you to be his mother."

Her braid brushed her shoulder as she shook her head. "I still don't understand."

"Willa, plain and simple, fairest to my heart, I'm asking you to marry me."

A flock of hummingbirds took up residence in her stomach. *Marry her?*

"What about Belle?"

Gideon blinked. Twice. "Belle?"

"Aren't the two you—" she stuttered "—you sent the letter— I thought she was your—"

Gideon looked momentarily perplexed and then laughed his soft laugh. "I thought we resolved that long ago. Belle is my friend and my business partner."

"Business partner?"

Hope sprouted wings and flew around inside her head until her brain whirled.

With a beleaguered sigh, he said, "My business ventures, and Belle, are a discussion for later. Will you please stop asking questions and allow yourself to be courted?"

"You're courting me?" she asked, stunned to her toenails. "I've never been courted before. I don't know how that works."

Gideon rested his forehead against hers, chuckling. "Ah, Willa. My warrior, my persistent gnat, my dearest love. You try the patience of a saint, but you also give me such great hope. Do you love me?"

Suddenly as shy as the boy clinging to her skirt-tail, Willa nodded. She could not look away from Gideon's eyes. The blue depths were filled with humor and the one thing she'd dreamed of but never expected to see.

He was courting her. He loved her.

Lips trembling, she whispered, "I do."

"And I love you, Willa Malone, 'to the depth and breadth and heights my soul can reach.' Though I will never be worthy of you, I am a better man for knowing you, for loving you. Will you do me the honor of becoming my wife?"

Shocked and thrilled and filled with wonder, Willa could only say, "I will. Yes, I will."

As if she were fragile and beautiful, and wonder of wonders she felt exactly that way, Gideon drew her into his arms and placed his smiling lips on hers.

Epilogue

A wagonload of lumber from Faragate Mill rumbled onto the grass next to the large home Gideon was building for his bride. Hammer in hand and Grady at his side, he looked around the vast green space he'd purchased for them and found Willa with a clutch of other ladies.

In a purple flounced dress and the new boots he'd bought for her, her long shining braid over one shoulder, she took his breath away. But then plain and simple Willa had captivated him in worn-out boots and a dirty brown skirt.

He wanted to give her the world but all she'd asked of him was a home in which to raise the children they hoped would join Grady, the gentle little boy who now called him Daddy.

Every morning when Gideon awakened with Willa at his side, gratitude and joy overwhelmed him. His love, his wife, a gift he'd never expected to have in his life, she filled him with such pride and pleasure and made him strive all the harder to be the man she thought he was.

He had not had a drink in a year, and when temptation

came, he shunned it with prayer and reminders of how much better his life had become without the alcohol. He was, as the Bible claimed, a different man, a new creation.

Hammers rang out, and around him the men of Sweet Clover gathered for an old-fashioned house-raising. Among them were a now hale and healthy Isaiah Baker along with Matthew, Reverend Danforth and Liam O'Shea, men he was proud to claim as friends.

He had become, to his great shock, a pillar of Sweet Clover because of his part in Theodore Pierce's arrest.

They'd even asked him to become their sheriff, though he'd refused. He preferred to keep his investigations, such as they were, in the hands of Belle Holbrook. For it was she who'd secretly made contact with the women inside Madam Frenchy's brothel and learned the crucial facts about Coy Ling and two other young girls like her.

Though the town applauded her brave actions, Belle, in deflecting the praise, had managed to keep her secrets intact.

He smiled in her direction. She tilted her parasol.

Next to Belle, Mary Baker and her flock of children assisted Willa, her sisters and other ladies in setting out prepared food and drink. The final wall was about to go up and the men would be starving soon.

He was starving, all right. For time alone with his beautiful bride. He had something to tell her.

Willa waved as the last wagon disappeared into the waning evening. The walls were up. The roof was on. Tomorrow, they'd start on the interior. She still had to pinch herself to believe all the changes in her life over the past few months. In Gideon's life, too, she mused as her handsome husband walked toward where she was clearing away the last of the food dishes and loading them into the wagon.

"Where's Grady?" she asked.

"With Liam O'Shea and his boy. We can fetch him when we go back to the hotel. I wanted to speak to you alone."

The seriousness in his tone caught her attention. "Is something wrong?"

"Got some news today. Hank Fleming brought out the mail."

"What kind of news?" He was making her anxious.

He fished a large envelope from his vest and withdrew a stack of papers. "A friend in Fort Smith sent this."

Willa peered at the missive, amazed and proud to make out some of the words. That she was learning to read from Gideon's tutelage of both her and Grady thrilled her.

"Under mounting evidence and Pierce's arrest, Charlie Bangs confessed that he and Idaho Tom were connected with a gang that brought girls to the Red Diamond and other brothels against their will."

She let out the breath she'd been holding. Regardless of Gideon's serious tone, this was good news.

"Idaho Tom was the man in the alley that night who attacked me and whispered the warning about Papa. I still don't understand what he meant. What did Papa have to do with any of that brothel business?"

"According to Bangs's testimony, Pierce believed your father overheard a conversation between Pierce and Madam Frenchy concerning the girls they were buying from Becker and Tom."

"Papa would never have allowed that to happen if he'd known."

"That was exactly what our sanctimonious banker was afraid of. He thought your father had found out and would inform authorities in Guthrie. So, the conniving Pierce told a much dumber Charlie Bangs about a silver mine Finn Malone had supposedly discovered. He offered Bangs the mine in exchange for killing your father."

"Are you saying Papa really owned a silver mine?"

Gideon wrapped an arm around her waist as if bracing her for bad news. "From all we can learn, the mine didn't exist. It was a ruse to coerce Bangs into murdering your papa."

Willa's fingers went to her lips. "Oh, Papa. Sweet Papa. I wonder if he actually overheard anything at all."

"We'll never know for sure, but Pierce thought he did."

"And it cost him his life." She sighed, gazing toward the skeletal house, sad at heart. Papa would have been so pleased for her. He'd have danced a merry jig.

"I'm sorry, Willa." Gideon tugged her close and planted a kiss on her hair. She loved when he did that. "Though money is no compensation for a lost life, I wanted that mine to exist for you and your sisters."

She tilted her face toward his, loving his heart, loving the way he sheltered her, even though they both knew she could stand on her own two feet. He made her feel feminine and treasured, two words she'd never ascribed to herself. But Gideon did.

"Those men are in jail and Coy Ling is free. That's good enough for me. I think it would be for Papa, too."

"I'm glad. I never want you to be sad. I'd do anything to make you happy. Do you know that yet?"

"Oh, Gideon, my love, my husband, you make me happy in so many ways." She held out her left hand for both of them to see. Diamonds sparkled above a gold band. "When you put this ring on my finger, when you made me your wife, when you rode all the way to Buffalo Gap to get Grady and make him our son. And now, you've done another spectacular thing that brings me great joy."

"The house?" he asked, that half smile tilting his lips.

Willa stretched tall and kissed the corner of that mouth she loved so dearly.

"I love the house, but this is even better."

He frowned. "You have me at a loss, dear lady. I am, I admit, flummoxed."

Feeling suddenly tender and vulnerable and near to weeping, a silly, useless behavior, Willa smiled into the face of her beloved.

Without words, she took his hand and placed it on her flat belly. And held it there.

Gideon blinked. Slowly, his confusion turned to wonder. His expression softened, melted as he looked from her face to her stomach and back again.

"A baby?" he whispered.

Lips pressed tight in case she did something foolish like cry, she could only nod. For months now, they'd talked of having another child. At times, she'd worried she was too old to give him that precious gift.

"A baby?" he murmured again, awestruck. "We're having a baby?"

In the next instant, she was in his embrace. His hands cradled her face, his eyes holding hers and he was laughing with such delight that Willa joined him.

"Willa plain and simple," he said when the rush of exuberance calmed. "When I was nothing, you found me and dragged me back to life, believing in me when I didn't. With your fiery determination and unwavering compassion, you filled all the cold empty rooms inside my soul. You and the faith I thought I'd lost." His hand went once more to that place where their child grew. "And now this exquisite gift."

Heart full to overflowing, Willa said nothing as she basked in his loving words. He was the wordsmith, her poet, her husband, her eternal love.

She leaned into him, feeling his heartbeat, hearing him breathe, in no hurry to release this special moment.

Darkness faded the day, and stars began to emerge, one by one.

Man and wife stood together in front of their soon-to-be home, a union of hearts, rejoicing for what neither had once thought possible.

And they were complete.

★ ★ ★ ★ ★

Look for more books from New York Times *bestselling author Linda Goodnight later in 2022!*

LOVE INSPIRED

Stories to uplift and inspire

Fall in love with Love Inspired—
inspirational and uplifting stories of faith
and hope. Find strength and comfort in
the bonds of friendship and community.
Revel in the warmth of possibility and the
promise of new beginnings.

Sign up for the Love Inspired newsletter
at **LoveInspired.com** to be the first
to find out about upcoming titles,
special promotions and exclusive content.

*After a traumatic brain injury, military vet Behr Delgado
refuses the one thing that could help him—a service dog.
But charity head Ellery Watson knows the dog she selected
will improve his quality of life and vows to work with him
one-on-one. When their personal lives entwine with
their professional, can they trust each other long
enough to both heal?*

Read on for a sneak peek at
The Veteran's Vow *by Jill Lynn!*

Ellery approached and held out Margo's leash for him. She was so excited he was doing better. The thought of disappointing her cut Behr like a combat knife.

Margo stood by Ellery's side, her chocolate face toggling back and forth between them, questioning what she was supposed to do next. Waiting for his lead.

Behr reached out and took the leash. If Ellery noticed his shaking hand, she didn't say anything.

"I want to teach her to stand by your left side. That's it. She's just going to be there. We're going to take it slow." Ellery moved to Behr's left, leaving enough room for Margo to stand between them.

A tremble echoed through him, and Behr tensed his muscles in an effort to curb it.

Margo, on the other hand, would be the first image if someone searched the internet for the definition of *calm*.

"Heel." When he gave Margo the command and she obeyed, taking that spot, Behr's heart just about ricocheted out of his chest. *This effort is worth it.* Was it, though? He could get through life off-kilter, running into things, tripping, leaving items on the floor when they fell, willing his poor coordination to work instead of using Margo to create balance for him or grasp or retrieve things for him, couldn't he?

Ellery didn't say anything about his audible inhales or exhales, but she had to know what he was up to. The weakness that plagued Behr rose up to ridicule him. It was hard to reveal this side of himself to Ellery, not that she hadn't seen it already. Hard to know that he couldn't just snap his fingers and make his body right again. Hard to remember that he needed this dog and that was why his mom and sisters had signed him up for one.

"You're doing great." Ellery's focus was on Behr, but Margo's tail wagged as if the compliment had been directed to her.

They both laughed, and the tension dissipated like a deployment care package.

"You, too, girl." Ellery offered Margo a treat. "Do you want me to put the balance harness on her so you can feel what it's like?" she asked Behr.

He gave one determined nod.

Ellery strode over to the storage cabinets that lined the back wall. She returned with the harness and knelt, sliding it on Margo, adjusting it. Behr should probably be watching how to do the same, but right now he was concentrating on standing next to Margo and not having his knees liquefy.

Ellery stood. "See what you think."

Behr gripped the handle, his knuckles turning white. The handle was the right height, and it did make him feel sturdy. Supported.

Like the woman beaming at him from the other side of the dog.

Don't miss
The Veteran's Vow by *Jill Lynn,*
available March 2022 wherever Love Inspired books
and ebooks are sold.

LoveInspired.com

Sometimes a broken heart just needs a little mending...

Don't miss this uplifting new story of faith, forgiveness and hope from bestselling author

JO ANN BROWN

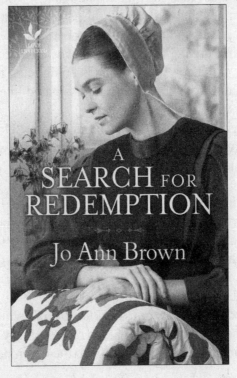

"Brown is a gifted writer who makes unforgettable characters that invite the reader to join them on their journey."
—*Publishers Weekly* bestselling author Marie E. Bast

Coming soon from Love Inspired!

LOVE INSPIRED
LoveInspired.com